Shino Can't Say Her Name

Translator: Molly Rabbitt
Proofreading: Patrick Sutton
Production: Glen Isip
                Nicole Dochych
                Lauren Eldon

SHINOCHAN WA JIBUN NO NAMAE GA IENAI
©Shuzo Oshimi 2013
All rights reserved
First Published in Japan in 2013 by Ohta Publishing Co., Tokyo
English translation rights arranged with Ohta Publishing Co.
through Tuttle-Mori Agency, Inc., Tokyo

Published in English by Denpa, LLC., Portland, Oregon, 2021.

Originally published in Japanese as *Shino-chan wa Jibun no Namae ga Ienai*
by Ohta Publishing Co., 2013.
Shino Can't Say Her Name first serialized in *Pocopoco*, Ohta Publishing Co.,
December 2011 through October 2012.

This is a work of fiction.

ISBN-13: 978-1-63442-968-9
Library of Congress Control Number: 2020947276
Printed in the USA

First Edition

Denpa, LLC.
625 NW 17th Ave
Portland, OR 97209
www.denpa.pub

Afterword

Thank you very much for reading thus far.

The plot of this manga is based on my own experiences.

I think the first time I felt that I was unable to talk was in my second year of middle school. However, I did not know the proper name of this condition until after that. It's called dysphemia, or quite simply put, stuttering.

Anyway, I figured out that at some point, that even my first words wouldn't come out correctly. So, whenever I spoke with my friends, I found that suddenly I would become unable to speak, and everyone would laugh at me. Apparently, they thought I was just messing around. I didn't really pay it much mind at the time.

But when it came to speaking on the phone with people or when I was chosen to introduce myself in class, or if I was picked in class to answer a question... I noticed that my problem with speaking began to increase.

What readily comes to mind was one experience in math class. I was called upon to answer a math problem. And I knew the answer was 1. But I just couldn't seem to get it out of my mouth. Not even the "ON" part would come out. The more I tried to say it, the more my face would contort, my eyes would widen, and I would put more force behind trying to say it. But the more I did that, the more I became unable to speak. Suddenly, I'd become enveloped in a cloud of riotous laughter.

When it comes to stuttering, there are two types: clonal (continuous) and tonal (spasms which cause intermittent stuttering). An example of clonal dysphemia would be something like, "I-I-I-I- w-want an o-onigiri." In other words, a continuous string of stuttering throughout the sentence. With tonal dysphemia, however, the initial words in a sentence wouldn't come out. I would go, "...Uh..." The type of dysphemia I have is the latter.

The thing that terrified me the most, though, was when someone asked for my name. My chest would tighten in fear. It would happen even more over phone calls. I wouldn't be able to say my name, and I could start to feel the person at the other end of the line start to worry. Sometimes they would act with suspicion, so I would feel the urge to run away.

But even within tonal dysphemia there are waves. There are times when things go smoothly, and times when they don't. Even when relaxing with family, though, I would still become utterly unable to speak.

Increasingly, feelings of guilt started to pile up in my heart. Feelings that I was worthless; that I couldn't be normal like everyone else; that I felt bad for whoever was talking to me... would seize me.

But at the same time, when I did manage to speak normally, I felt like I was on top of the world. When I spoke with people, sometimes I thought to myself, "Well, this is where I'd make an interesting statement, but I don't know how the other person would receive it. So, I better not say anything." When I got lost in those thoughts, someone else would say whatever witty thing I had wanted to instead of me anyway. So whenever that happened, I would laugh along with my friends, yet still couldn't help but feel a sense of defeat.

Over time, I became more introverted. I became afraid of everything, but especially of speaking to people. So, I stopped doing it. Speaking to people became the one thing I could do without. When I did have to speak

Shuzo Oshimi

Shino Can't
Say Her Name

Contents

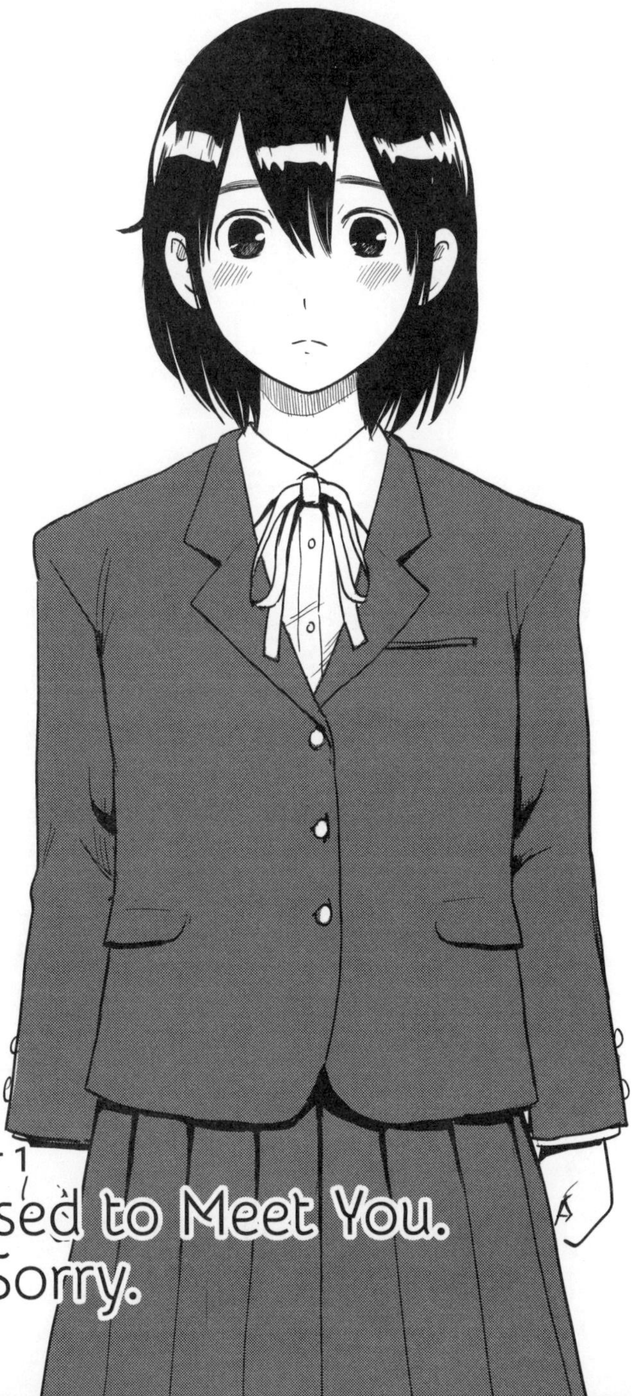

Chapter 1

Pleased to Meet You. I'm Sorry.

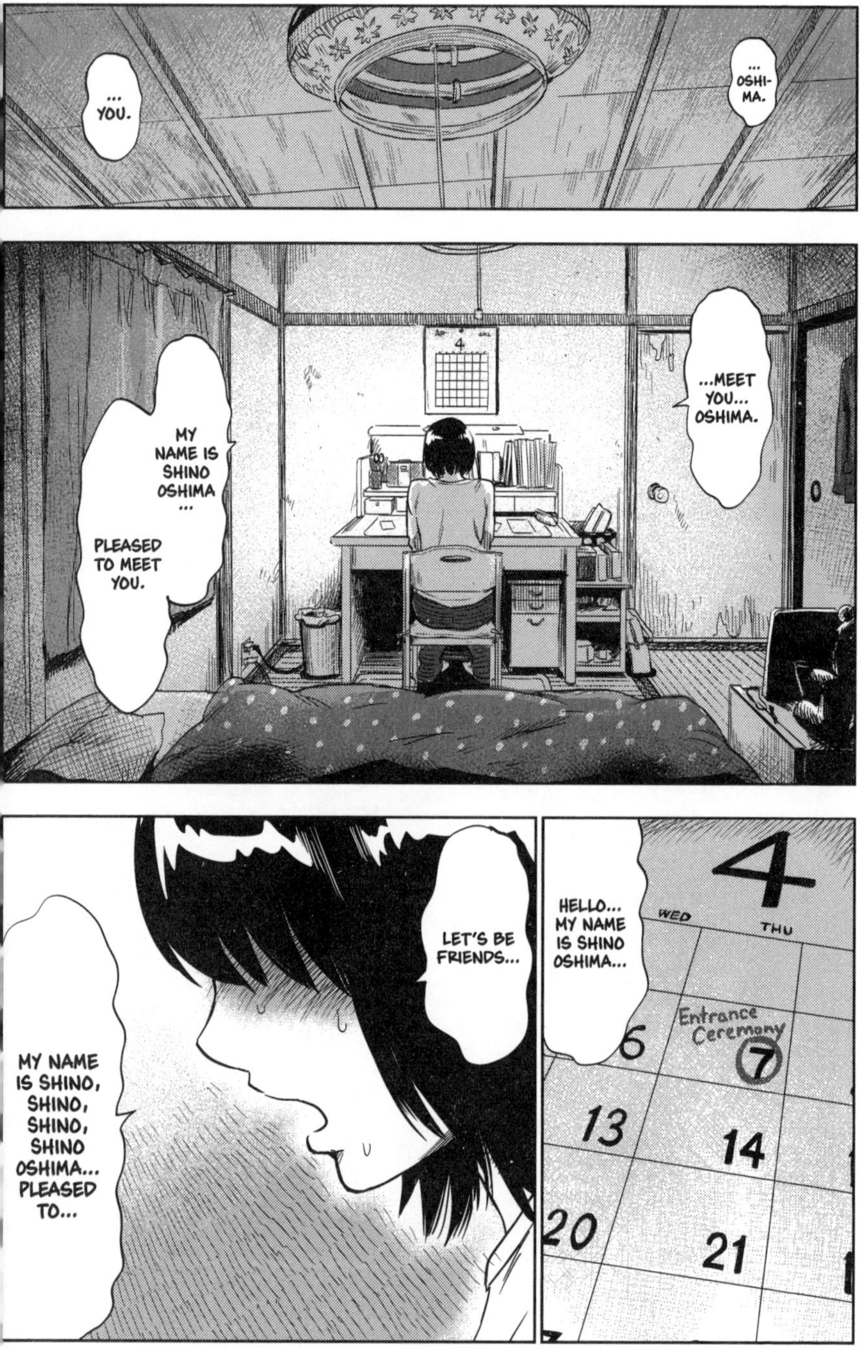
... OSHI-MA.
... YOU.
...MEET YOU... OSHIMA.
MY NAME IS SHINO OSHIMA ... PLEASED TO MEET YOU.
HELLO... MY NAME IS SHINO OSHIMA...
4
WED
THU
Entrance Ceremony
LET'S BE FRIENDS...
MY NAME IS SHINO, SHINO, SHINO, SHINO OSHIMA... PLEASED TO...

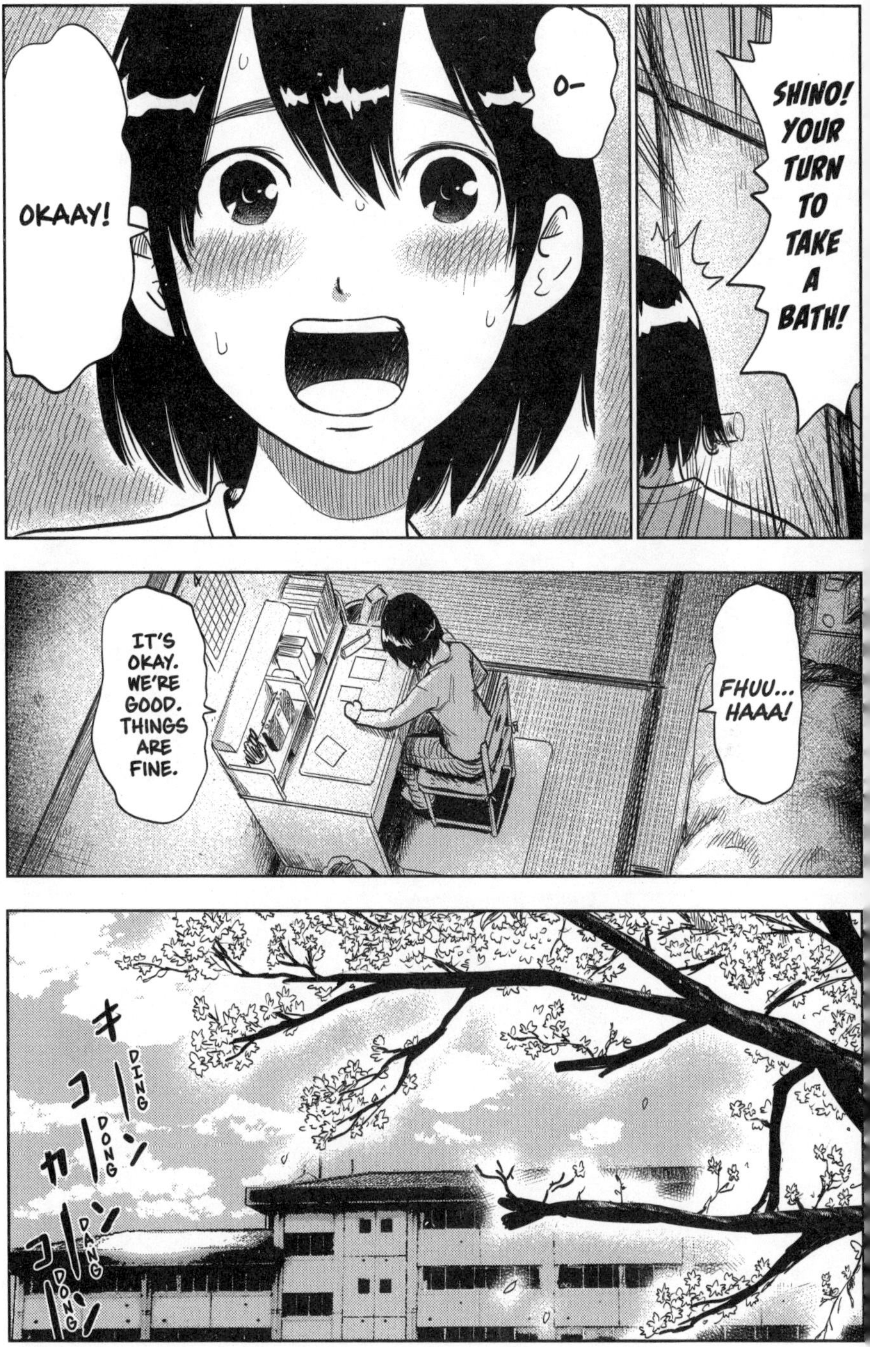
SHINO! YOUR TURN TO TAKE A BATH!
O-
OKAAY!
FHUU... HAAA!
IT'S OKAY. WE'RE GOOD. THINGS ARE FINE.
キーンコーンカーンコーン
DING DONG DANG DONG

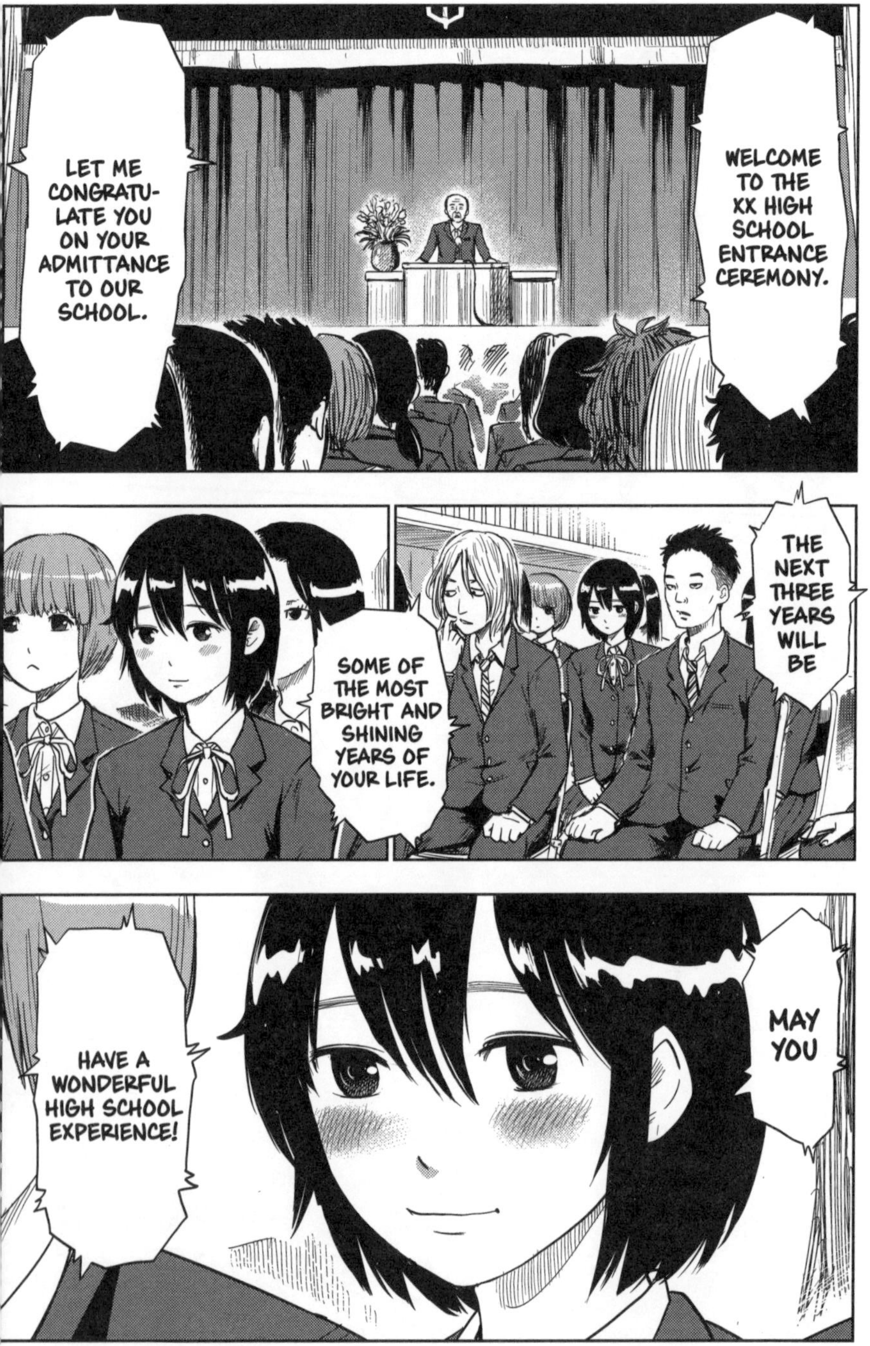
WELCOME TO THE XX HIGH SCHOOL ENTRANCE CEREMONY.
LET ME CONGRATU-LATE YOU ON YOUR ADMITTANCE TO OUR SCHOOL.
THE NEXT THREE YEARS WILL BE
SOME OF THE MOST BRIGHT AND SHINING YEARS OF YOUR LIFE.
MAY YOU
HAVE A WONDERFUL HIGH SCHOOL EXPERIENCE!

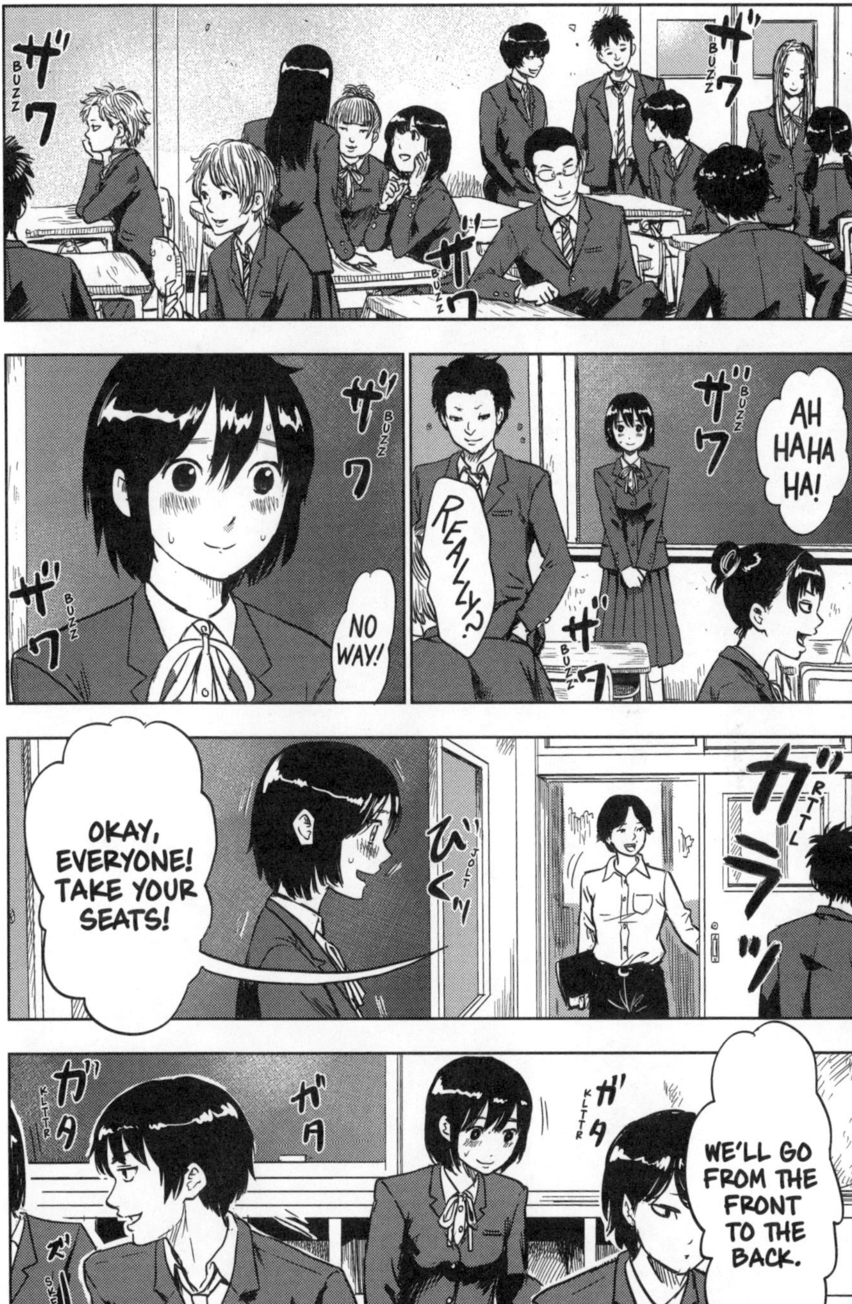
ザワ
BUZZ
ザワ
BUZZ
ザワ
BUZZ
AH HAHA HA!
ザワ
BUZZ
REALLY?
ザワ
BUZZ
ザワ
BUZZ
NO WAY!
ザワ
BUZZ
ガラッ
RTTL
ビクッ
JOLT
OKAY, EVERYONE! TAKE YOUR SEATS!
WE'LL GO FROM THE FRONT TO THE BACK.
ガタ
KLTTR
ガタ
ガタ
KLTTR
ズ
SKFF

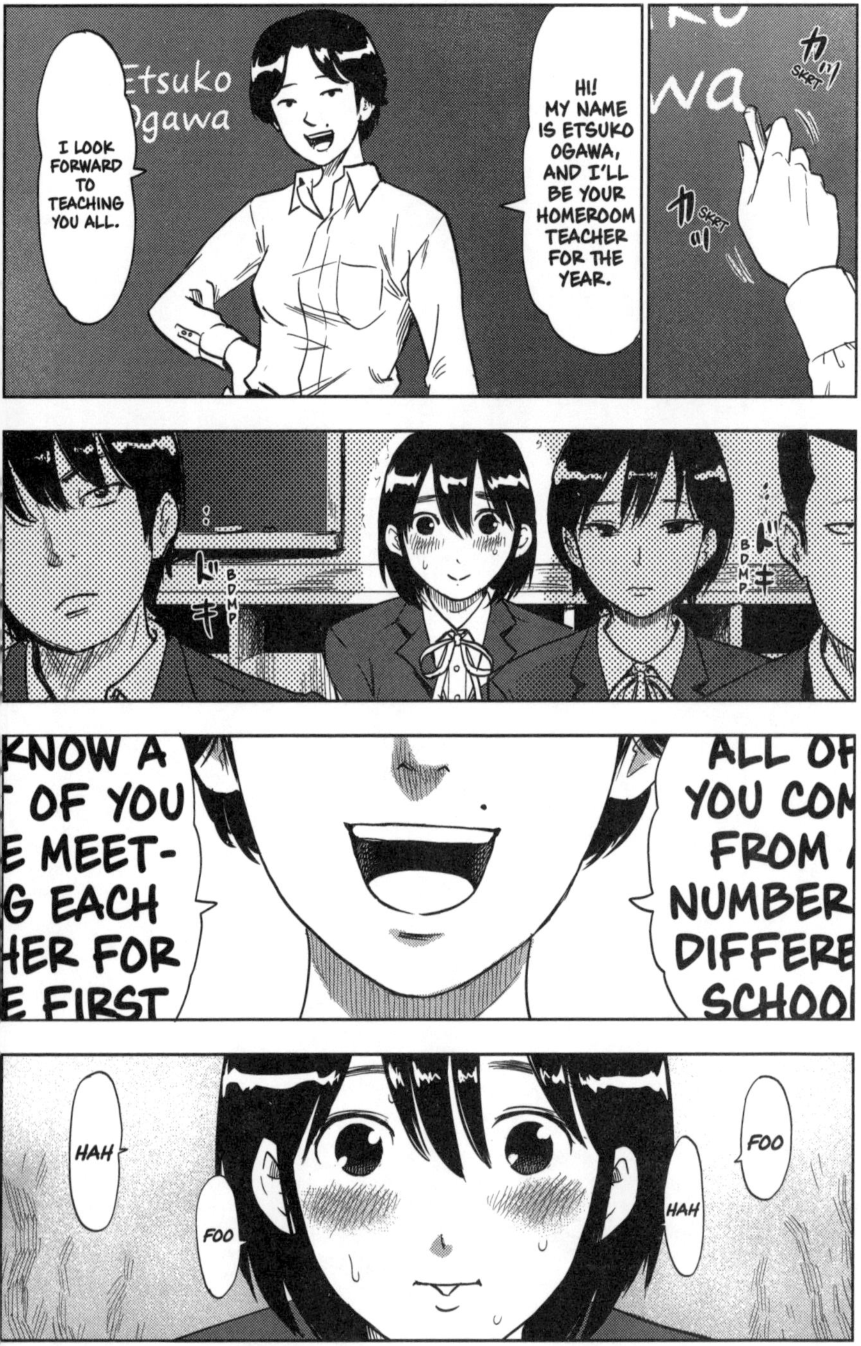
カッ SKRT
カッ SKRT
Etsuko Ogawa
HI! MY NAME IS ETSUKO OGAWA, AND I'LL BE YOUR HOMEROOM TEACHER FOR THE YEAR.
I LOOK FORWARD TO TEACHING YOU ALL.
ドキ B.D.M.P.
ドキ BDMP
ALL OF YOU COM FROM NUMBER DIFFERE SCHOO
KNOW A T OF YOU E MEET- G EACH HER FOR E FIRST
FOO
HAH
HAH
FOO

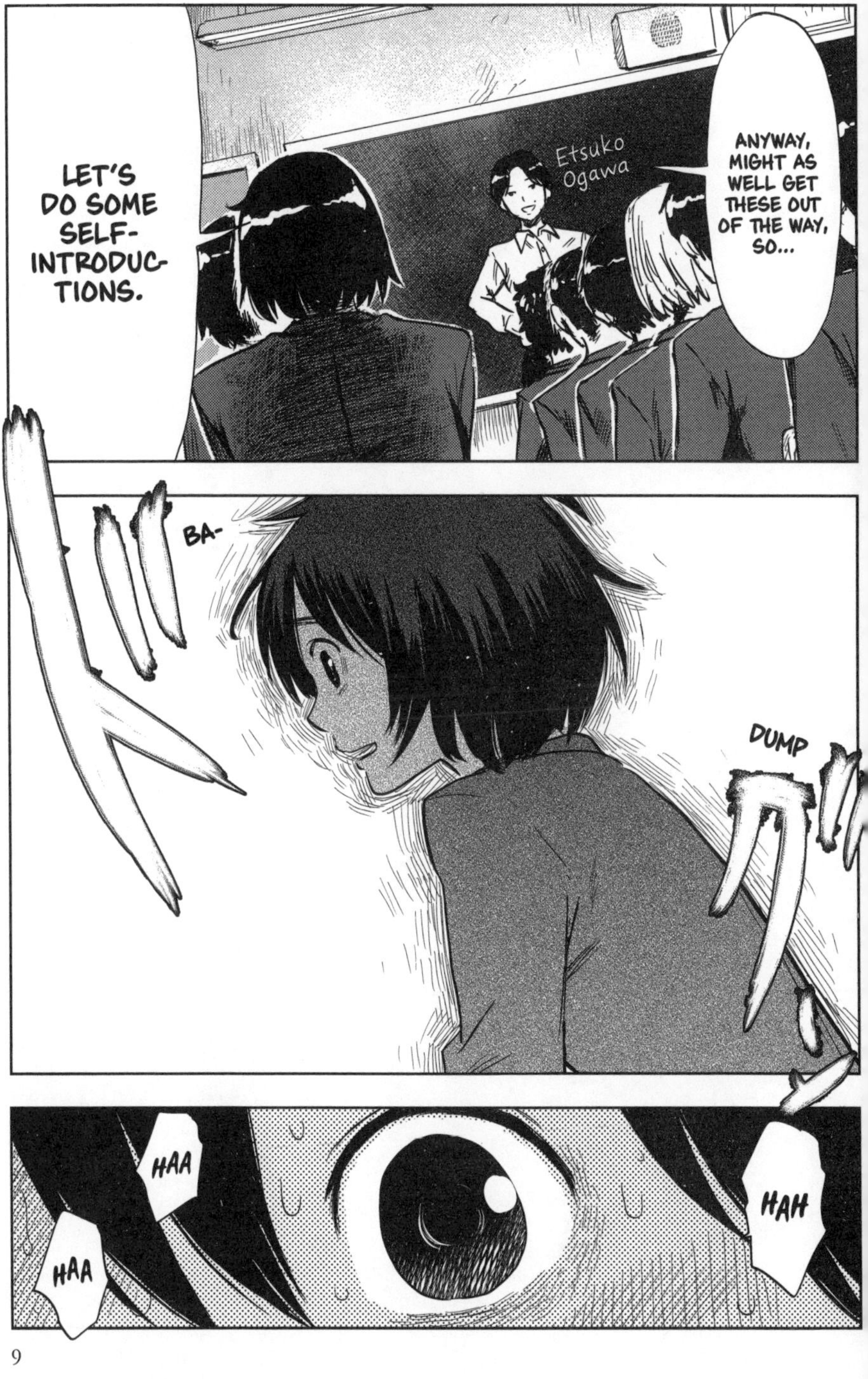
ANYWAY, MIGHT AS WELL GET THESE OUT OF THE WAY, SO...
Etsuko Ogawa
LET'S DO SOME SELF-INTRODUCTIONS.
DUMP
BA-
HAH
HAA
HAA

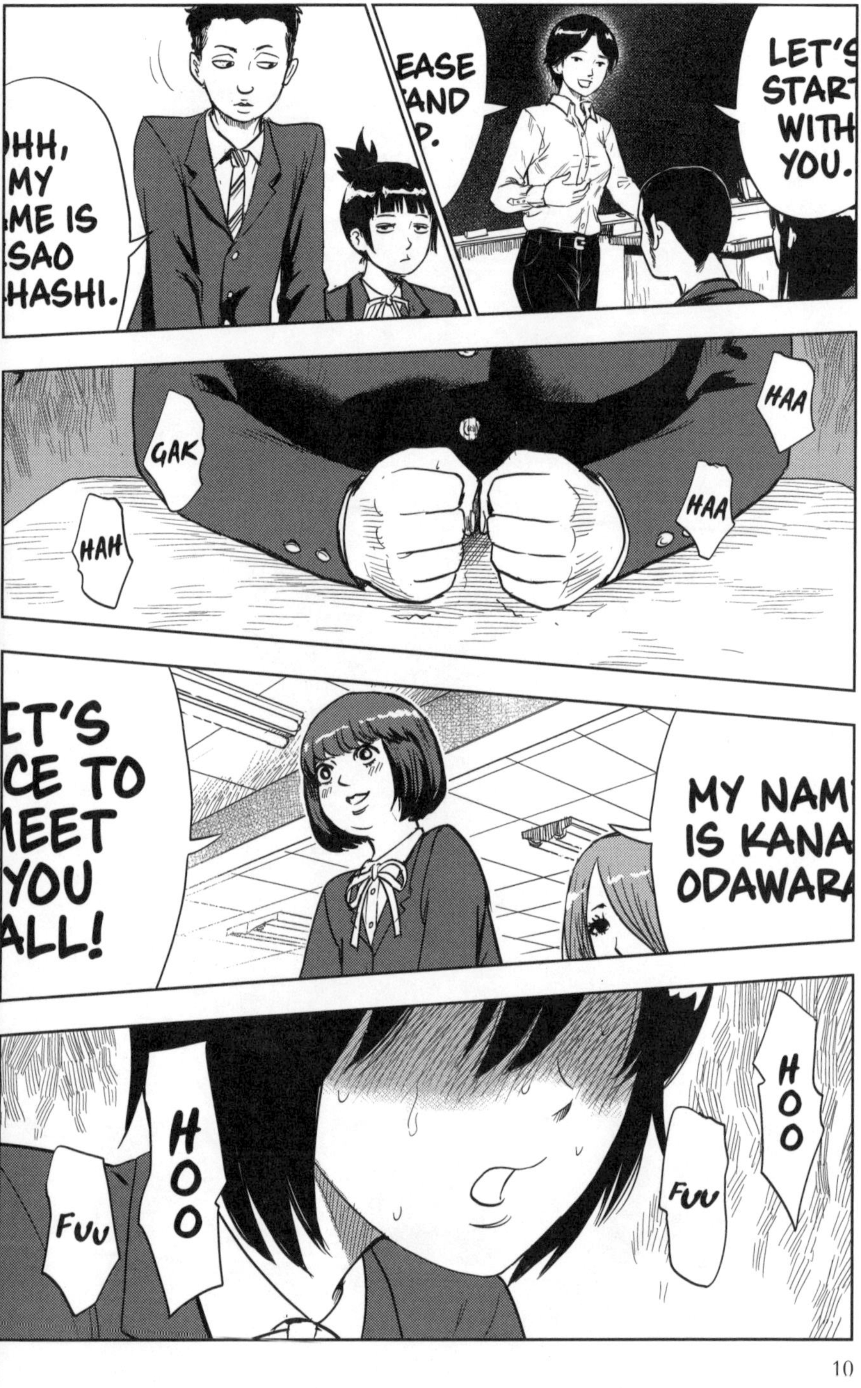
LET'S START WITH YOU.
EASE AND P.
HH, MY ME IS SAO HASHI.
HAA
HAA
GAK
HAH
MY NAM IS KANA ODAWARA
IT'S CE TO MEET YOU ALL!
HOO
FUU
HOO
FUU

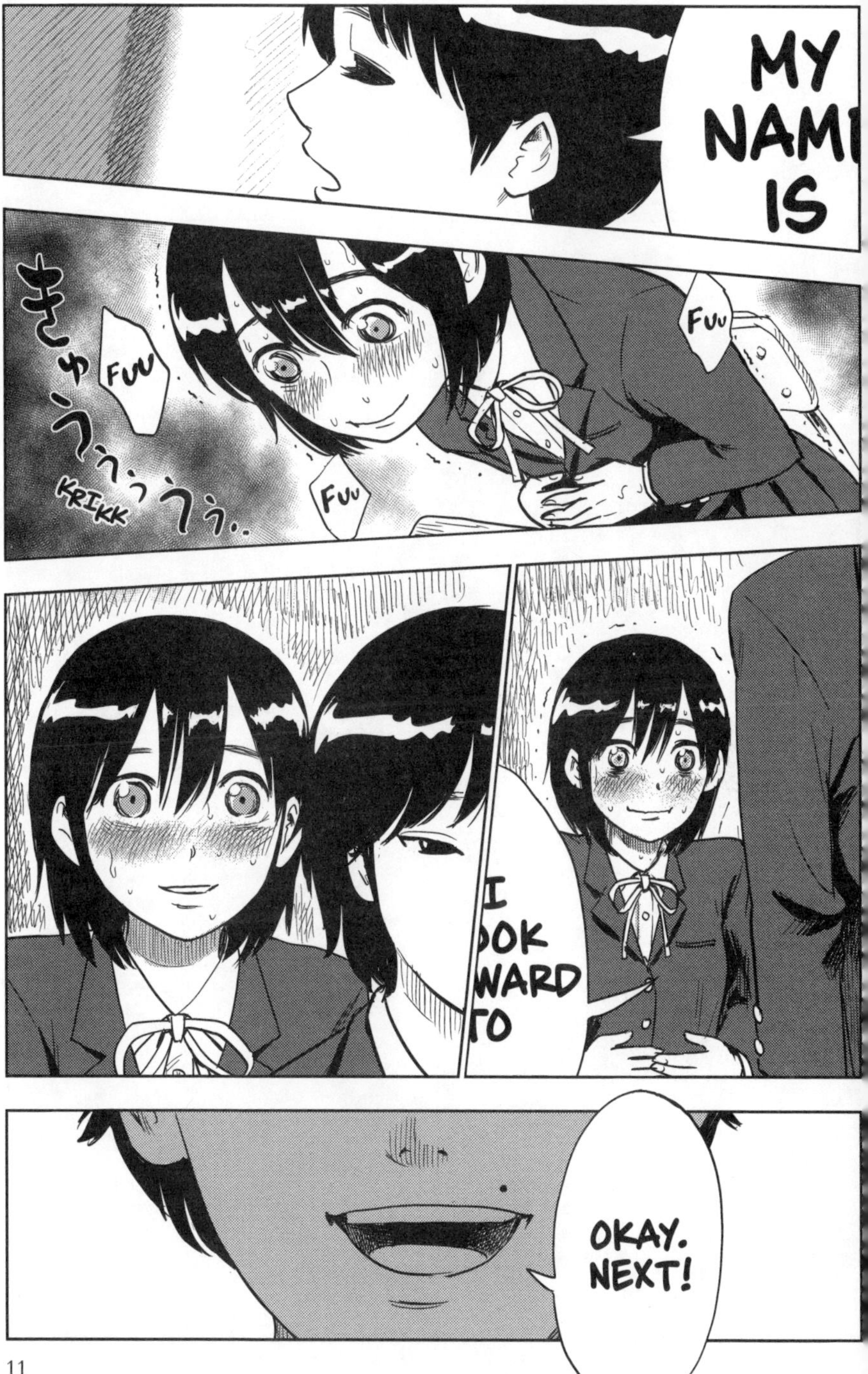

MY NAM
IS
FUU
FUU
FUU
きゅううううう..
KRIKK
I
OOK
WARD
TO
OKAY. NEXT!

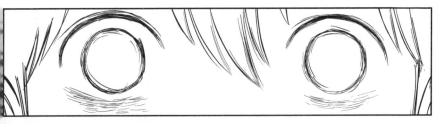

ズ
SKFF

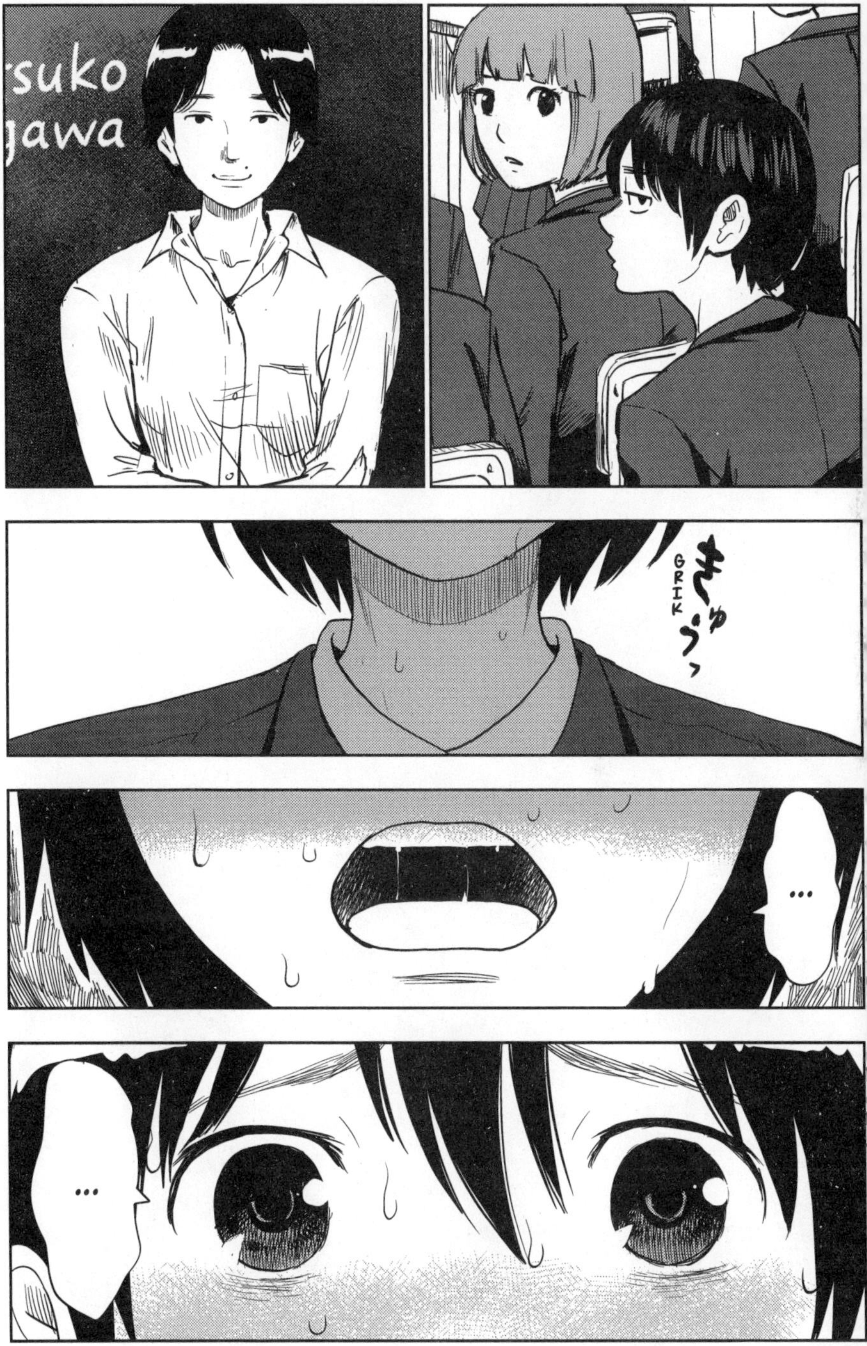
suko
gawa
きゅうっ
GRIK
...
...

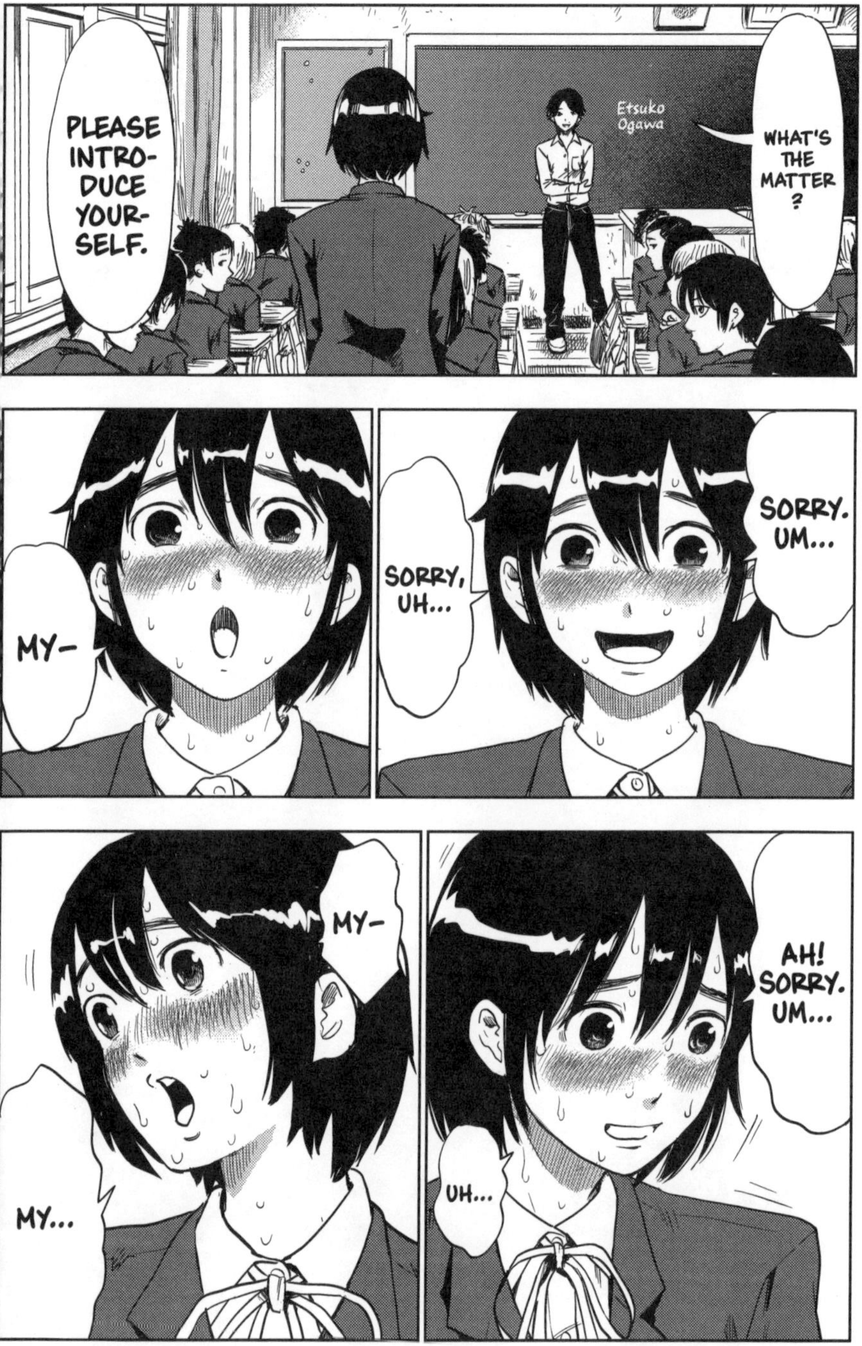
WHAT'S THE MATTER?
Etsuko Ogawa
PLEASE INTRO-DUCE YOUR-SELF.
SORRY. UM...
SORRY, UH...
MY-
AH! SORRY. UM...
UH...
MY-
MY...

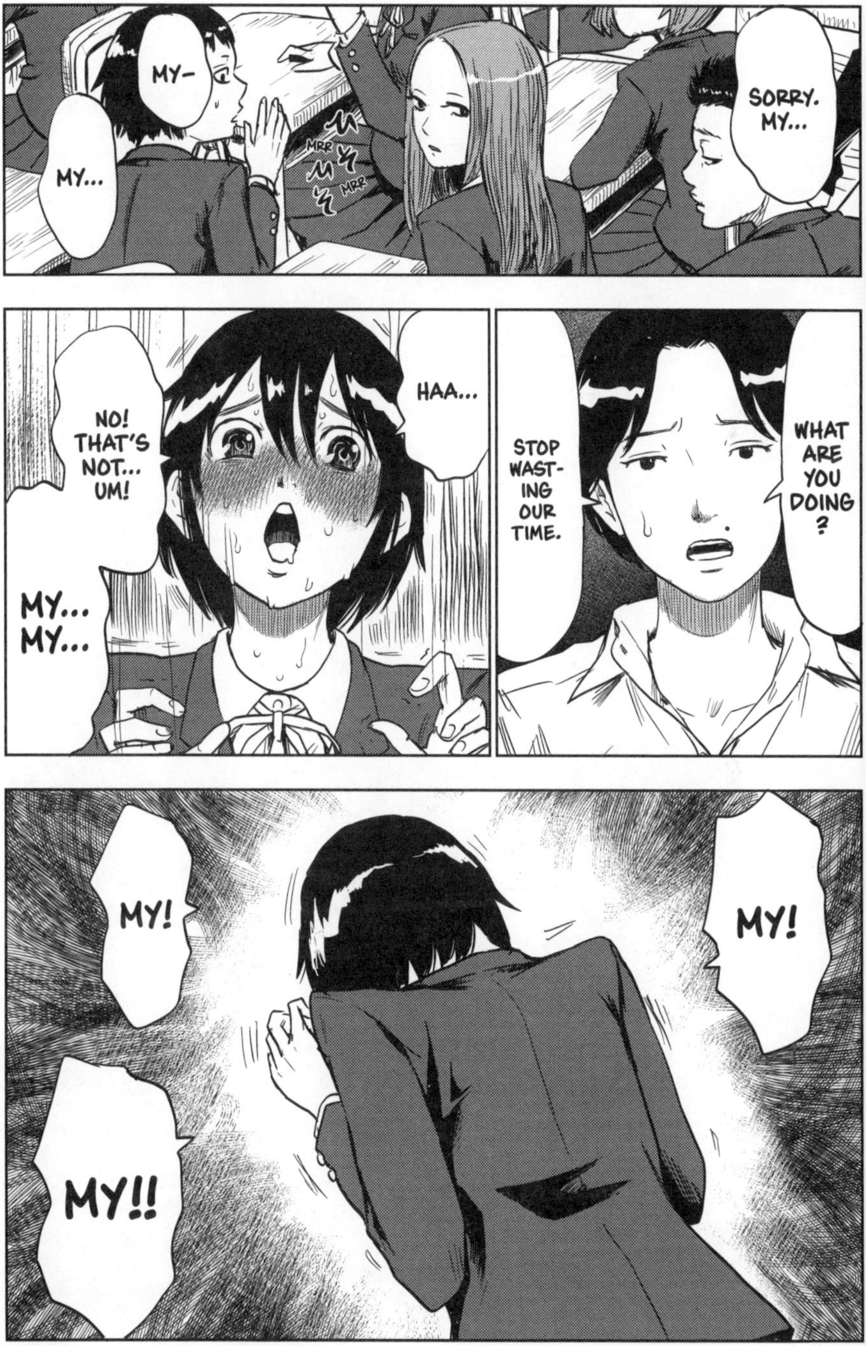
SORRY. MY...
MY-
MRR
MRR
MY...
WHAT ARE YOU DOING?
STOP WASTING OUR TIME.
HAA...
NO! THAT'S NOT... UM!
MY... MY...
MY!
MY!
MY!!

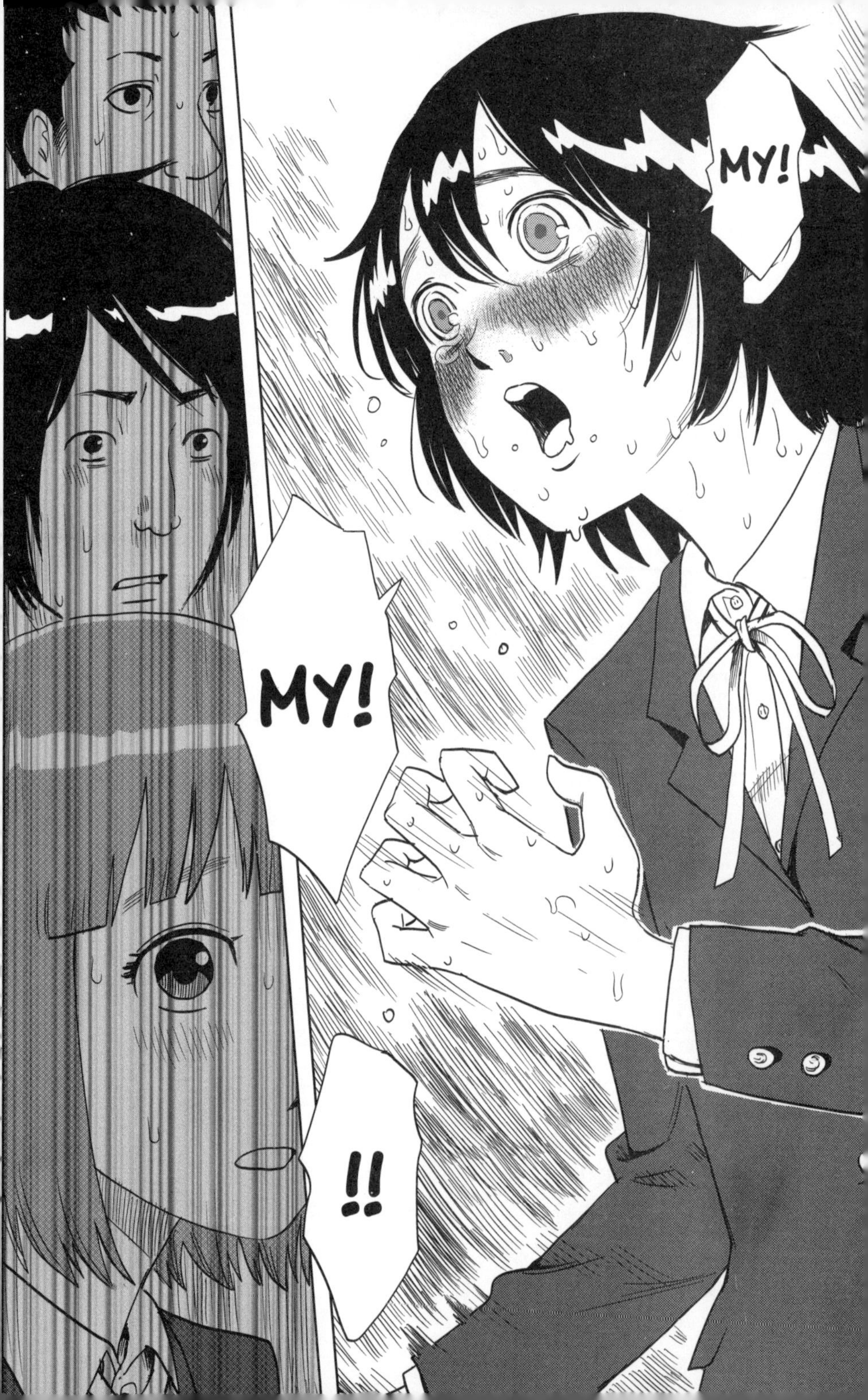
MY!
MY!
!!

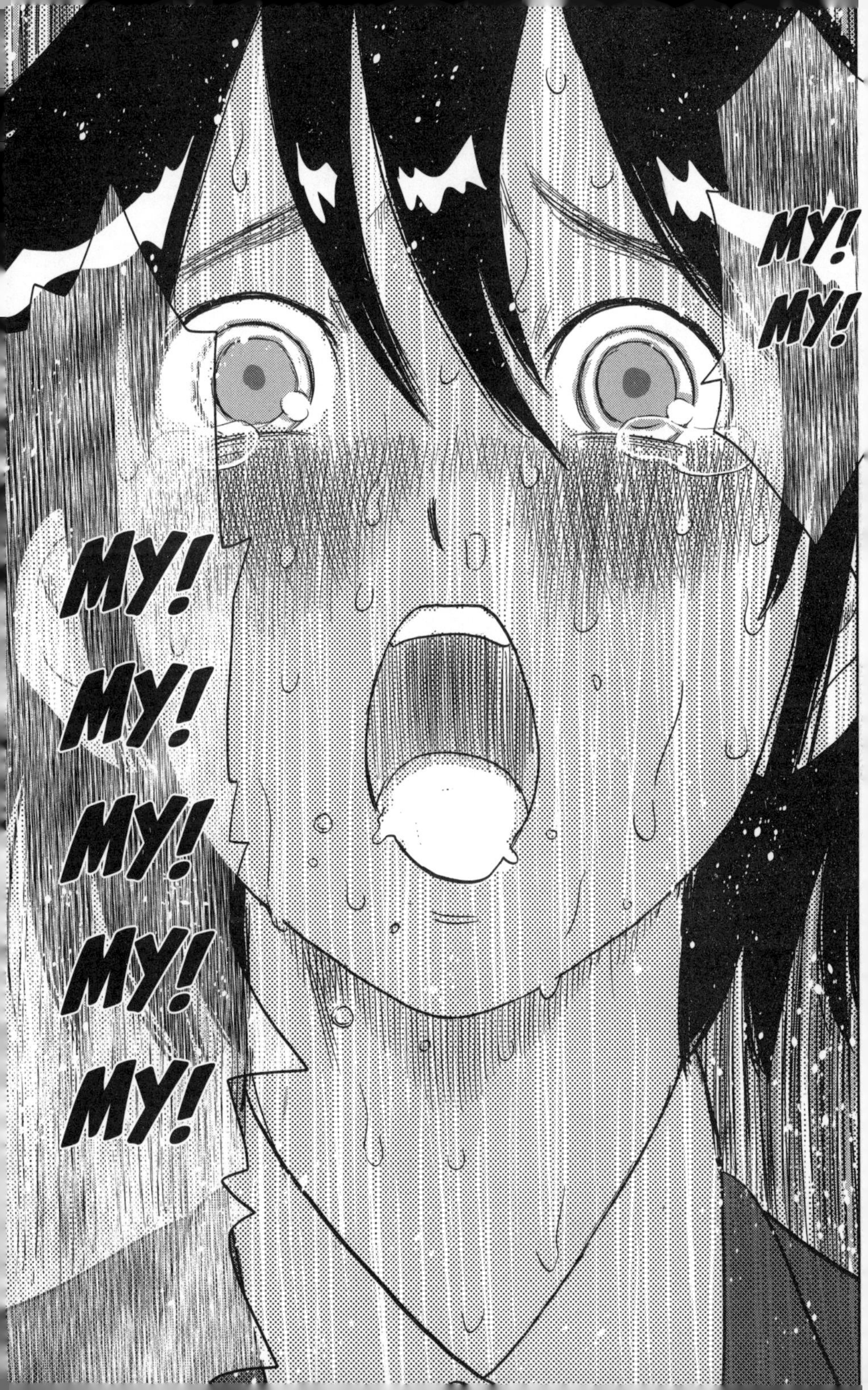
MY! MY!
MY! MY! MY! MY! MY!

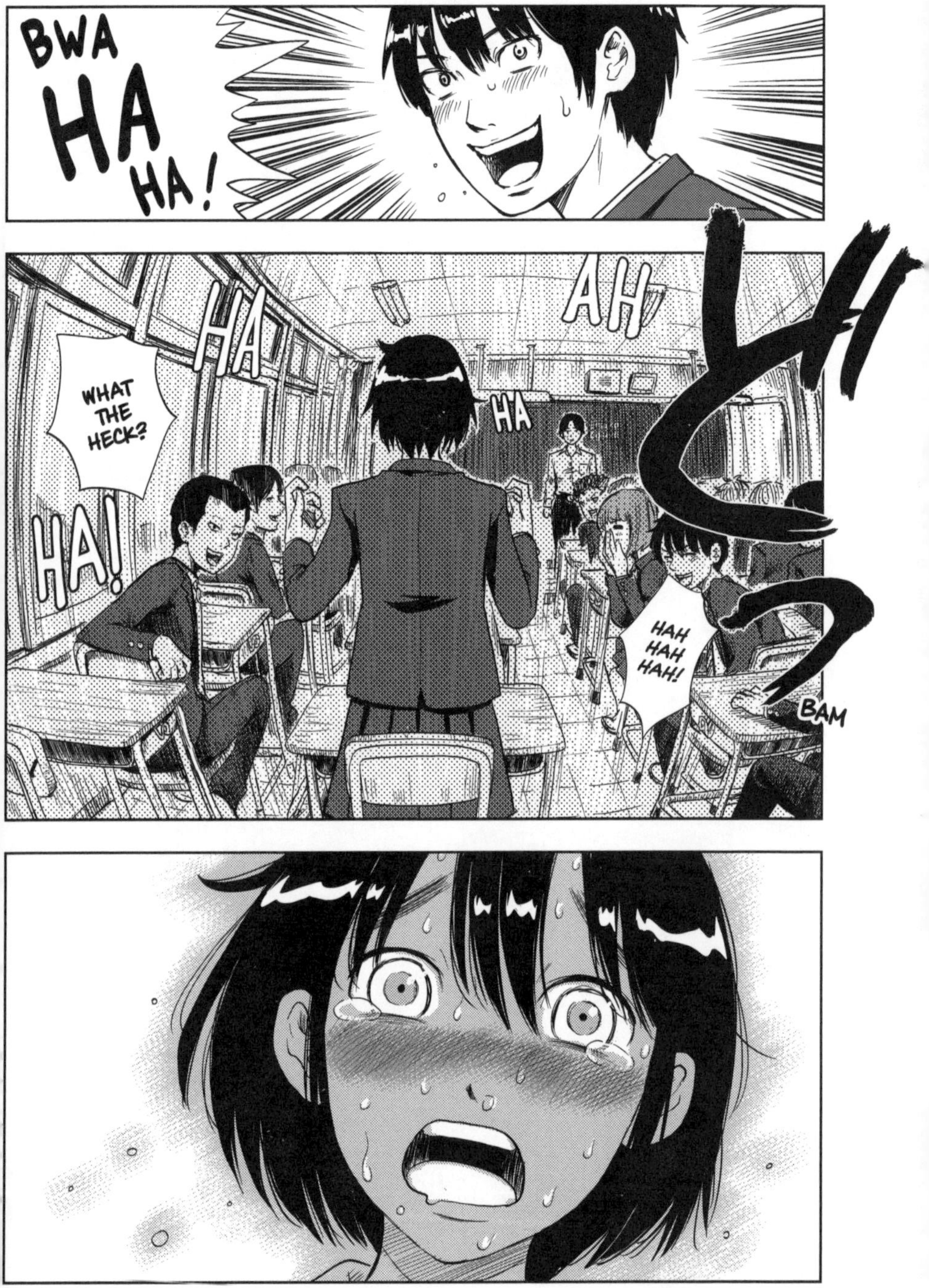
BWA HA HA!
AH
BAM
HAH HAH HAH!
HA
HA
WHAT THE HECK?
HA!

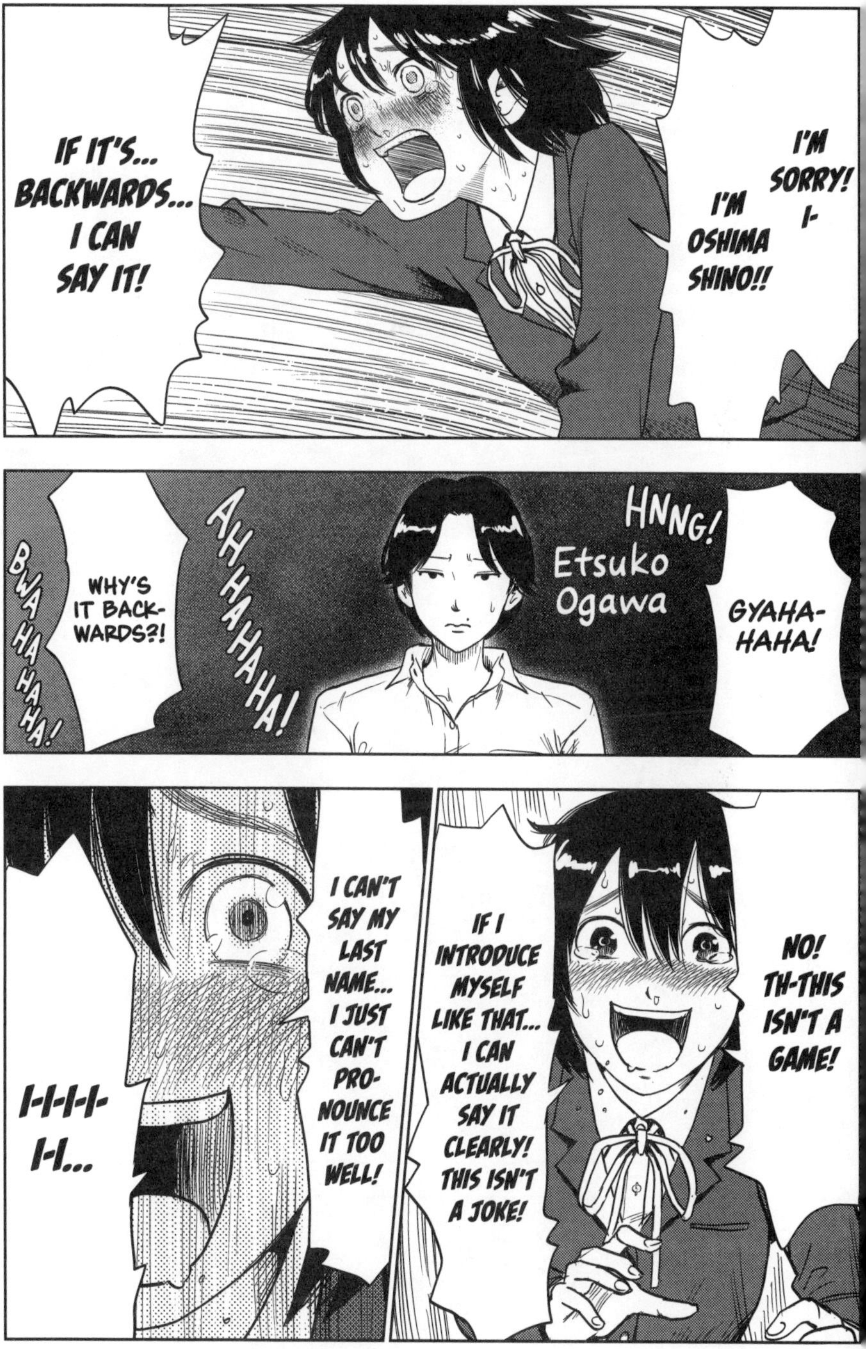
I'M SORRY! I-
I'M OSHIMA SHINO!!
IF IT'S... BACKWARDS... I CAN SAY IT!
GYAHA-HAHA!
HNNG!
Etsuko Ogawa
AHHAHAHAHA!
WHY'S IT BACK-WARDS?!
BWAHAHAHAHA!
NO! TH-THIS ISN'T A GAME!
IF I INTRODUCE MYSELF LIKE THAT... I CAN ACTUALLY SAY IT CLEARLY! THIS ISN'T A JOKE!
I CAN'T SAY MY LAST NAME... I JUST CAN'T PRO-NOUNCE IT TOO WELL!
I-I-I-I-I-I...

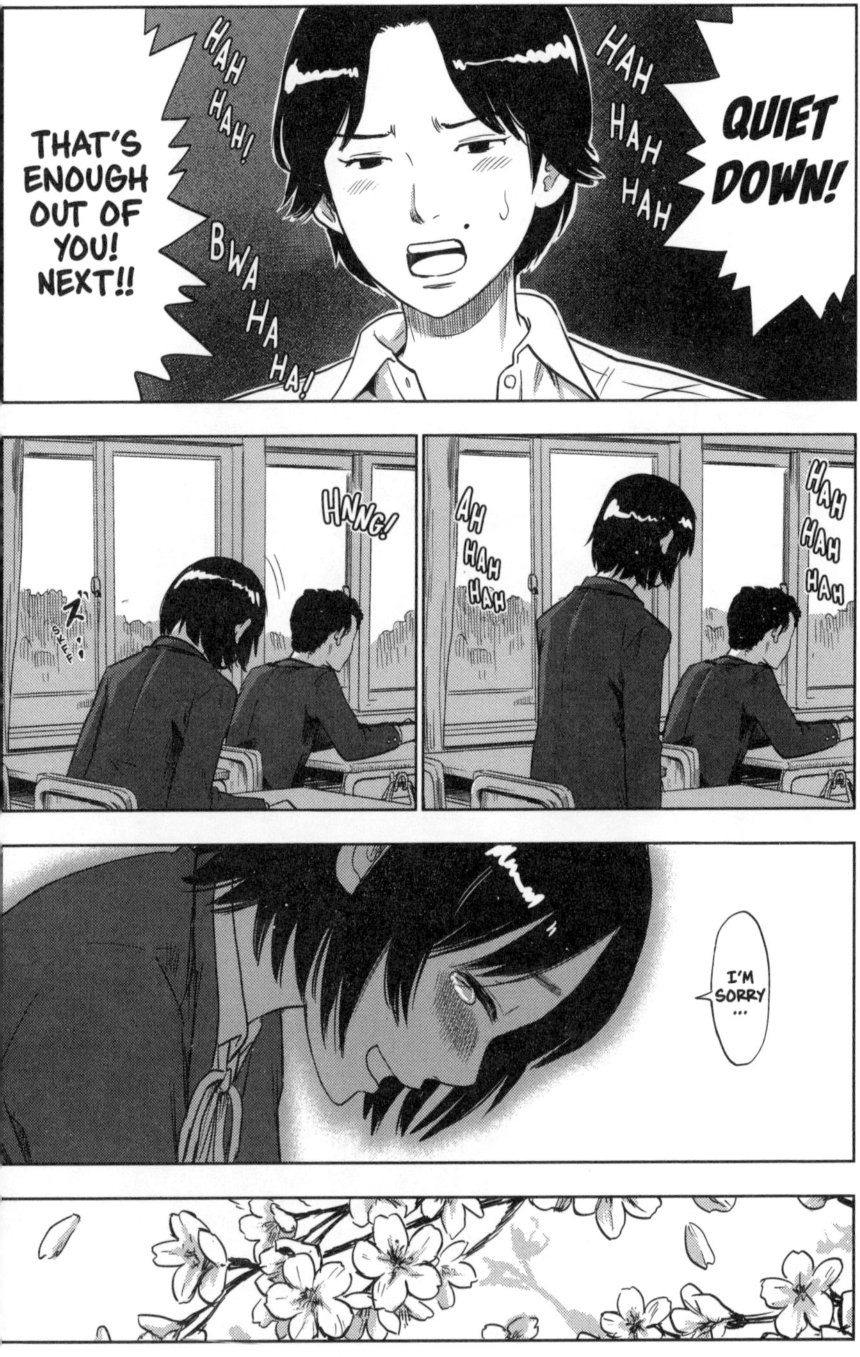
HAH HAH HAH HAH
QUIET DOWN!
HAH HAH!
THAT'S ENOUGH OUT OF YOU! NEXT!!
BWA HA HA HA!
HAH HAH HAH
AH HAH HAH
HNNG!
Z
I'M SORRY...

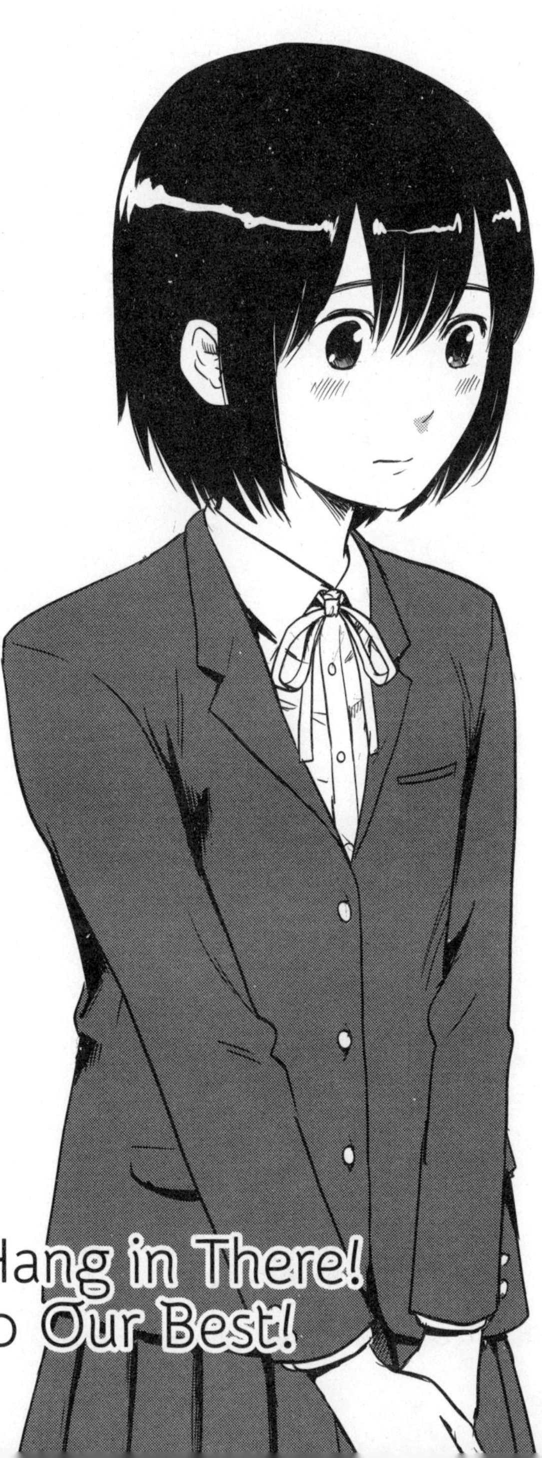

Chapter 2

Gotta Hang in There! Let's Do Our Best!

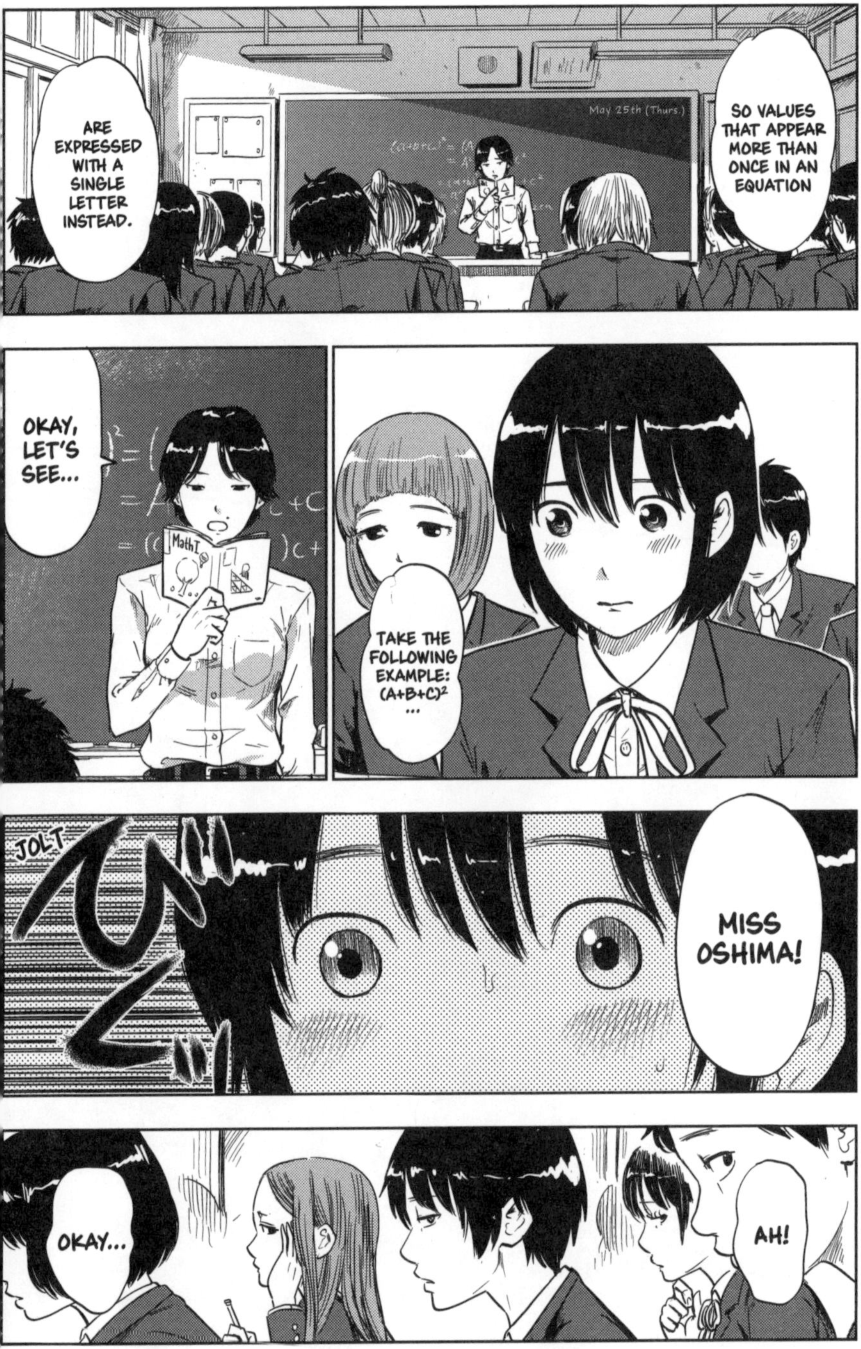
May 25th (Thurs.)
SO VALUES THAT APPEAR MORE THAN ONCE IN AN EQUATION
ARE EXPRESSED WITH A SINGLE LETTER INSTEAD.
TAKE THE FOLLOWING EXAMPLE: (A+B+C)² ...
OKAY, LET'S SEE...
Math I
MISS OSHIMA!
JOLT
AH!
OKAY...

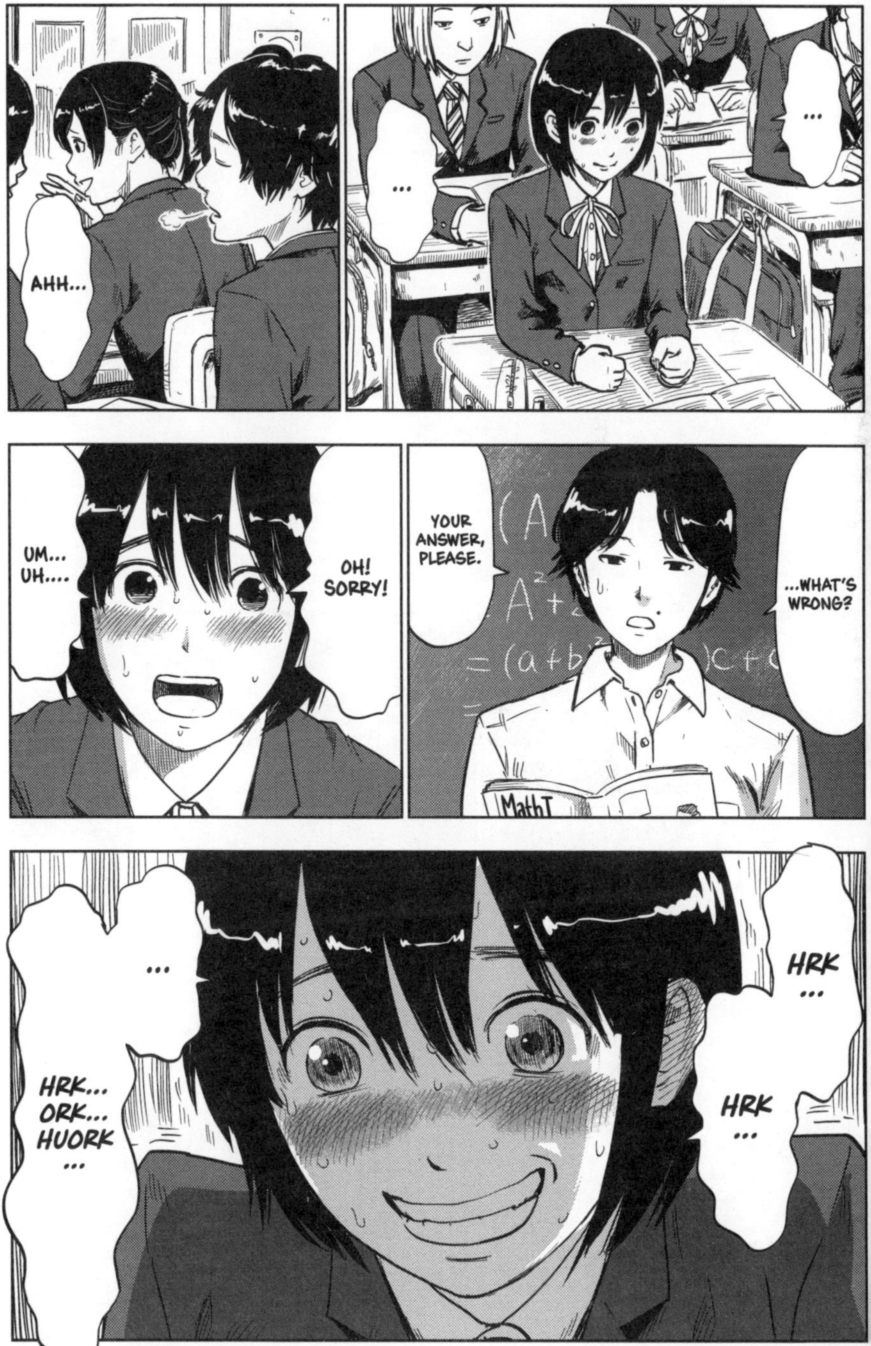
...
...
AHH...
...WHAT'S WRONG?
YOUR ANSWER, PLEASE.
OH! SORRY!
UM... UH....
HRK ...
HRK ...
...
HRK... ORK... HUORK ...

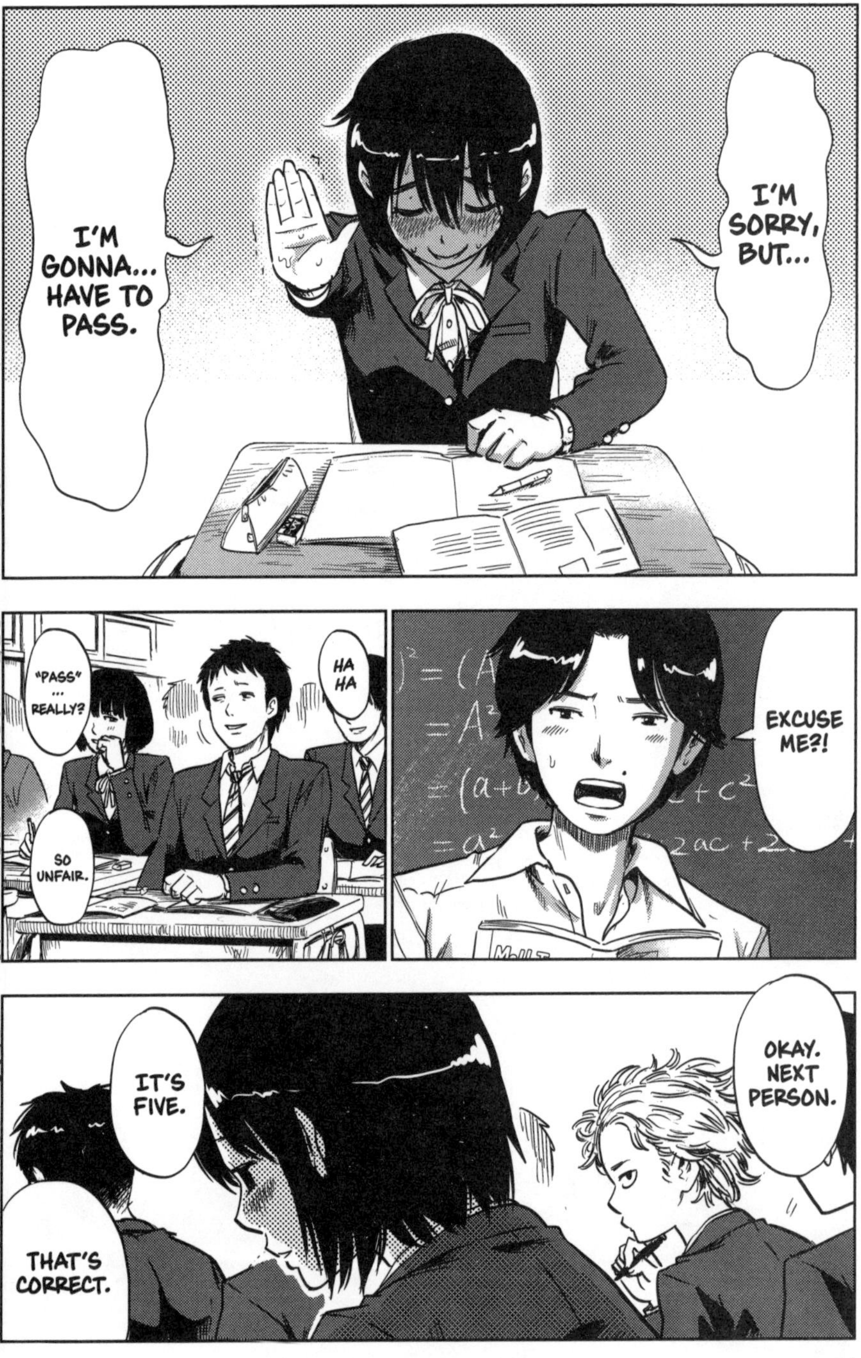
I'M SORRY, BUT...
I'M GONNA... HAVE TO PASS.
EXCUSE ME?!
HA HA
"PASS" ... REALLY?
SO UNFAIR.
OKAY. NEXT PERSON.
IT'S FIVE.
THAT'S CORRECT.

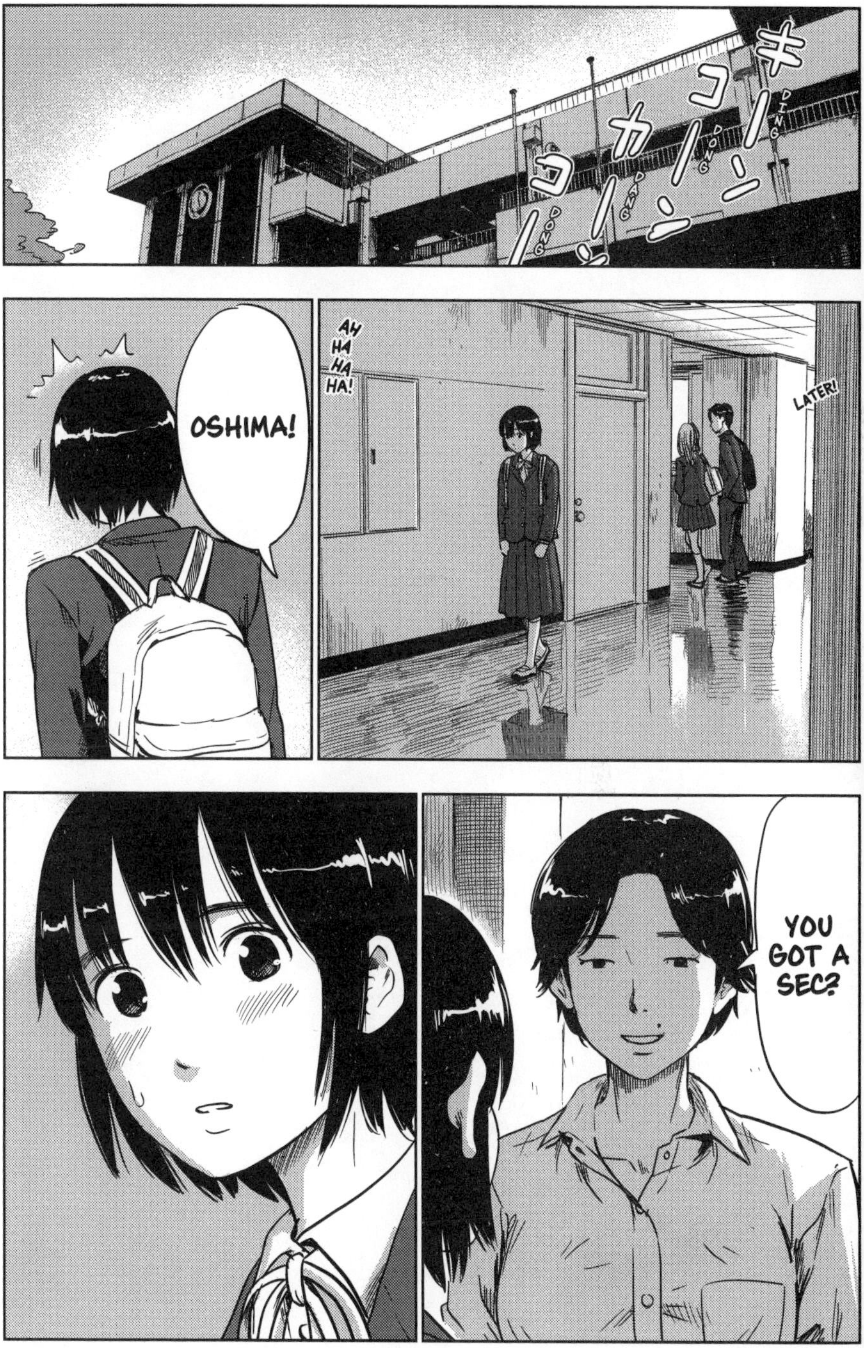
キーンコーン
カーンコーン
DING
DONG
DANG
DONG
LATER!
AH HA HA HA!
OSHIMA!
YOU GOT A SEC?

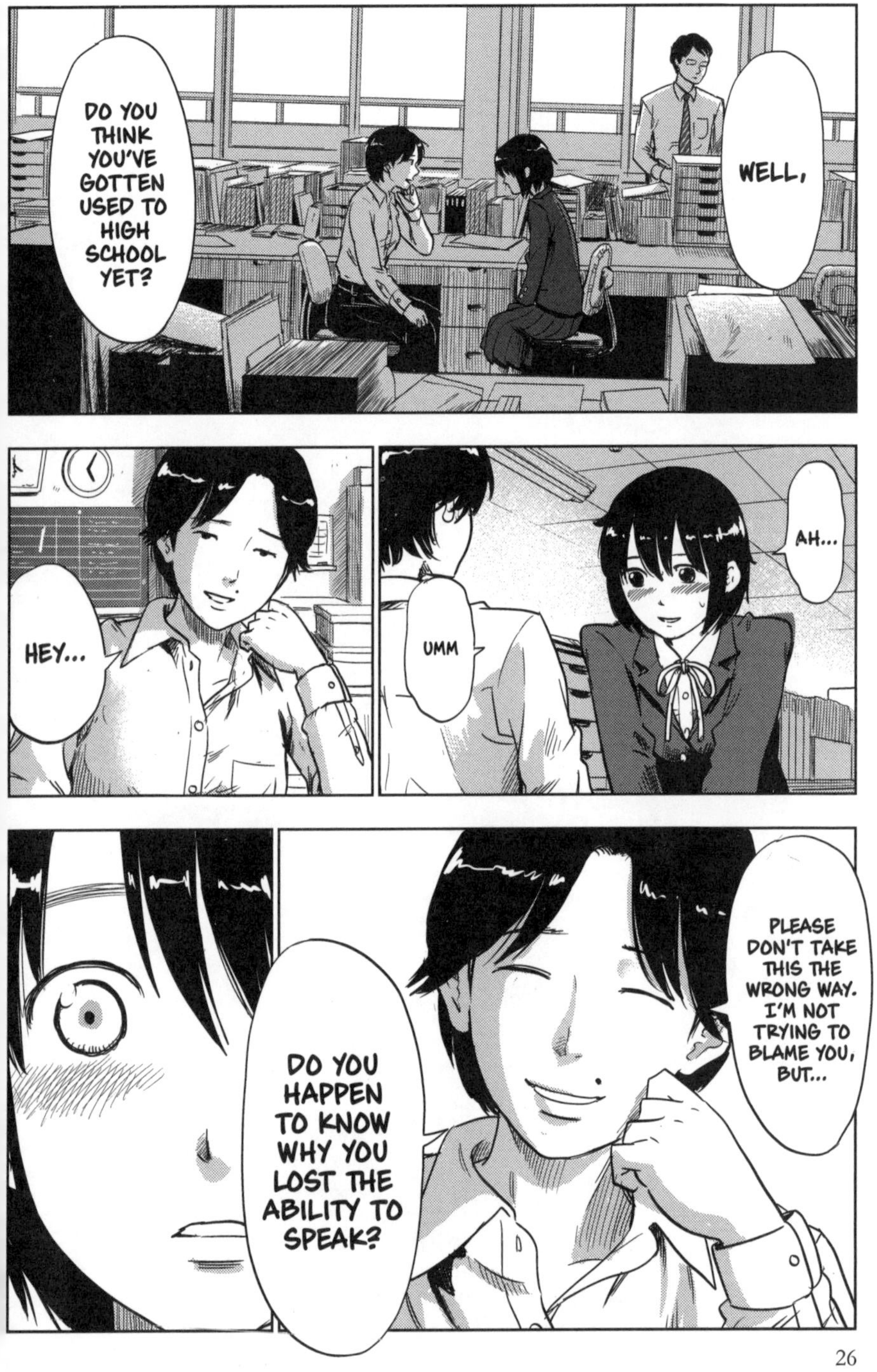
WELL,
DO YOU THINK YOU'VE GOTTEN USED TO HIGH SCHOOL YET?
AH...
UMM
HEY...
PLEASE DON'T TAKE THIS THE WRONG WAY. I'M NOT TRYING TO BLAME YOU, BUT...
DO YOU HAPPEN TO KNOW WHY YOU LOST THE ABILITY TO SPEAK?

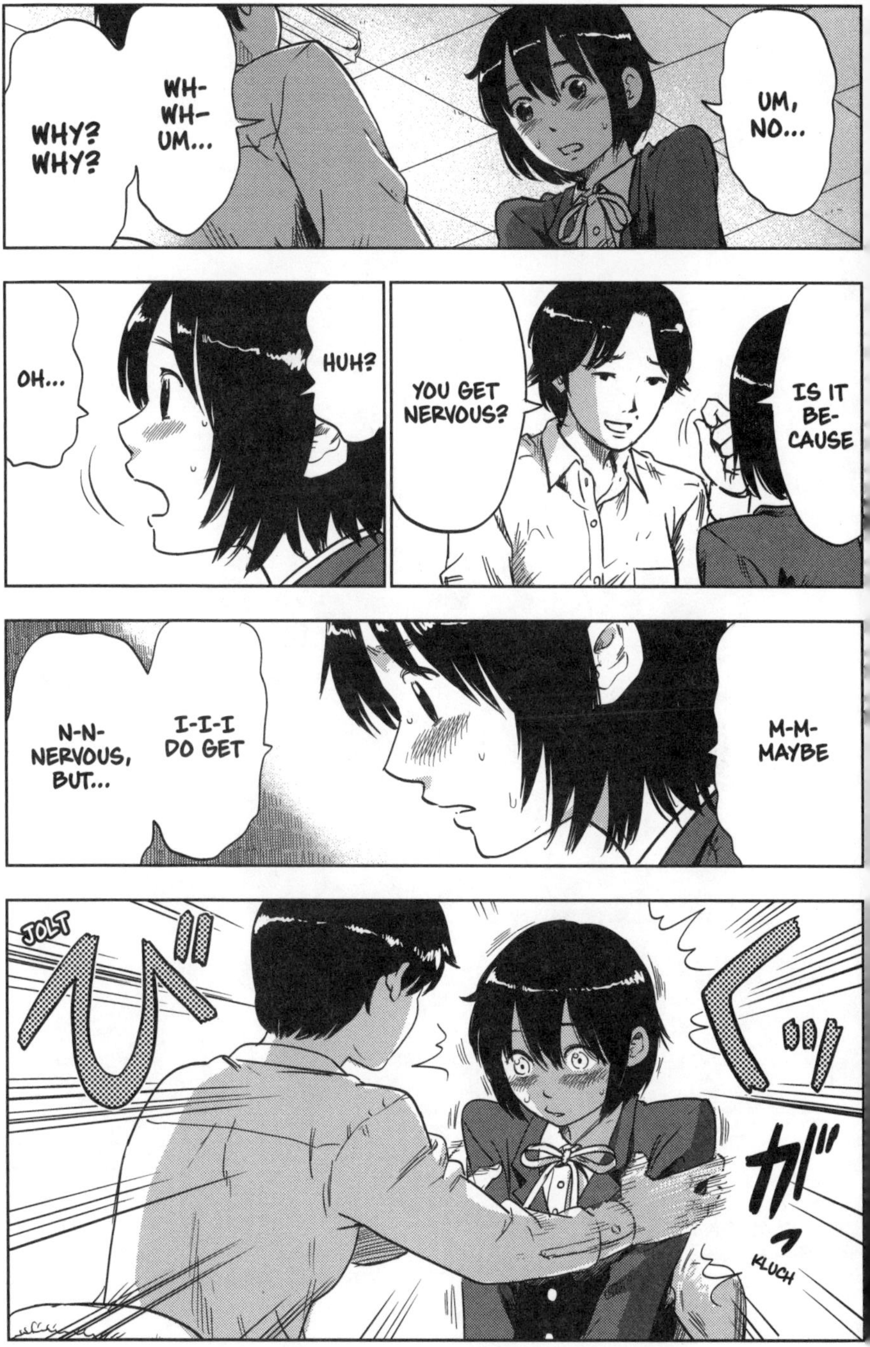
UM, NO...
WH- WH- UM...
WHY? WHY?
IS IT BE-CAUSE
YOU GET NERVOUS?
HUH?
OH...
M-M-MAYBE
I-I-I DO GET
N-N-NERVOUS, BUT...
JOLT
KLUCH

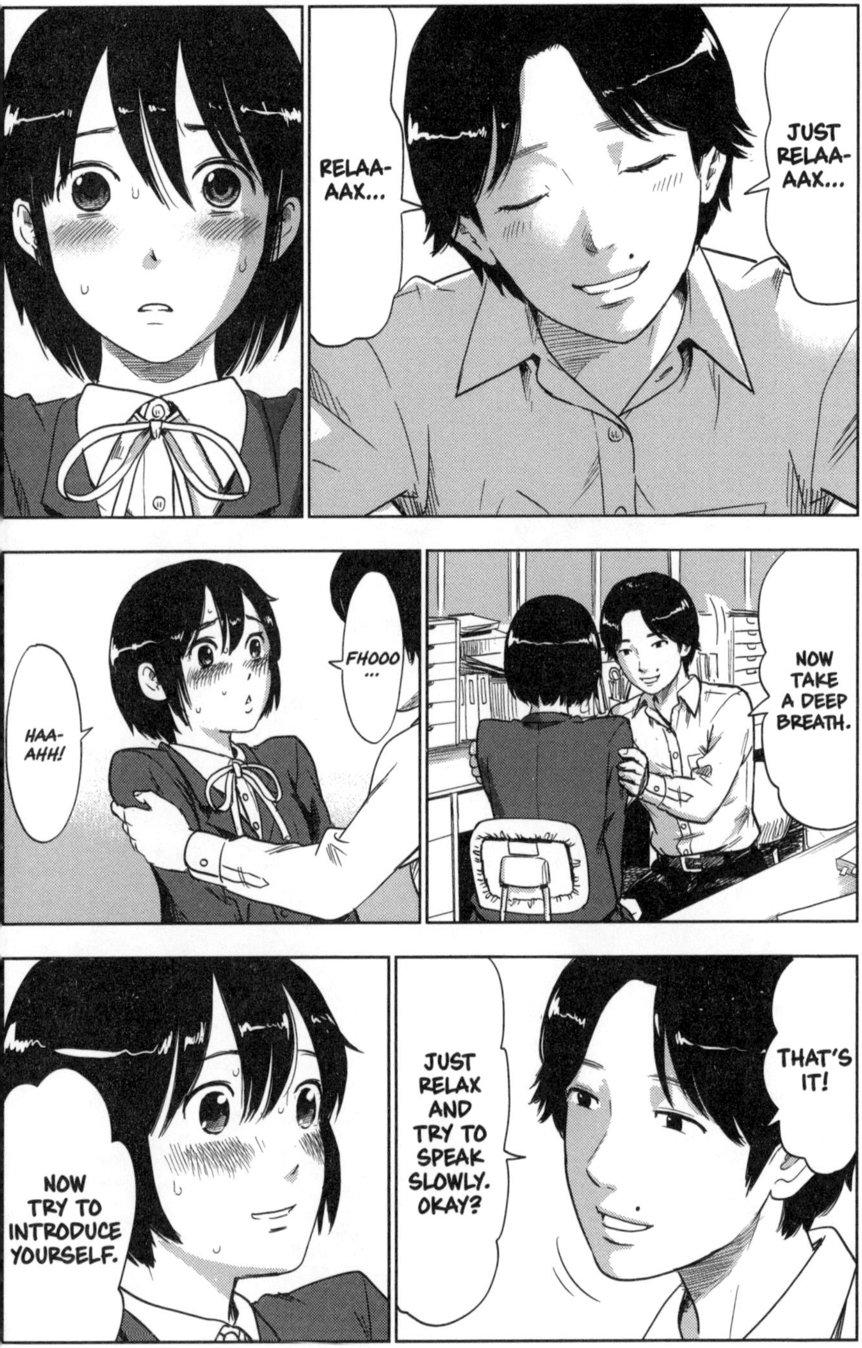
JUST RELAA-AAX...
RELAA-AAX...
NOW TAKE A DEEP BREATH.
FHOOO...
HAA-AHH!
THAT'S IT!
JUST RELAX AND TRY TO SPEAK SLOWLY. OKAY?
NOW TRY TO INTRODUCE YOURSELF.

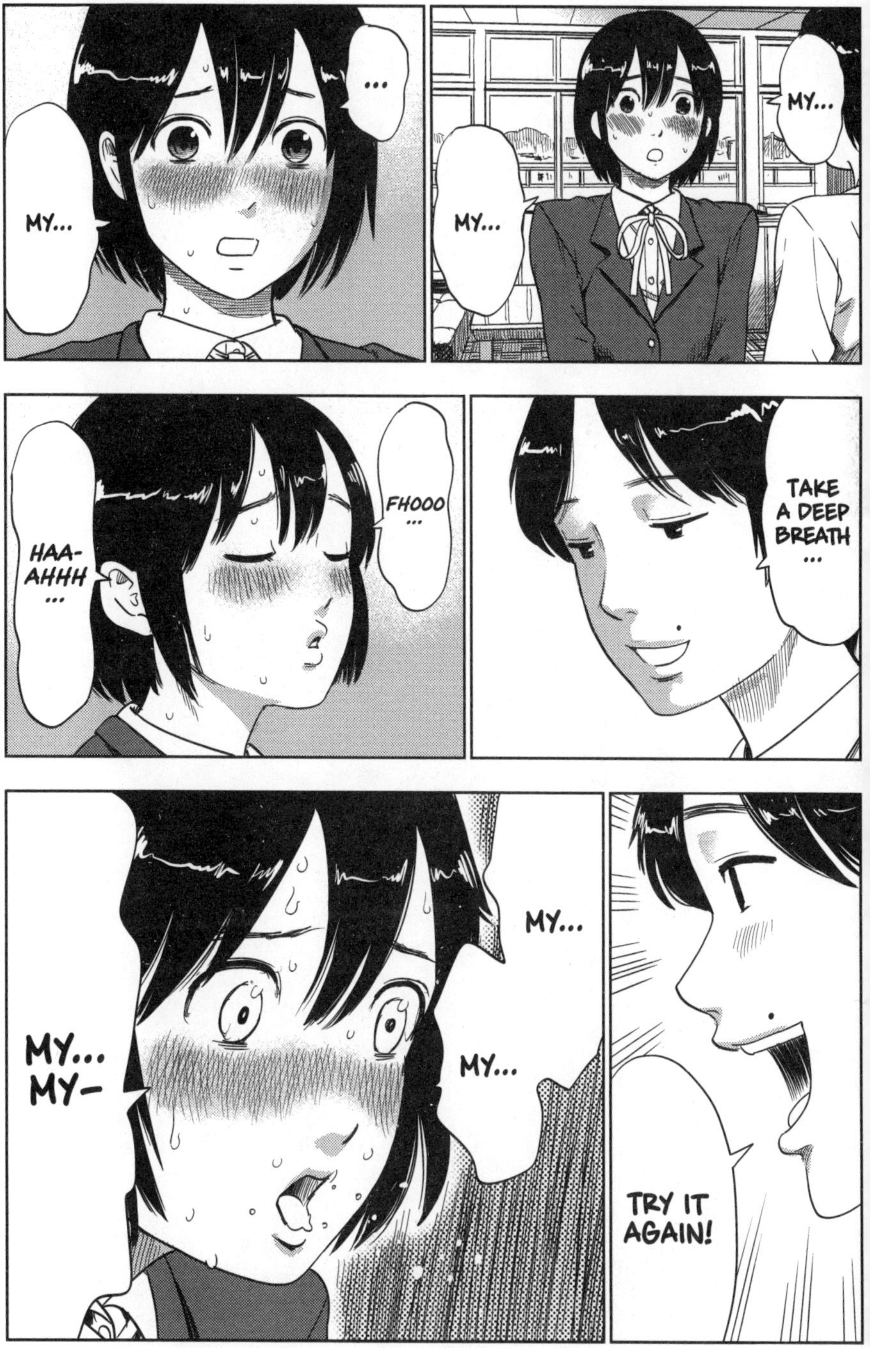

MY...
MY...
...
MY...
TAKE A DEEP BREATH ...
FHOOO ...
HAA-AHHH ...
TRY IT AGAIN!
MY...
MY...
MY... MY-

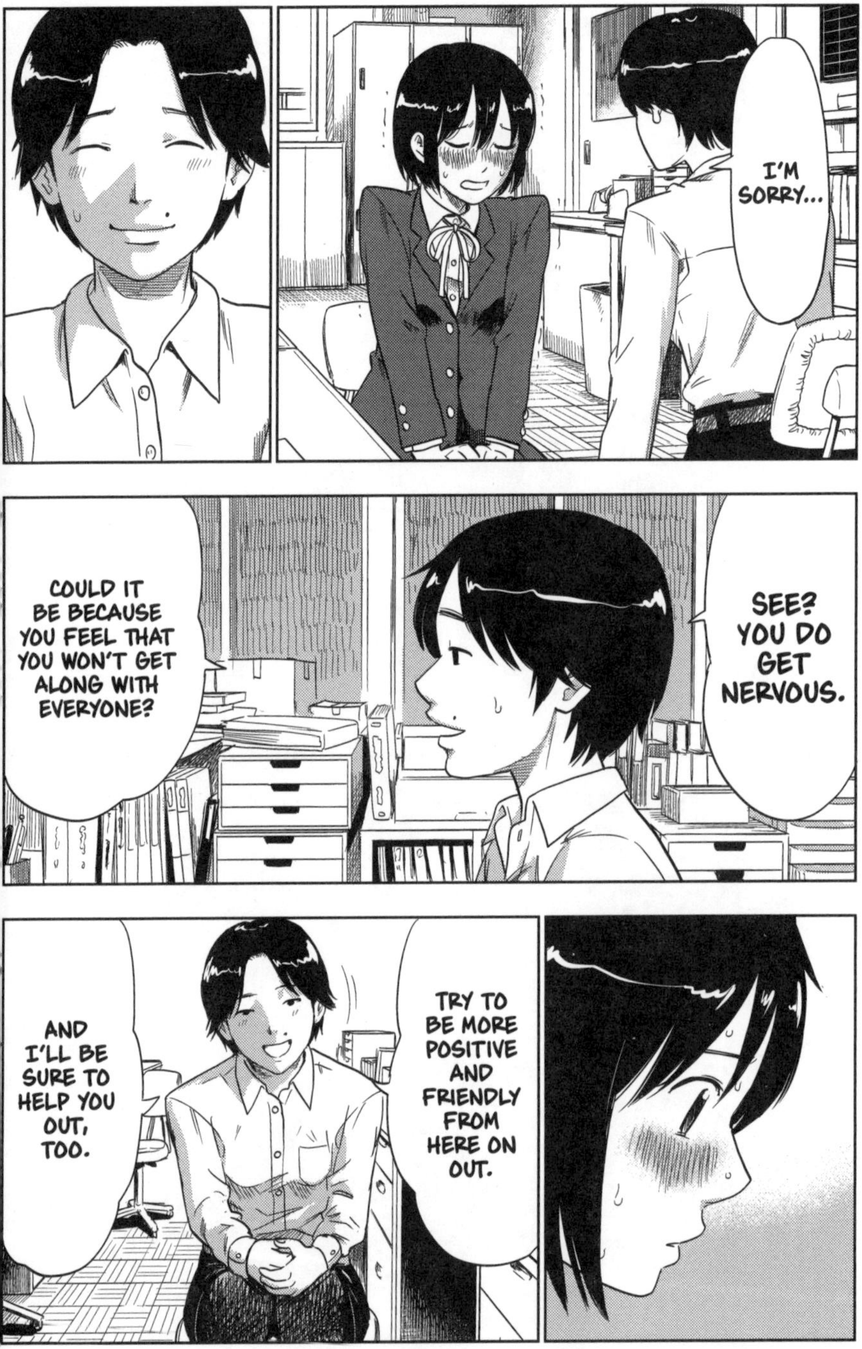
I'M SORRY...
SEE? YOU DO GET NERVOUS.
COULD IT BE BECAUSE YOU FEEL THAT YOU WON'T GET ALONG WITH EVERYONE?
TRY TO BE MORE POSITIVE AND FRIENDLY FROM HERE ON OUT.
AND I'LL BE SURE TO HELP YOU OUT, TOO.

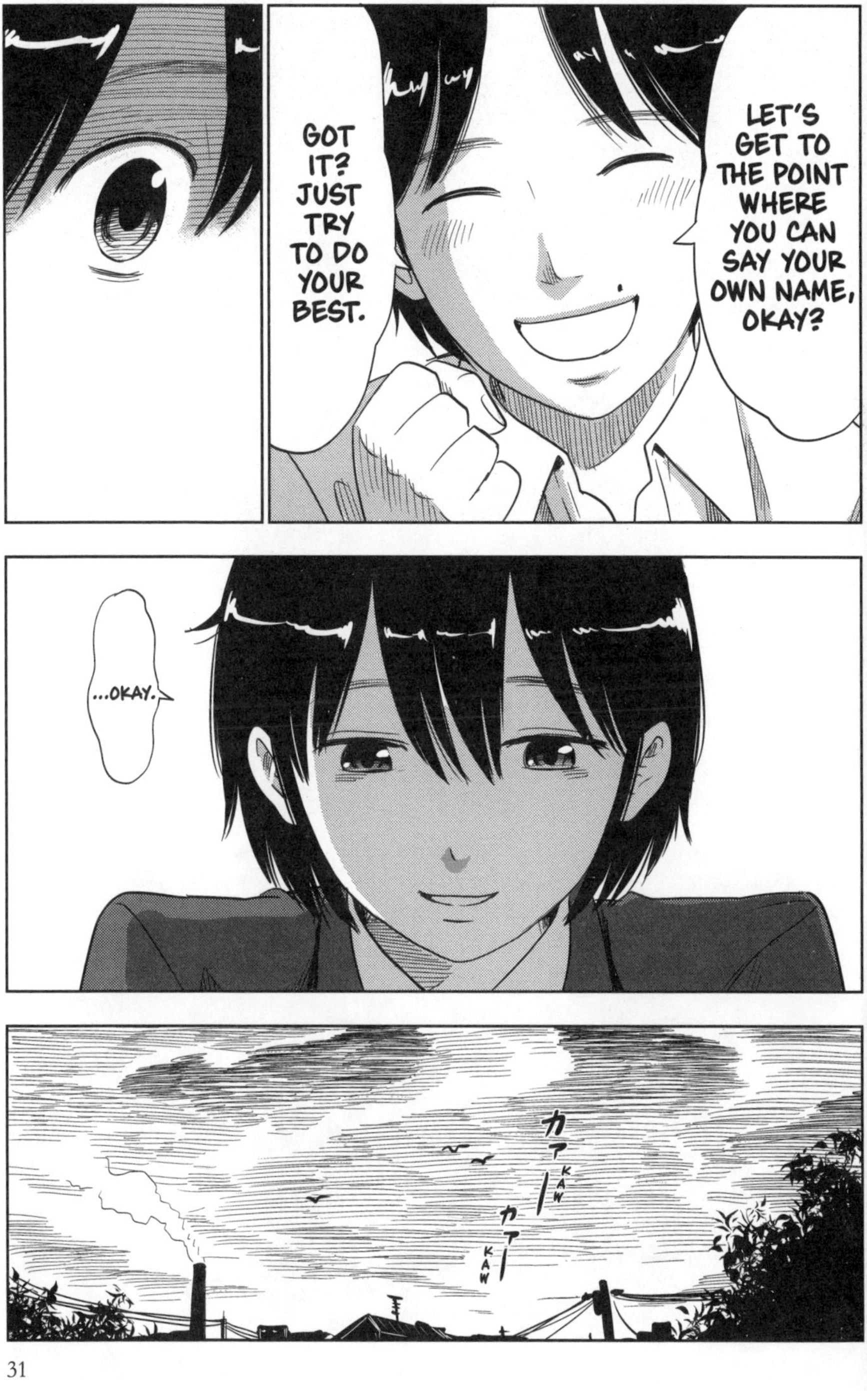
LET'S GET TO THE POINT WHERE YOU CAN SAY YOUR OWN NAME, OKAY?
GOT IT? JUST TRY TO DO YOUR BEST.
...OKAY.
カァー
KAW
カァー
KAW

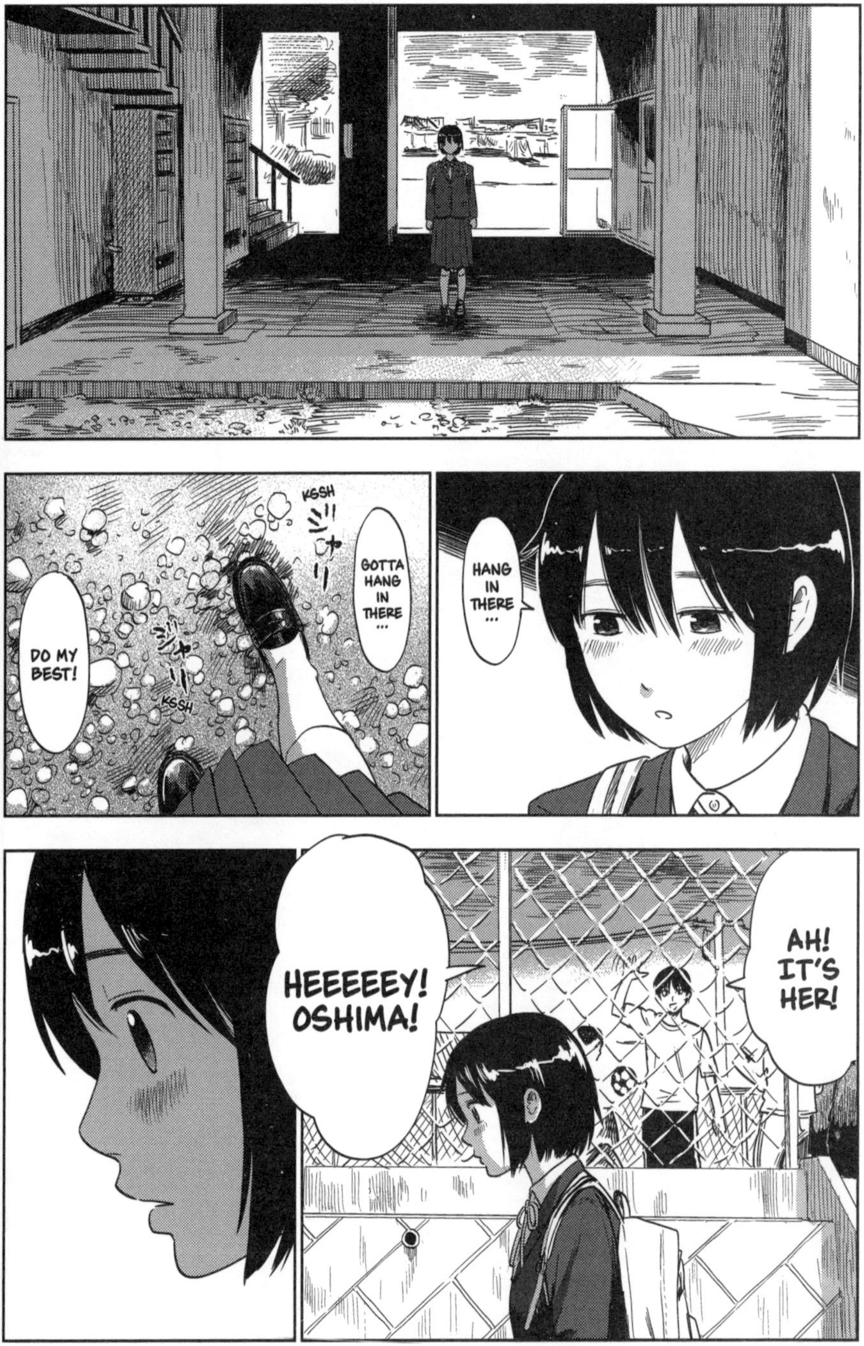
HANG IN THERE...
KSSH
GOTTA HANG IN THERE...
DO MY BEST!
KSSH
AH! IT'S HER!
HEEEEEY! OSHIMA!

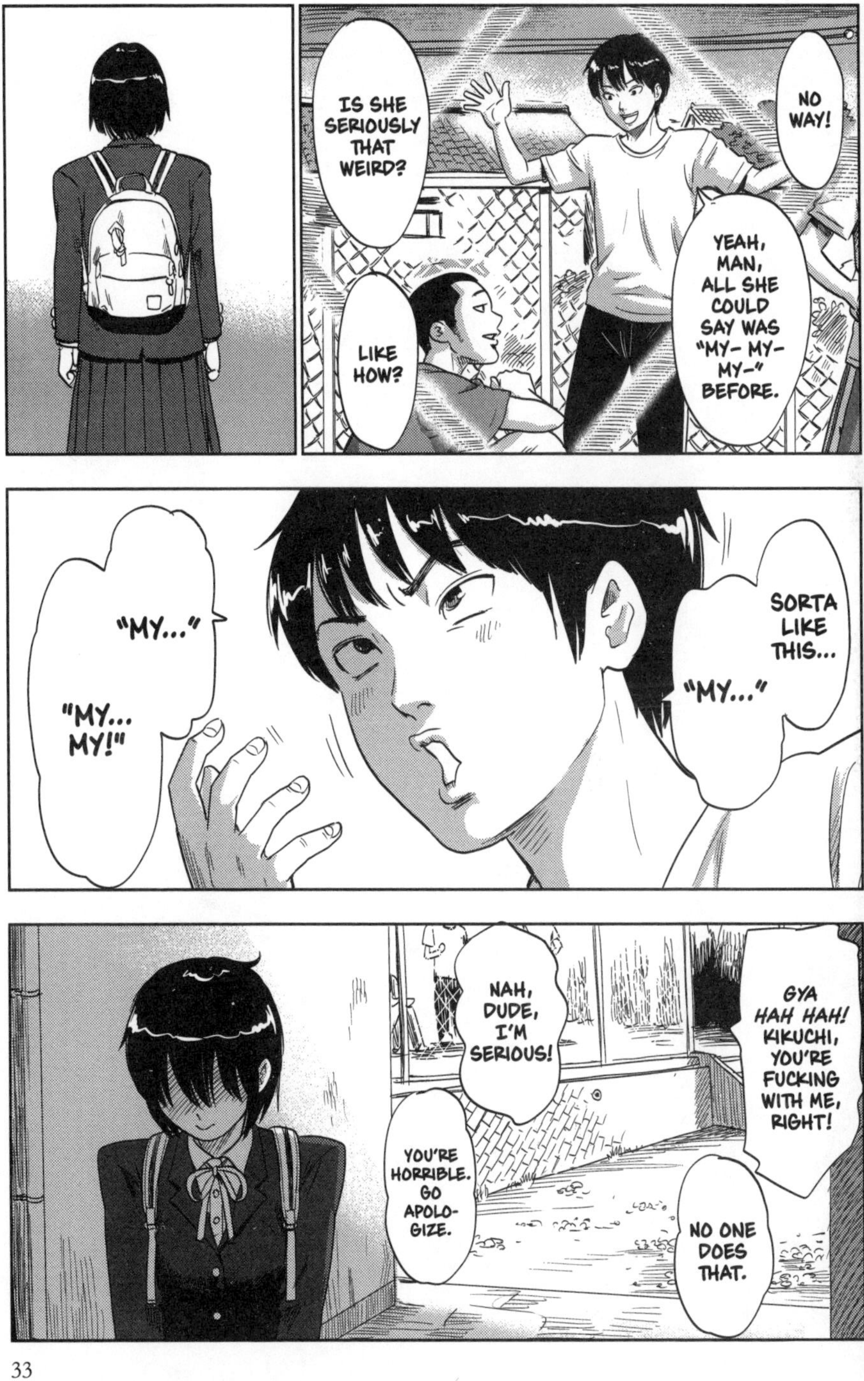
NO WAY!
IS SHE SERIOUSLY THAT WEIRD?
YEAH, MAN, ALL SHE COULD SAY WAS "MY- MY- MY-" BEFORE.
LIKE HOW?
SORTA LIKE THIS... "MY..."
"MY..."
"MY... MY!"
GYA HAH HAH! KIKUCHI, YOU'RE FUCKING WITH ME, RIGHT!
NAH, DUDE, I'M SERIOUS!
NO ONE DOES THAT.
YOU'RE HORRIBLE. GO APOLOGIZE.

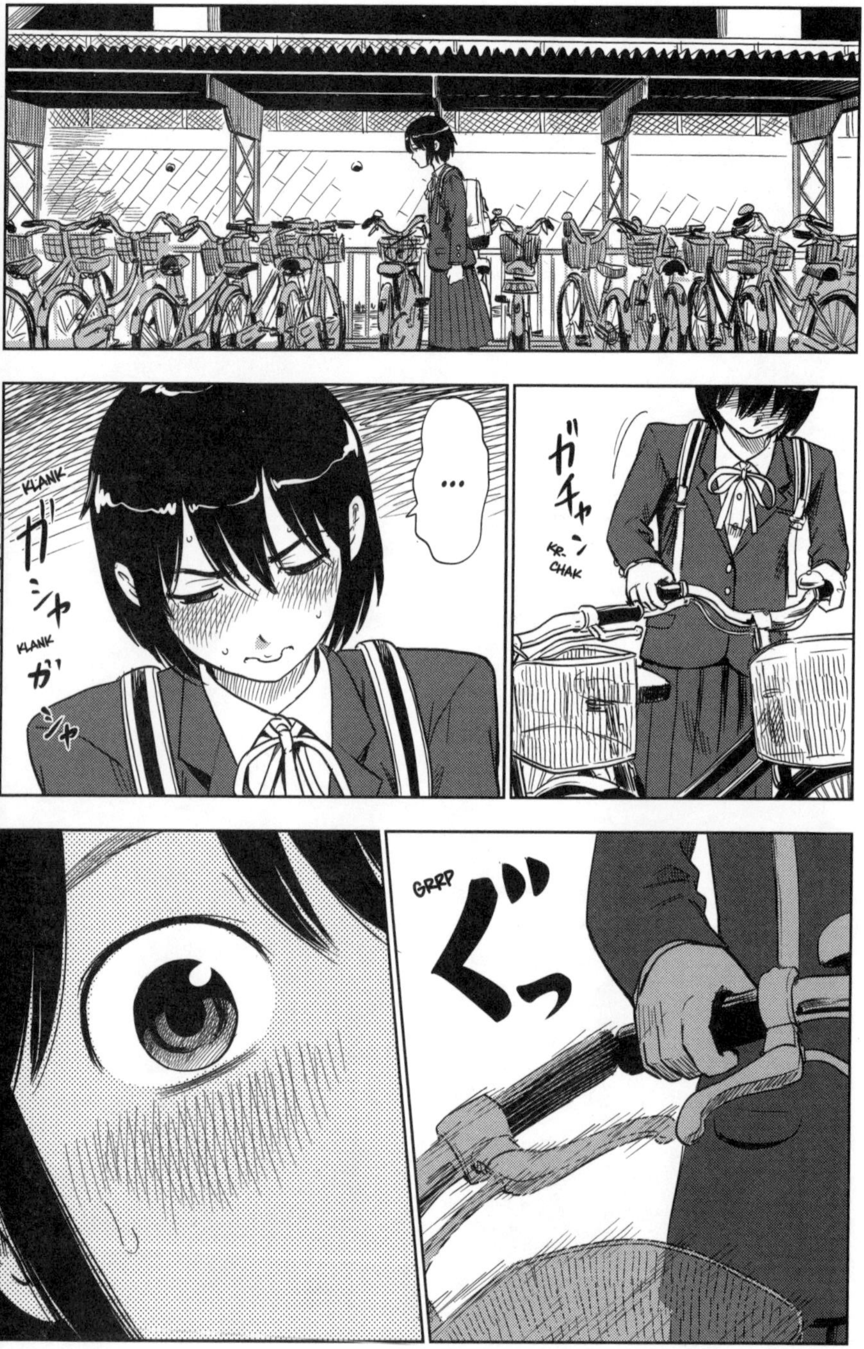
ガチャン
KR-CHAK
...
KLANK
ガシャ
KLANK
ガシャ
GRRP
ぐっ

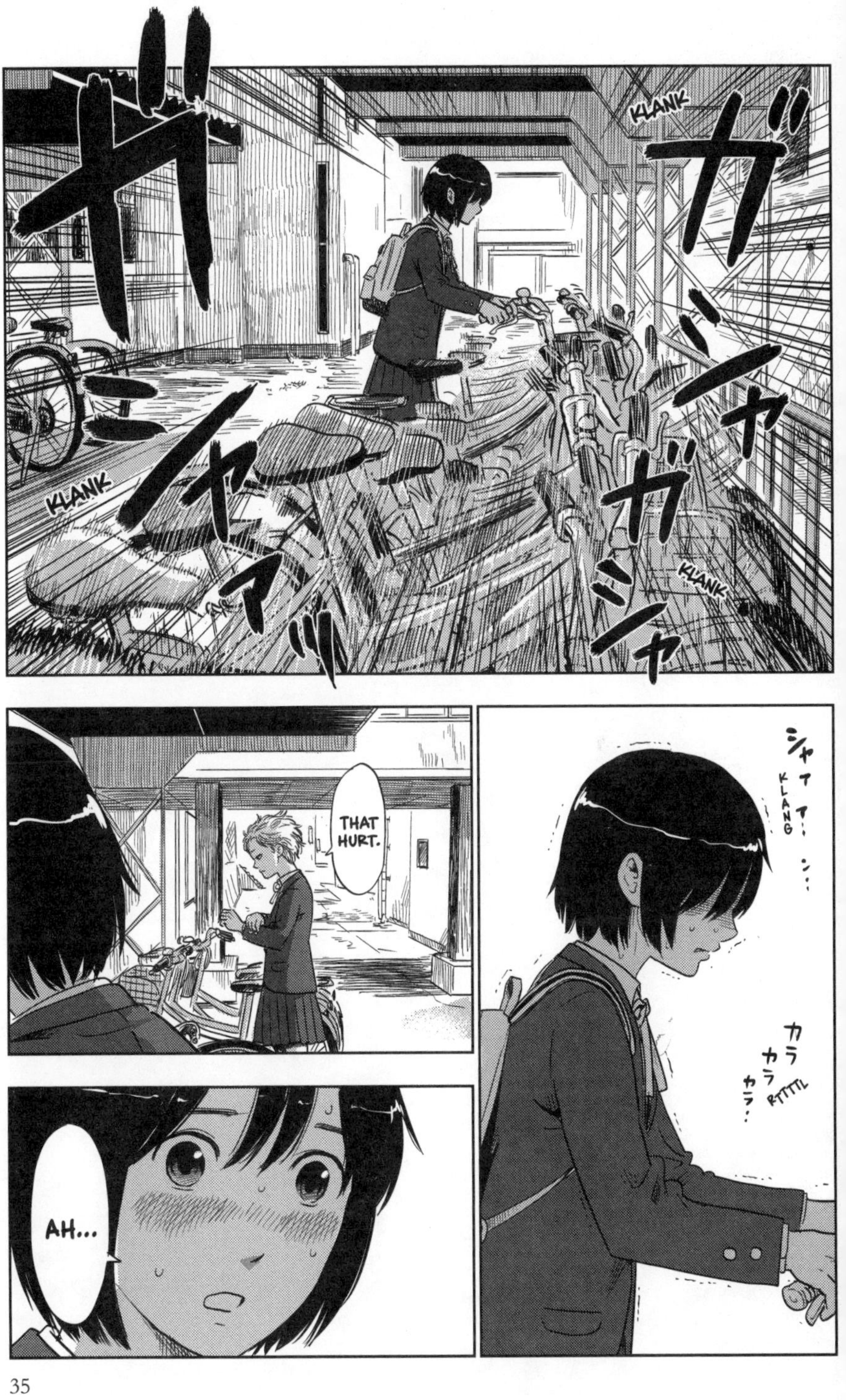
KLANK
KLANK
KLANK
シャァ…
KLANG
カラ
カラ
カラ…
RTTTTL
THAT HURT.
AH...

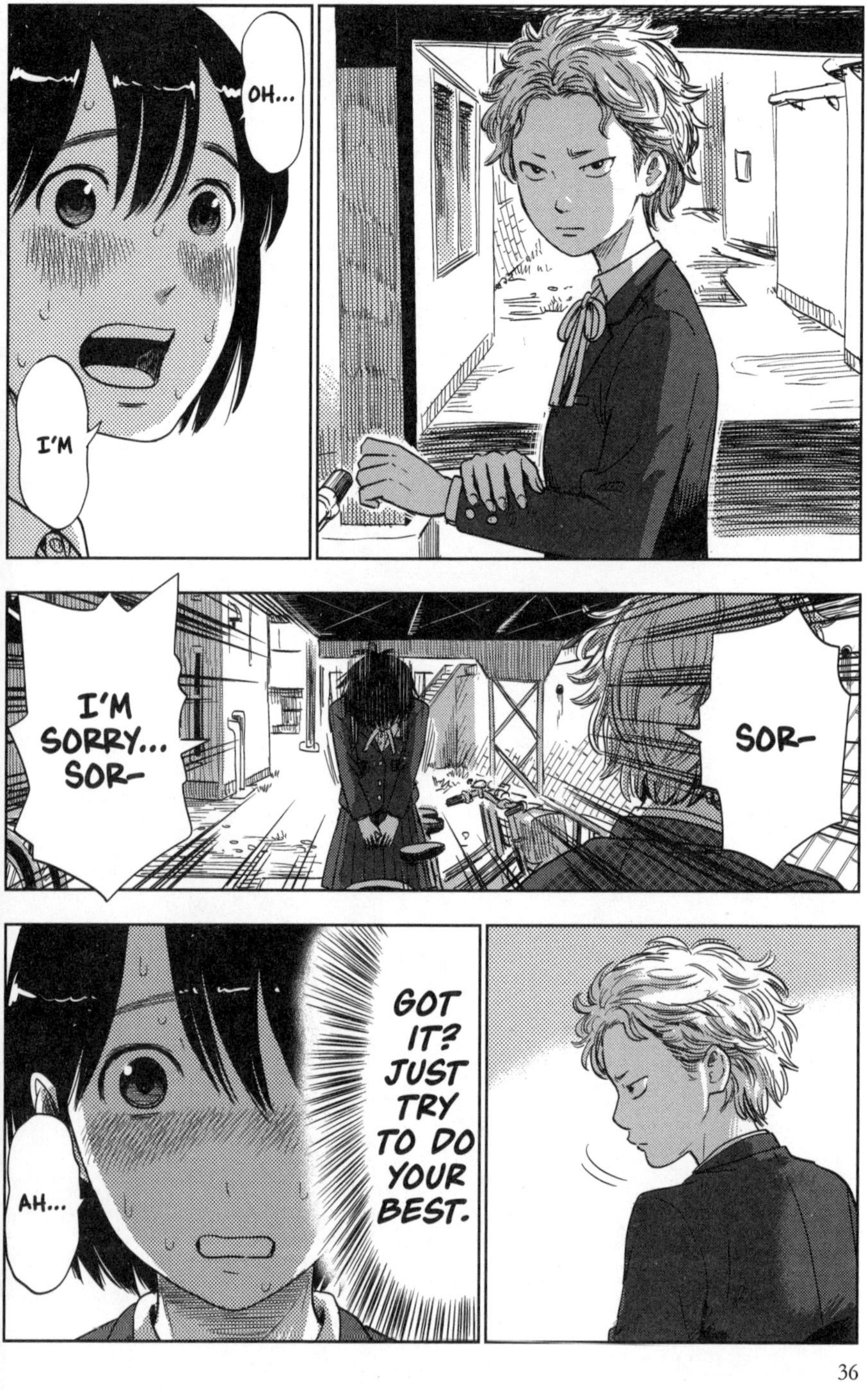
OH...
I'M
I'M SORRY... SOR-
SOR-
GOT IT? JUST TRY TO DO YOUR BEST.
AH...

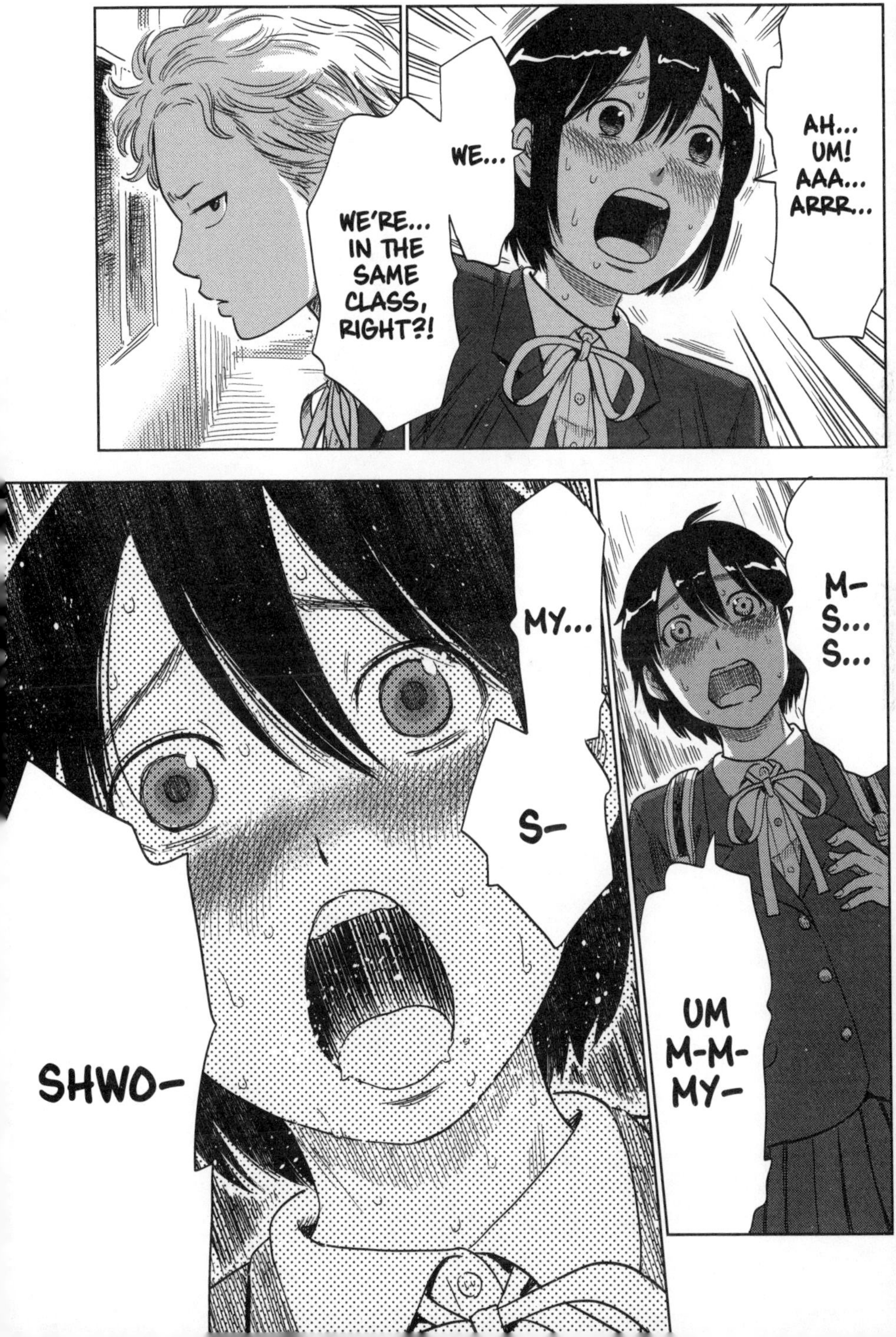
AH... UM! AAA... ARRR...
WE...
WE'RE... IN THE SAME CLASS, RIGHT?!
M-S... S...
UM M-M-MY-
MY...
S-
SHWO-

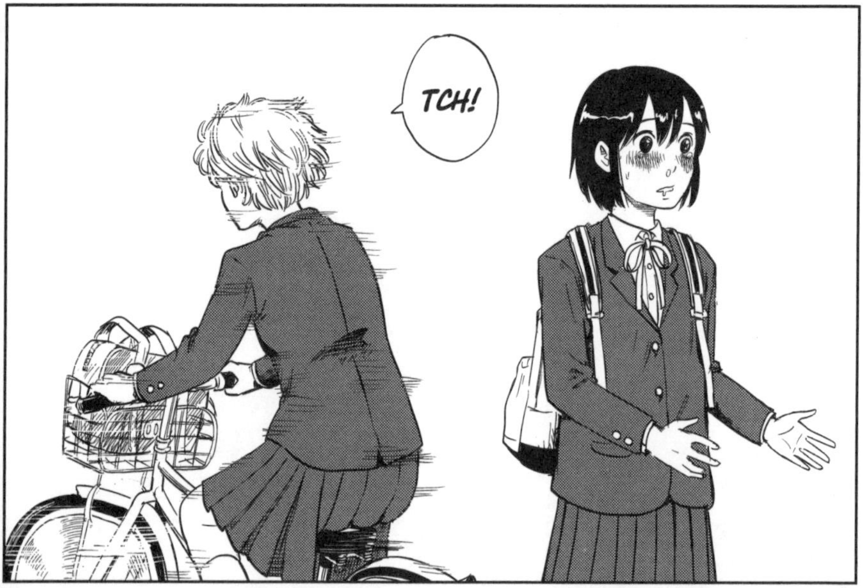
TCH!

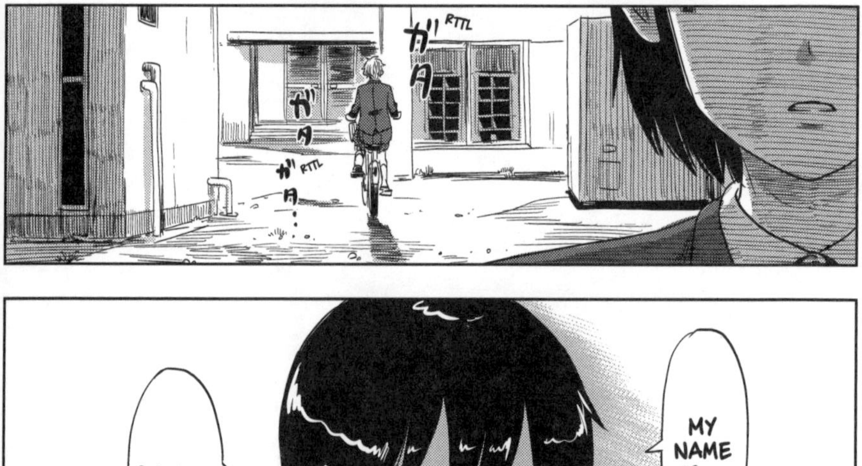
ガタ RTTL
ガタ RTTL

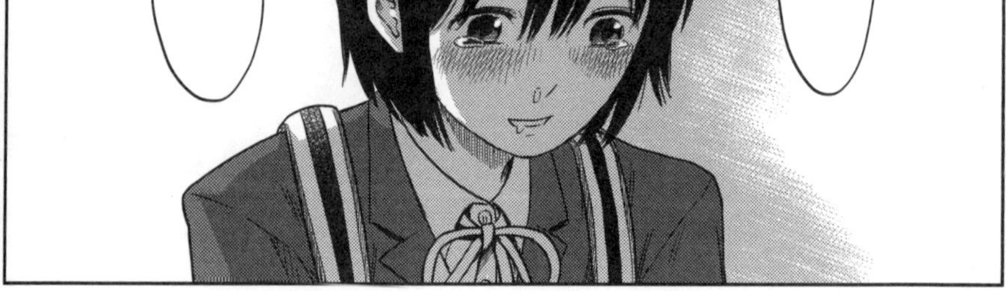
MY NAME IS...
SHINO...

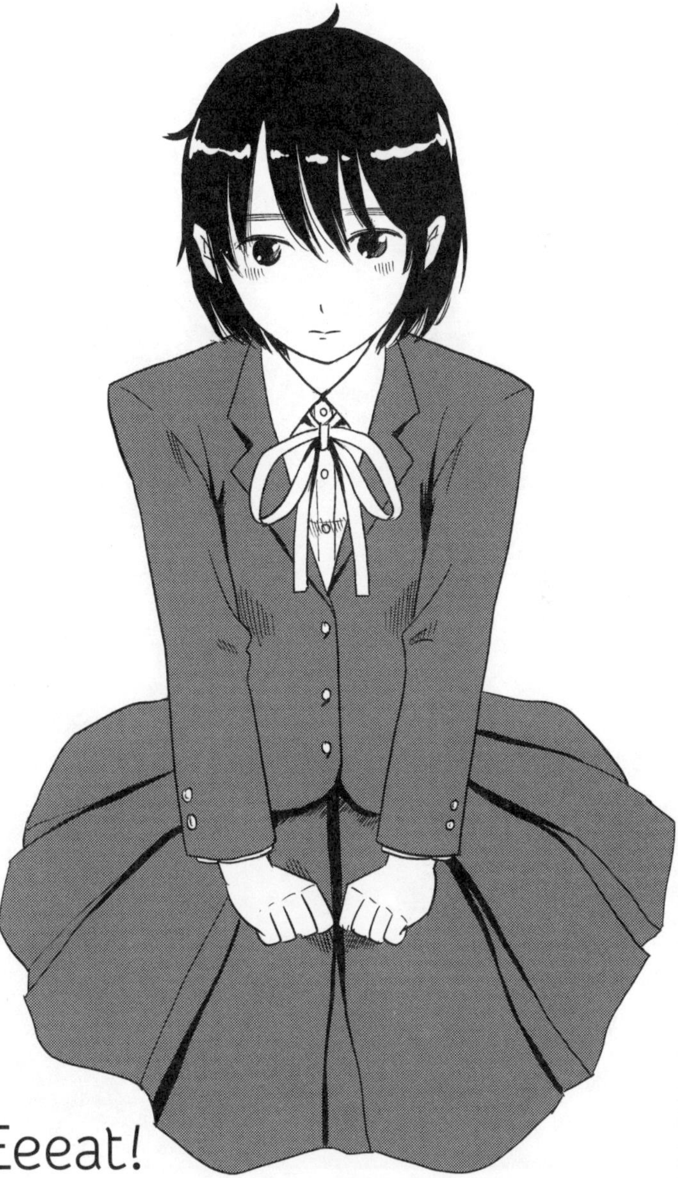

Chapter 3
Let's Eeeat!

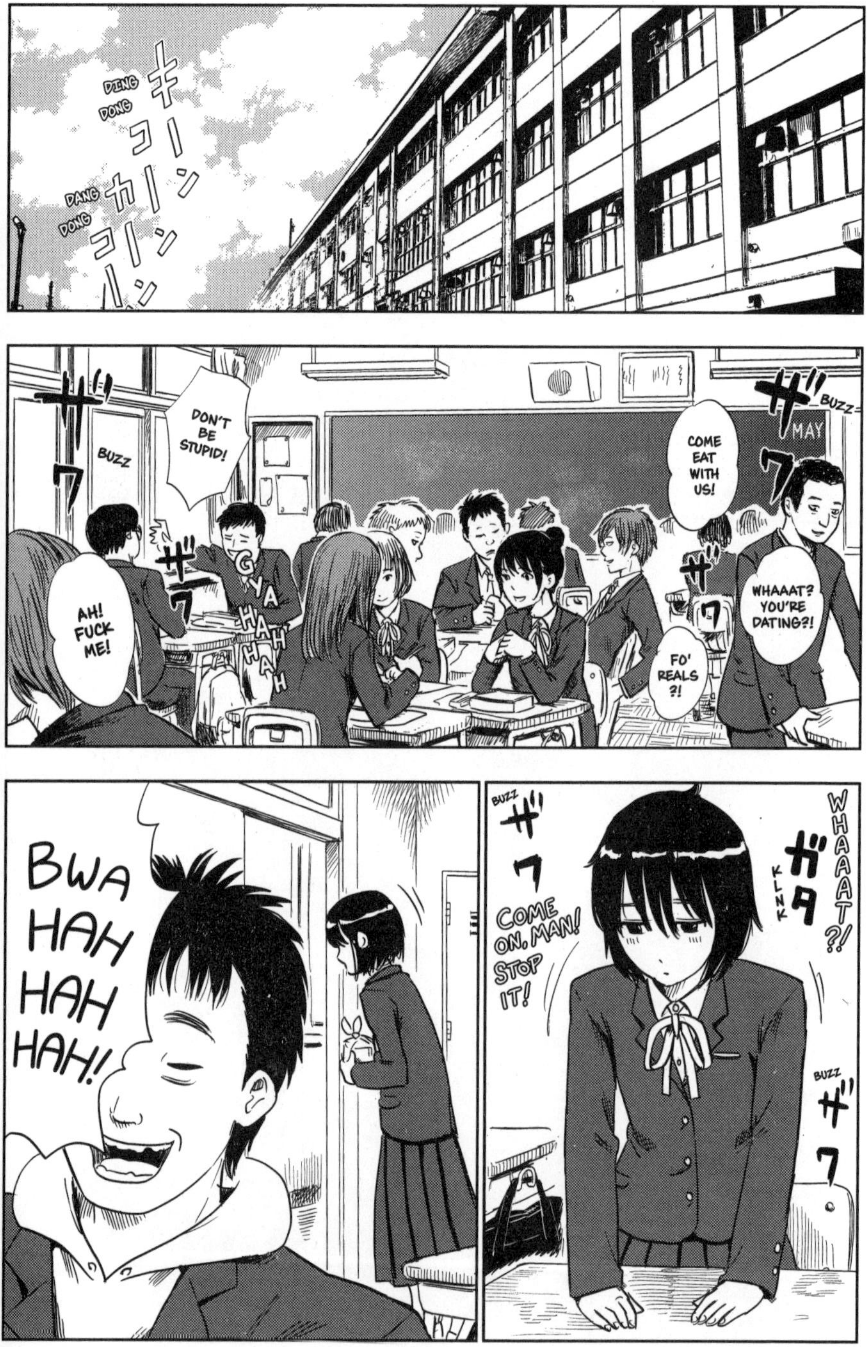
キーンコーンカーンコーン
DING DONG DANG DONG
ザワ
BUZZ
COME EAT WITH US!
WHAAAT? YOU'RE DATING?!
FO' REALS?!
GYAHAHHAH
DON'T BE STUPID!
ザワ
BUZZ
AH! FUCK ME!
WHAAAT?!
ガタ
KLNK
ザワ
BUZZ
COME ON, MAN! STOP IT!
ザワ
BUZZ
BWA HAH HAH HAH!

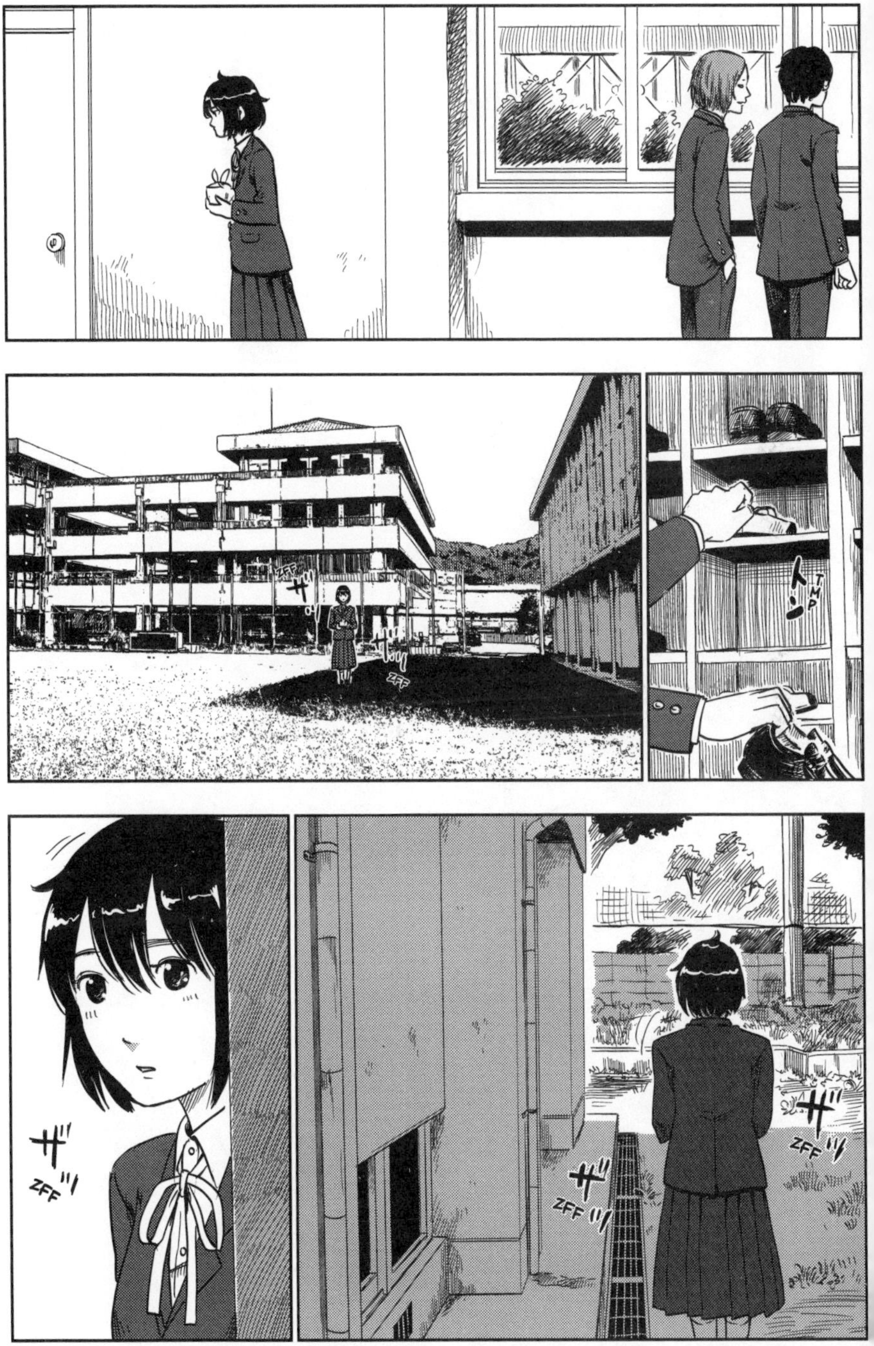
トン
TMP
ZFF
ザッ
ZFF
ザッ
ZFF
ザッ
ZFF
ザッ
ZFF

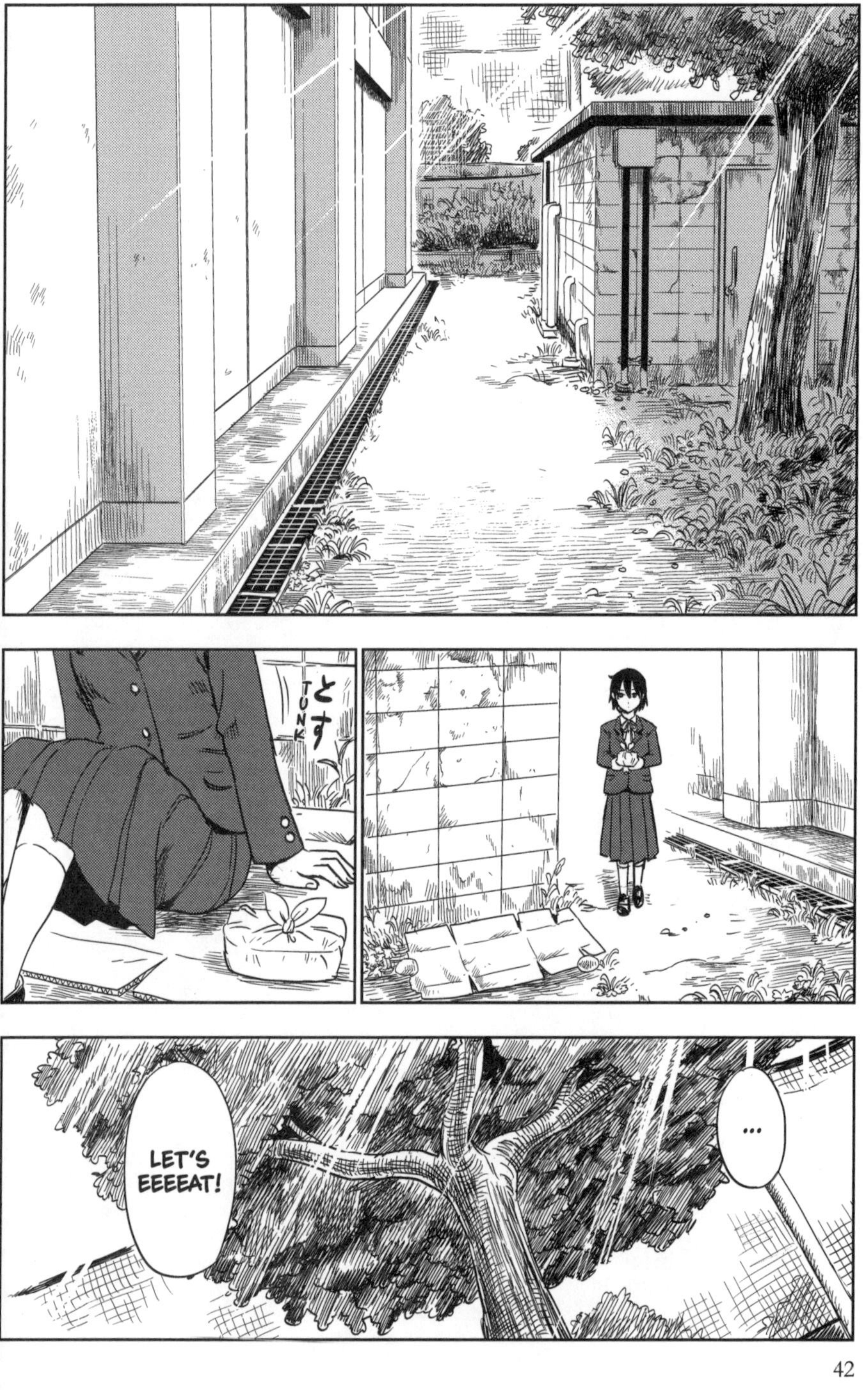
とす
TUNK
...
LET'S EEEEAT!

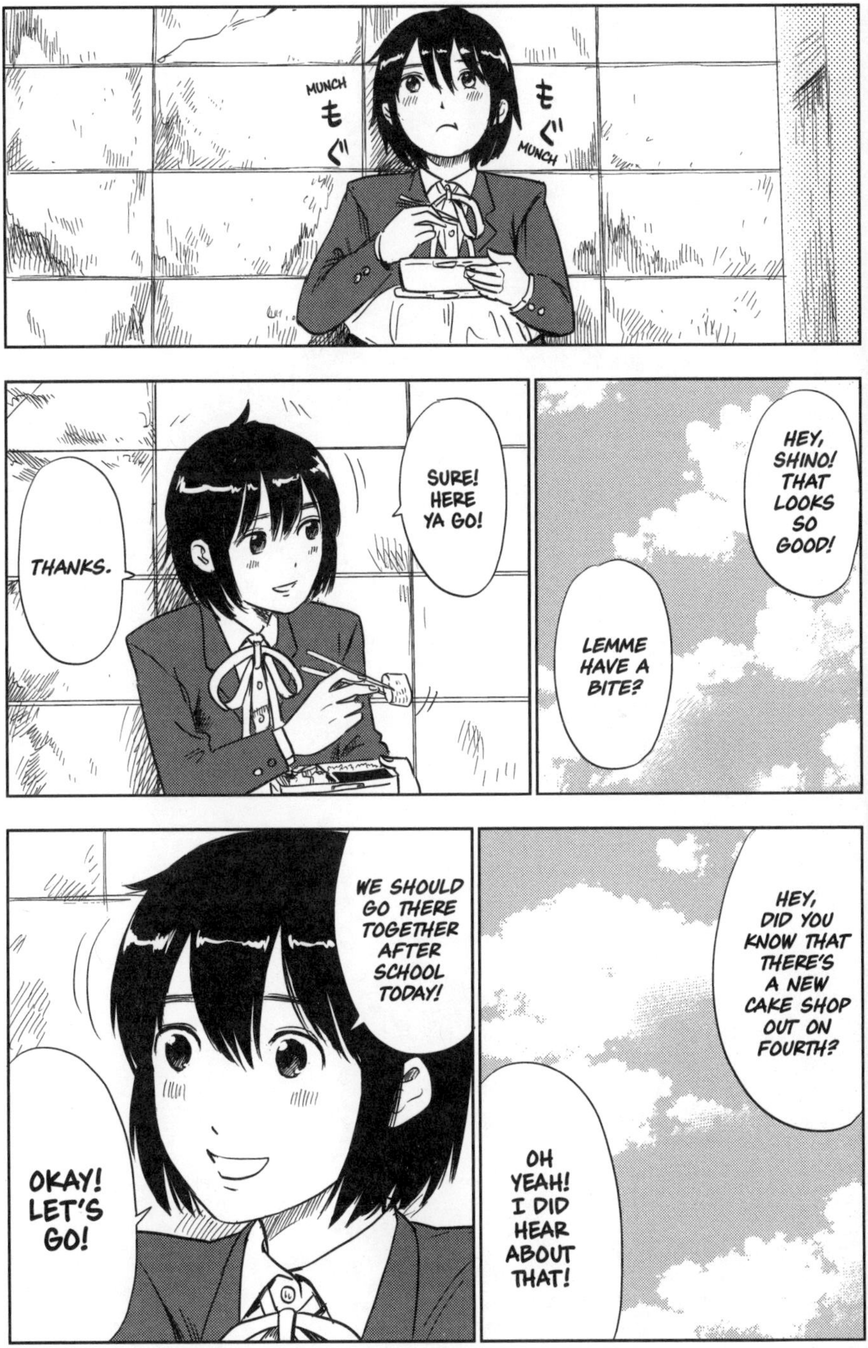
もぐ MUNCH
MUNCH もぐ
HEY, SHINO! THAT LOOKS SO GOOD!
LEMME HAVE A BITE?
SURE! HERE YA GO!
THANKS.
HEY, DID YOU KNOW THAT THERE'S A NEW CAKE SHOP OUT ON FOURTH?
OH YEAH! I DID HEAR ABOUT THAT!
WE SHOULD GO THERE TOGETHER AFTER SCHOOL TODAY!
OKAY! LET'S GO!

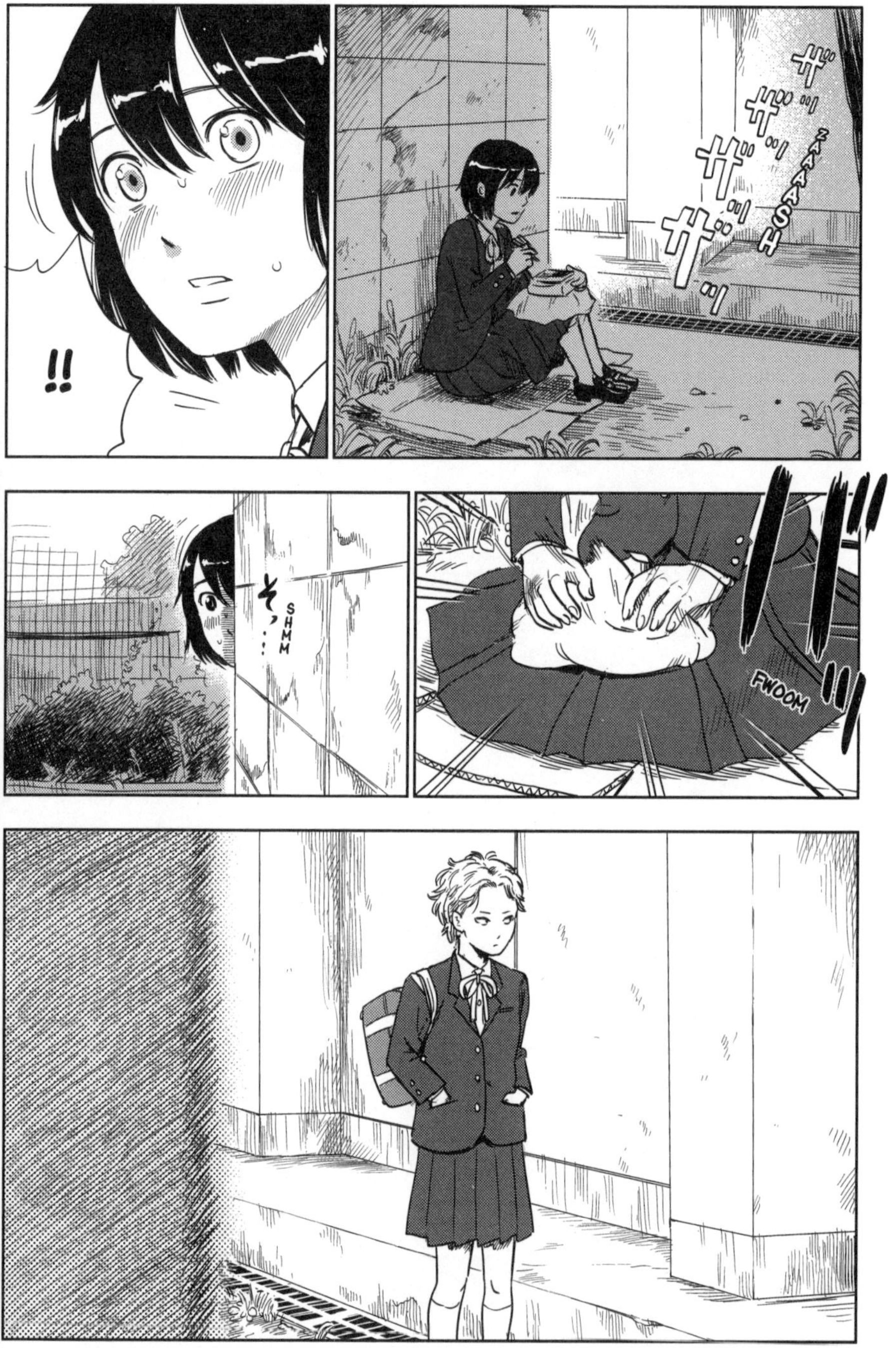
ザッ ザッ ザッ ザッ
ZAAAASH
!!
FWOOM
そ…
SHMM

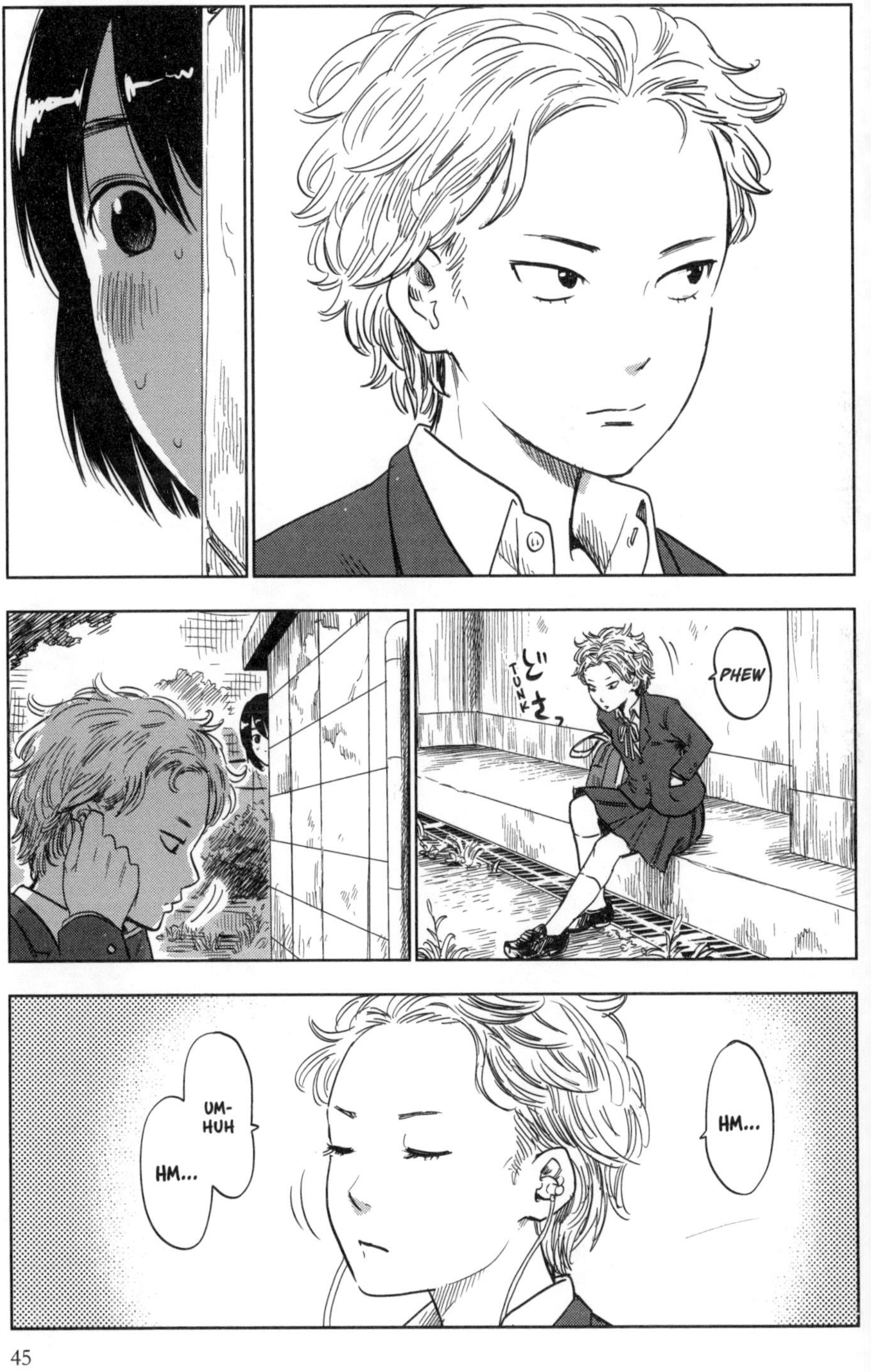
どさっ
TUNK
PHEW
HM...
UM-HUH
HM...

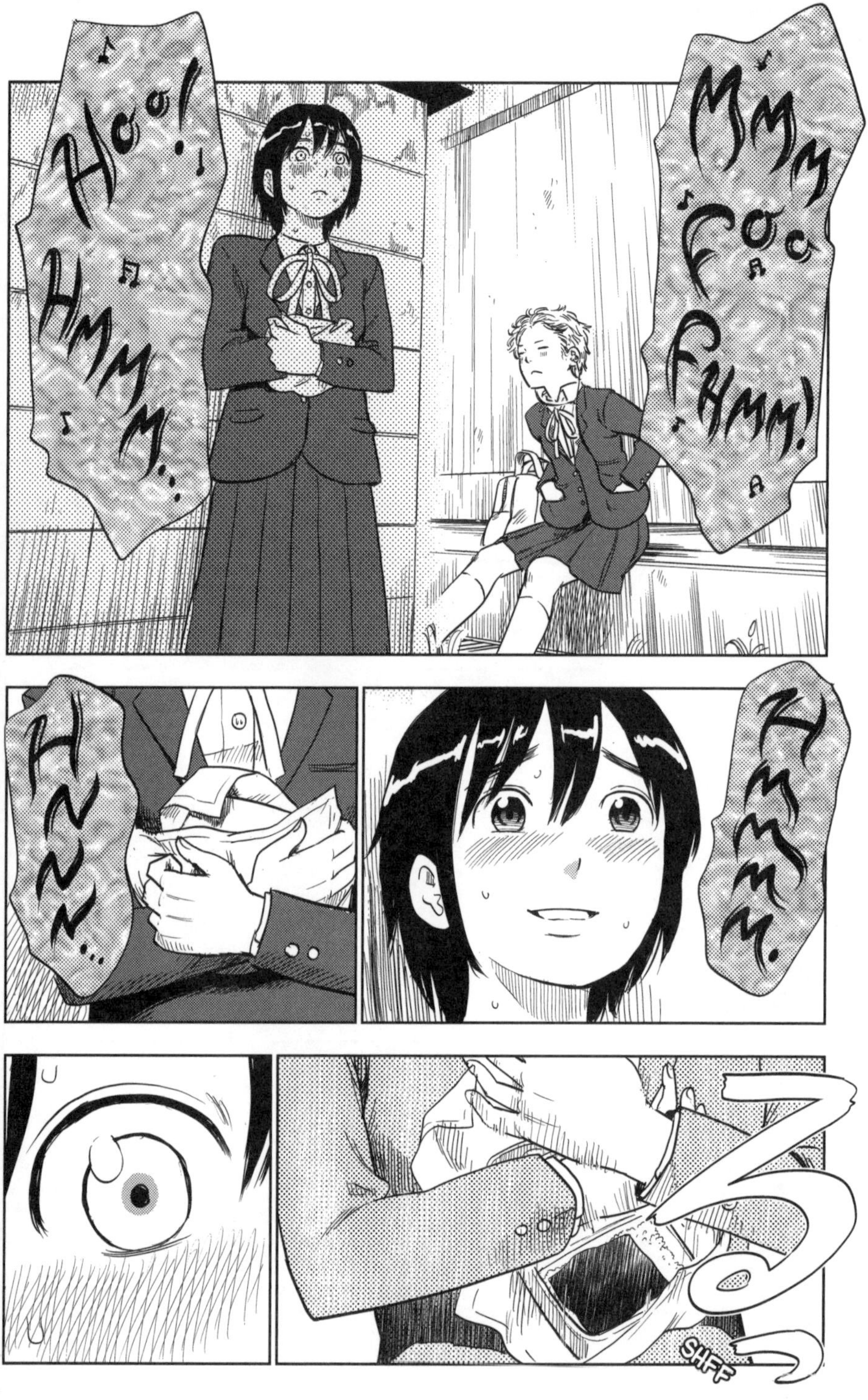
MMM FOO FHMM!
HOO! HMMM...
HMMMM.
HNNN...
SHFF

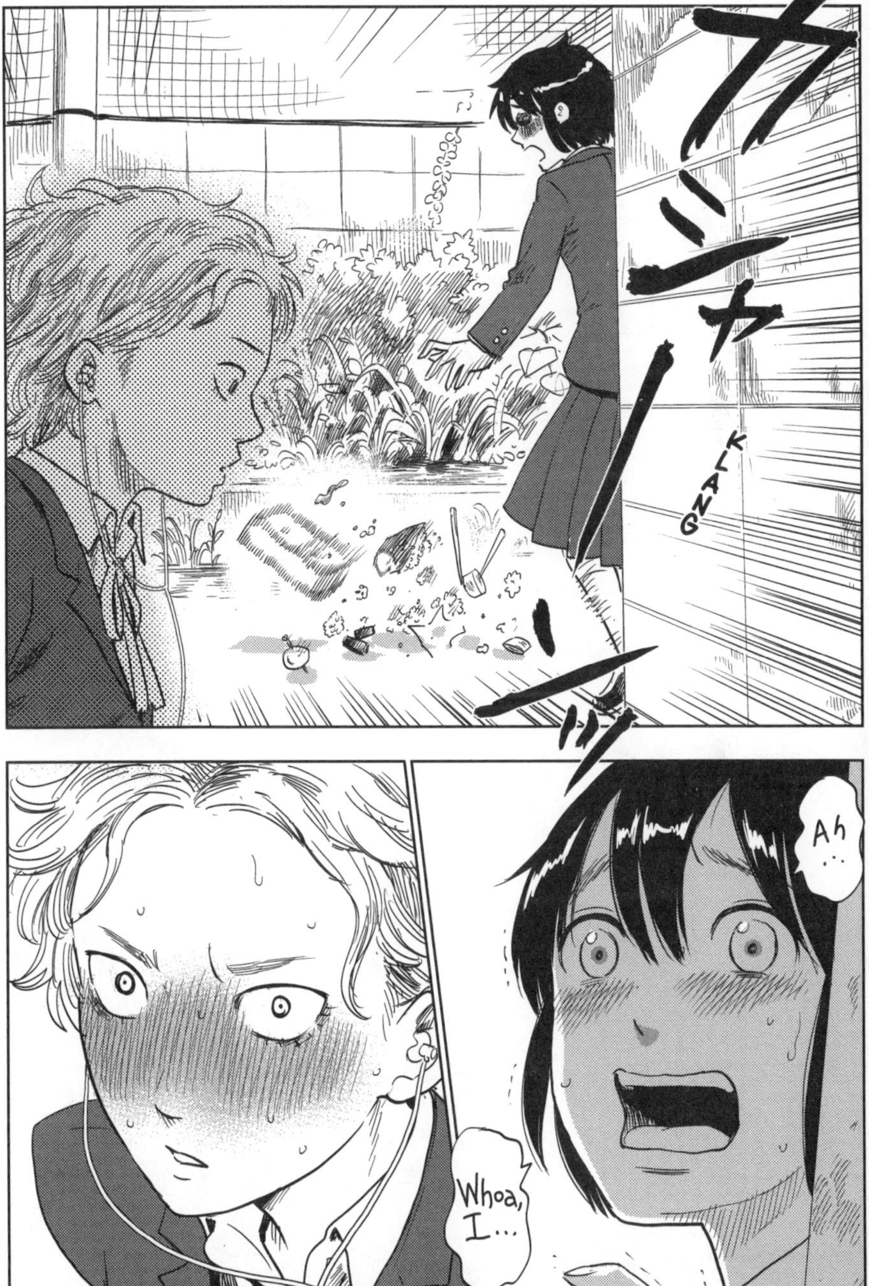
KLANG
Ah ...
Whoa, I...

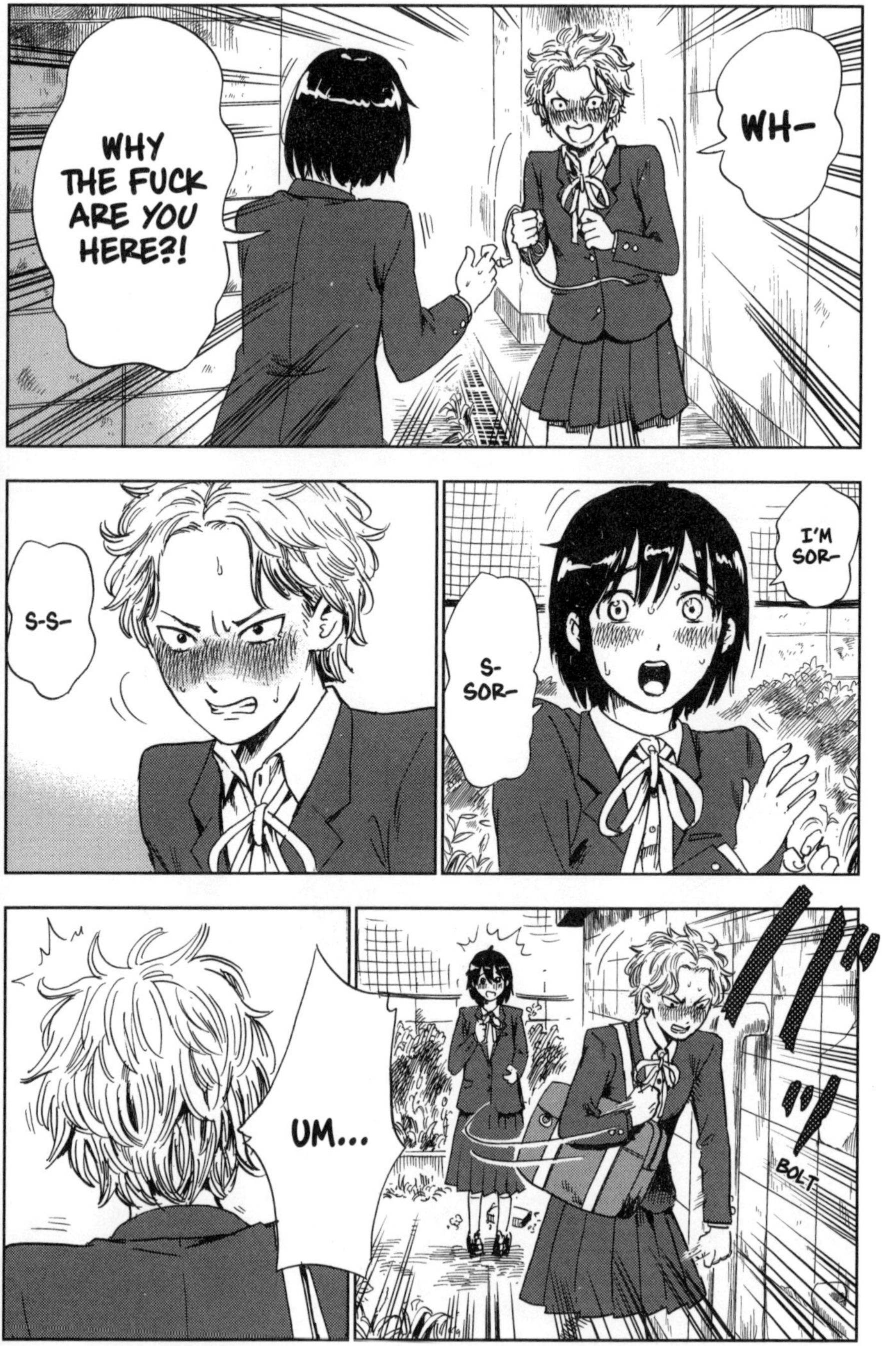
WH-
WHY THE FUCK ARE YOU HERE?!
I'M SOR-
S- SOR-
S-S-
BOLT
UM...

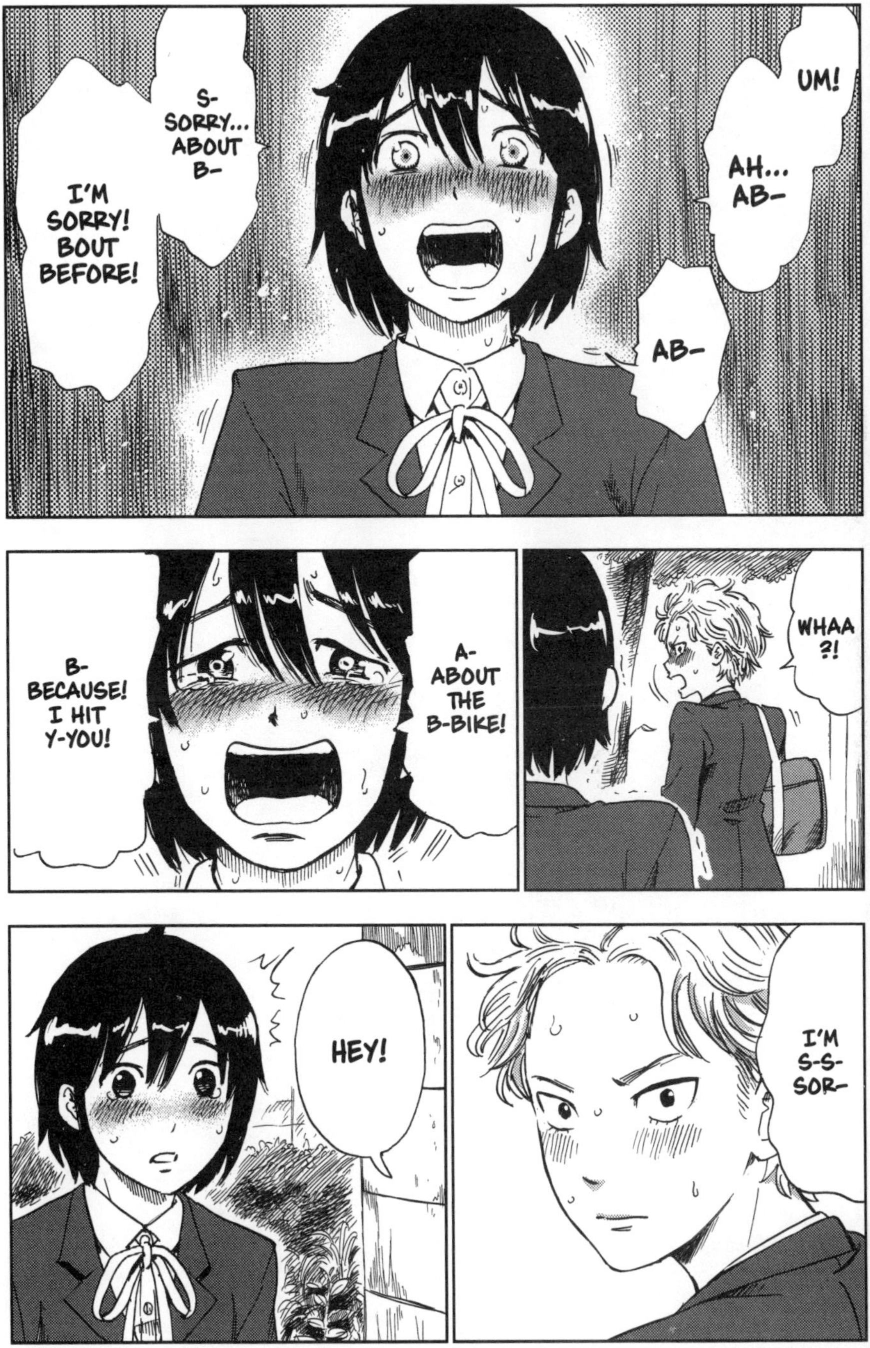
UM!
AH... AB-
AB-
S- SORRY... ABOUT B-
I'M SORRY! BOUT BEFORE!
WHAA?!
A- ABOUT THE B-BIKE!
B- BECAUSE! I HIT Y-YOU!
I'M S-S-SOR-
HEY!

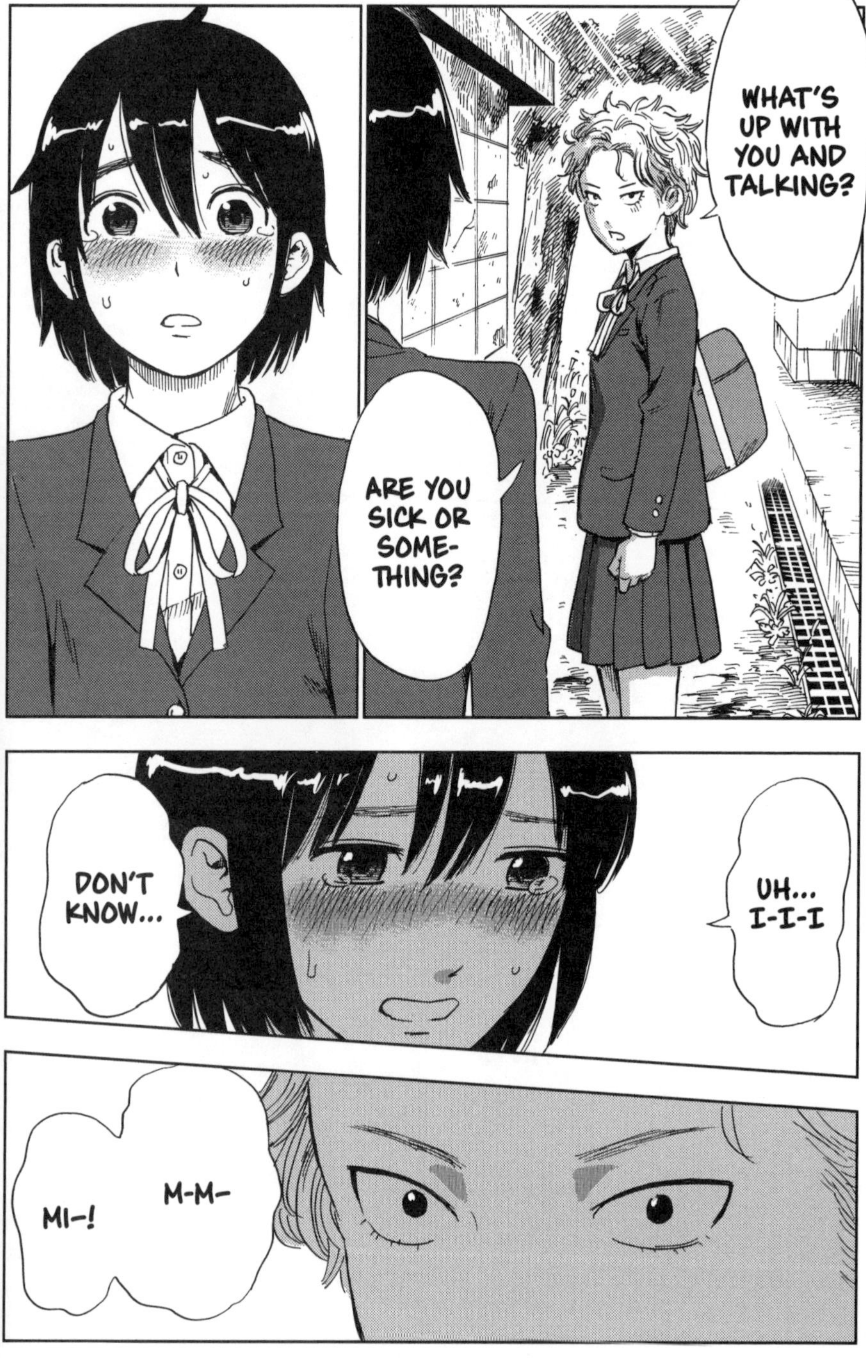
WHAT'S UP WITH YOU AND TALKING?
ARE YOU SICK OR SOME-THING?
UH... I-I-I
DON'T KNOW...
M-M-
MI-!

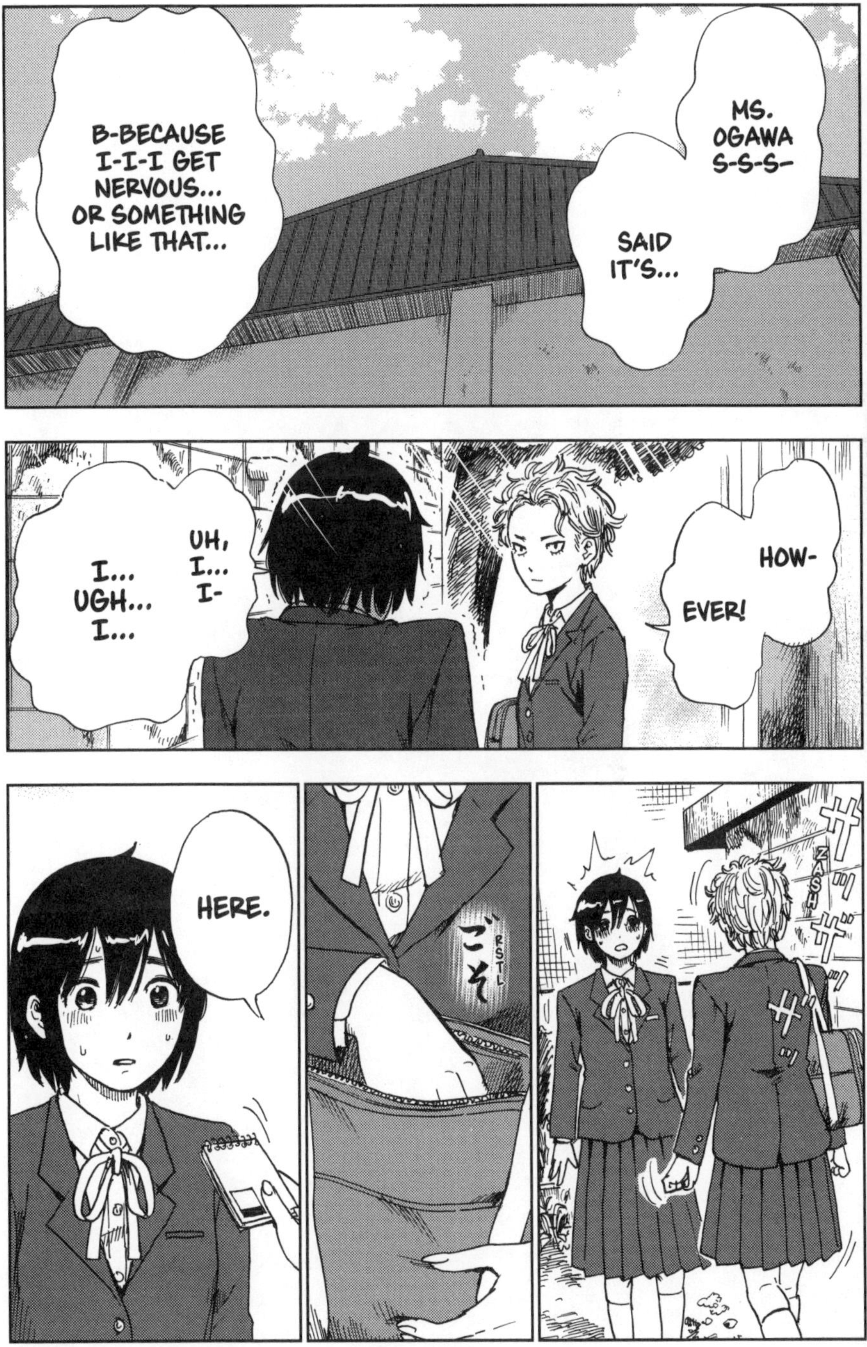
MS. OGAWA S-S-S-
SAID IT'S...
B-BECAUSE I-I-I GET NERVOUS... OR SOMETHING LIKE THAT...
HOW-EVER!
UH, I... I-
I... UGH... I...
ザッ
ZASH
ザザッ
ザッ
ごそ
RSTL
HERE.

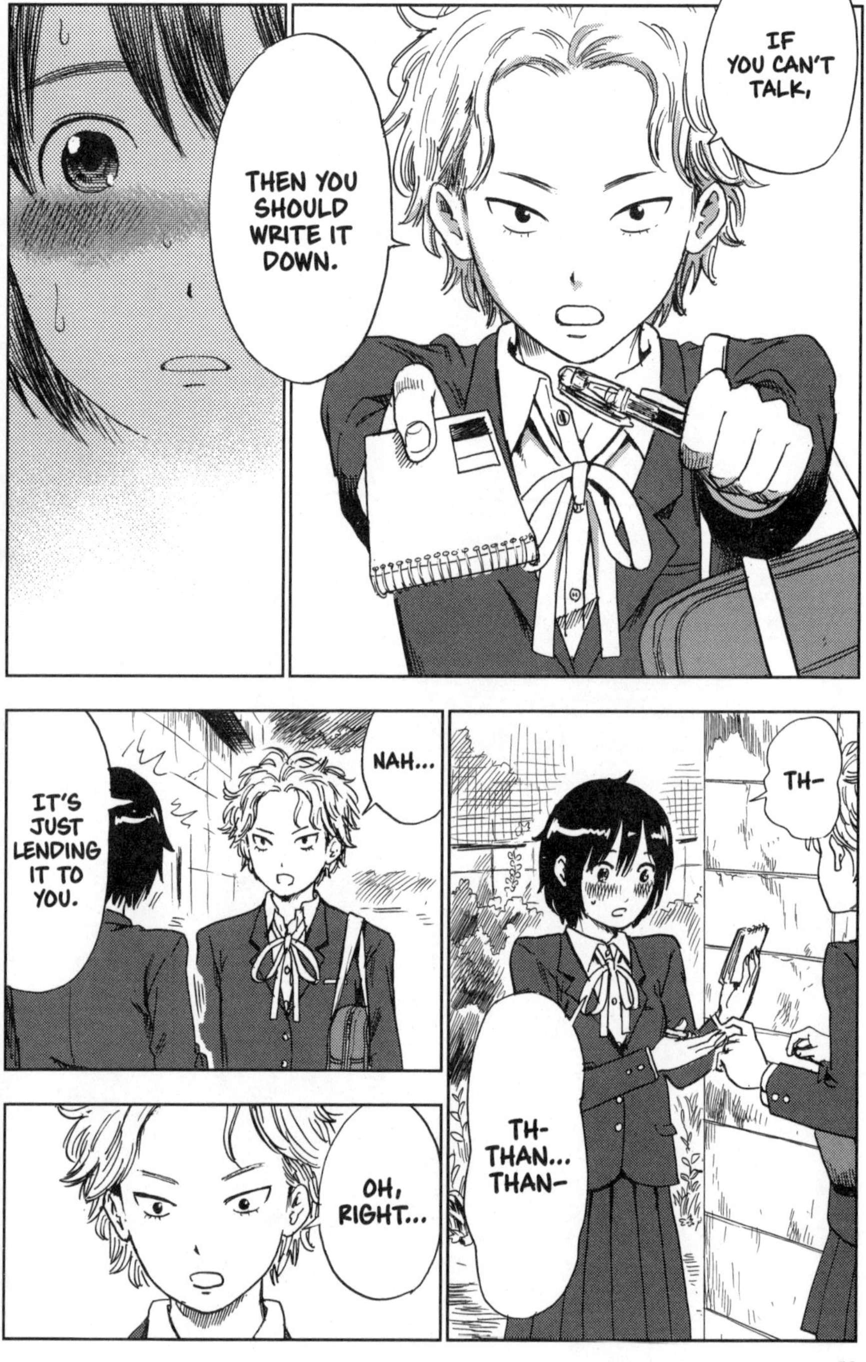
IF YOU CAN'T TALK,
THEN YOU SHOULD WRITE IT DOWN.
TH-
TH- THAN... THAN-
NAH...
IT'S JUST LENDING IT TO YOU.
OH, RIGHT...

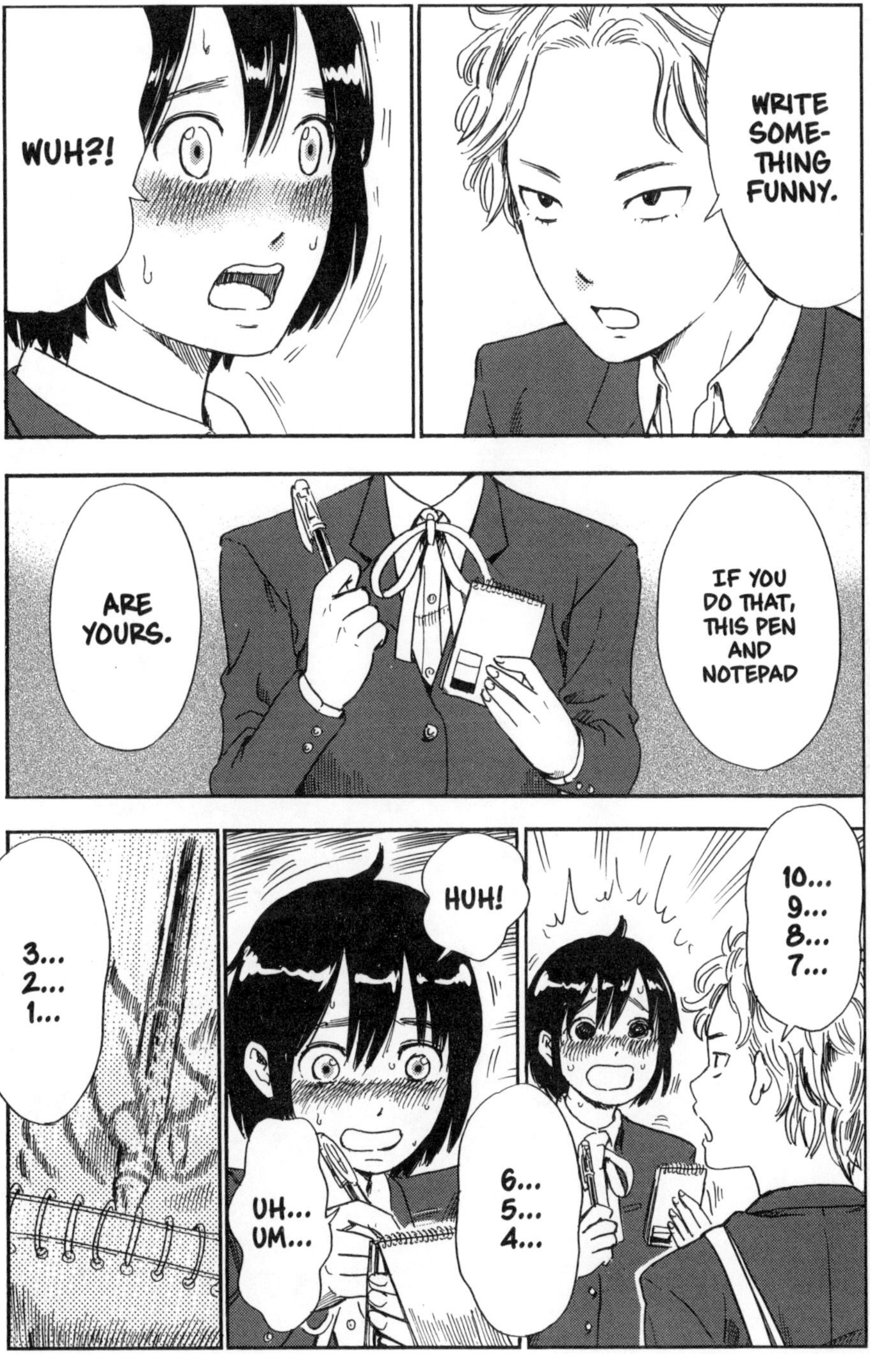
WRITE SOME-THING FUNNY.
WUH?!
IF YOU DO THAT, THIS PEN AND NOTEPAD
ARE YOURS.
10... 9... 8... 7...
6... 5... 4...
HUH!
UH... UM...
3... 2... 1...

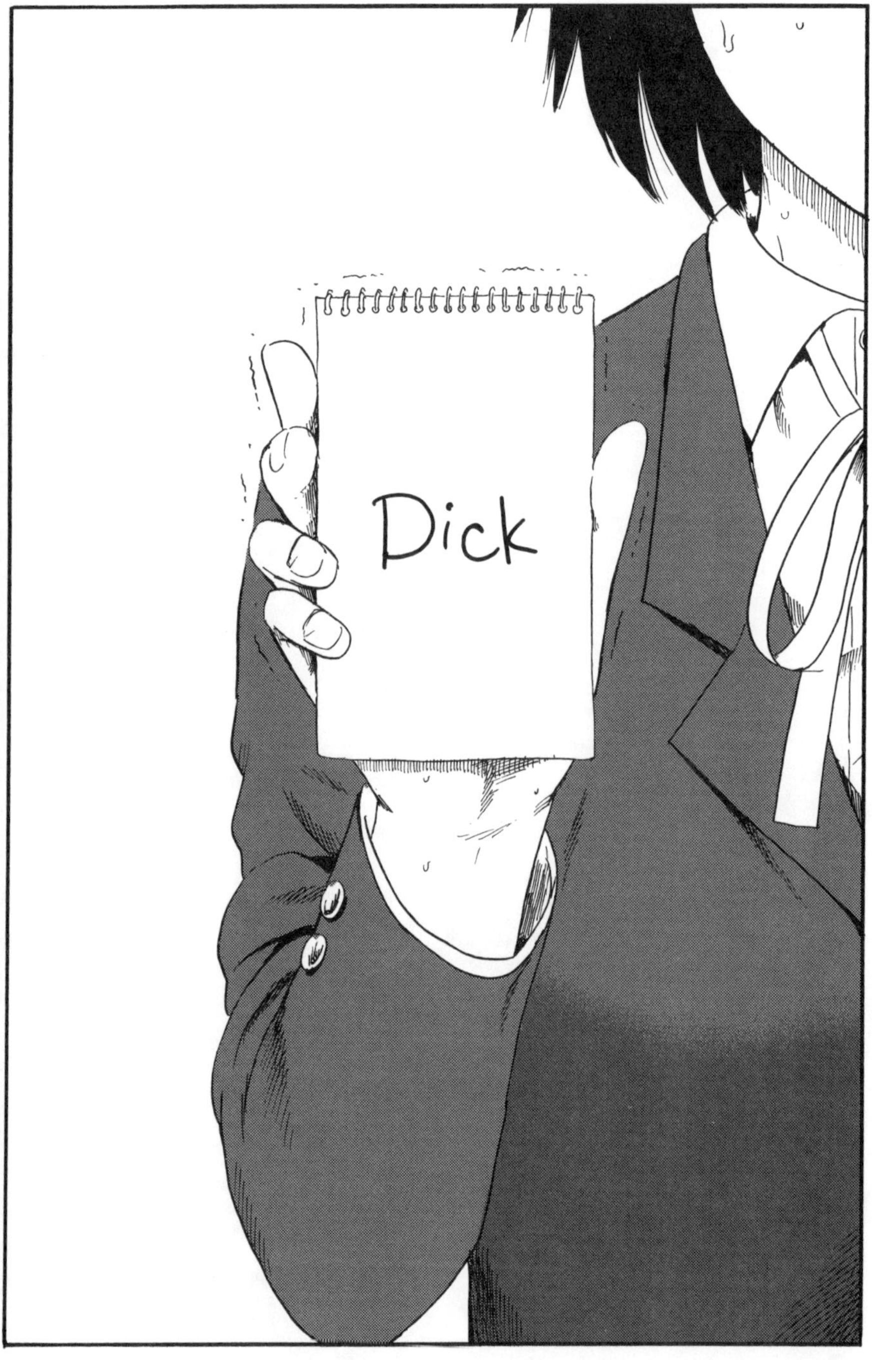
Dick

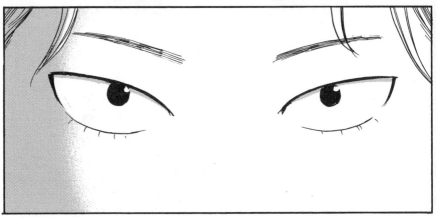

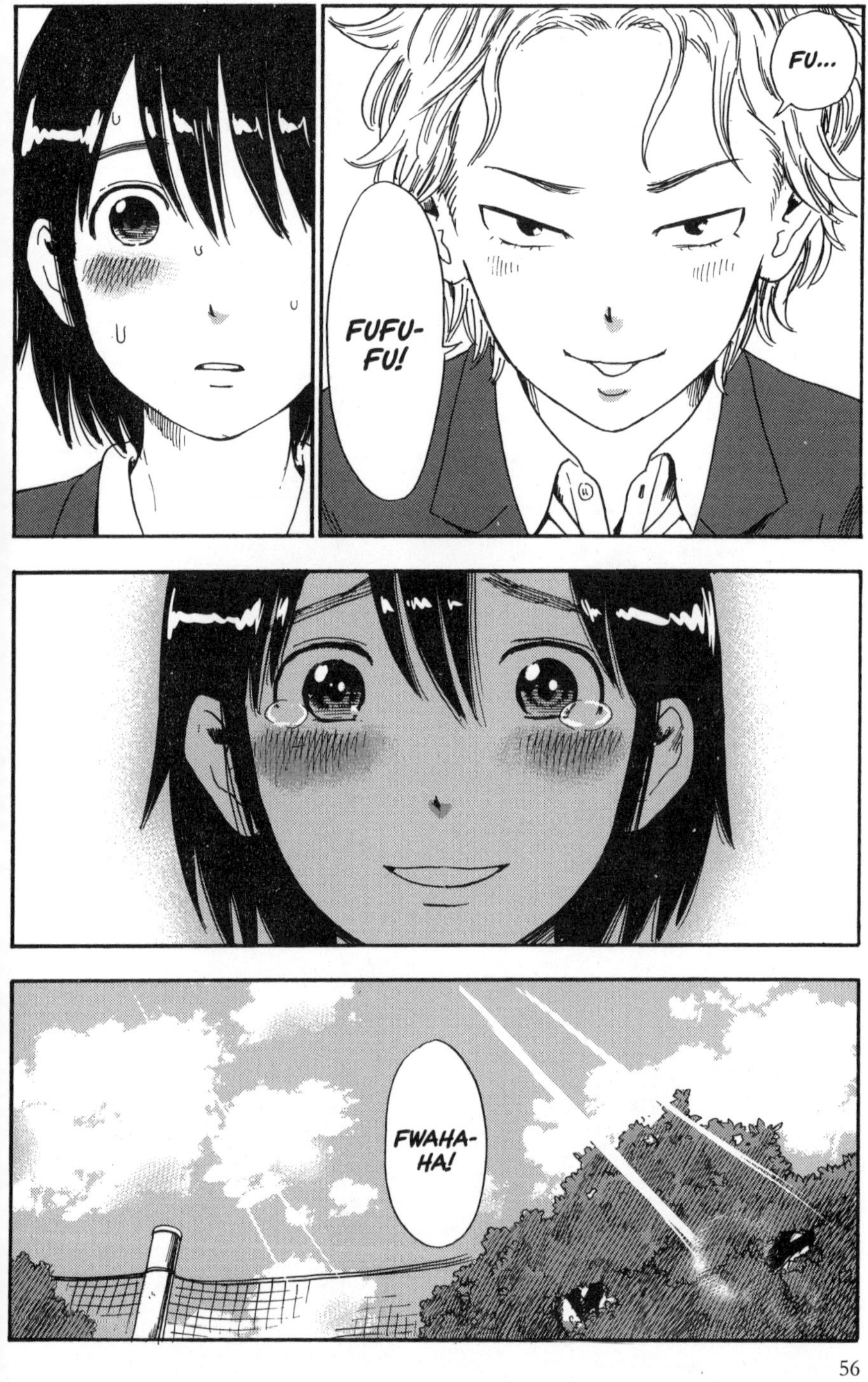
FU...
FUFU-FU!
FWAHA-HA!

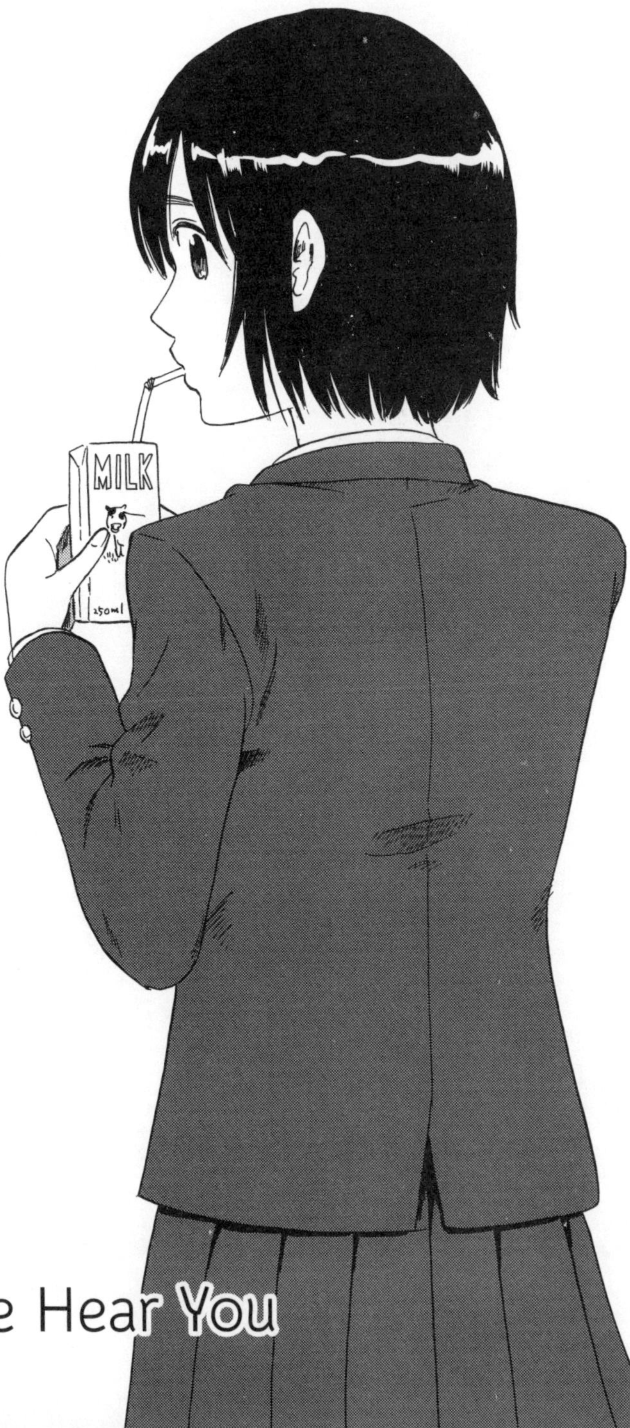
MILK
250ml

Chapter 4

Lemme Hear You

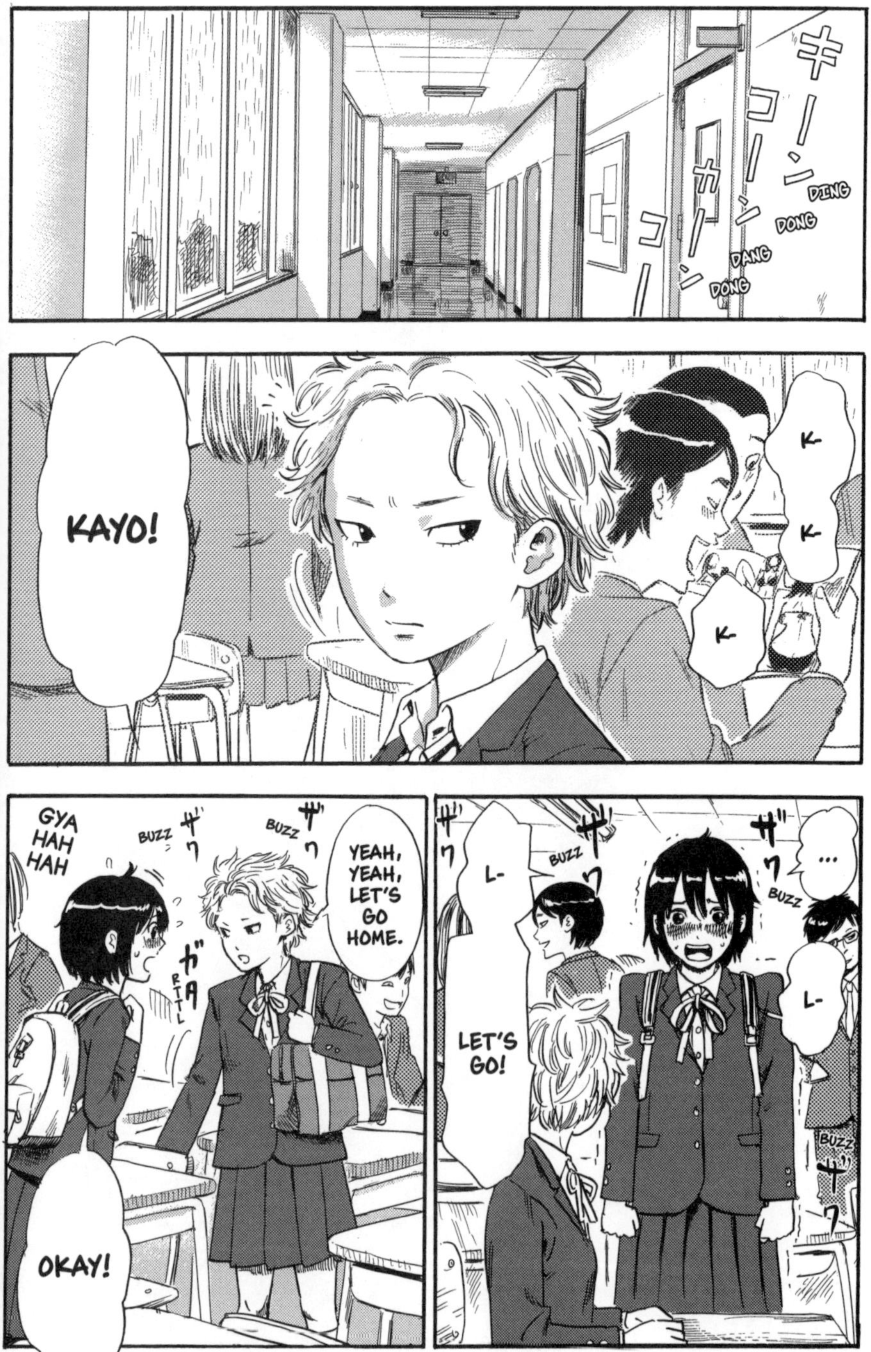
キーンコーンカーンコーン
DING
DONG
DANG
DONG
K- K- K-
KAYO!
...
L- L-
L-
LET'S GO!
BUZZ
OKAY!
YEAH, YEAH, LET'S GO HOME.
BUZZ
BUZZ
RTTL
GYA HAH HAH

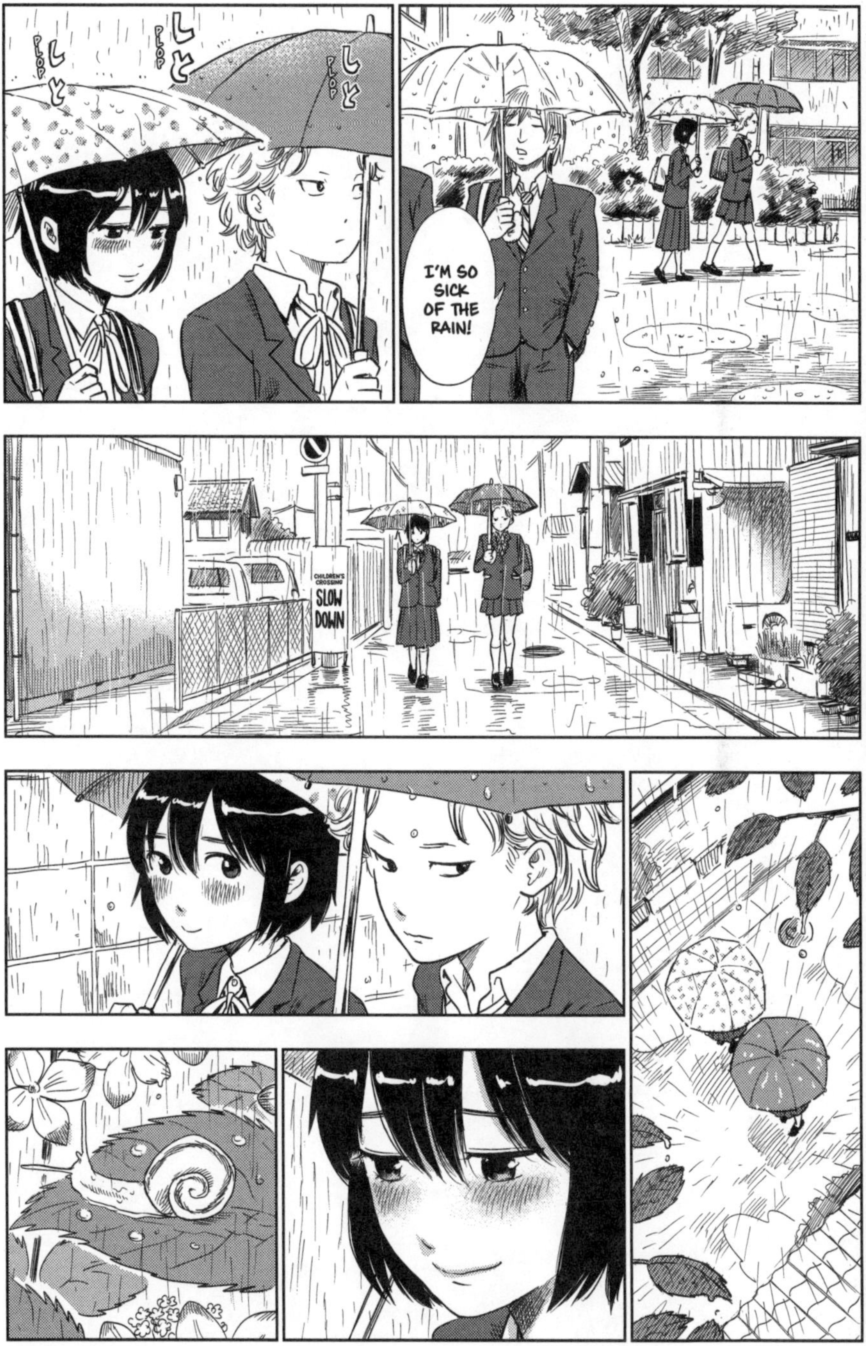
I'M SO SICK OF THE RAIN!
しと PLOP
しと PLOP
しと PLOP
CHILDREN'S CROSSING
SLOW DOWN

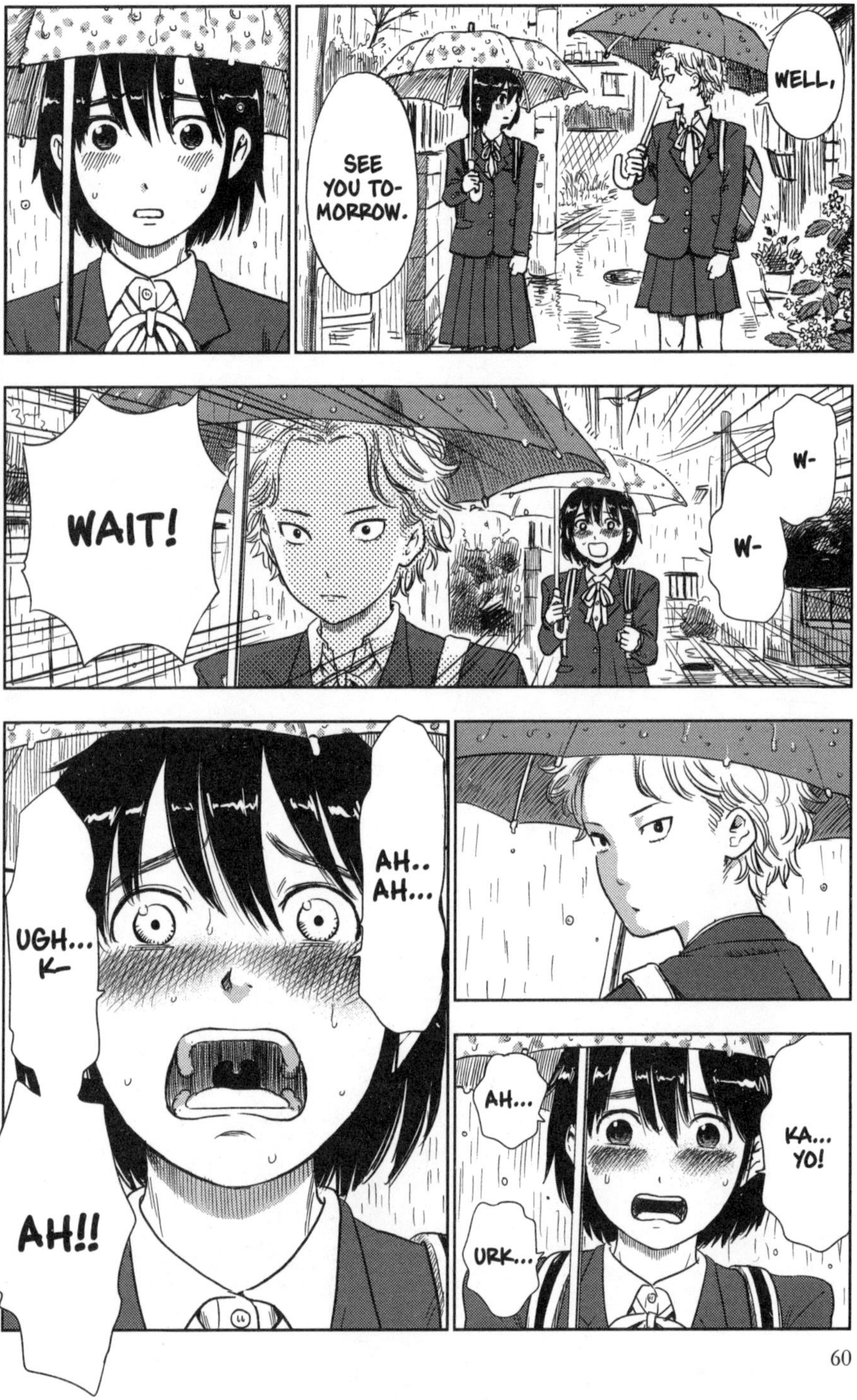
WELL,
SEE YOU TO-MORROW.
W-
W-
WAIT!
KA... YO!
AH...
URK...
AH.. AH...
UGH... K-
AH!!

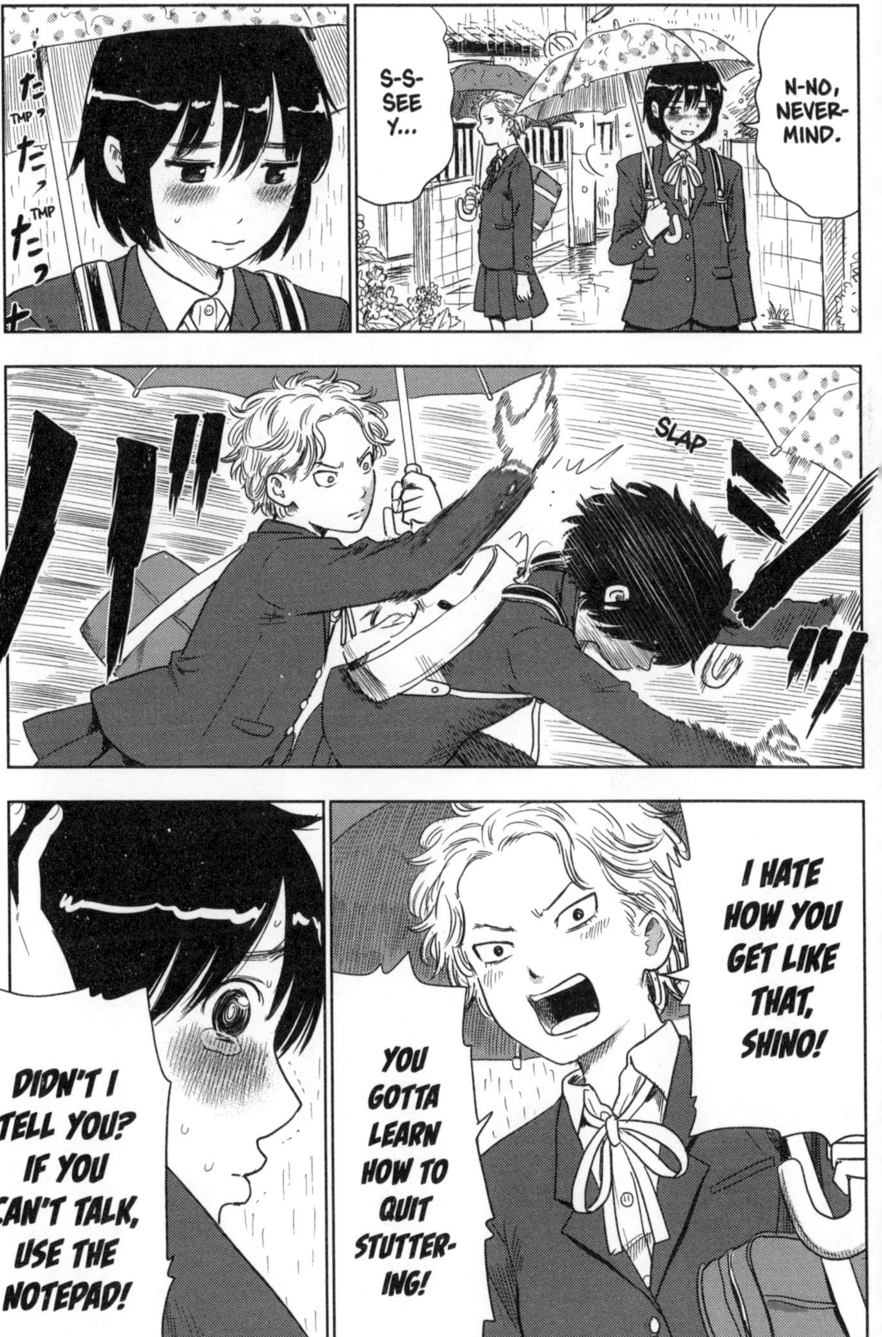
N-NO, NEVER-MIND.
S-S-SEE Y...
TMP
TMP
SLAP
I HATE HOW YOU GET LIKE THAT, SHINO!
YOU GOTTA LEARN HOW TO QUIT STUTTER-ING!
DIDN'T I TELL YOU? IF YOU CAN'T TALK, USE THE NOTEPAD!

B- BUT...
JUST WRITE IT DOWN!
...
Can I come over to your house to hang out?

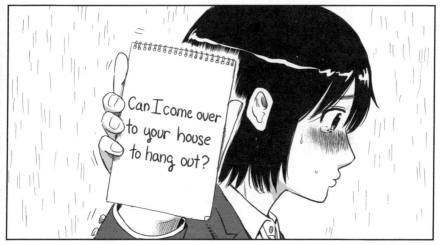

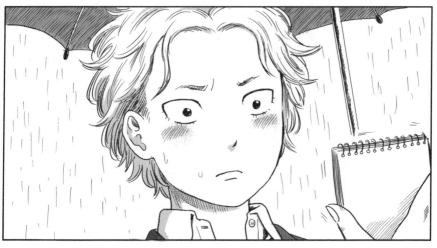

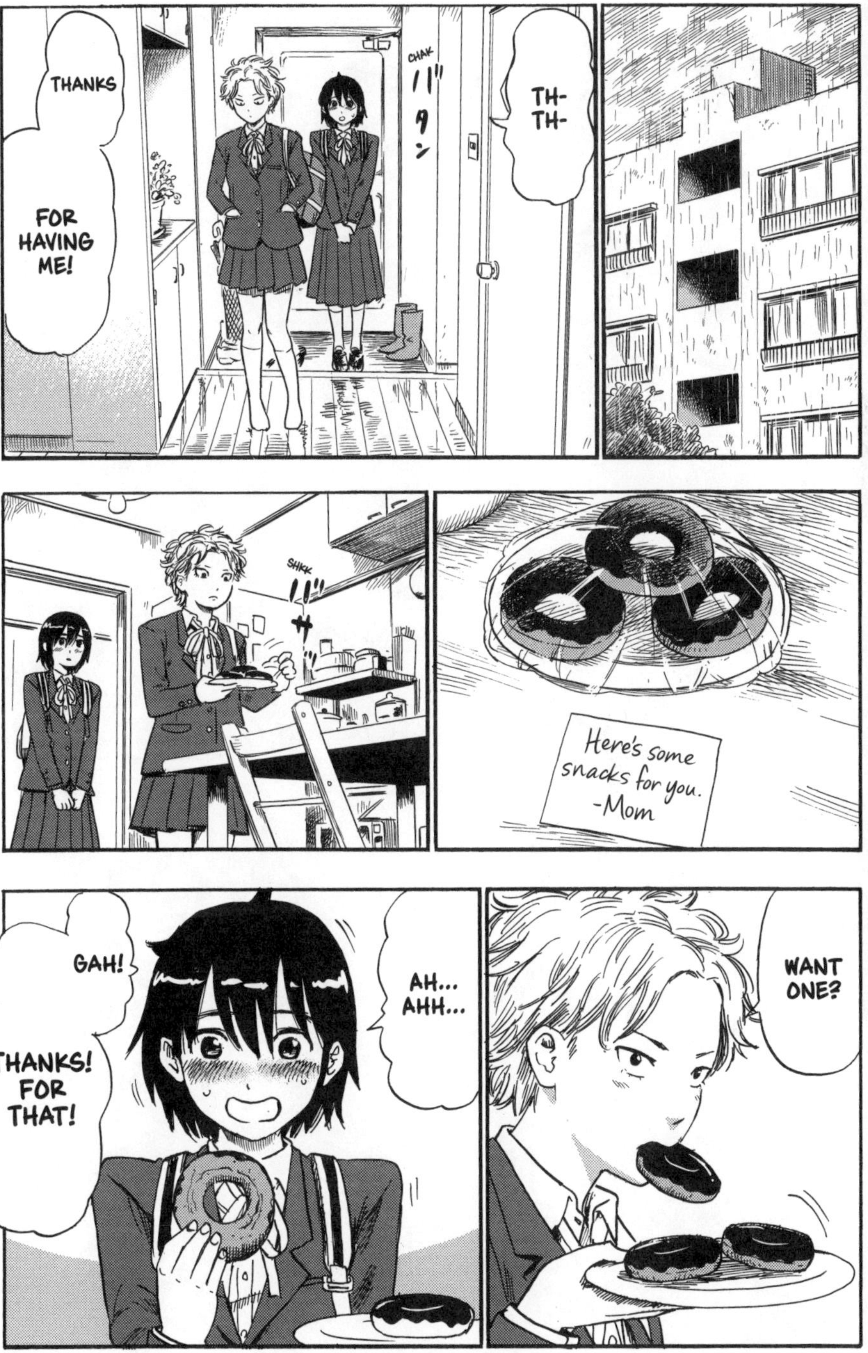
TH- TH-
CHAK
THANKS
FOR HAVING ME!
Here's some snacks for you. -Mom
SHKK
WANT ONE?
AH... AHH...
GAH!
THANKS! FOR THAT!

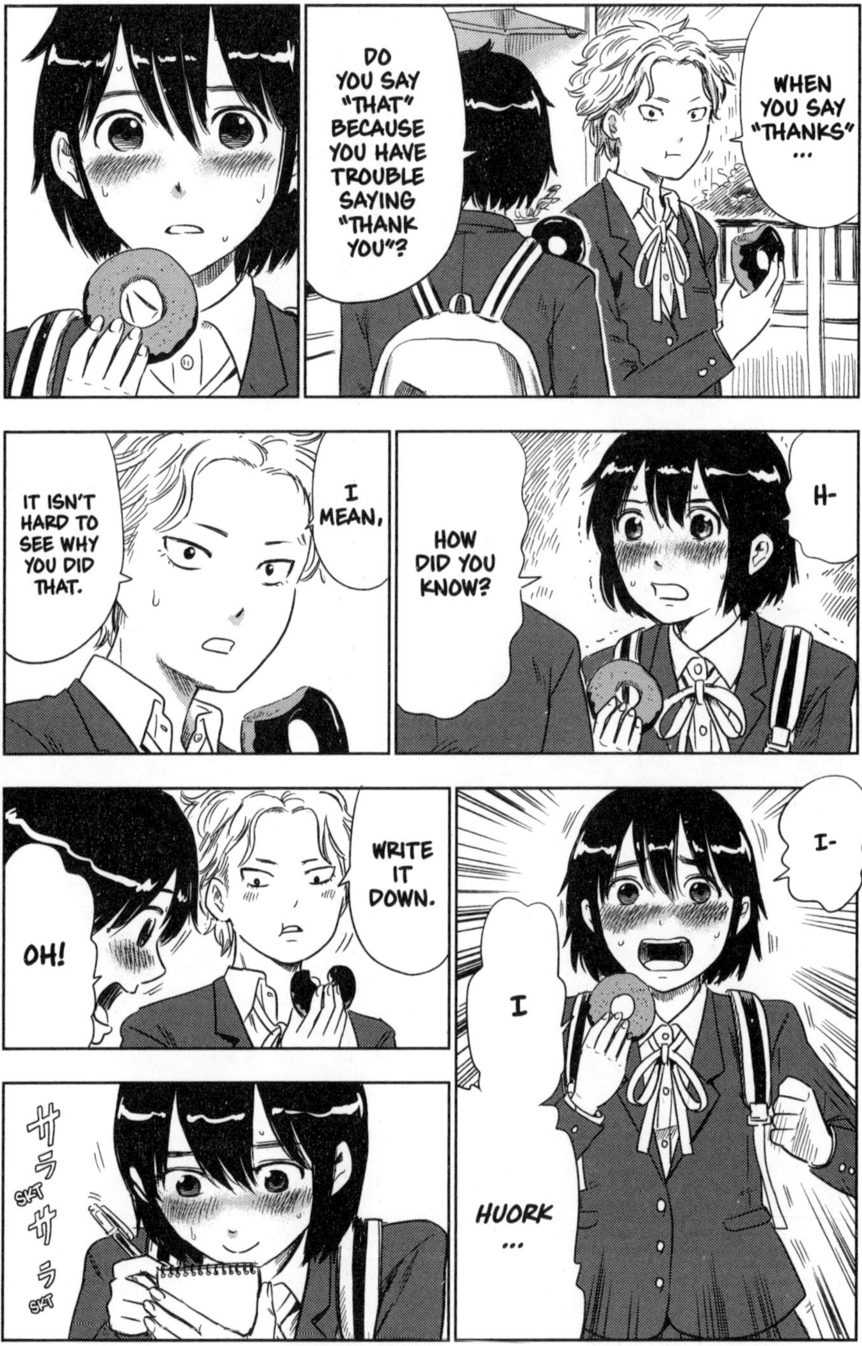
WHEN YOU SAY "THANKS"...
DO YOU SAY "THAT" BECAUSE YOU HAVE TROUBLE SAYING "THANK YOU"?
H-
HOW DID YOU KNOW?
I MEAN,
IT ISN'T HARD TO SEE WHY YOU DID THAT.
I-
I
HUORK...
WRITE IT DOWN.
OH!
サラ
SKT
サラ
SKT

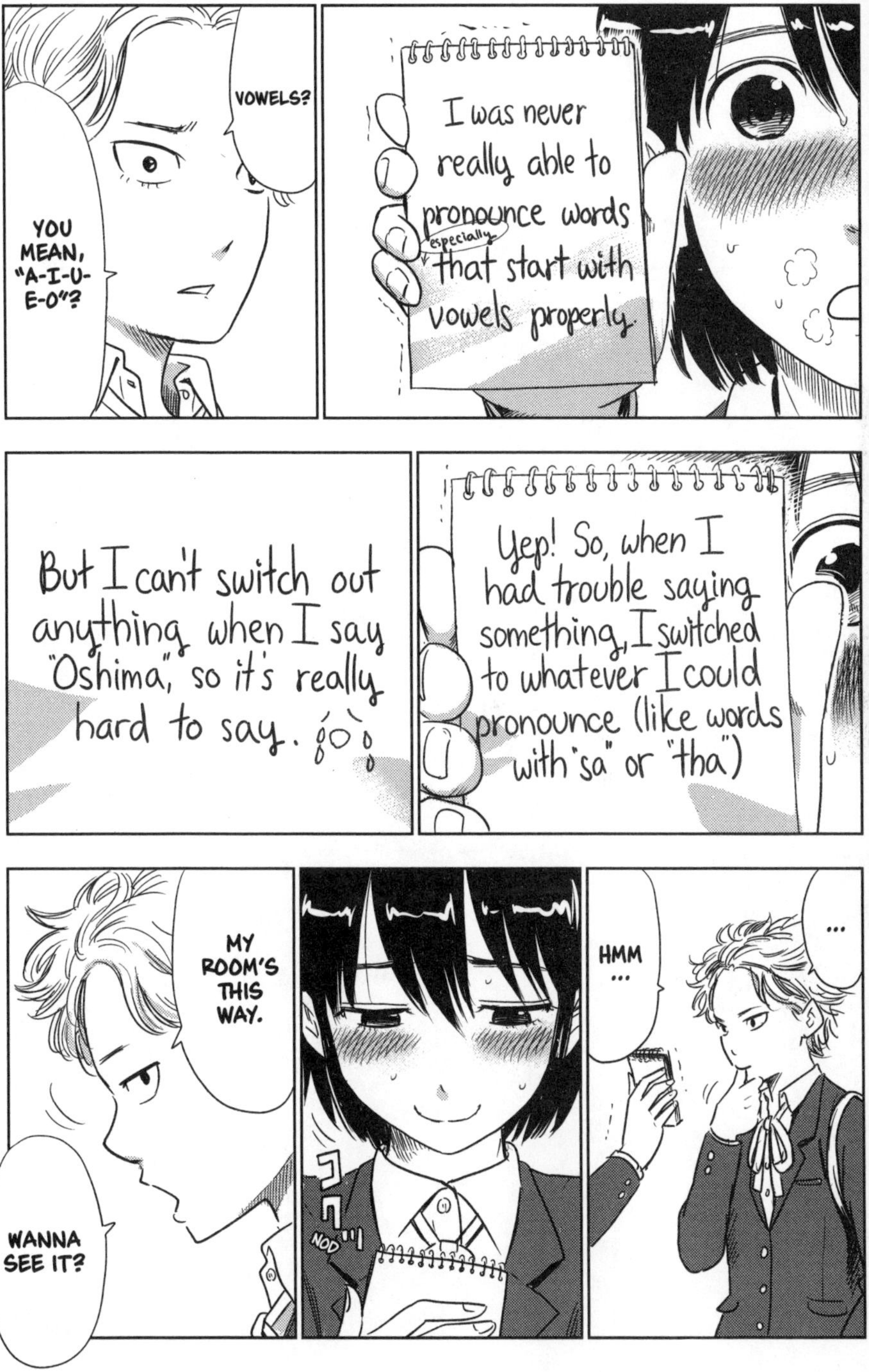
I was never really able to pronounce words especially that start with vowels properly.
VOWELS?
YOU MEAN, "A-I-U-E-O"?
Yep! So, when I had trouble saying something, I switched to whatever I could pronounce (like words with "sa" or "tha")
But I can't switch out anything when I say "Oshima," so it's really hard to say.
...
HMM ...
NOD
MY ROOM'S THIS WAY.
WANNA SEE IT?

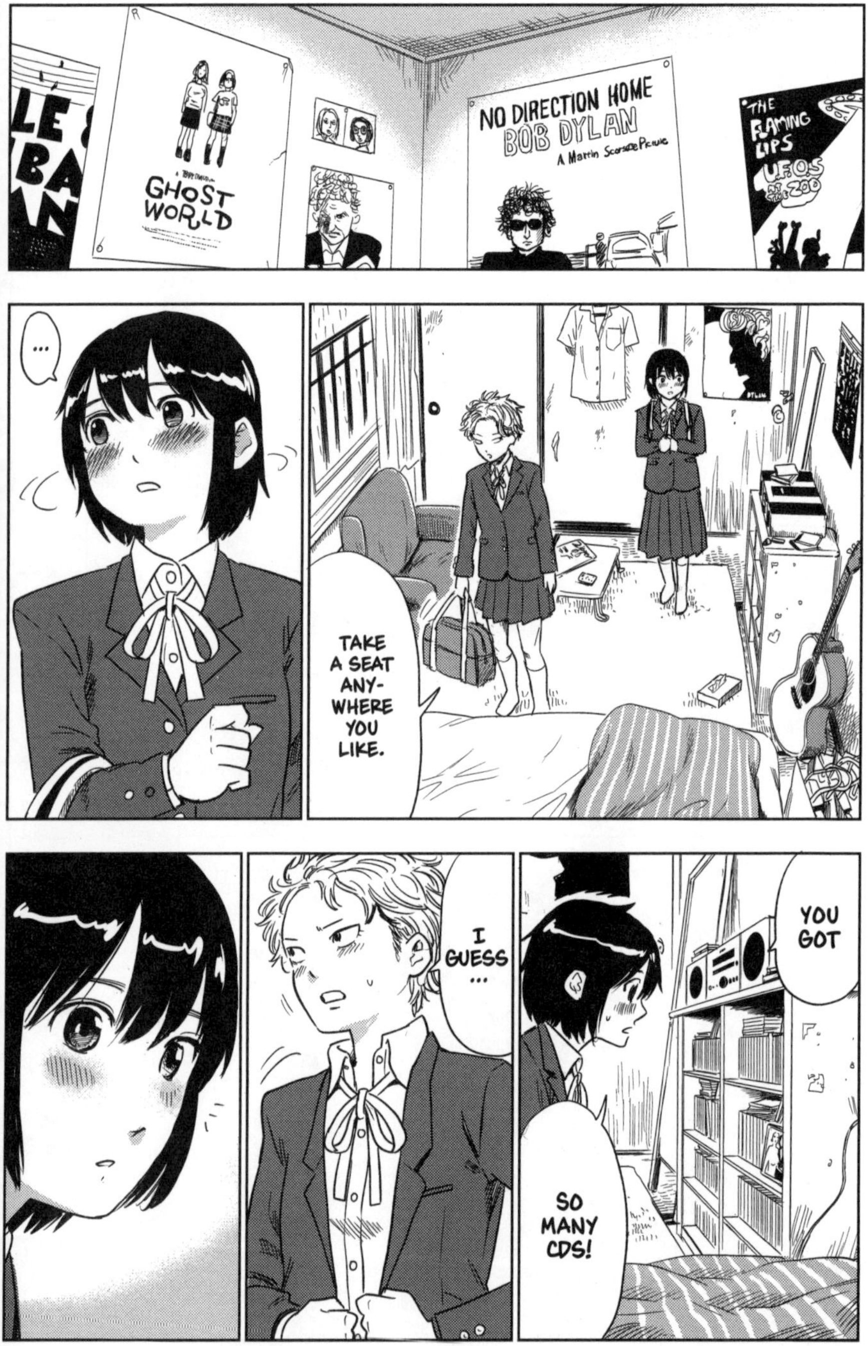
THE FLAMING LIPS
UFOS
NO DIRECTION HOME
BOB DYLAN
A Martin Scorsese Picture
GHOST WORLD
TAKE A SEAT ANY-WHERE YOU LIKE.
...
YOU GOT
SO MANY CDS!
I GUESS ...

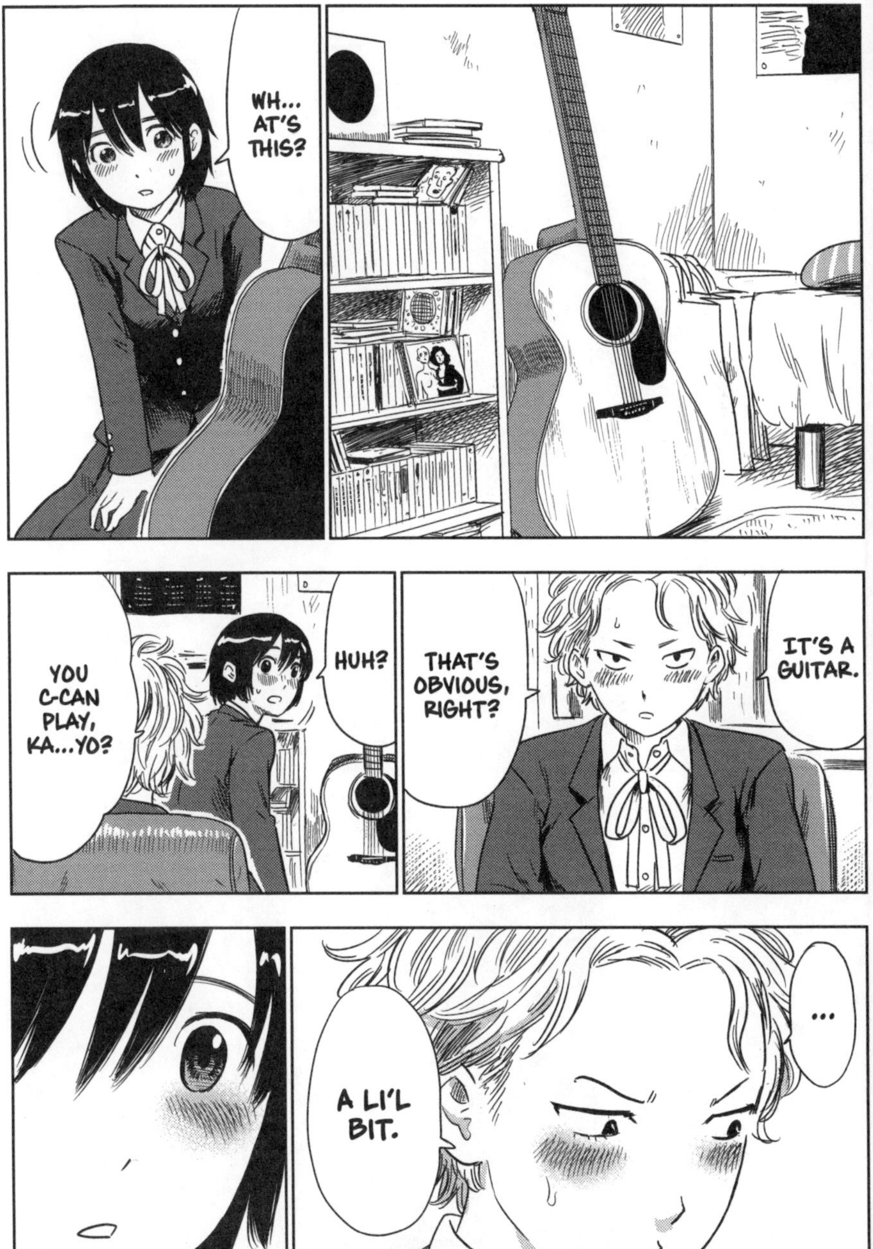
WH... AT'S THIS?
IT'S A GUITAR.
THAT'S OBVIOUS, RIGHT?
HUH?
YOU C-CAN PLAY, KA...YO?
...
A LI'L BIT.

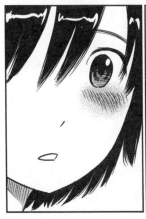

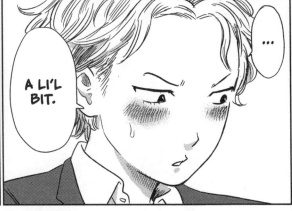

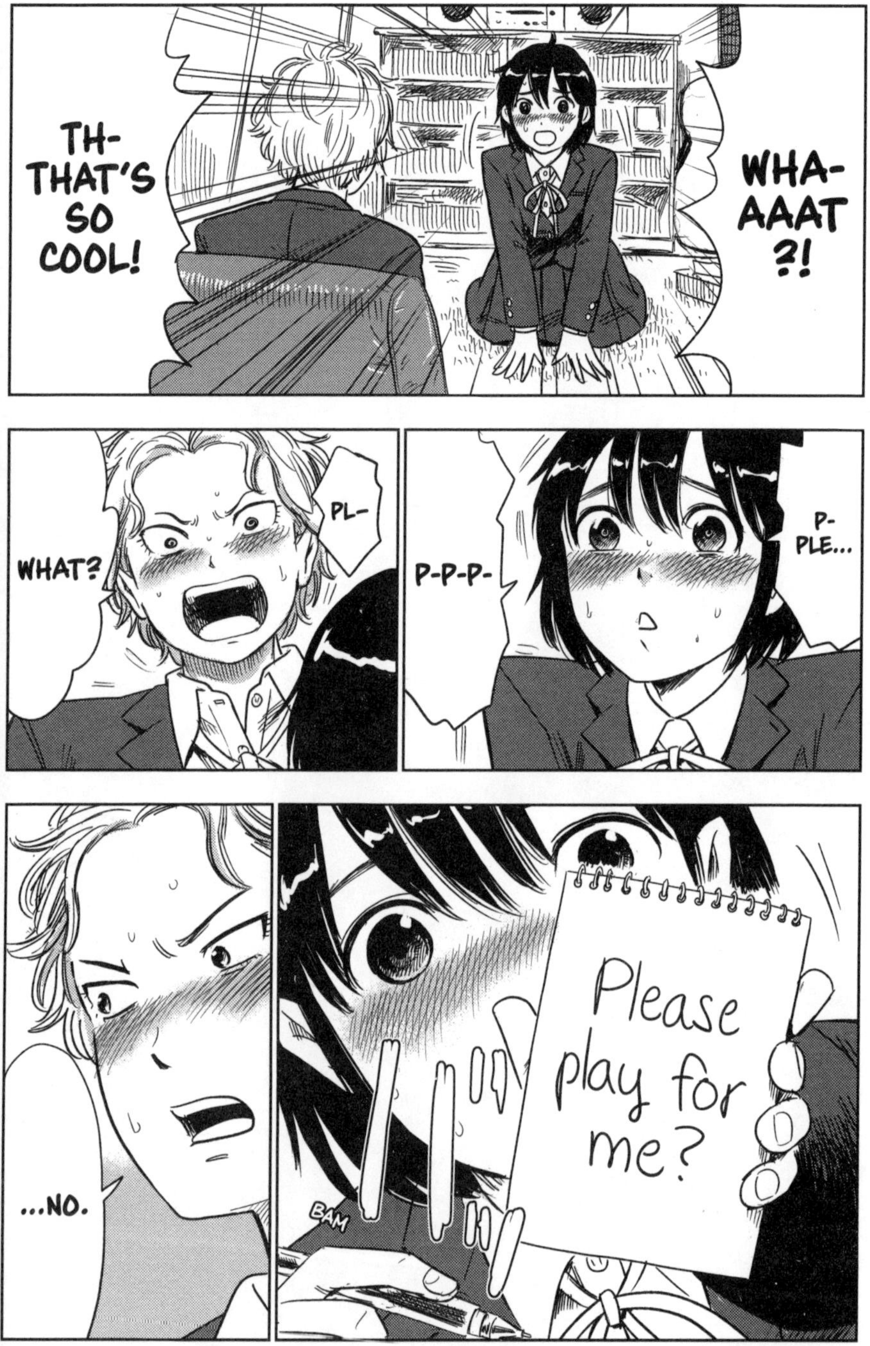
WHA-AAAT?!
TH-THAT'S SO COOL!
P-PLE...
P-P-P-
PL-
WHAT?
Please play for me?
BAM
...NO.

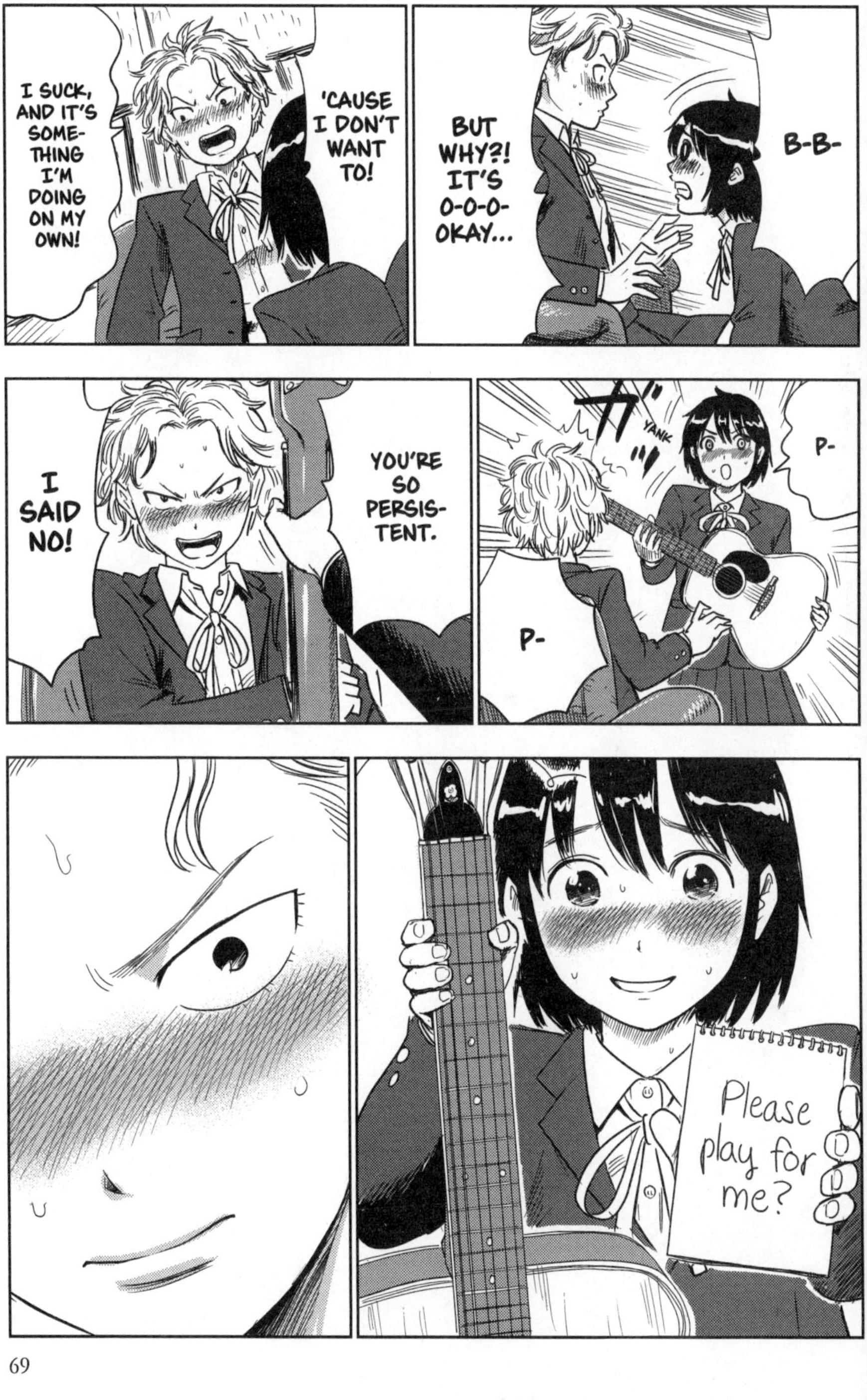
B-B-
BUT WHY?! IT'S O-O-O-OKAY...
'CAUSE I DON'T WANT TO!
I SUCK, AND IT'S SOME-THING I'M DOING ON MY OWN!
P-
ガッ
YANK
P-
YOU'RE SO PERSIS-TENT.
I SAID NO!
Please play for me?

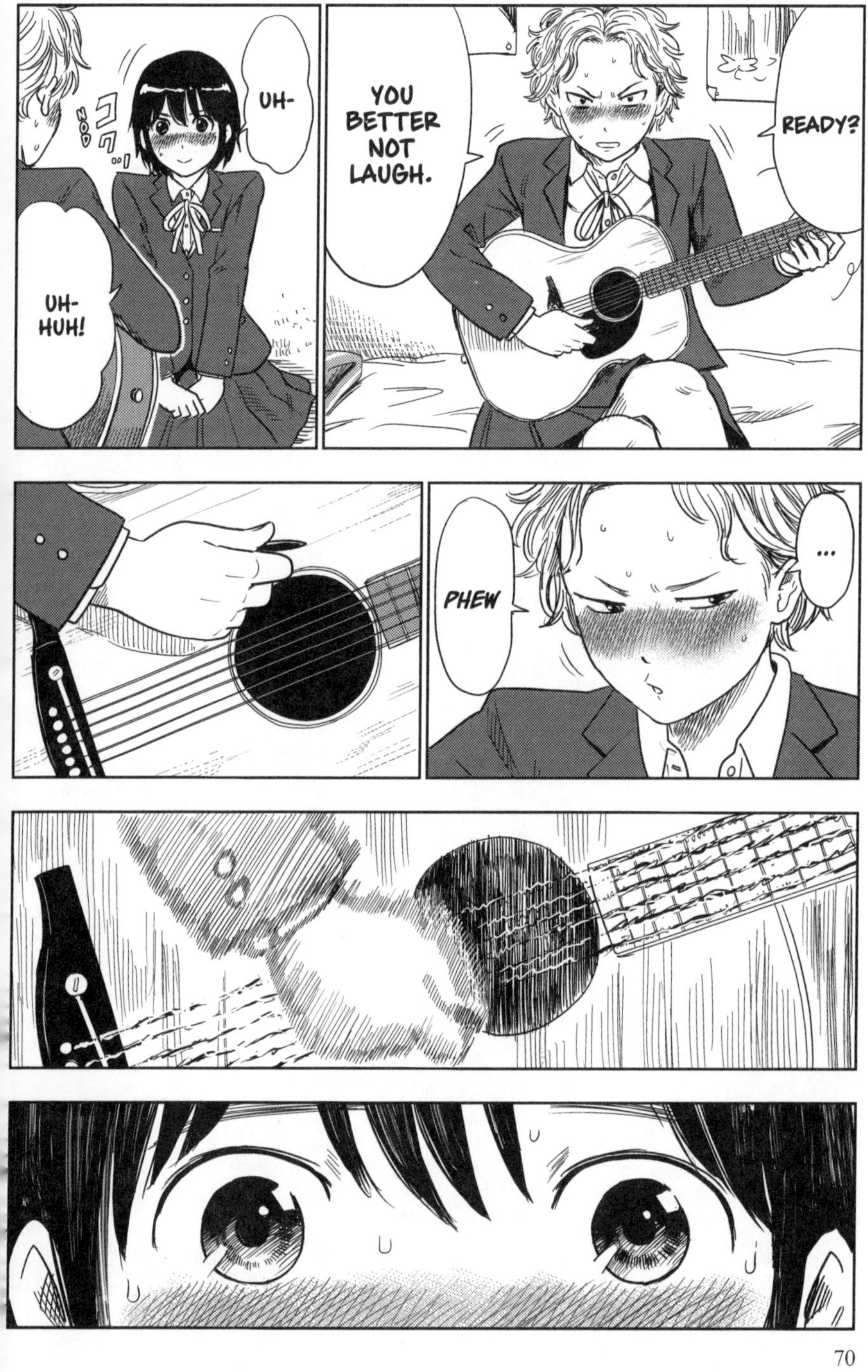
READY?
YOU BETTER NOT LAUGH.
UH-
NOD
UH-HUH!
...
PHEW

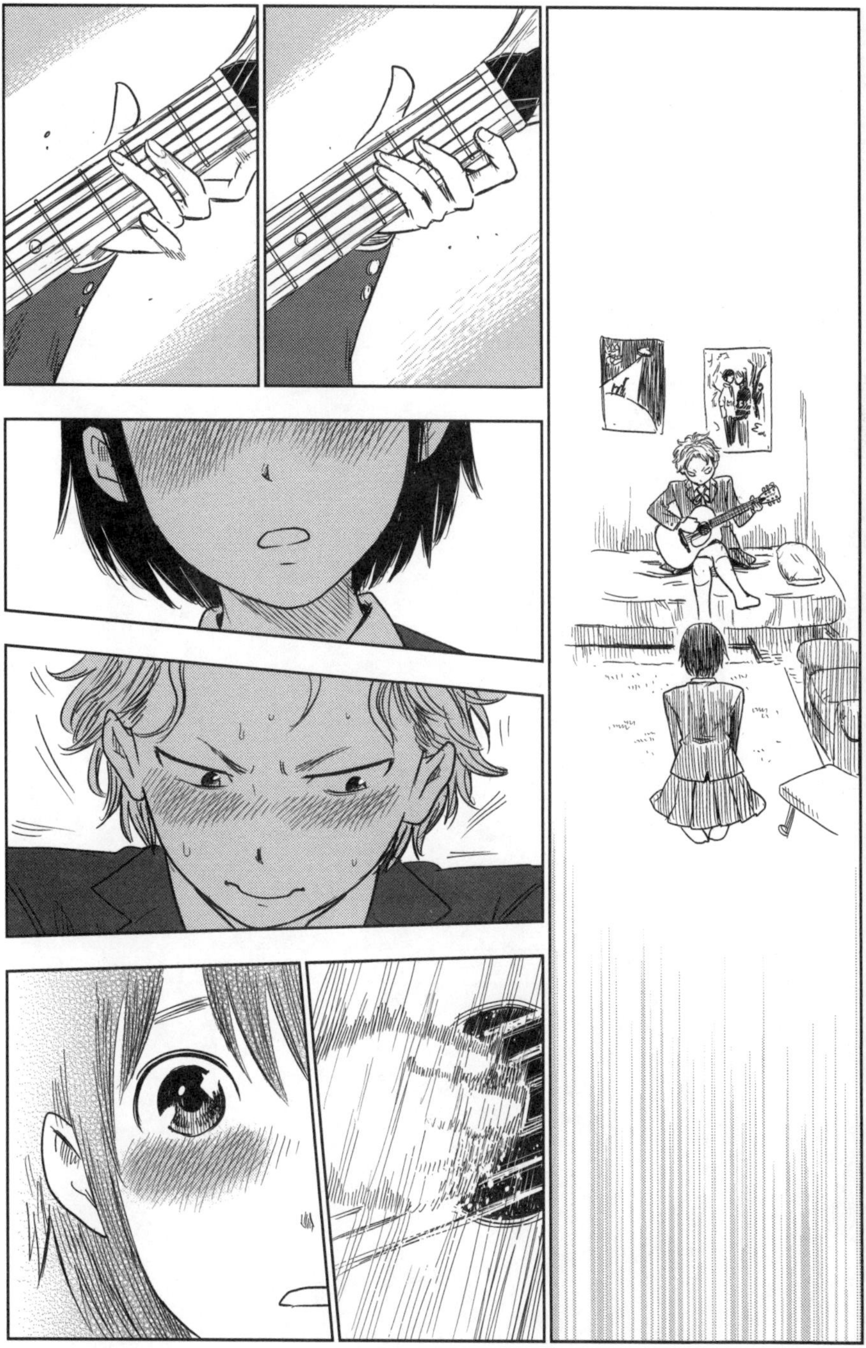

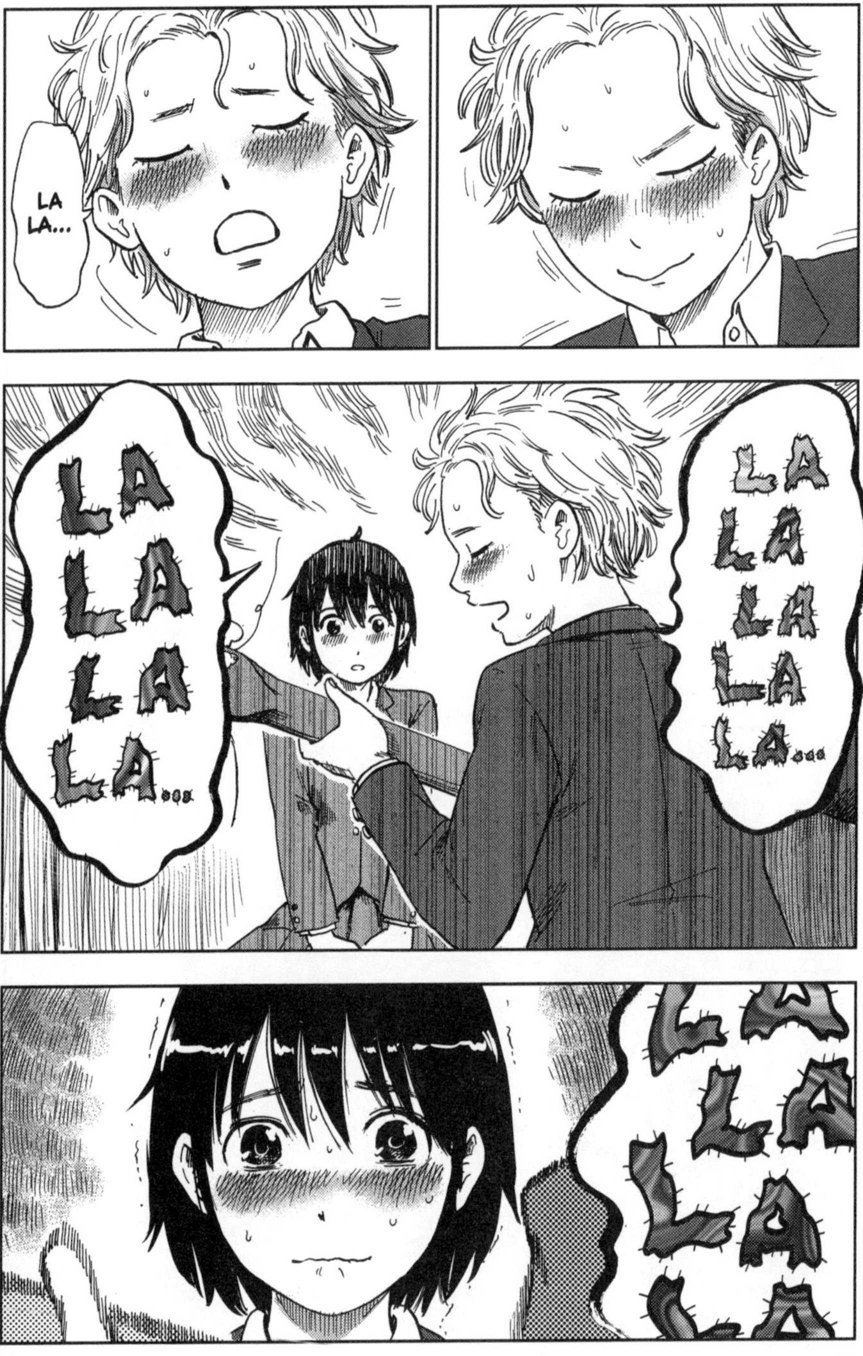
LA LA...
LA LA LA LA LA...
LA LA LA LA LA...
LA LA LA LA LA

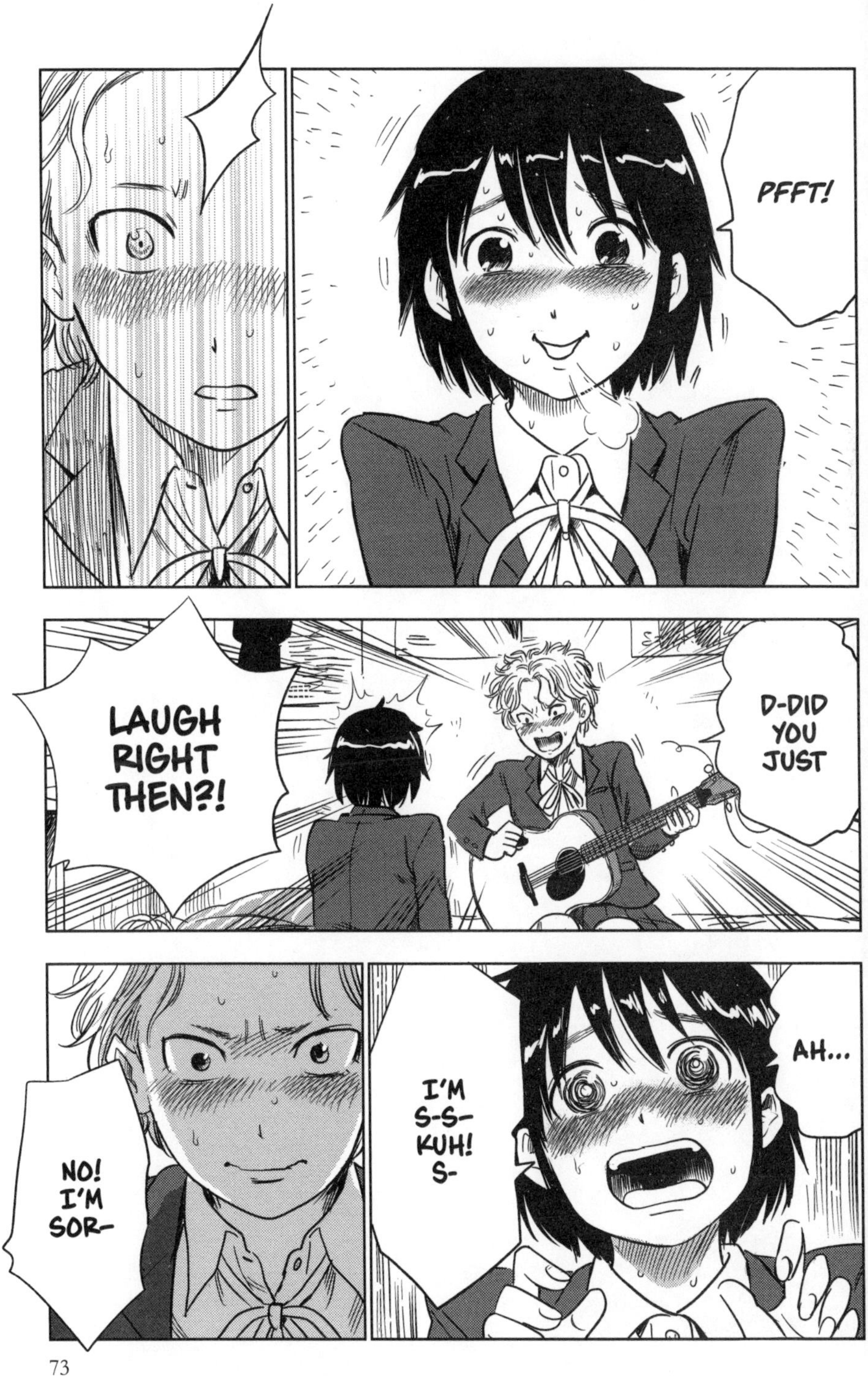
PFFT!
D-DID YOU JUST
LAUGH RIGHT THEN?!
AH...
I'M S-S-KUH! S-
NO! I'M SOR-

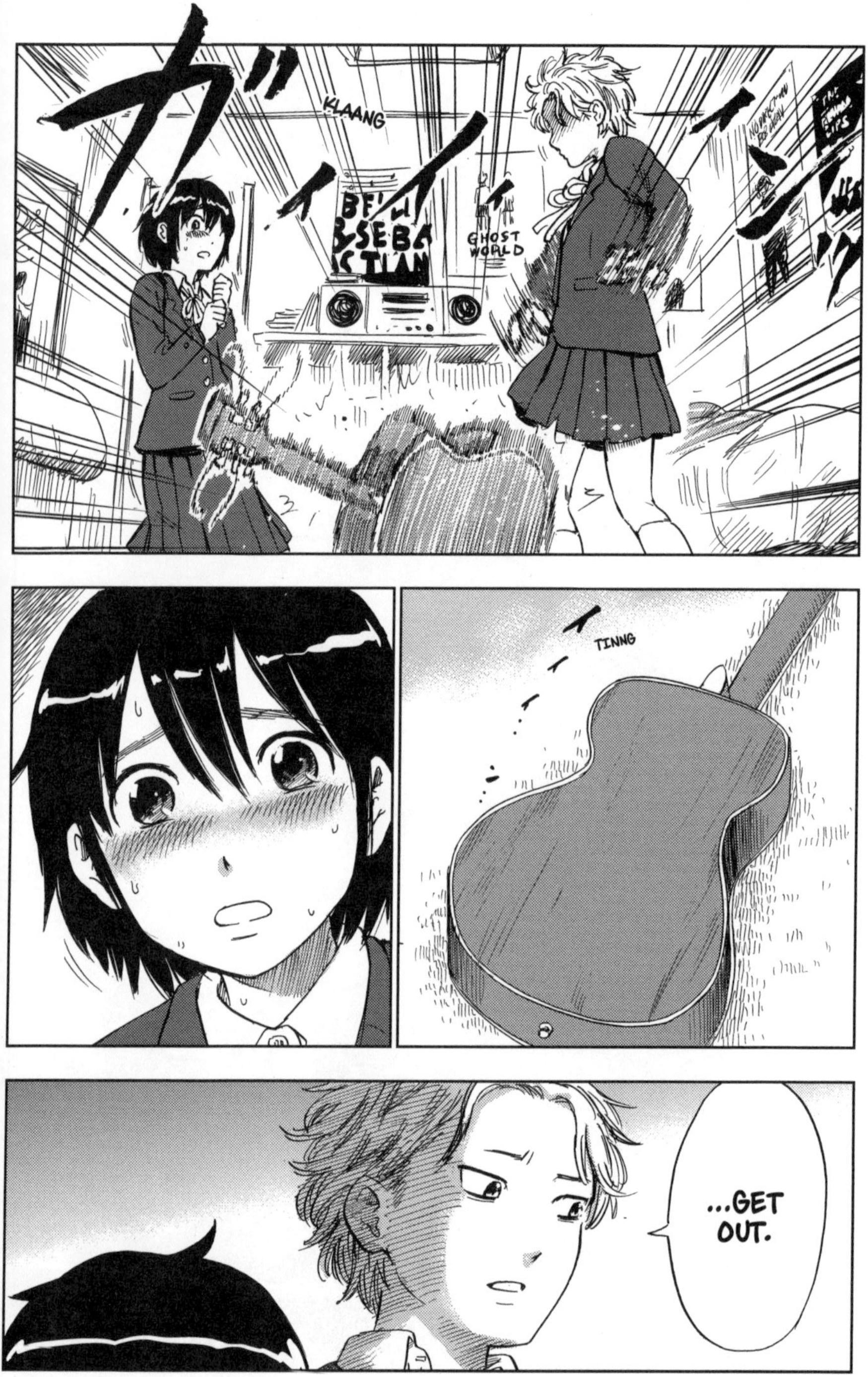
KLAANG
GHOST WORLD
TINNG
...GET OUT.

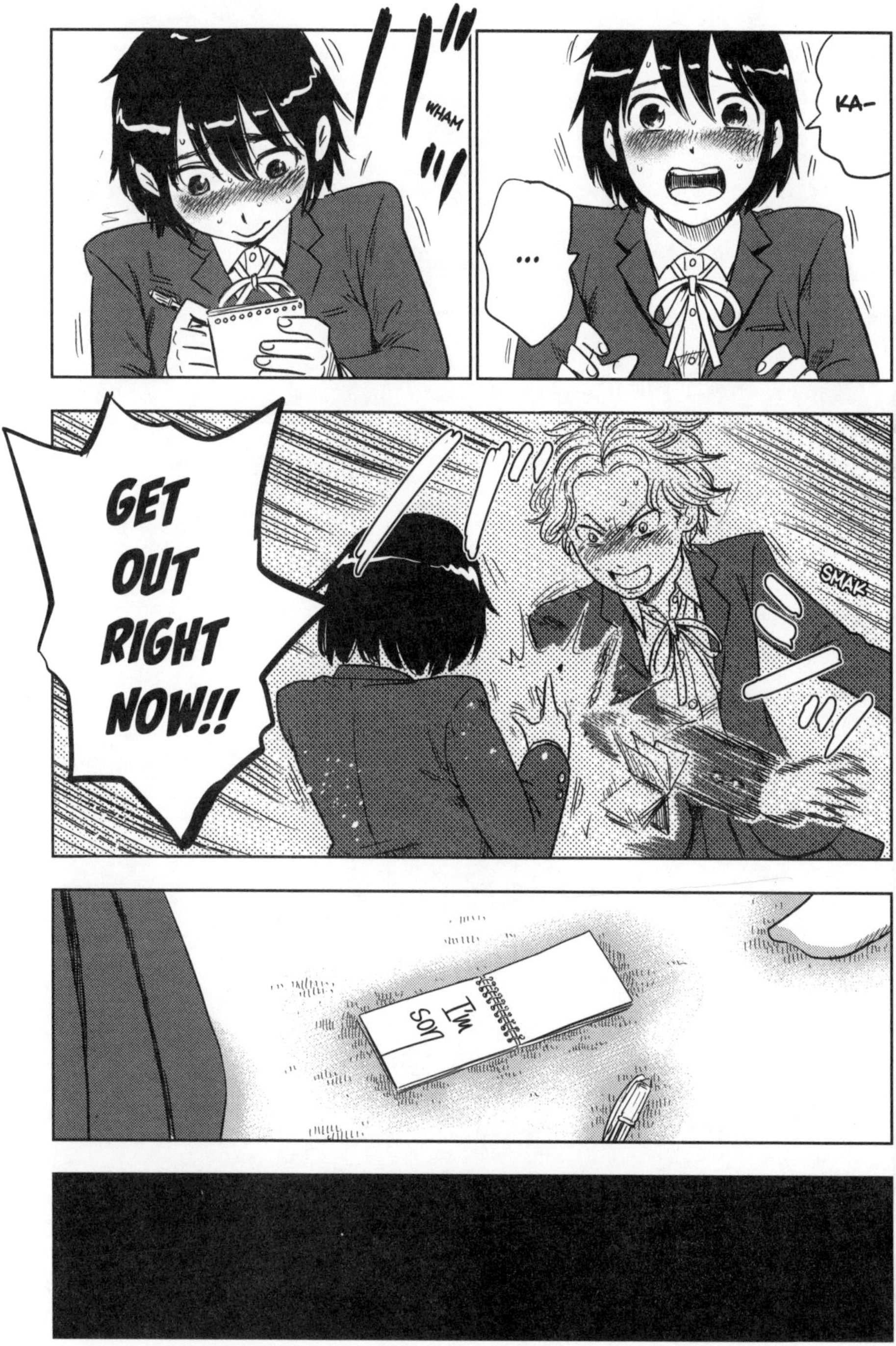
KA-
...
WHAM
GET OUT RIGHT NOW!!
SMAK
I'm sor

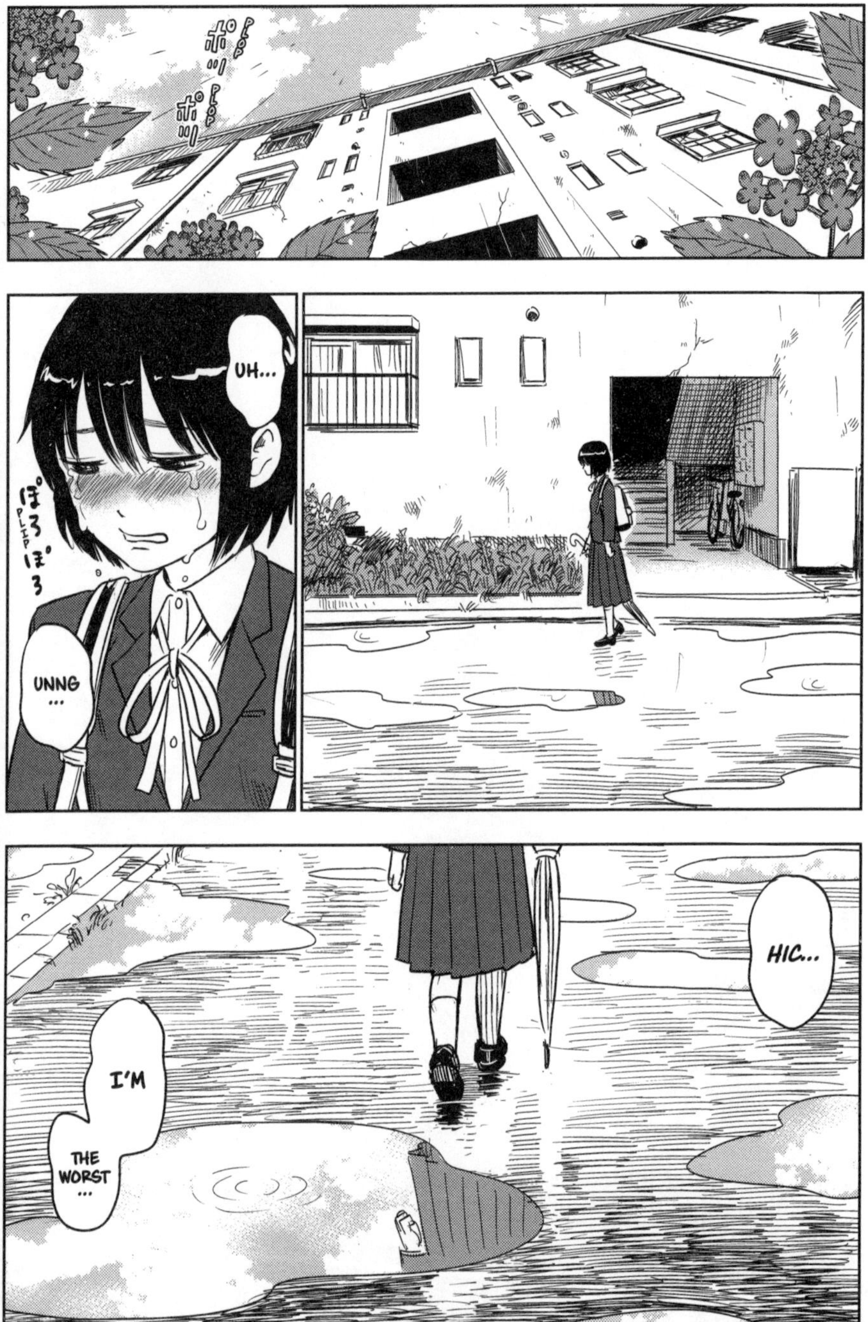
PLOP
ポツ
PLOP
ポツ
UH...
ぽろぽろ
PLIP
UNNG...
HIC...
I'M
THE WORST...

Chapter 5
The Worst

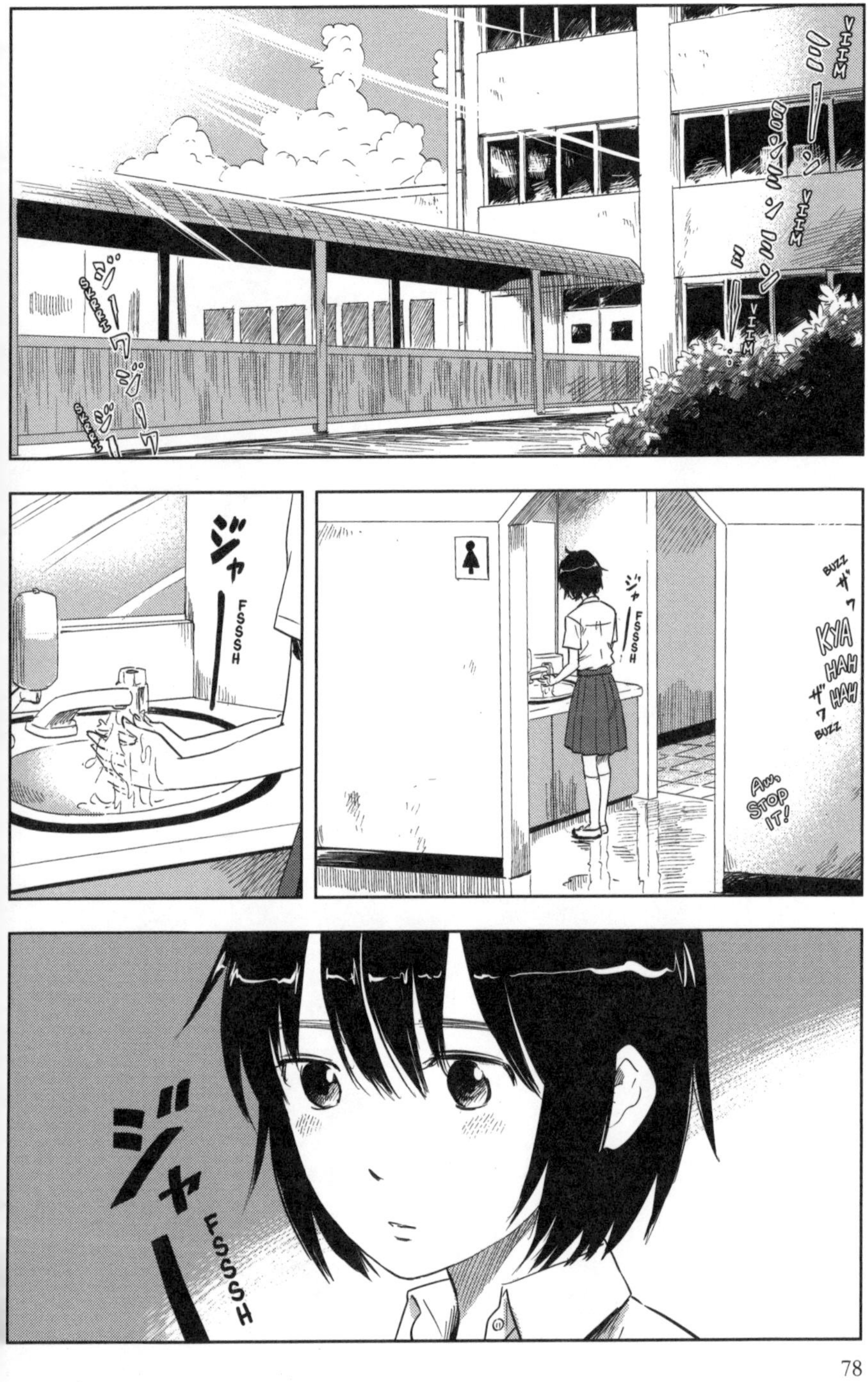
VIIM
VIIM
VIIM
SKREEH
SKREEH
BUZZ
KYA HAH HAH
BUZZ
Aw, STOP IT!
ジャー
FSSSH
ジャー
FSSSH
ジャー
FSSSH

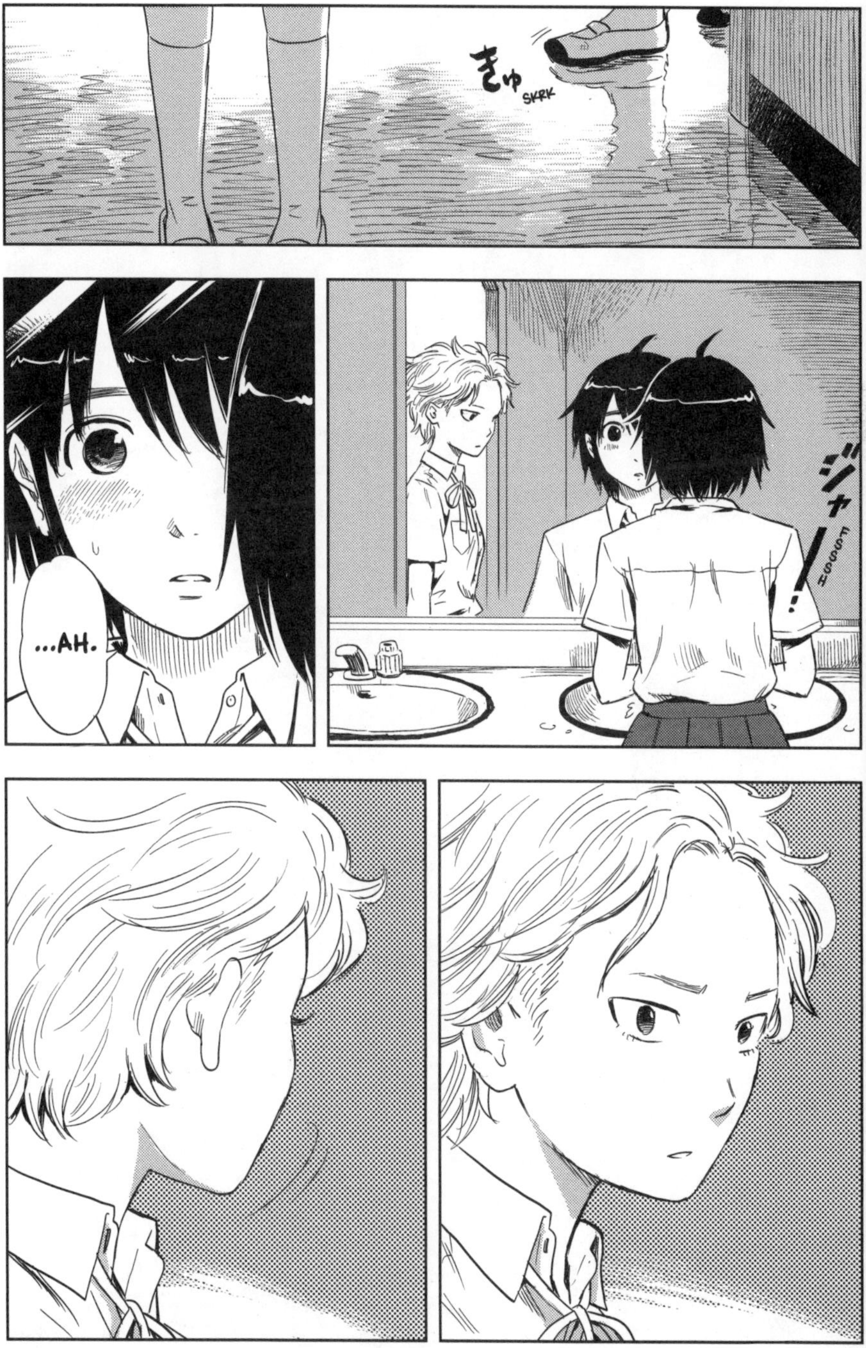
きゅ
SKRK
ジャー!
FSSSH
...AH.

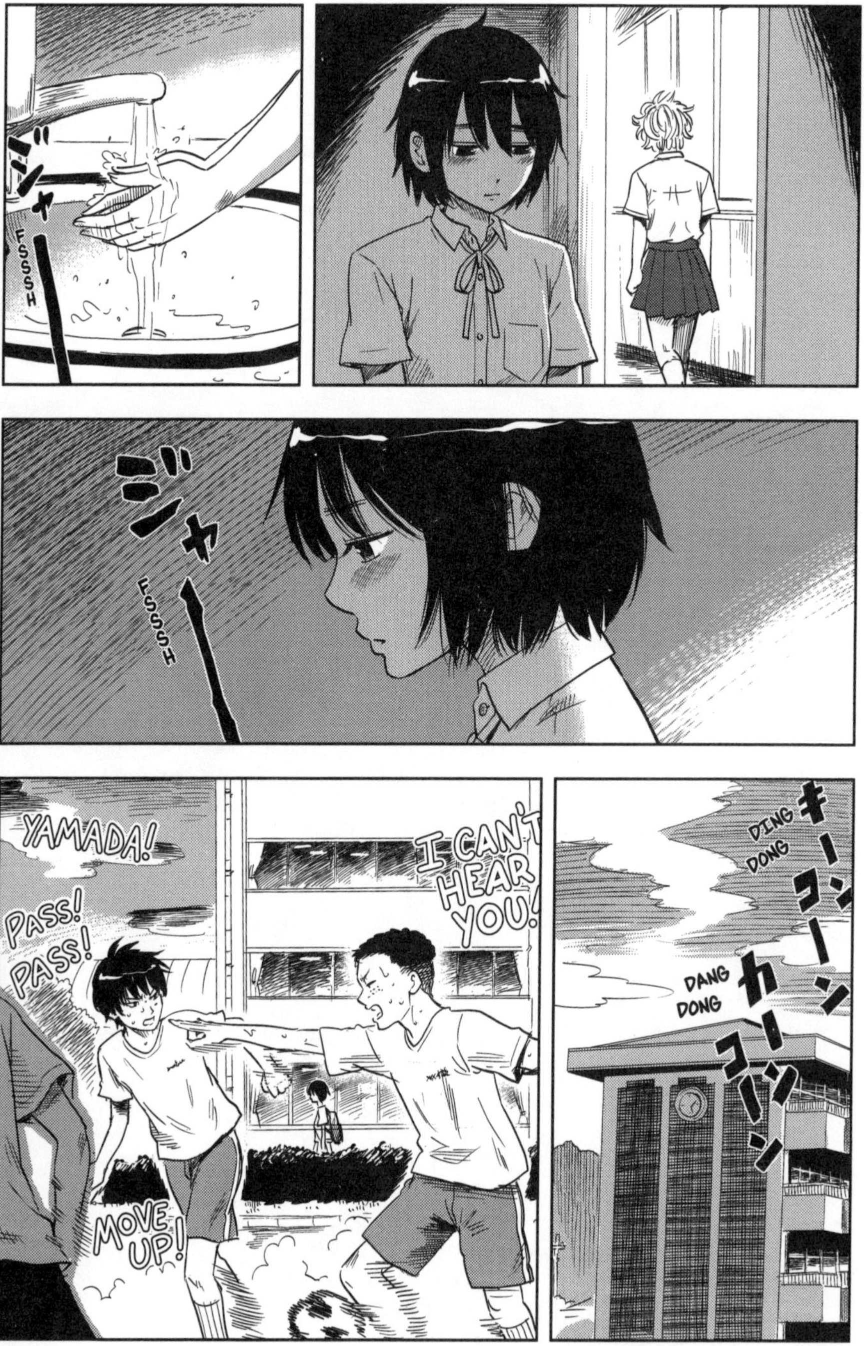
ジャ
FSSSH
ジャ
FSSSH
キーンコーン
DING DONG
カーンコーン
DANG DONG
I CAN'T HEAR YOU!
YAMADA!
PASS! PASS!
MOVE UP!

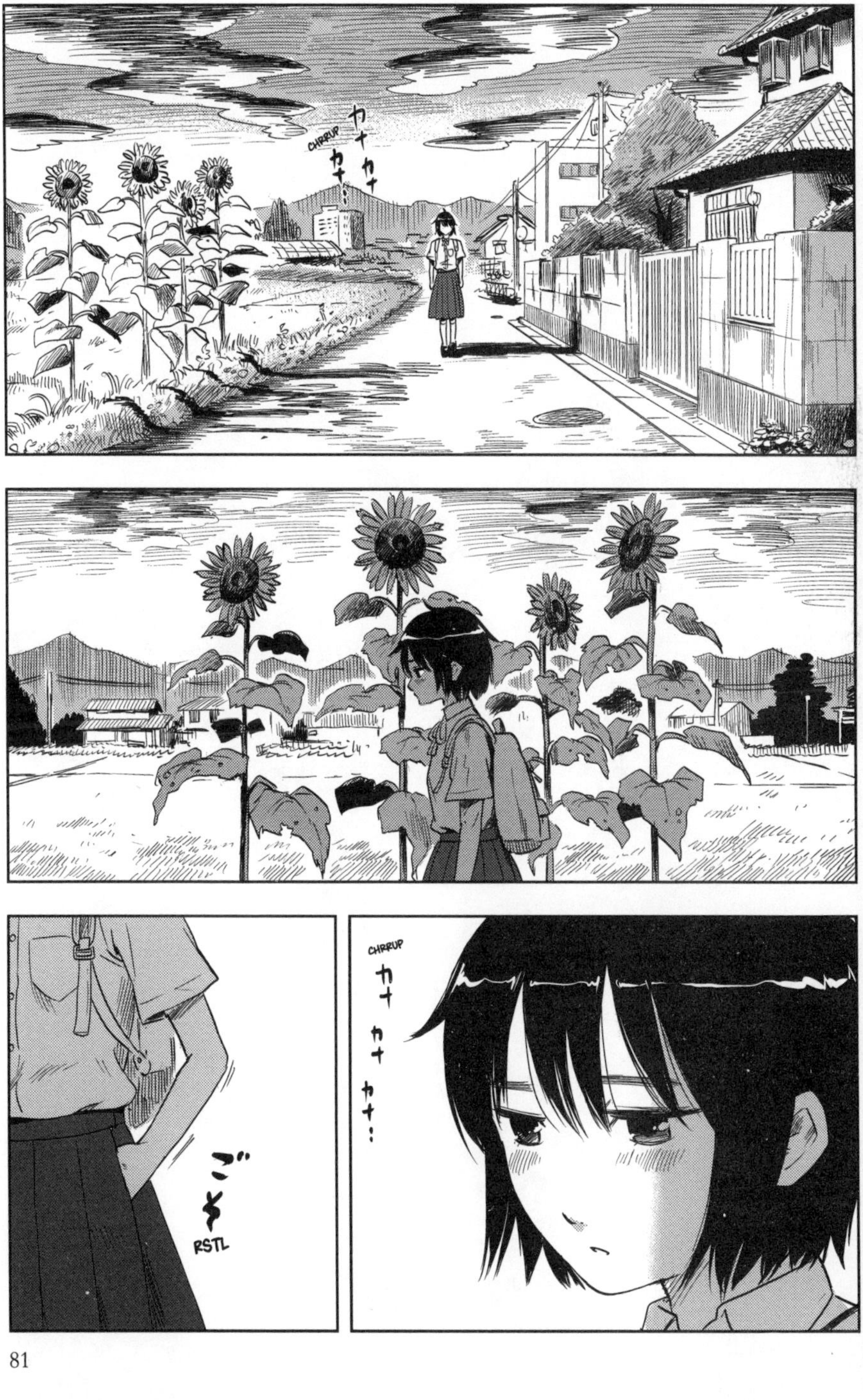
CHRRUP
カナカナ カナ…
CHRRUP
カナ カナ カナ…
ごそ
RSTL

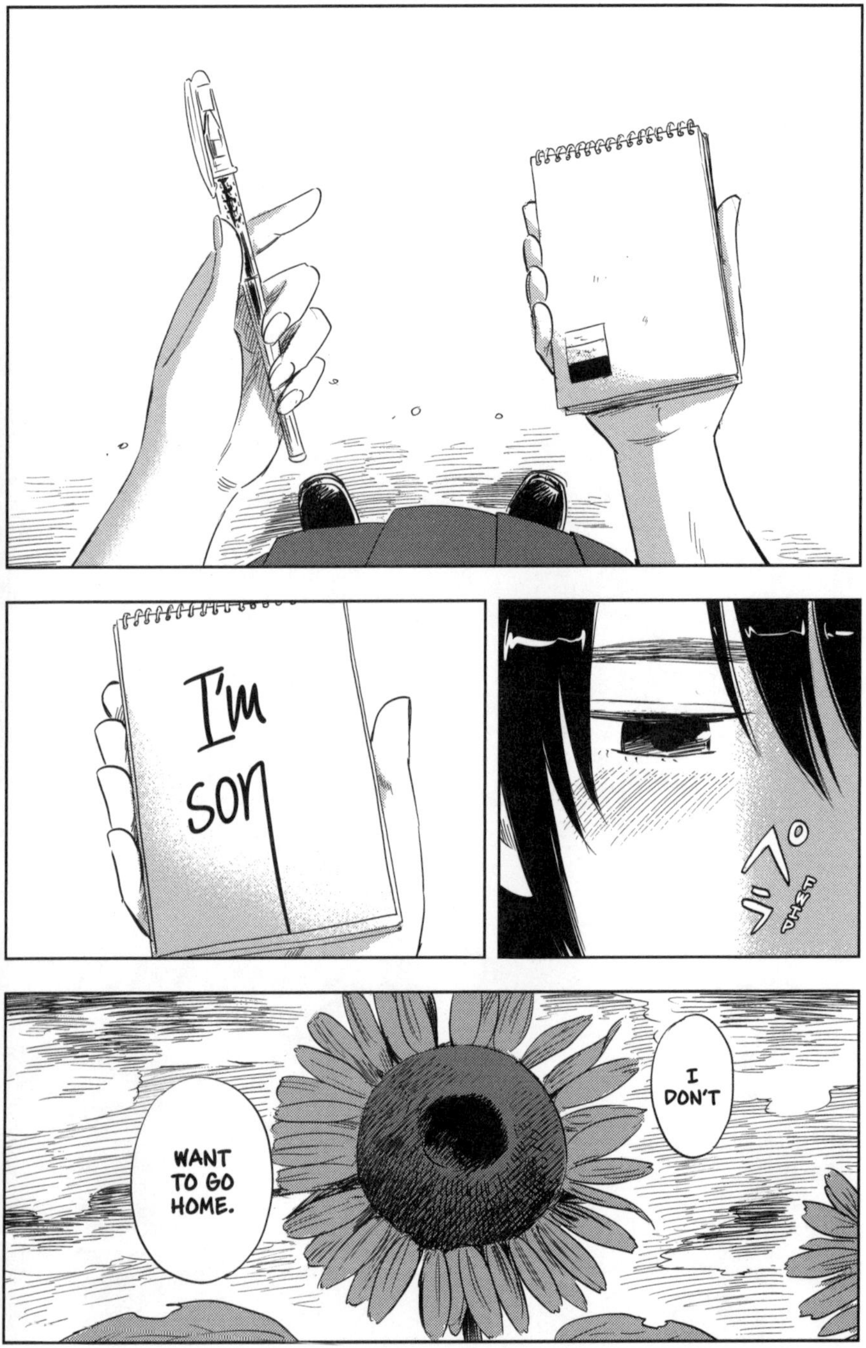
FWIP
I'm
son
I DON'T
WANT TO GO HOME.

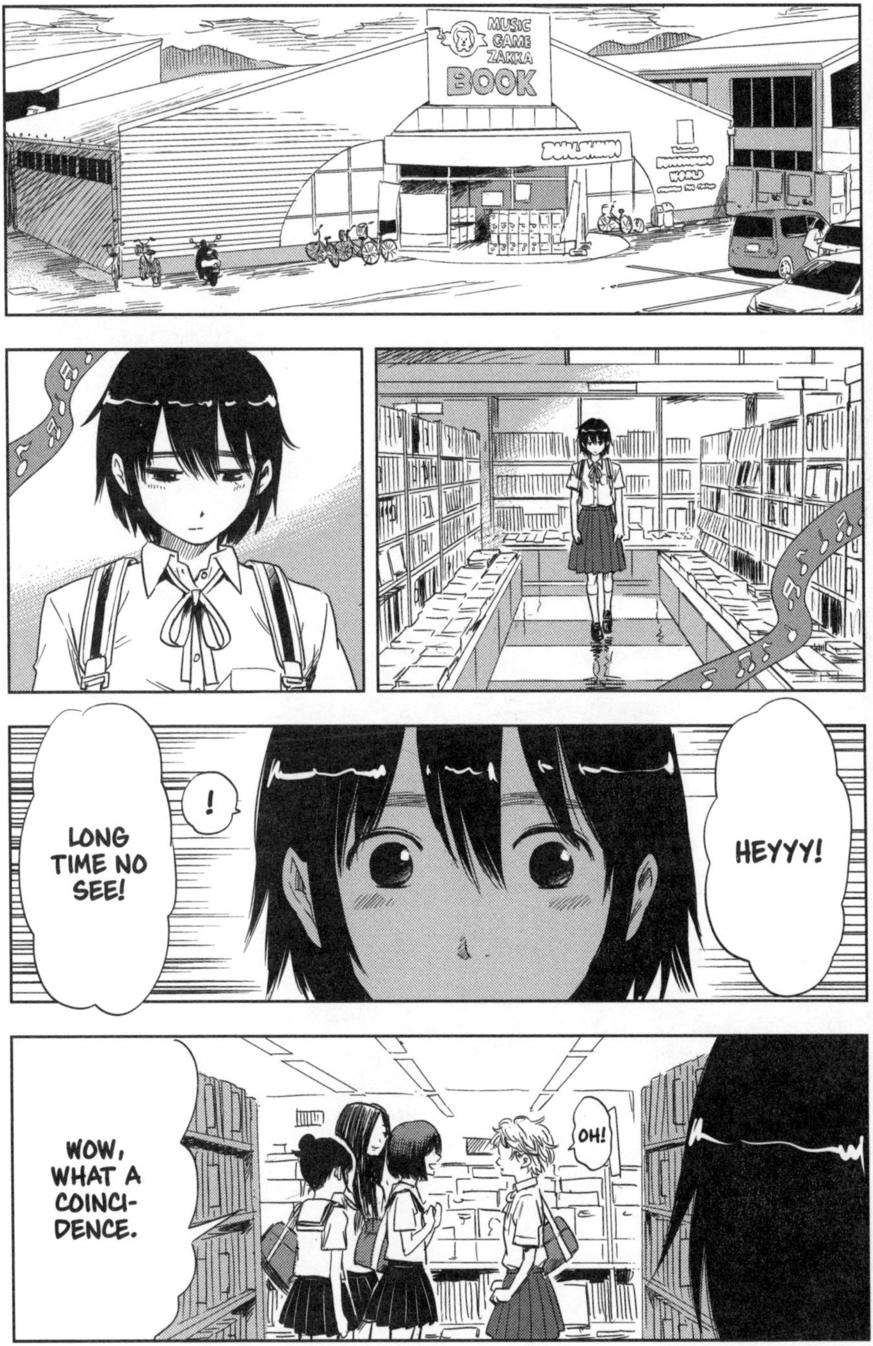
MUSIC GAME ZAKKA
BOOK
HEYYY!
!
LONG TIME NO SEE!
OH!
WOW, WHAT A COINCI-DENCE.

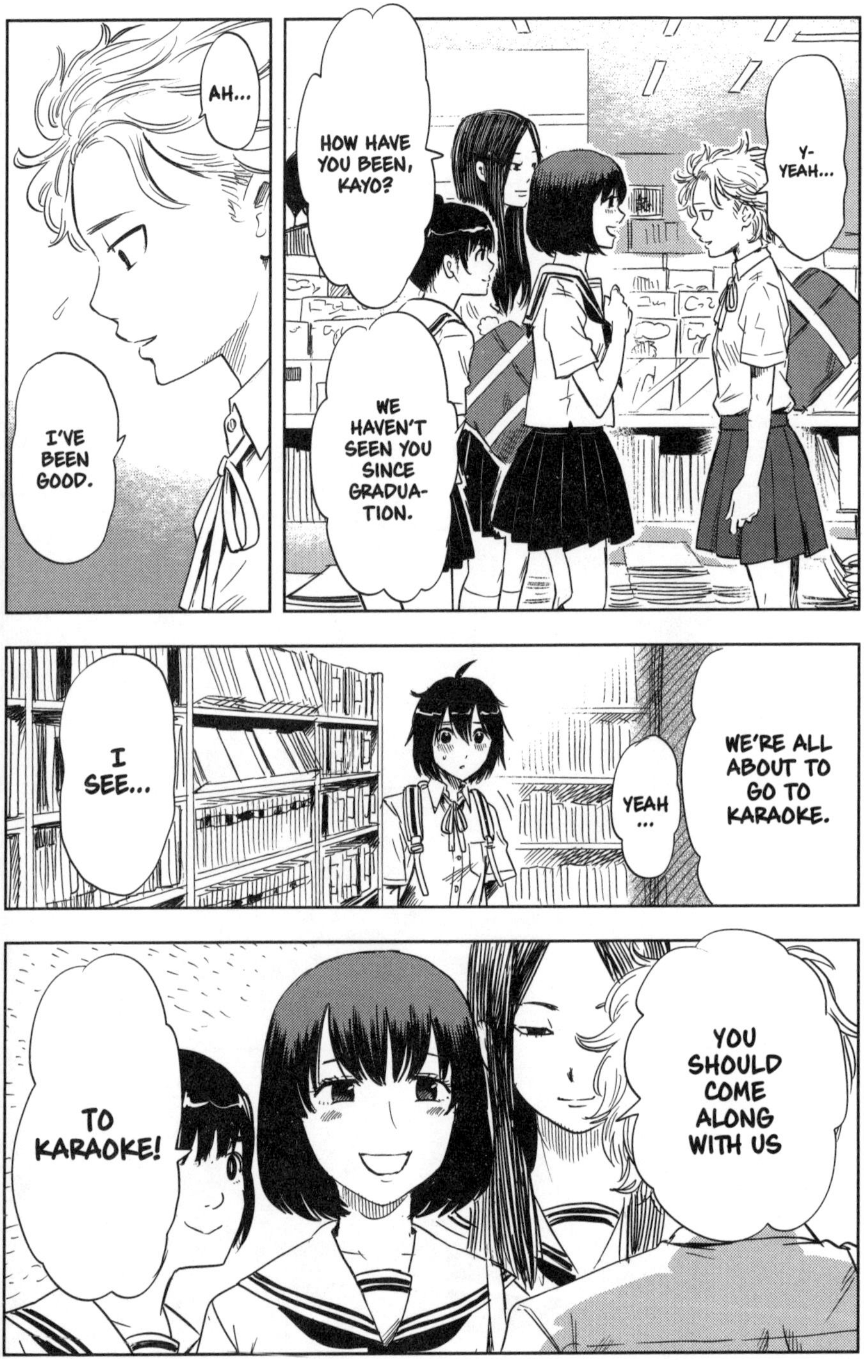
Y-YEAH...
HOW HAVE YOU BEEN, KAYO?
WE HAVEN'T SEEN YOU SINCE GRADUATION.
AH...
I'VE BEEN GOOD.
WE'RE ALL ABOUT TO GO TO KARAOKE.
YEAH ...
I SEE...
YOU SHOULD COME ALONG WITH US
TO KARAOKE!

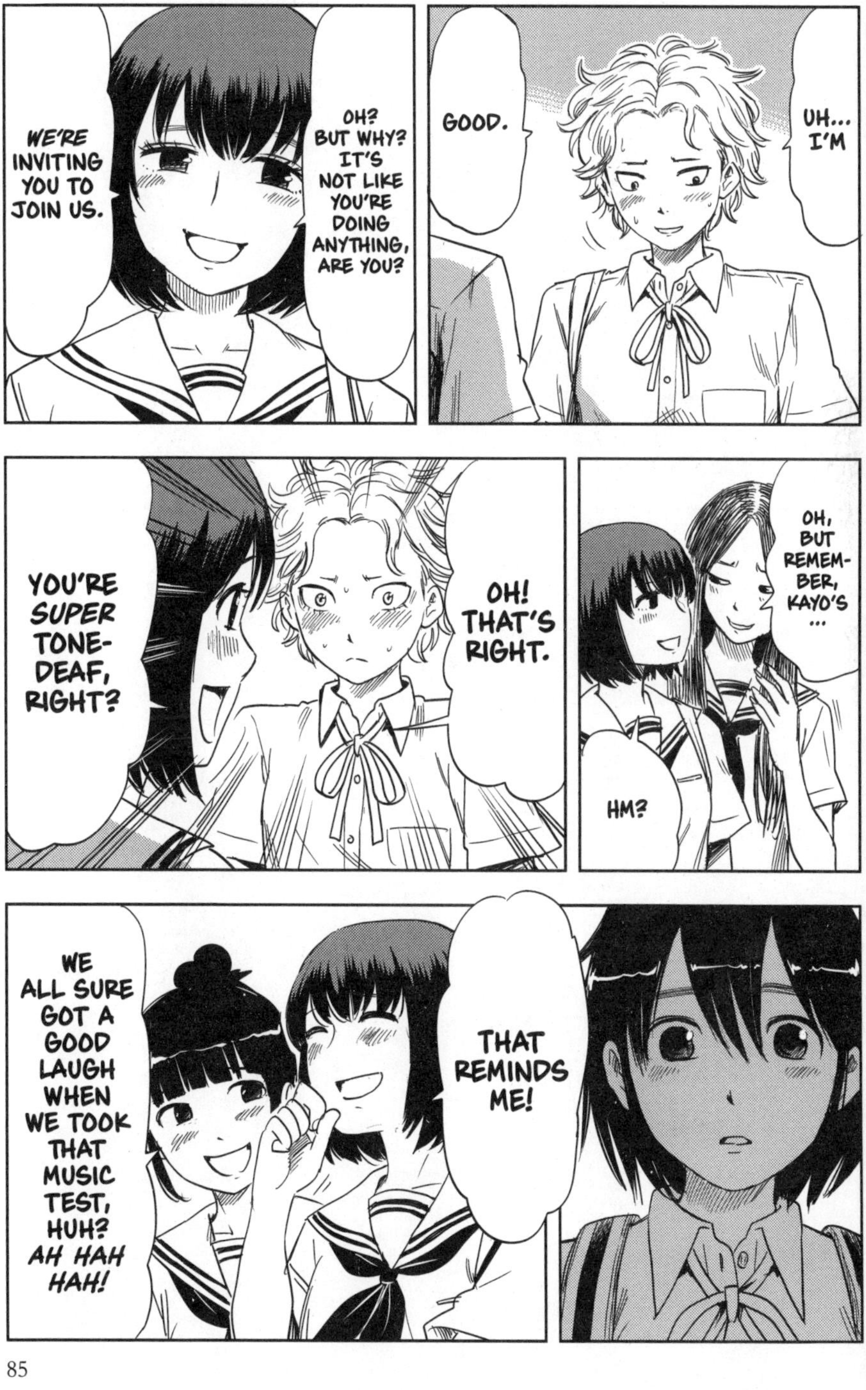
UH... I'M
GOOD.
OH? BUT WHY? IT'S NOT LIKE YOU'RE DOING ANYTHING, ARE YOU?
WE'RE INVITING YOU TO JOIN US.
OH, BUT REMEMBER, KAYO'S ...
HM?
OH! THAT'S RIGHT.
YOU'RE SUPER TONE-DEAF, RIGHT?
THAT REMINDS ME!
WE ALL SURE GOT A GOOD LAUGH WHEN WE TOOK THAT MUSIC TEST, HUH? AH HAH HAH!

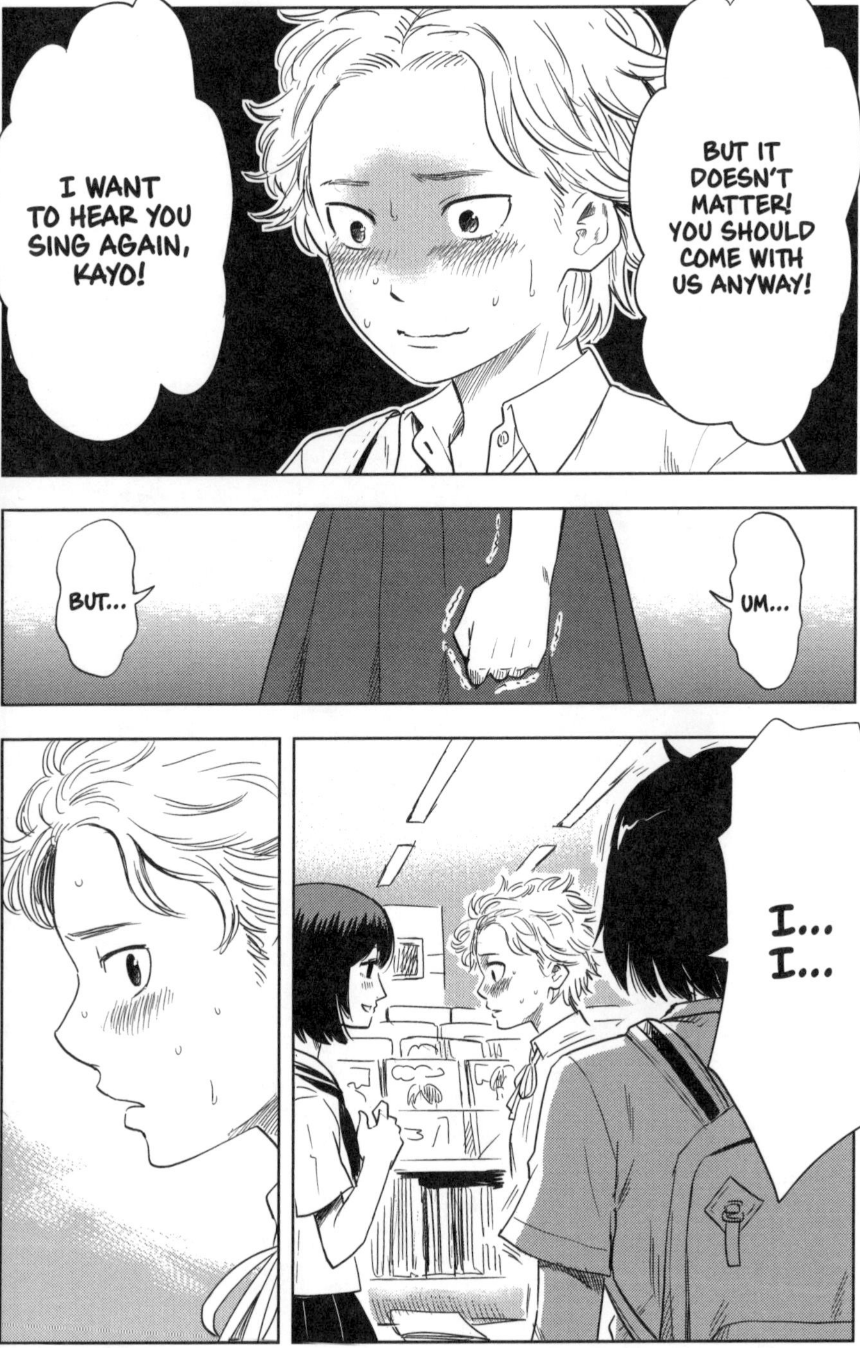
BUT IT DOESN'T MATTER! YOU SHOULD COME WITH US ANYWAY!
I WANT TO HEAR YOU SING AGAIN, KAYO!
UM...
BUT...
I... I...

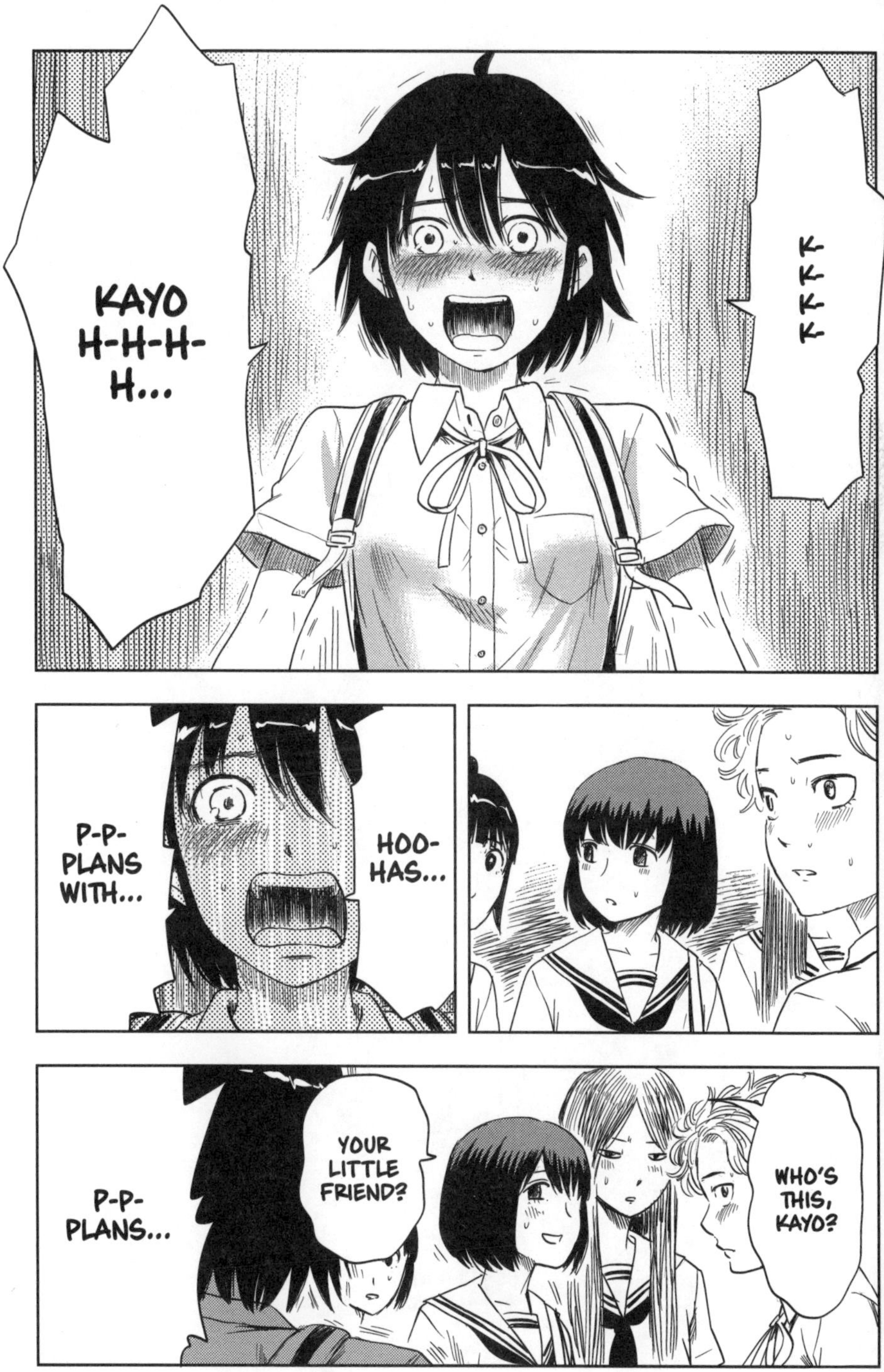
K-K-K-K-
KAYO H-H-H-H...
HOO-HAS...
P-P-PLANS WITH...
WHO'S THIS, KAYO?
YOUR LITTLE FRIEND?
P-P-PLANS...

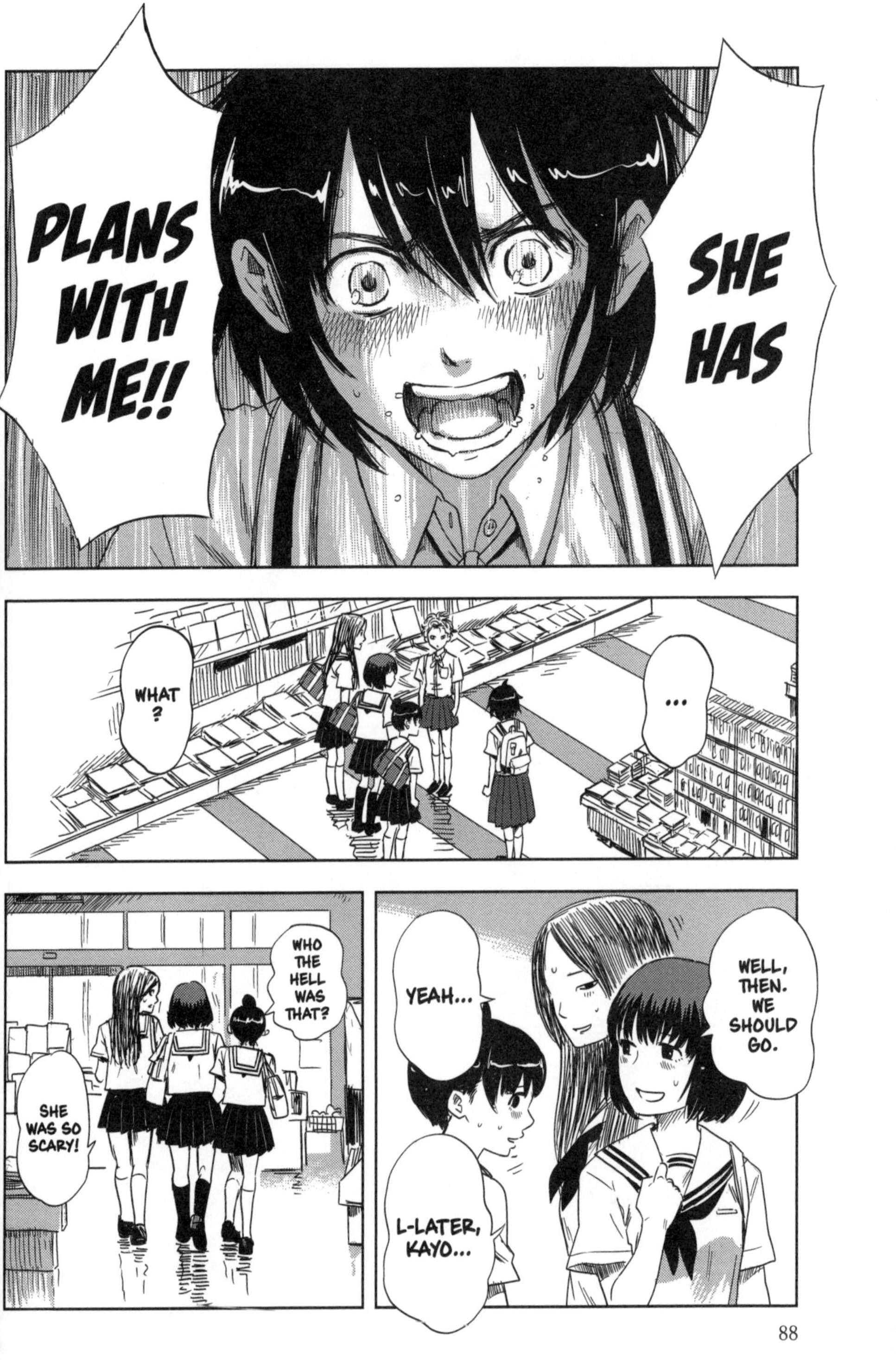
SHE HAS
PLANS WITH ME!!
...
WHAT?
WELL, THEN. WE SHOULD GO.
YEAH...
L-LATER, KAYO...
WHO THE HELL WAS THAT?
SHE WAS SO SCARY!

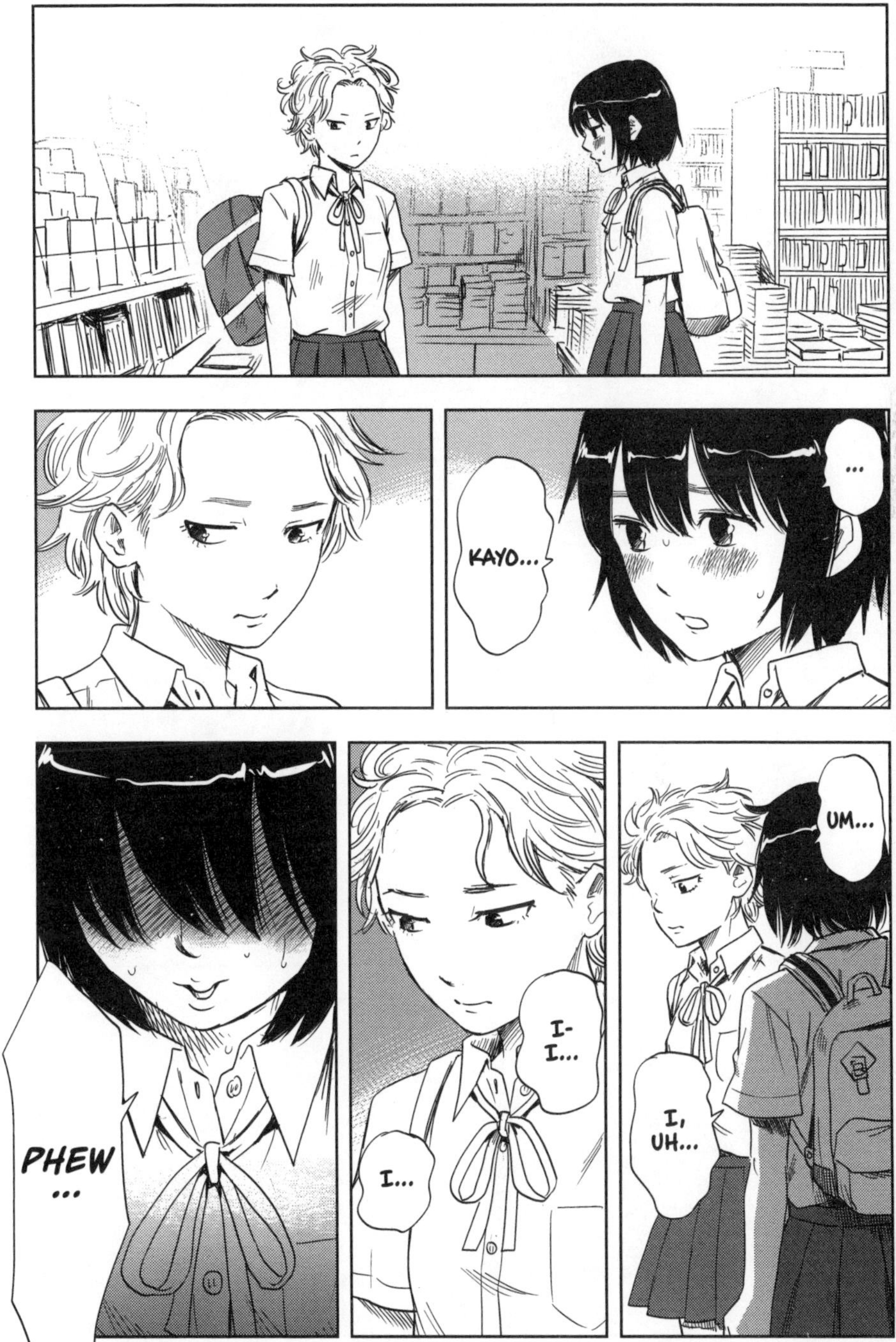
...
KAYO...
UM...
I, UH...
I- I...
I...
PHEW ...

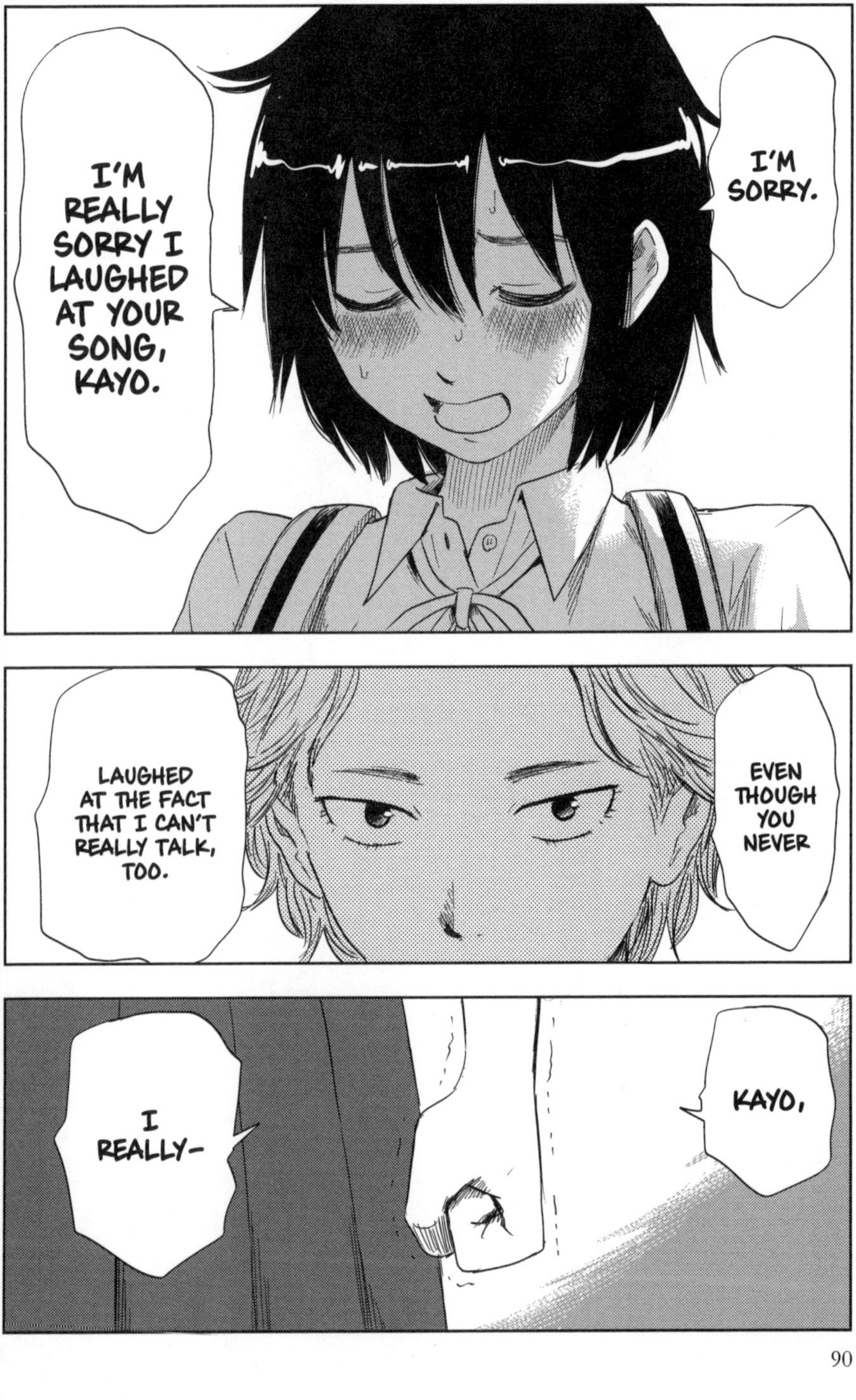
I'M SORRY.
I'M REALLY SORRY I LAUGHED AT YOUR SONG, KAYO.
EVEN THOUGH YOU NEVER
LAUGHED AT THE FACT THAT I CAN'T REALLY TALK, TOO.
KAYO,
I REALLY-

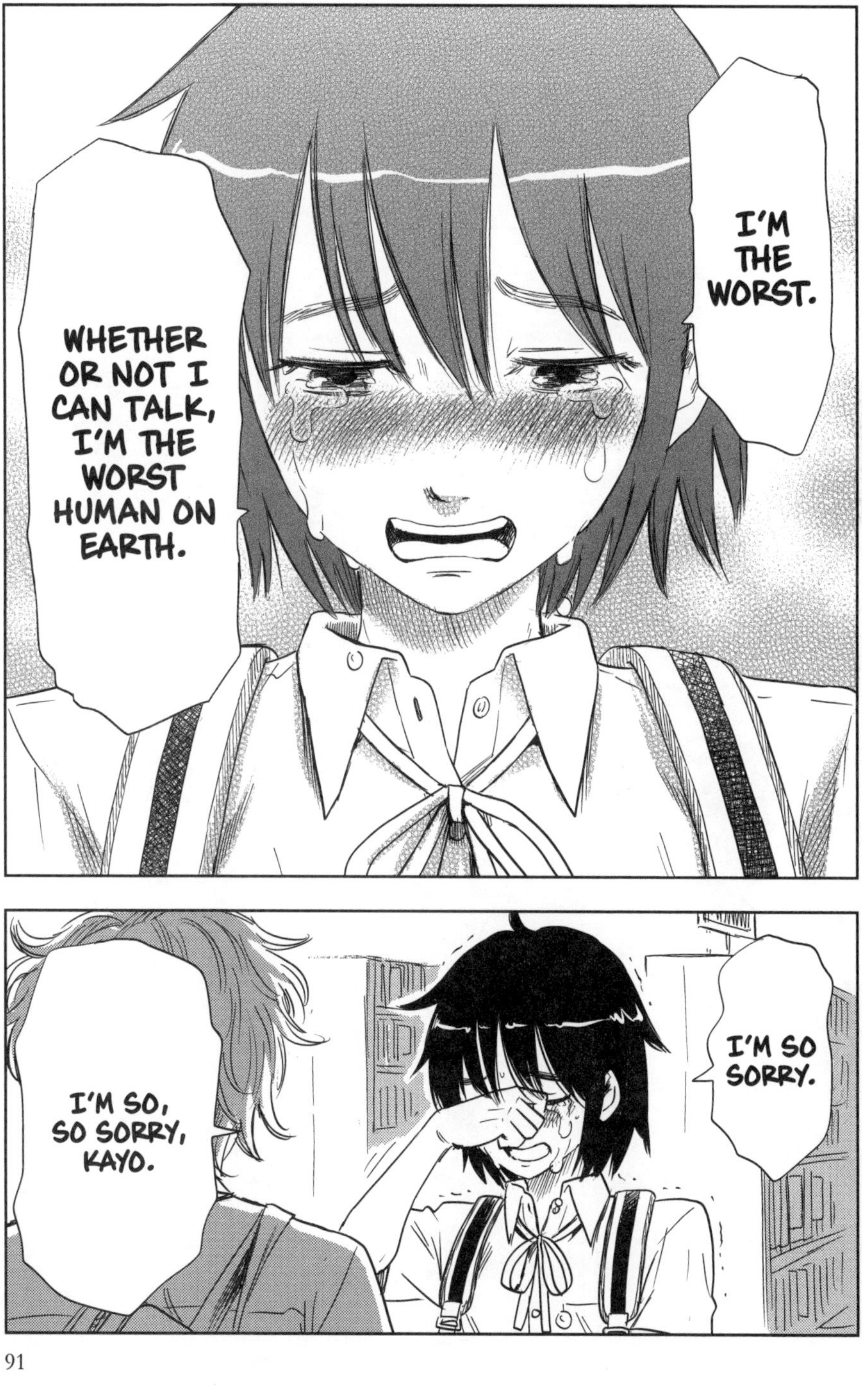
I'M THE WORST.
WHETHER OR NOT I CAN TALK, I'M THE WORST HUMAN ON EARTH.
I'M SO SORRY.
I'M SO, SO SORRY, KAYO.

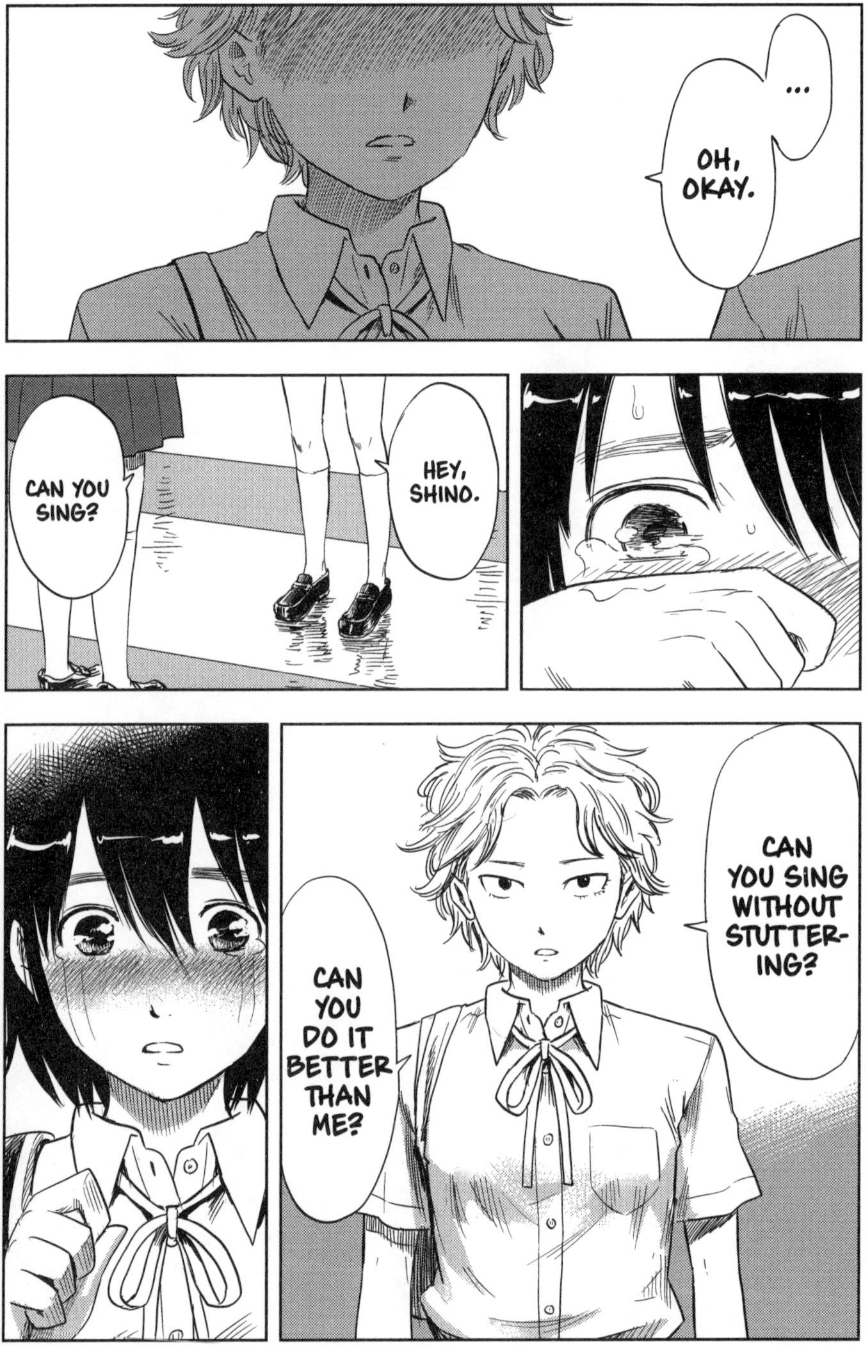
...
OH, OKAY.
HEY, SHINO.
CAN YOU SING?
CAN YOU SING WITHOUT STUTTER-ING?
CAN YOU DO IT BETTER THAN ME?

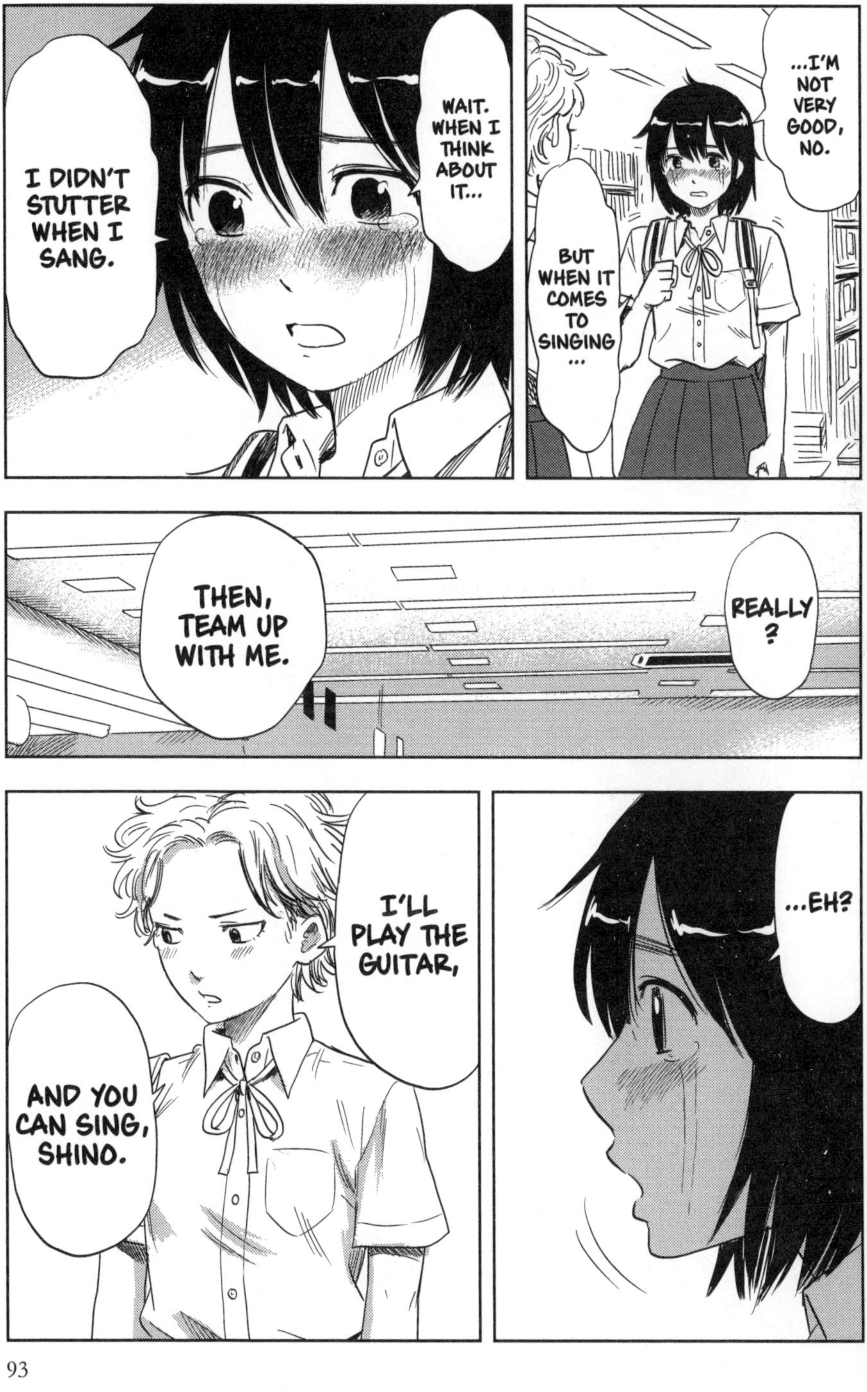
...I'M NOT VERY GOOD, NO.
BUT WHEN IT COMES TO SINGING...
WAIT. WHEN I THINK ABOUT IT...
I DIDN'T STUTTER WHEN I SANG.
REALLY?
THEN, TEAM UP WITH ME.
...EH?
I'LL PLAY THE GUITAR,
AND YOU CAN SING, SHINO.

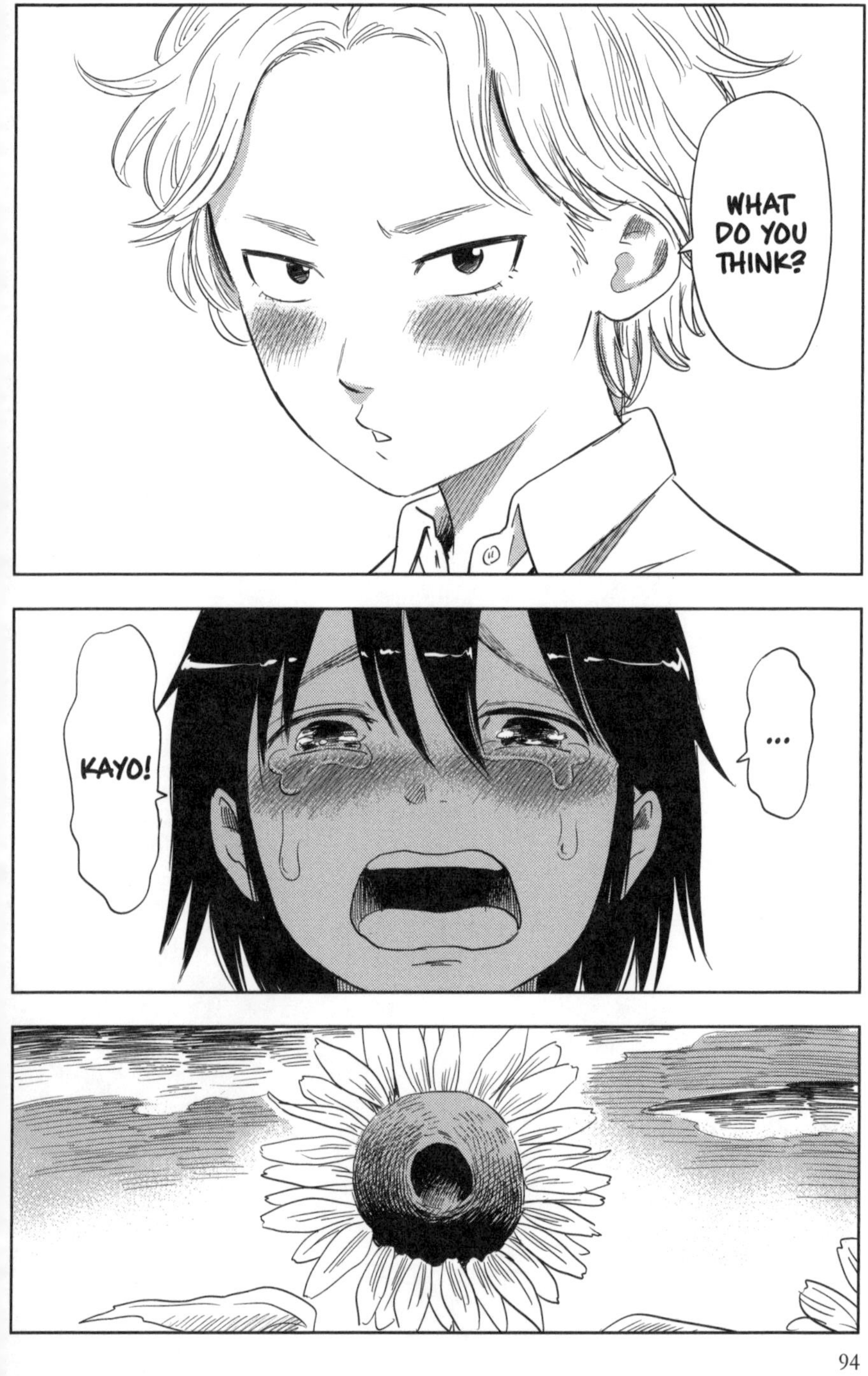
WHAT DO YOU THINK?
...
KAYO!

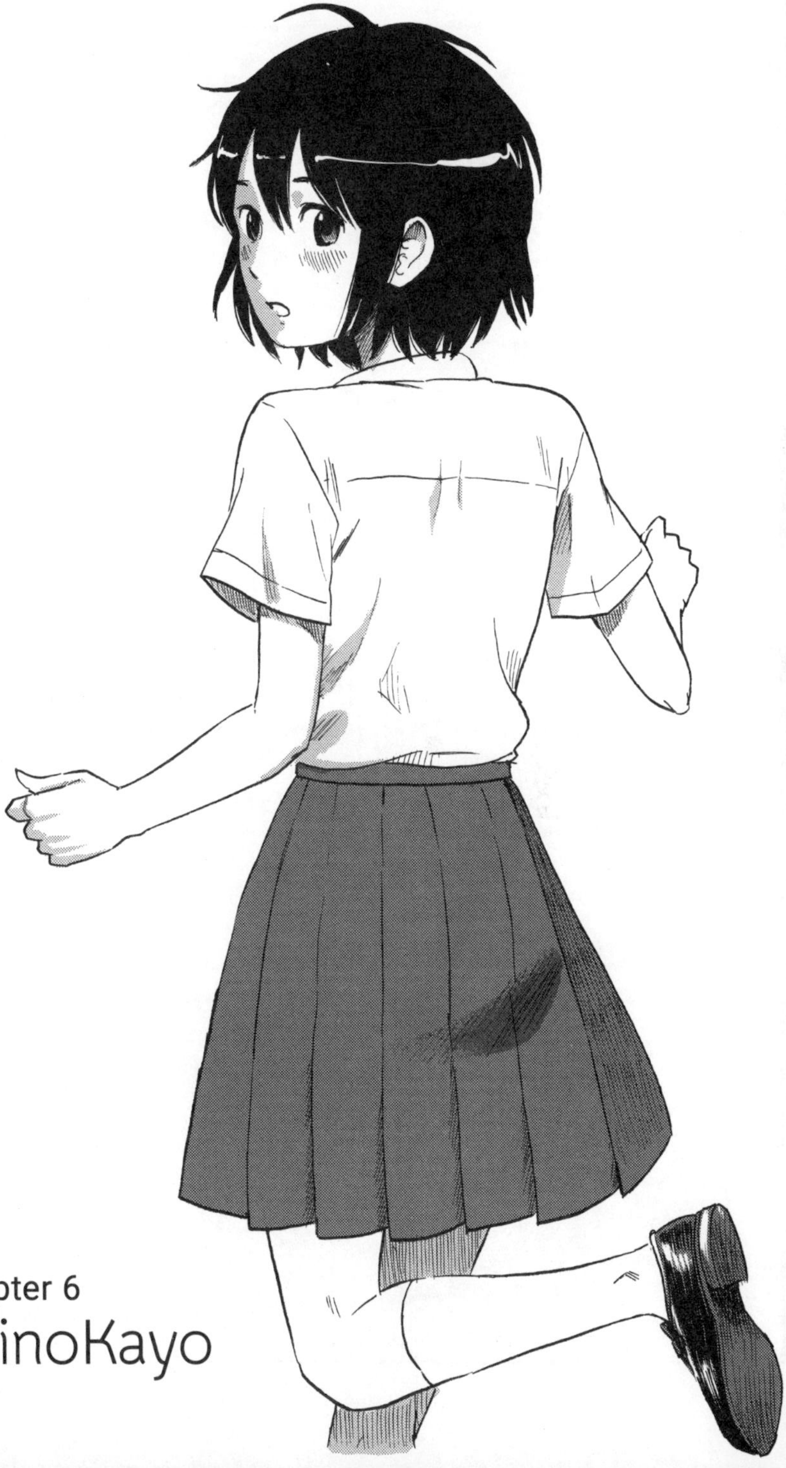

Chapter 6
ShinoKayo

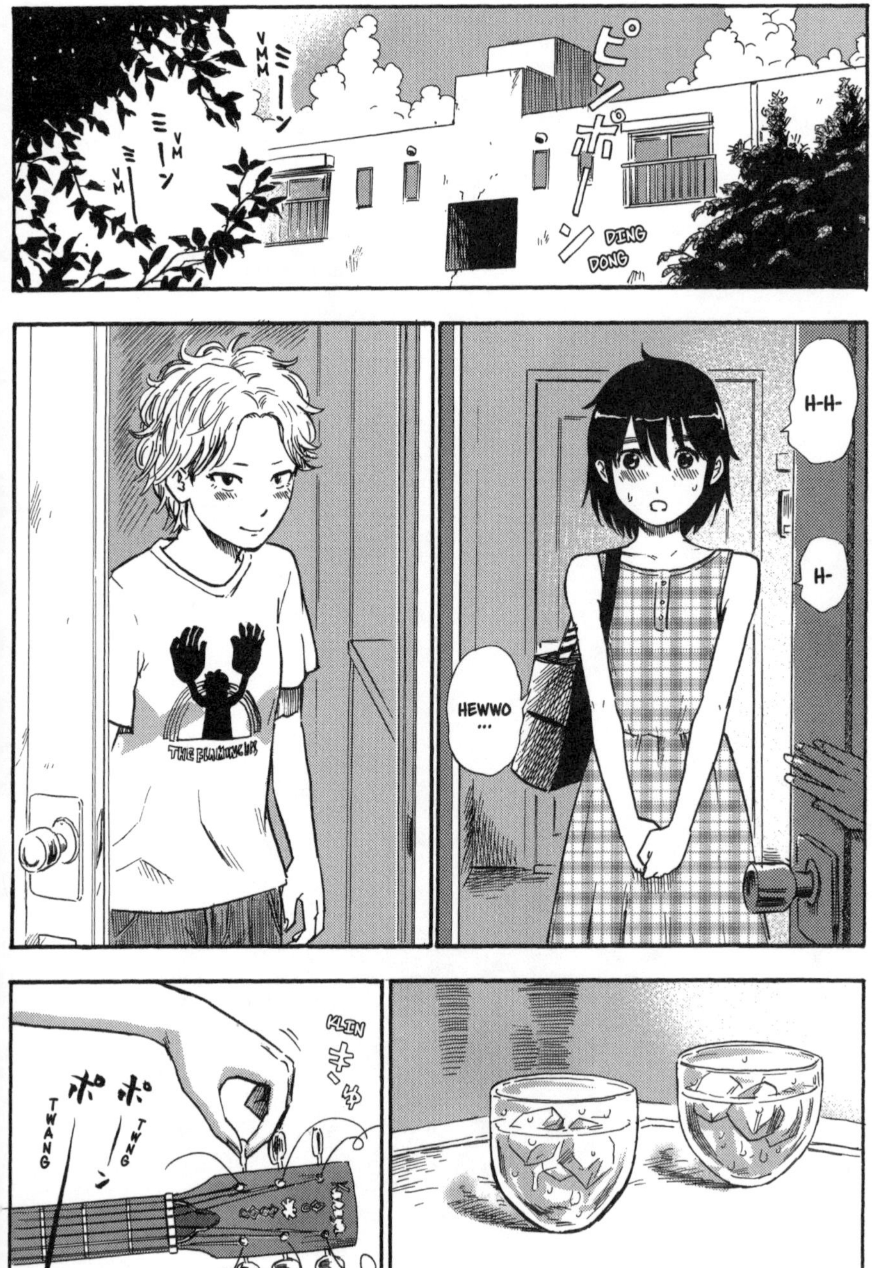
ピンポーン
DING DONG
ミーン
VMM
ミーン
VM
ミー
VM
H-H-
H-
HEWWO ...
キュ
KLIN
ポーン
TWNG
ポーン
TWANG

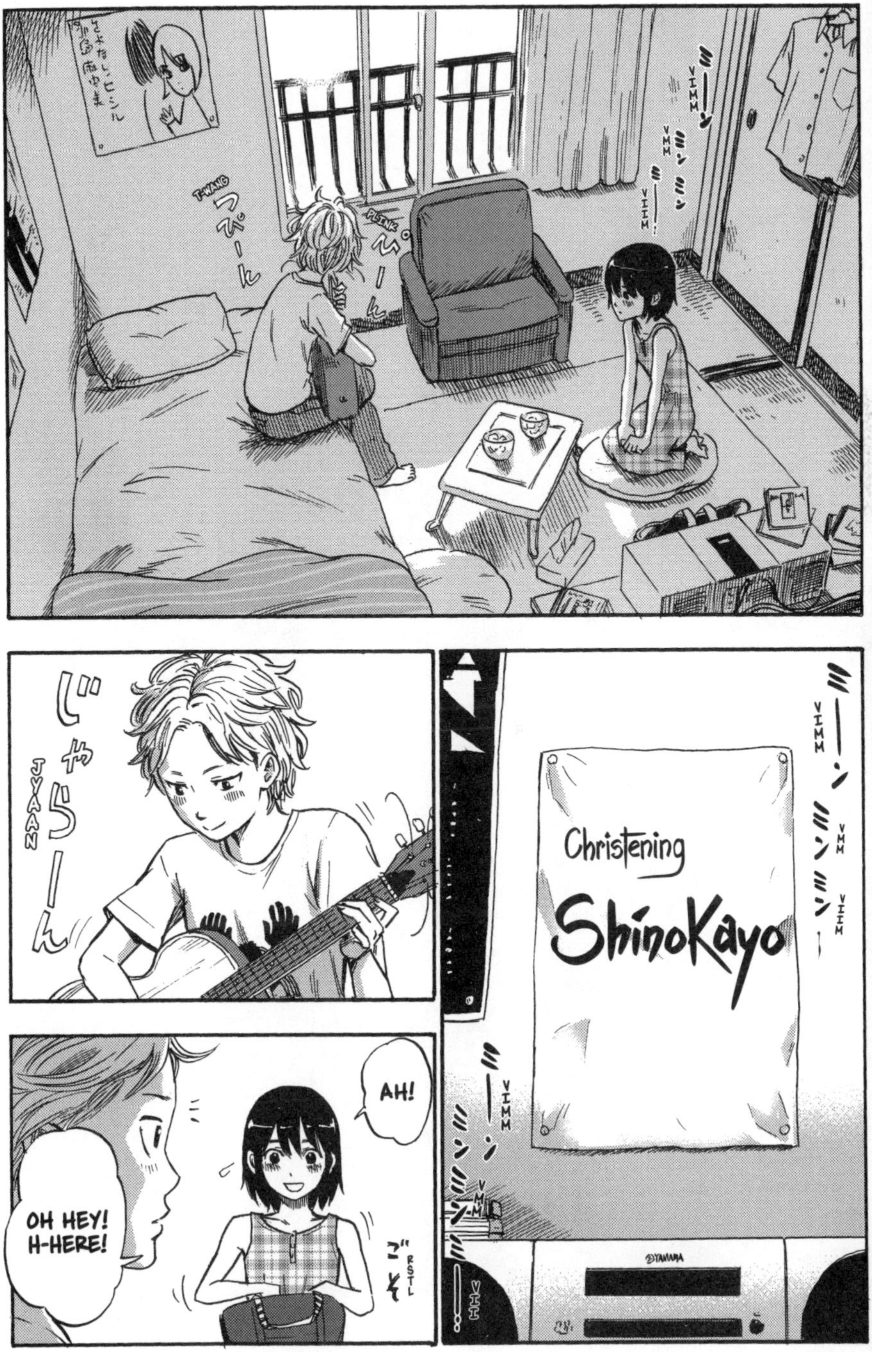
ミーン VIMM
ミンミン VMM
ミー…! VIIM
ぴーん PLINK
つぴーん T-WANG
ミーン VIMM
ミンミン VMM
ミン… VIIM
Christening
ShinoKayo
ミーン VIMM
ミンミン VMM
ミー…! VII
じゃらーん JYAAAN
AH!
ごそ RSTL
OH HEY! H-HERE!

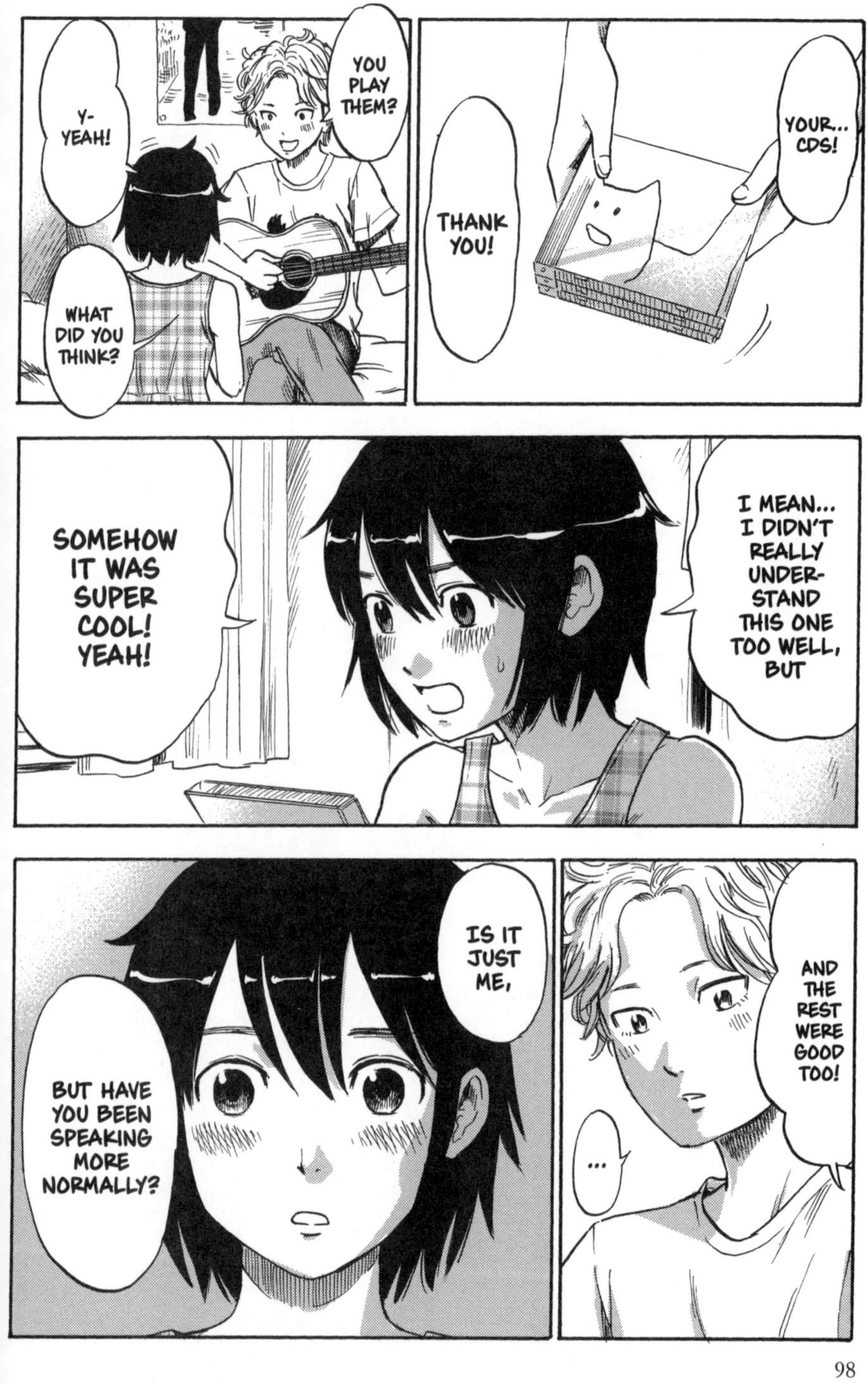
YOUR... CDS!
THANK YOU!
YOU PLAY THEM?
Y- YEAH!
WHAT DID YOU THINK?
I MEAN... I DIDN'T REALLY UNDER-STAND THIS ONE TOO WELL, BUT
SOMEHOW IT WAS SUPER COOL! YEAH!
AND THE REST WERE GOOD TOO!
...
IS IT JUST ME,
BUT HAVE YOU BEEN SPEAKING MORE NORMALLY?

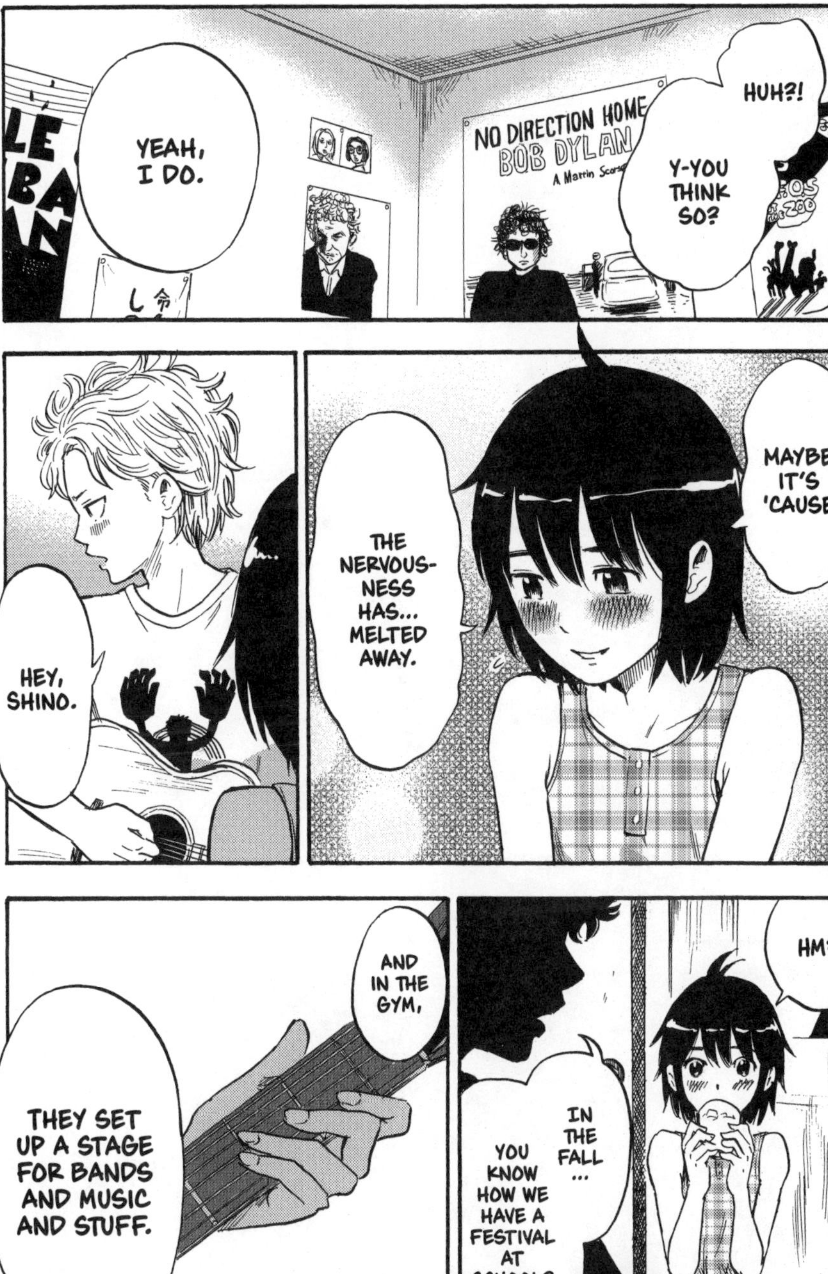
HUH?!
Y-YOU THINK SO?
NO DIRECTION HOME
BOB DYLAN
YEAH, I DO.
MAYBE IT'S 'CAUSE
THE NERVOUS-NESS HAS... MELTED AWAY.
HEY, SHINO.
HM?
IN THE FALL ...
YOU KNOW HOW WE HAVE A FESTIVAL AT SCHOOL?
AND IN THE GYM,
THEY SET UP A STAGE FOR BANDS AND MUSIC AND STUFF.

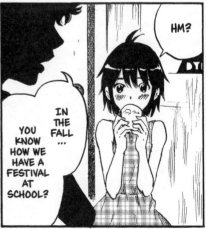

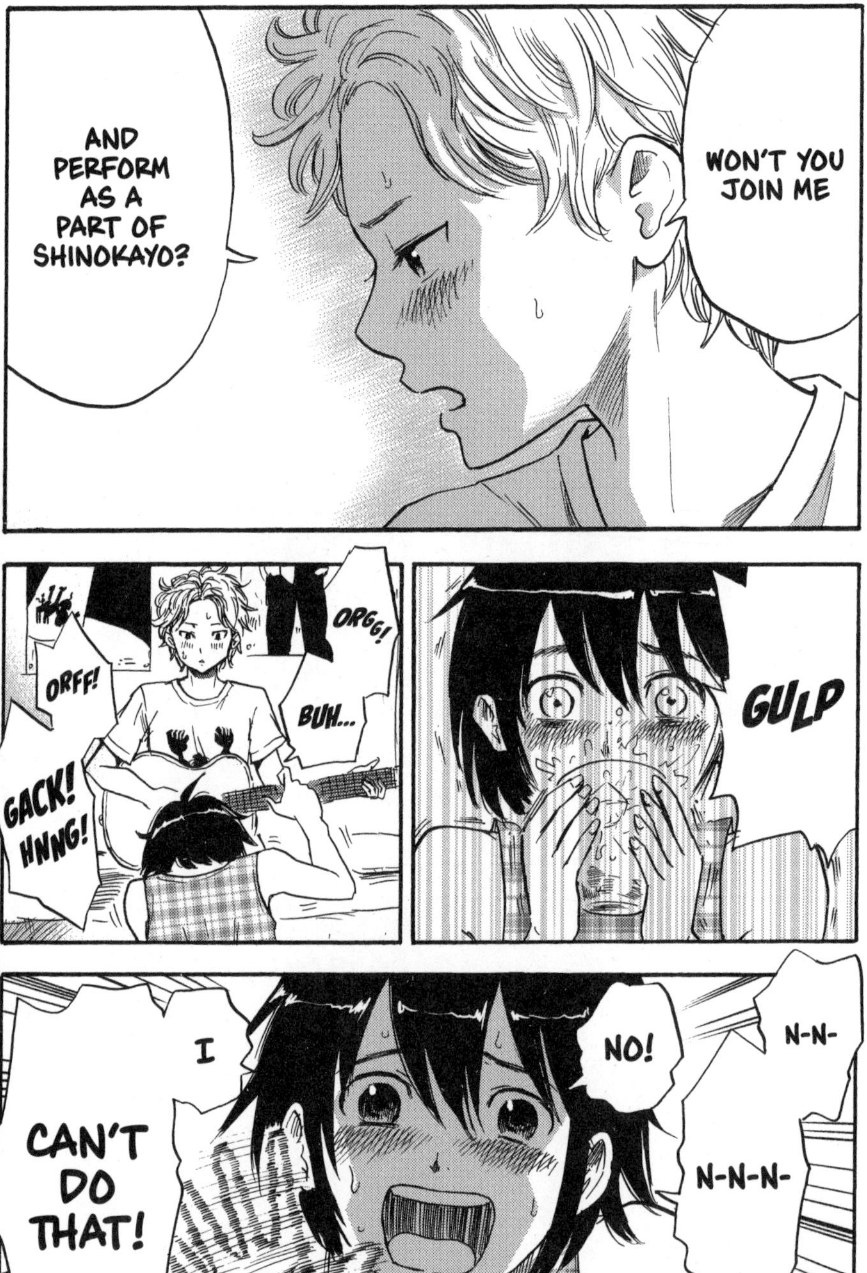
WON'T YOU JOIN ME
AND PERFORM AS A PART OF SHINOKAYO?
GULP
ORGG!
BUH...
ORFF!
GACK! HNNG!
N-N-
N-N-N-
NO!
I
CAN'T DO THAT!

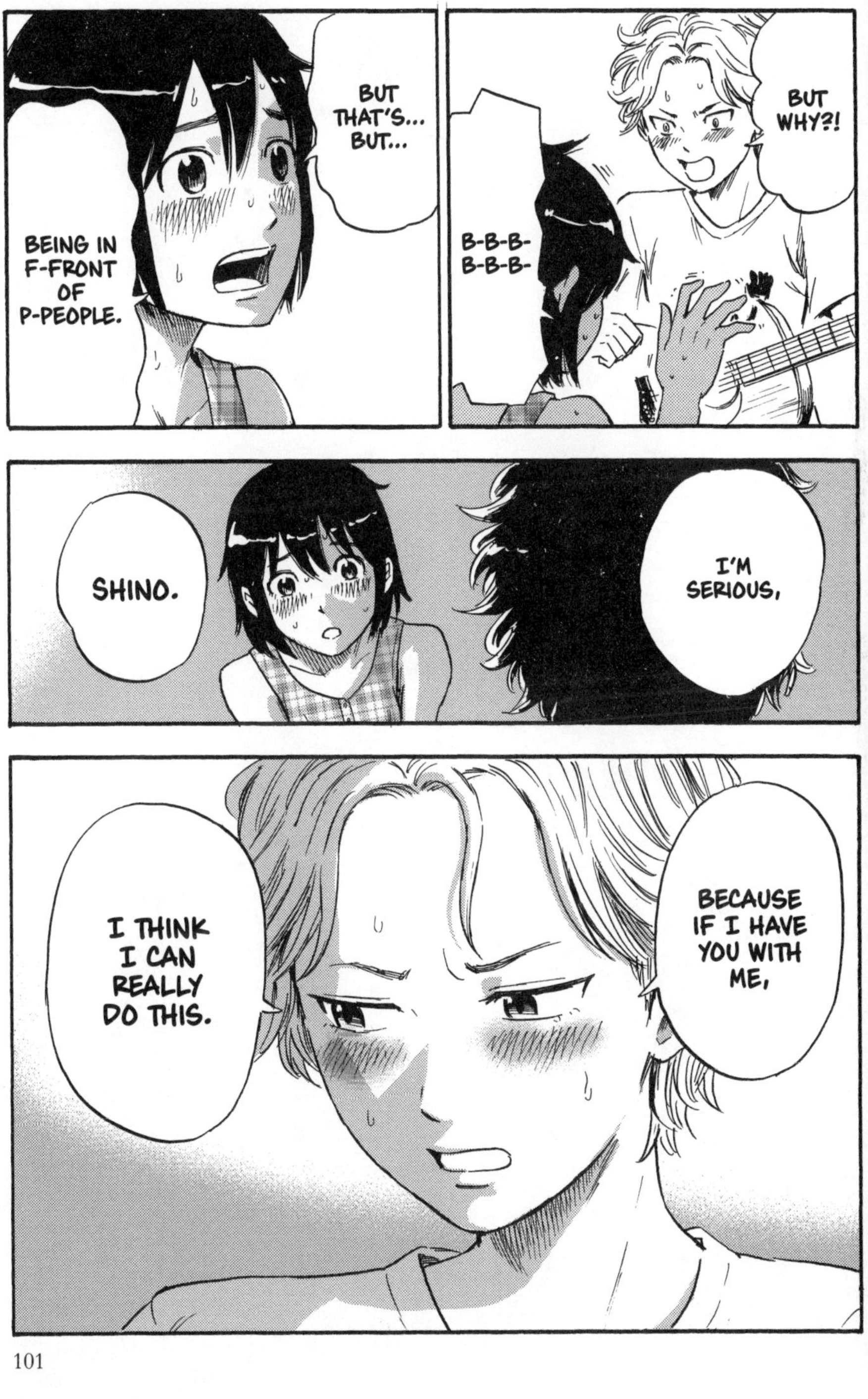
BUT WHY?!
B-B-B-B-B-B-
BUT THAT'S... BUT...
BEING IN F-FRONT OF P-PEOPLE.
I'M SERIOUS,
SHINO.
BECAUSE IF I HAVE YOU WITH ME,
I THINK I CAN REALLY DO THIS.

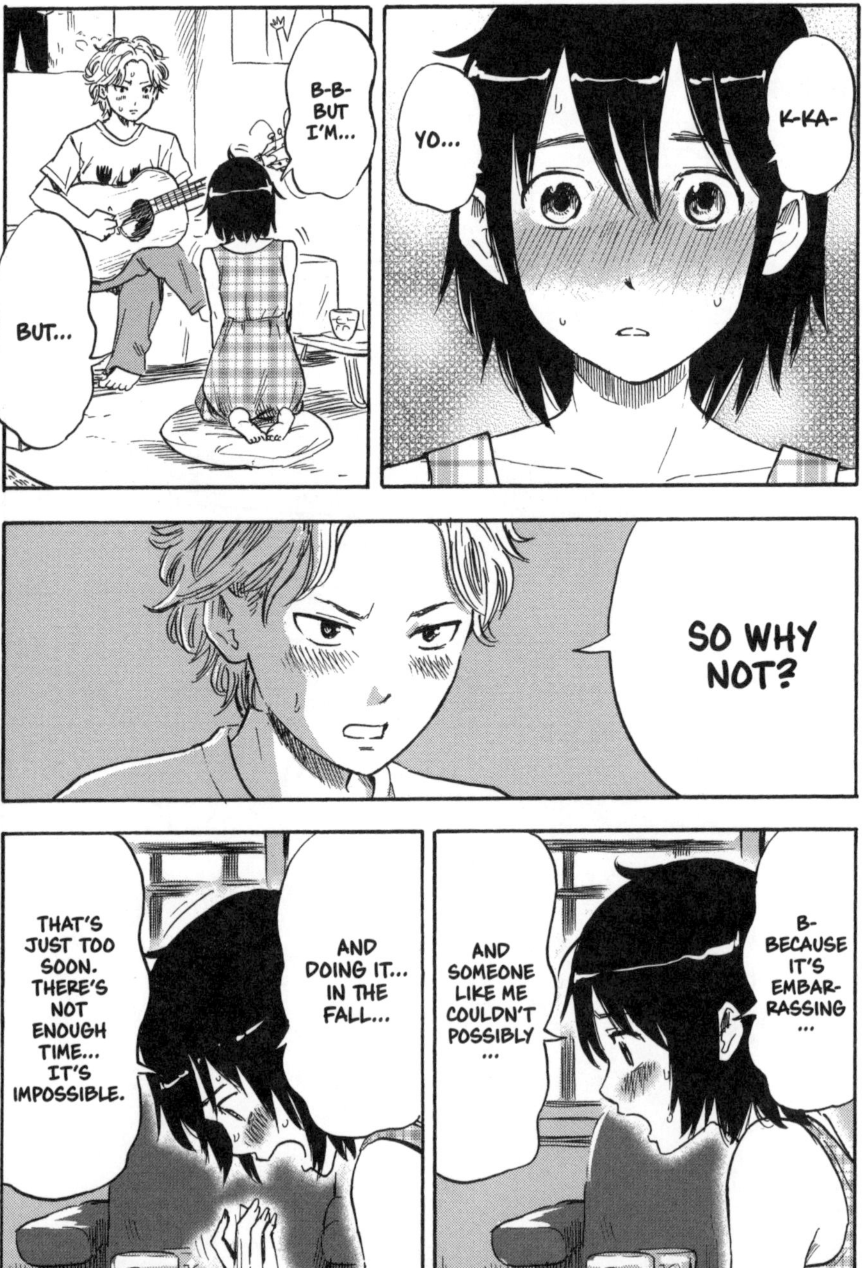
K-KA-
YO...
B-B-BUT I'M...
BUT...
SO WHY NOT?
B-BECAUSE IT'S EMBARRASSING...
AND SOMEONE LIKE ME COULDN'T POSSIBLY...
AND DOING IT... IN THE FALL...
THAT'S JUST TOO SOON. THERE'S NOT ENOUGH TIME... IT'S IMPOSSIBLE.

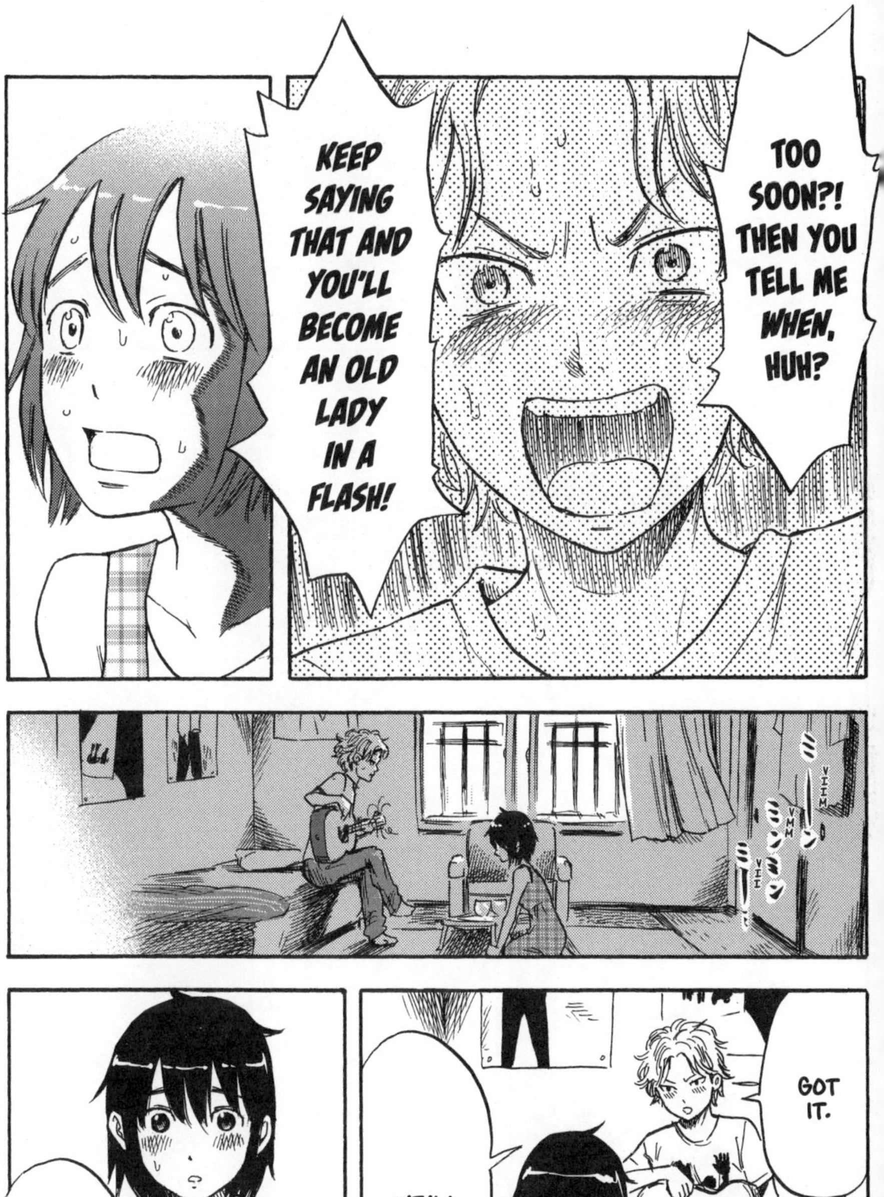
TOO SOON?! THEN YOU TELL ME WHEN, HUH?
KEEP SAYING THAT AND YOU'LL BECOME AN OLD LADY IN A FLASH!
VIIM
VMM
VII
GOT IT.
WE'LL PRACTICE, OKAY?
HUH?

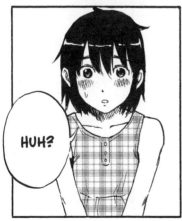

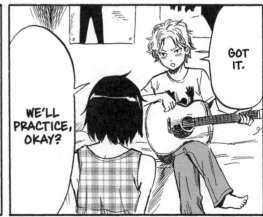

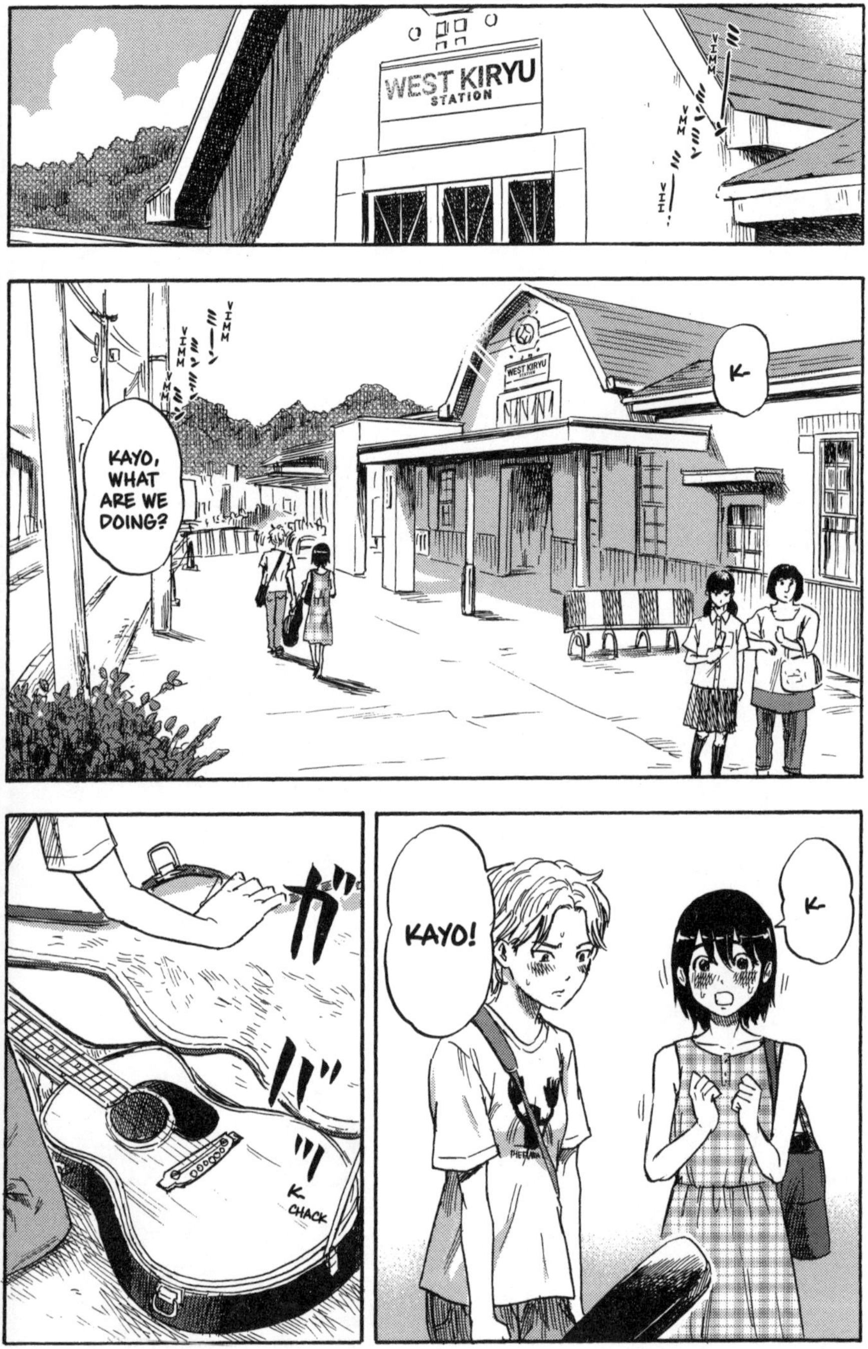
WEST KIRYU
STATION
VIMM
VMM
VII
VIMM
VIMM
VMM
K-
KAYO, WHAT ARE WE DOING?
WEST KIRYU
STATION
K-
KAYO!
K-
CHACK

WE'RE GONNA PLAY HERE.
IT'LL BE A STREET SHOW.
S-
STREET ?!
I... DON'T THINK THIS IS A GOOD IDEA...
I'VE NEVER SEEN THESE PEOPLE BEFORE!
Big Book of Songs
I BROUGHT MY SONG BOOK WITH ME.
WHICH ONE SHOULD WE PLAY?
FWIP
Big Book

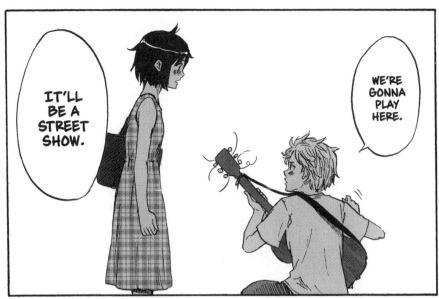

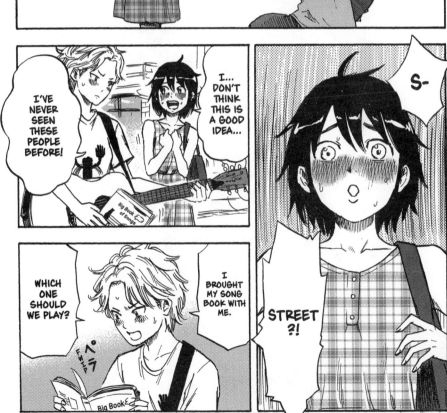

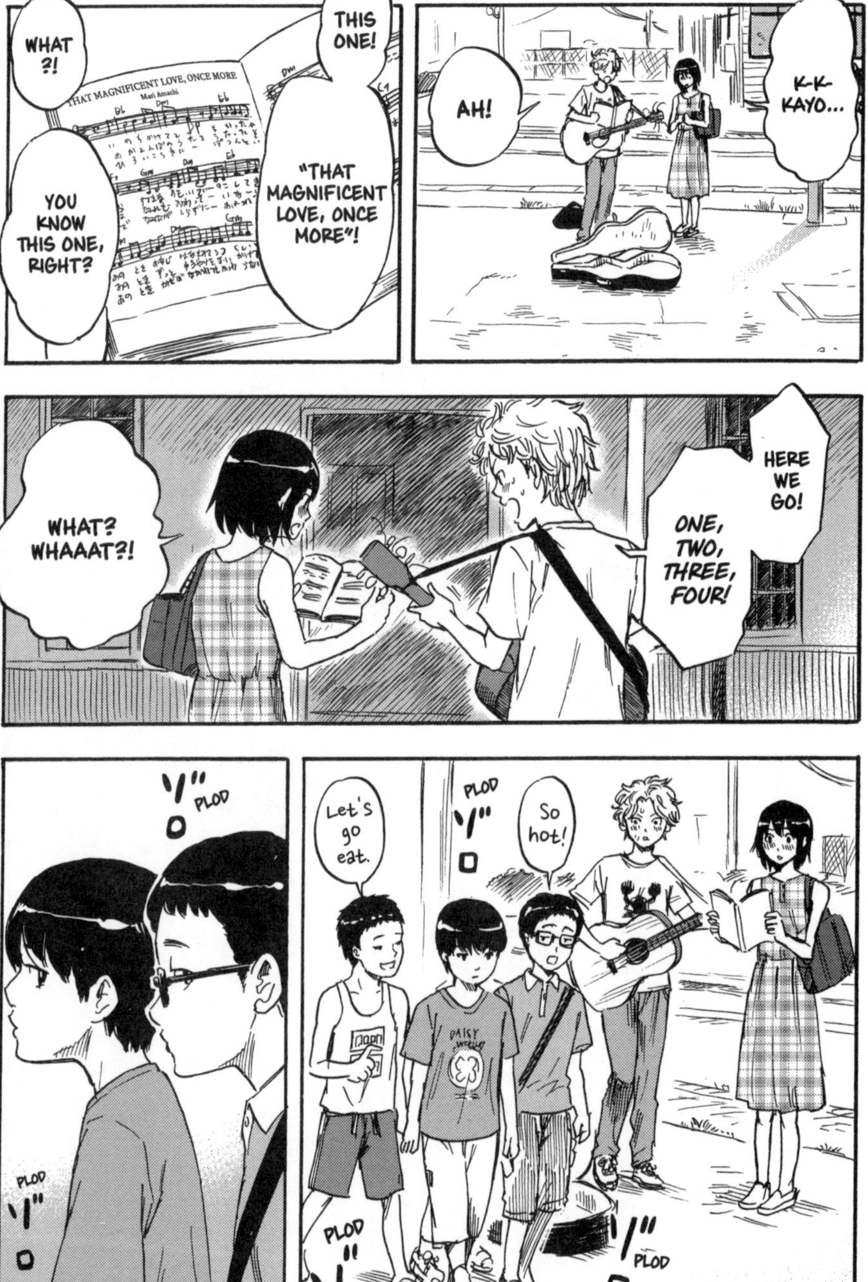
K-K KAYO...
AH!
THIS ONE!
"THAT MAGNIFICENT LOVE, ONCE MORE"!
WHAT ?!
THAT MAGNIFICENT LOVE, ONCE MORE
Mari Amachi
YOU KNOW THIS ONE, RIGHT?
HERE WE GO!
ONE, TWO, THREE, FOUR!
WHAT? WHAAAT?!
So hot!
PLOD
Let's go eat.
PLOD
PLOD
PLOD
PLOD

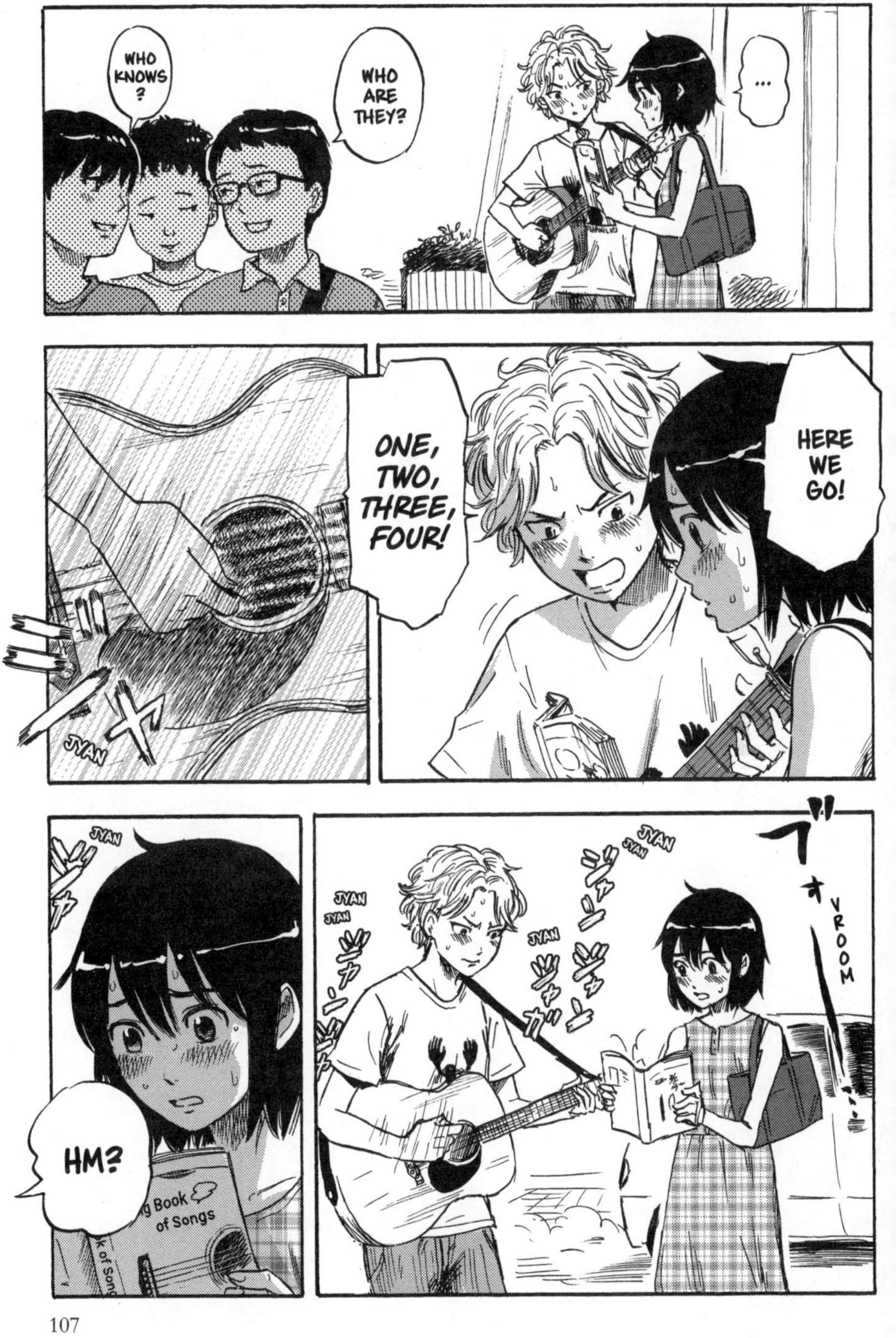
...
WHO ARE THEY?
WHO KNOWS ?
HERE WE GO!
ONE, TWO, THREE, FOUR!
JYAN
VROOM
JYAN
JYAN
JYAN
JYAN
JYAN
JYAN
HM?
Book
of Songs

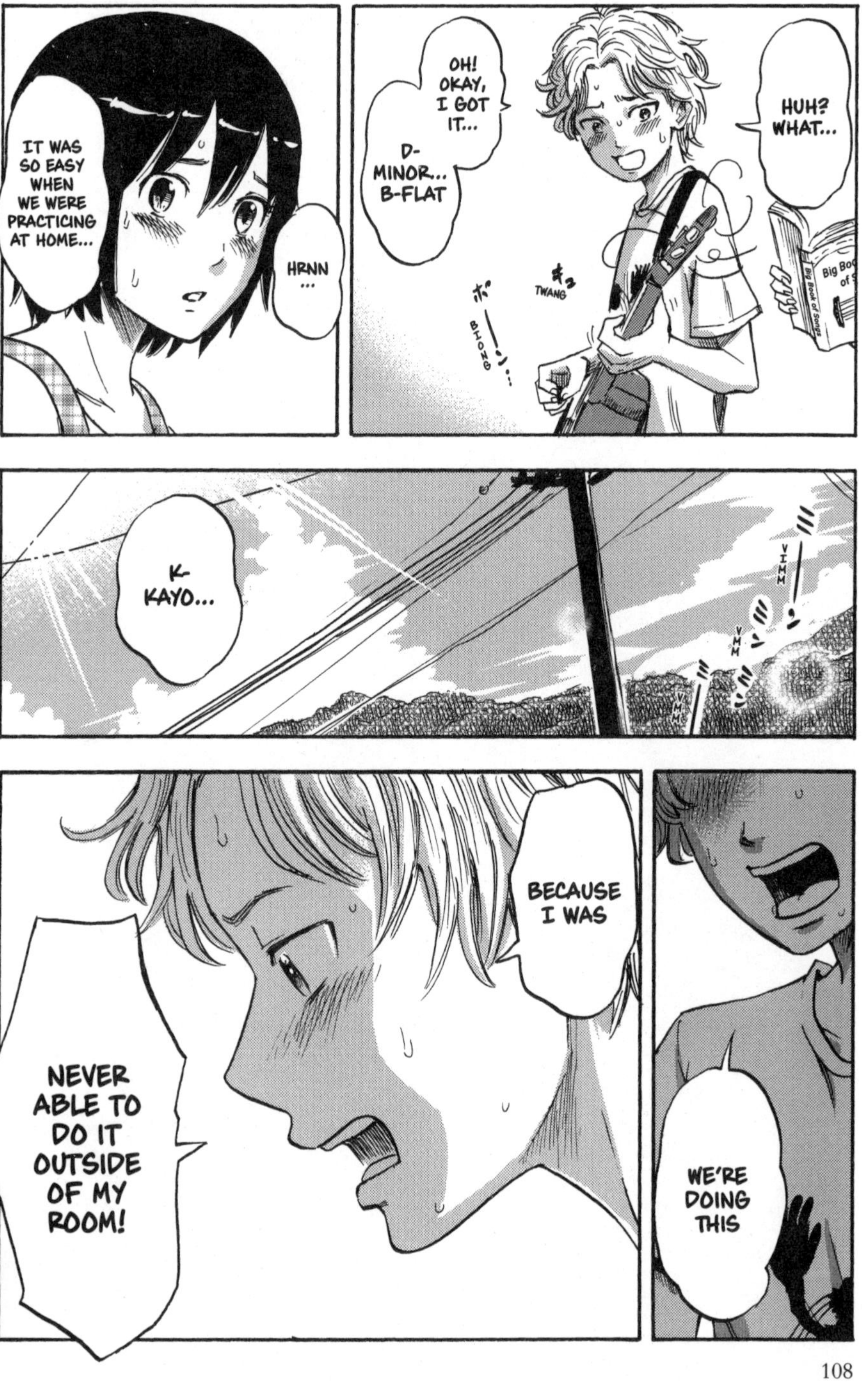
HUH? WHAT...
OH! OKAY, I GOT IT...
D- MINOR... B-FLAT
Big Book of Songs
TWANG
BIONG
HRNN...
IT WAS SO EASY WHEN WE WERE PRACTICING AT HOME...
VIMM
VIMM
VIMM
K- KAYO...
WE'RE DOING THIS
BECAUSE I WAS
NEVER ABLE TO DO IT OUTSIDE OF MY ROOM!

...
HERE WE GO!
JYAN JYAN
JYAN
JYAN JYAN
JYAN JYAN
JYAN
JYAN JYAN
JYAN
Big Book
GO!

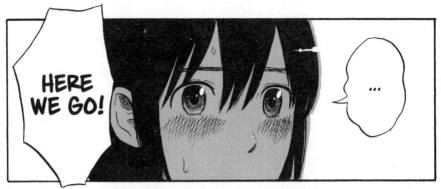

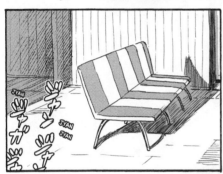

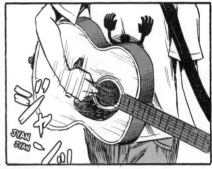

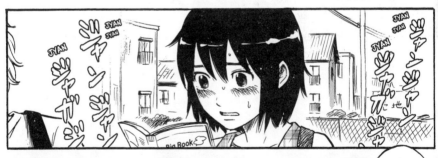

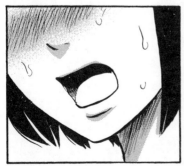

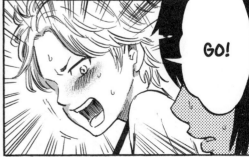

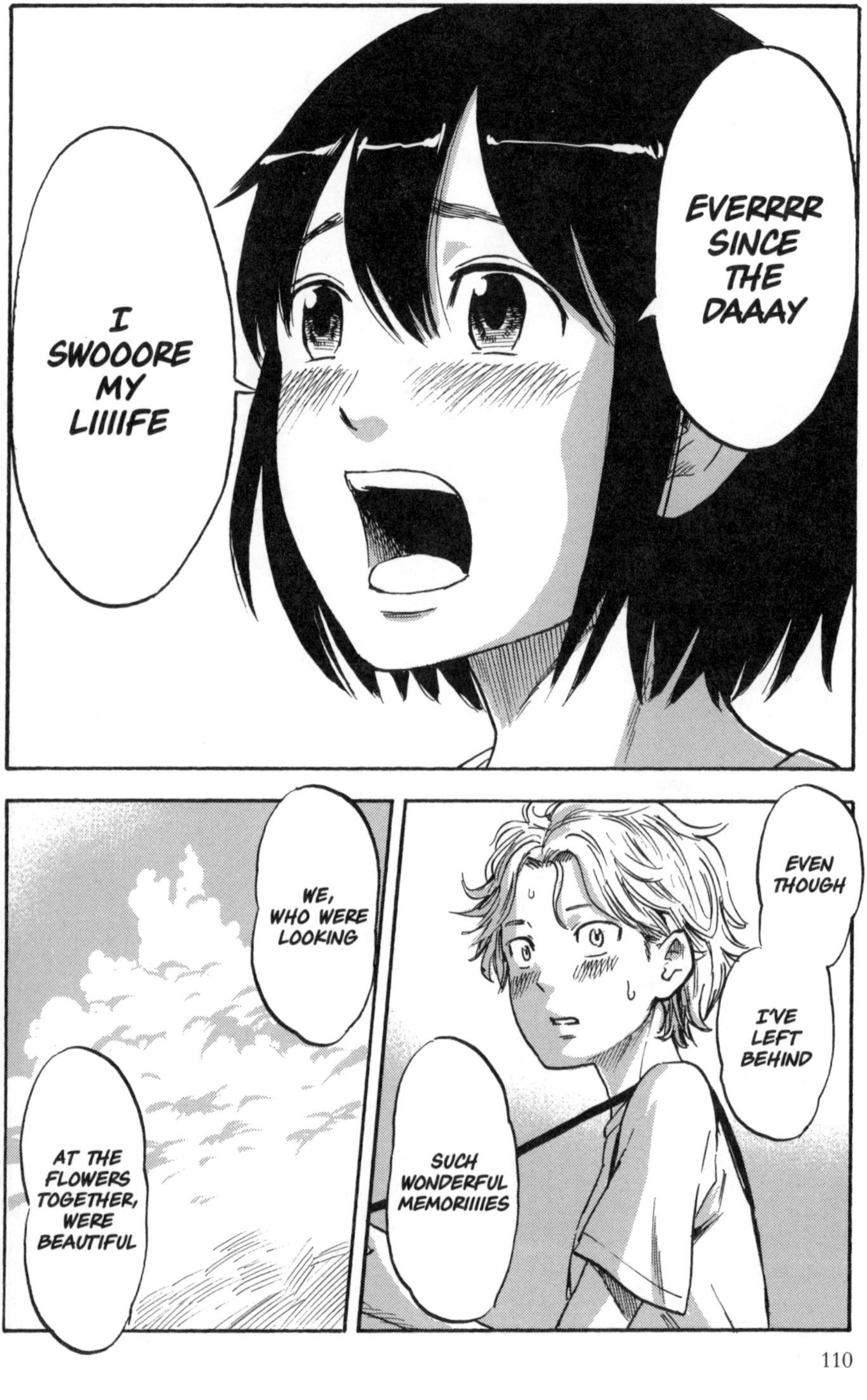
EVERRRR SINCE THE DAAAY
I SWOOORE MY LIIIIFE
EVEN THOUGH
I'VE LEFT BEHIND
SUCH WONDERFUL MEMORIIIIES
WE, WHO WERE LOOKING
AT THE FLOWERS TOGETHER, WERE BEAUTIFUL

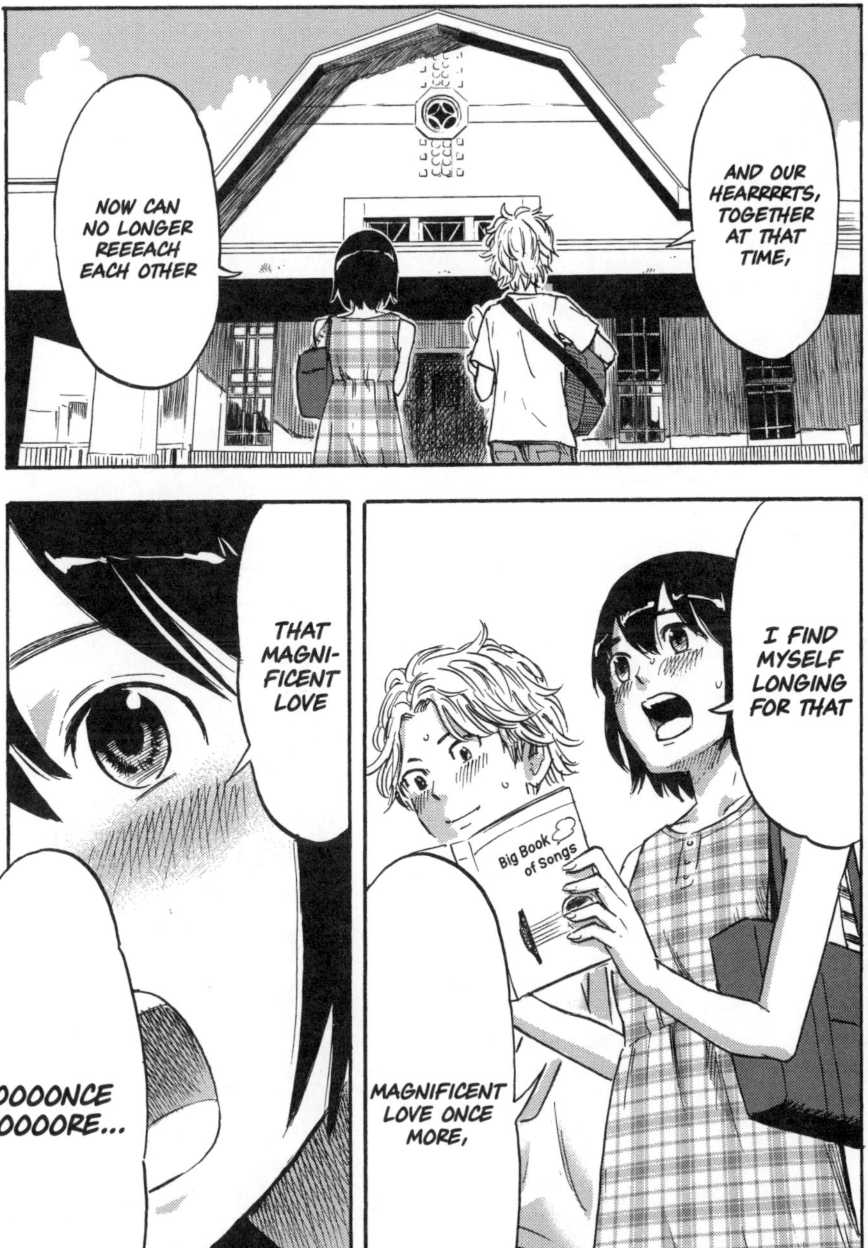
AND OUR HEARRRRTS, TOGETHER AT THAT TIME,
NOW CAN NO LONGER REEEACH EACH OTHER
I FIND MYSELF LONGING FOR THAT
Big Book of Songs
MAGNIFICENT LOVE ONCE MORE,
THAT MAGNI-FICENT LOVE
OOOONCE MOOOORE...

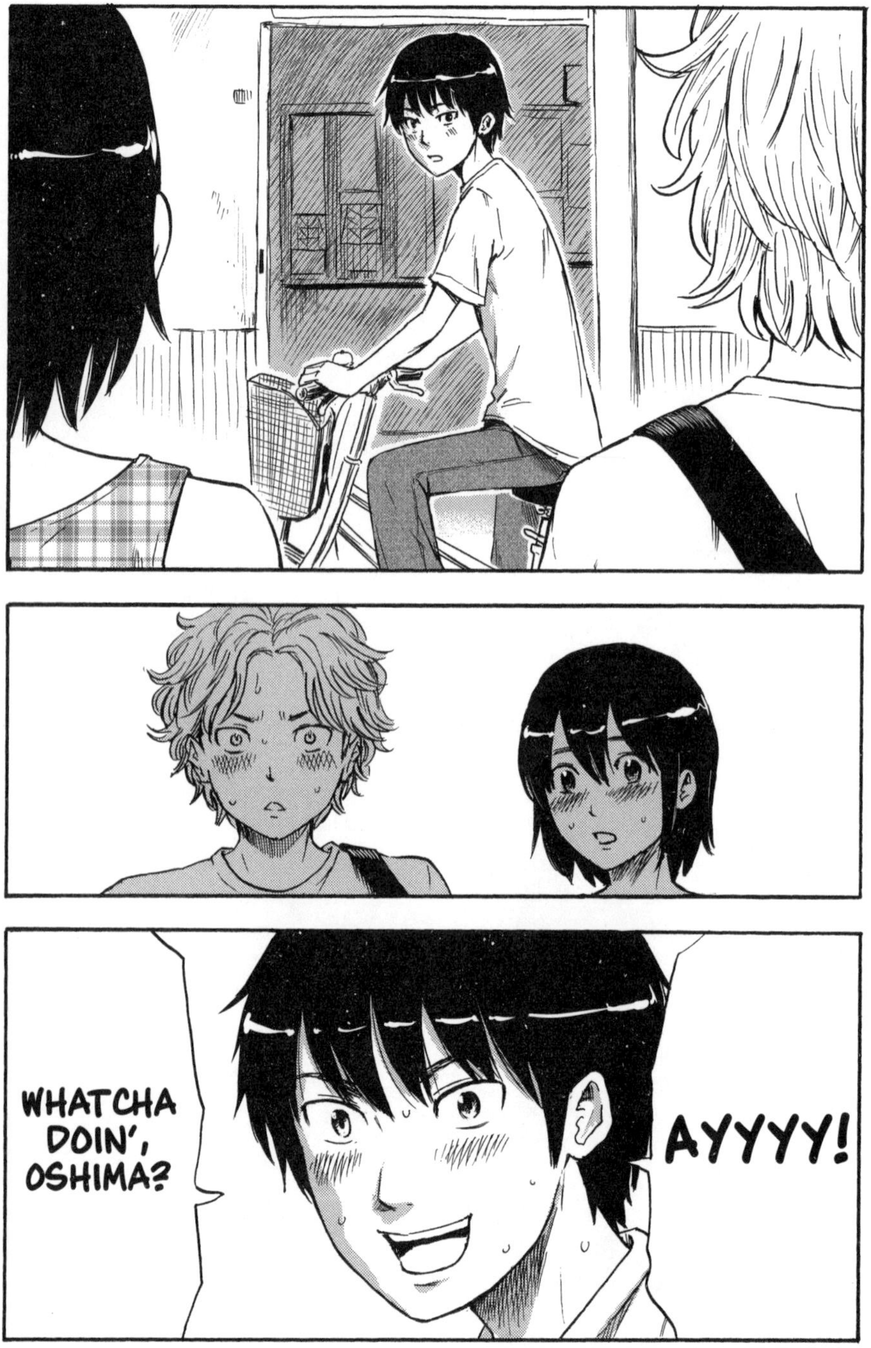
AYYYY!
WHATCHA DOIN', OSHIMA?

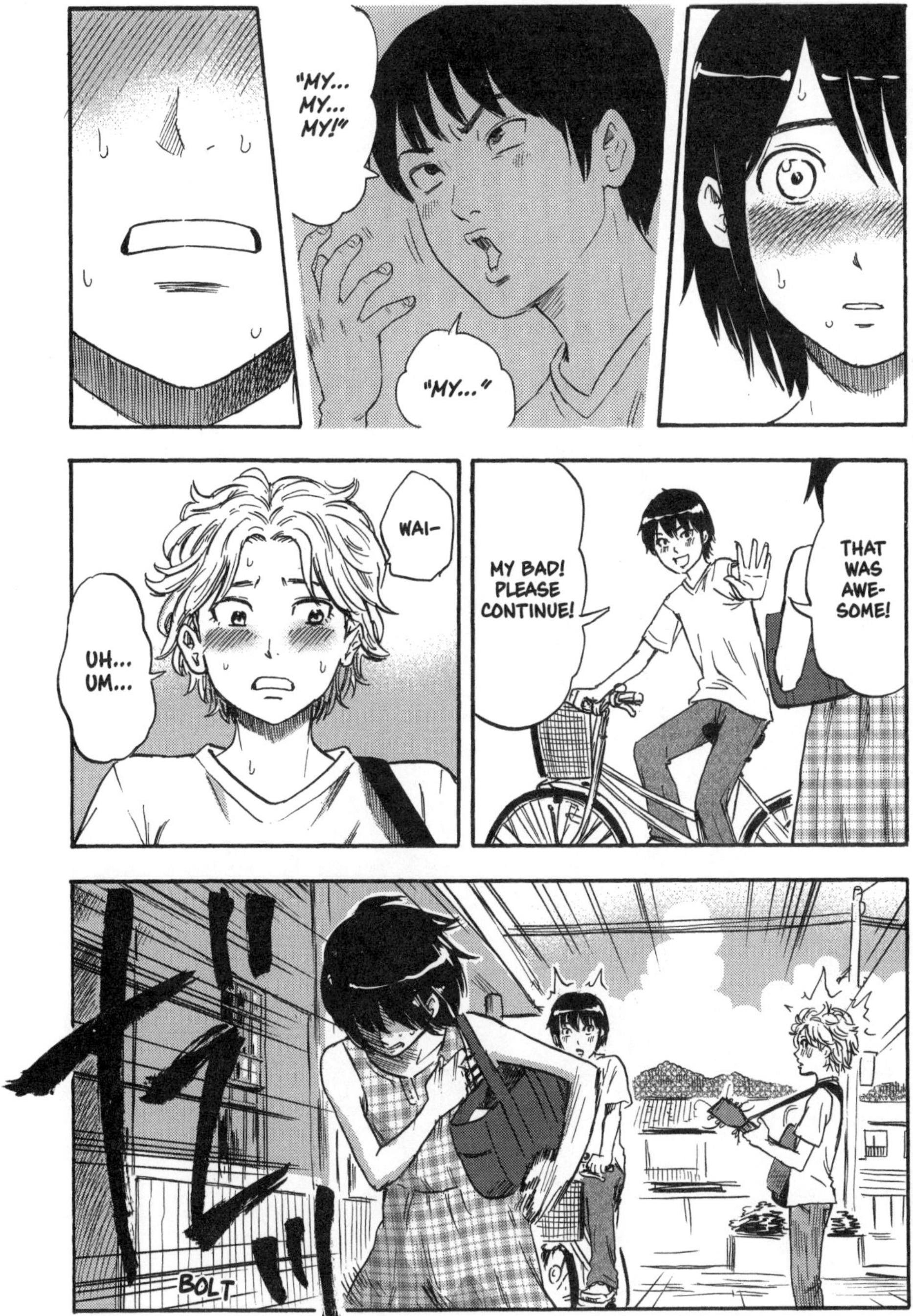
"MY... MY... MY!"
"MY..."
THAT WAS AWE-SOME!
MY BAD! PLEASE CONTINUE!
WAI-
UH... UM...
BOLT

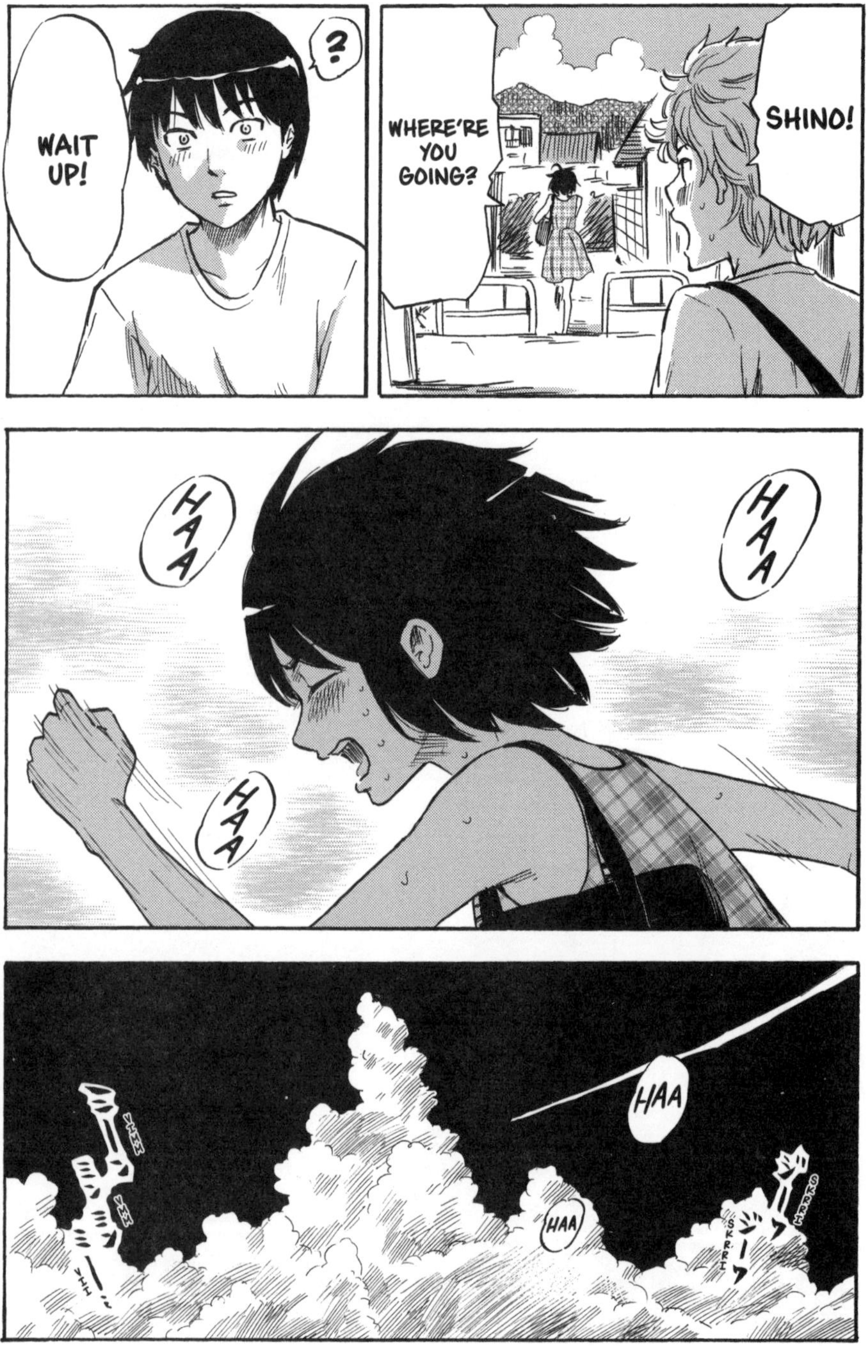
SHINO!
WHERE'RE YOU GOING?
?
WAIT UP!
HAA
HAA
HAA
HAA
SKRRI
SKRRI
HAA
VIMM
VMM
VII

Chapter 7
Just Gotta
Practice Some More

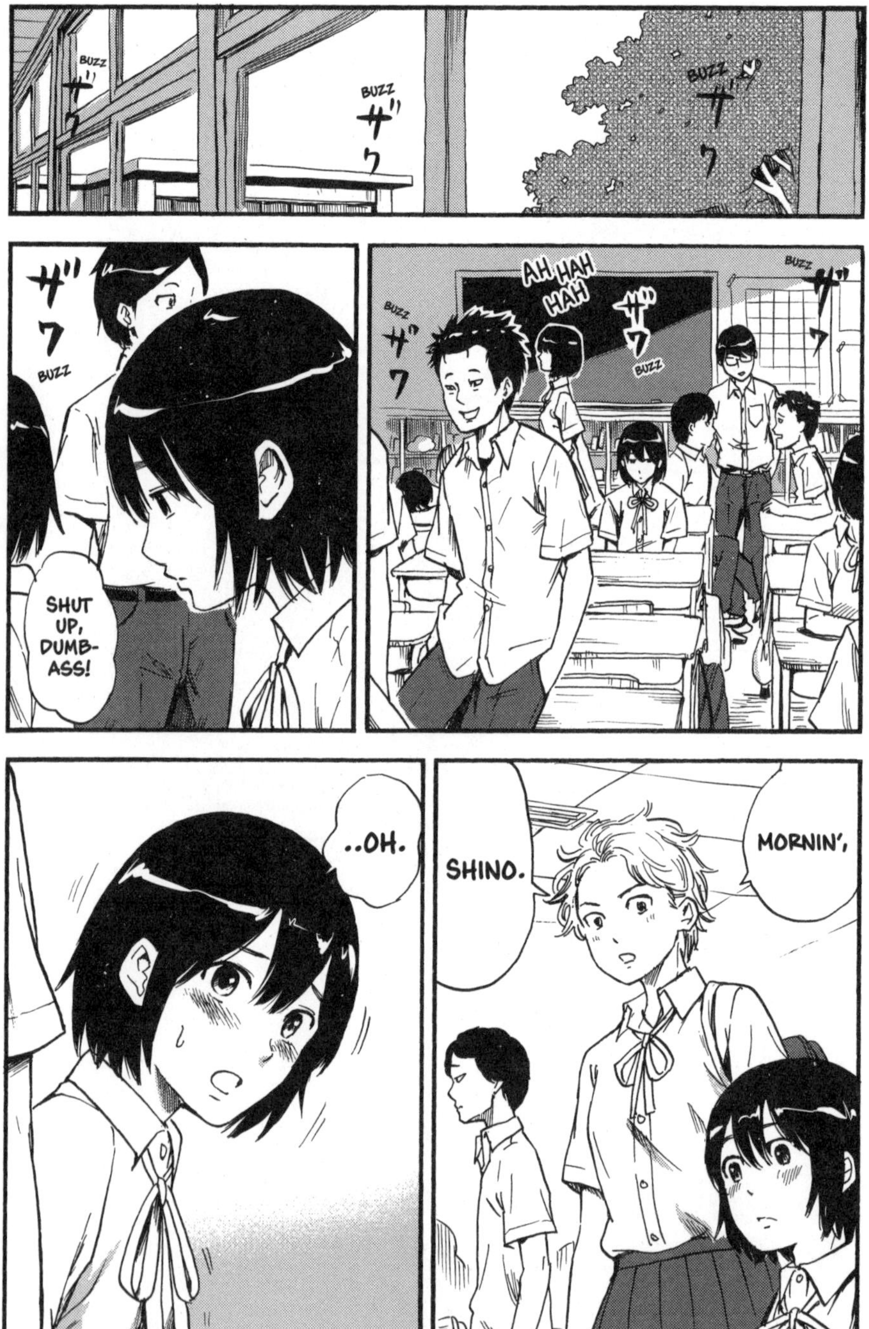
BUZZ
BUZZ
BUZZ
BUZZ
AH HAH HAH
BUZZ
BUZZ
BUZZ
SHUT UP, DUMB-ASS!
MORNIN',
SHINO.
..OH.

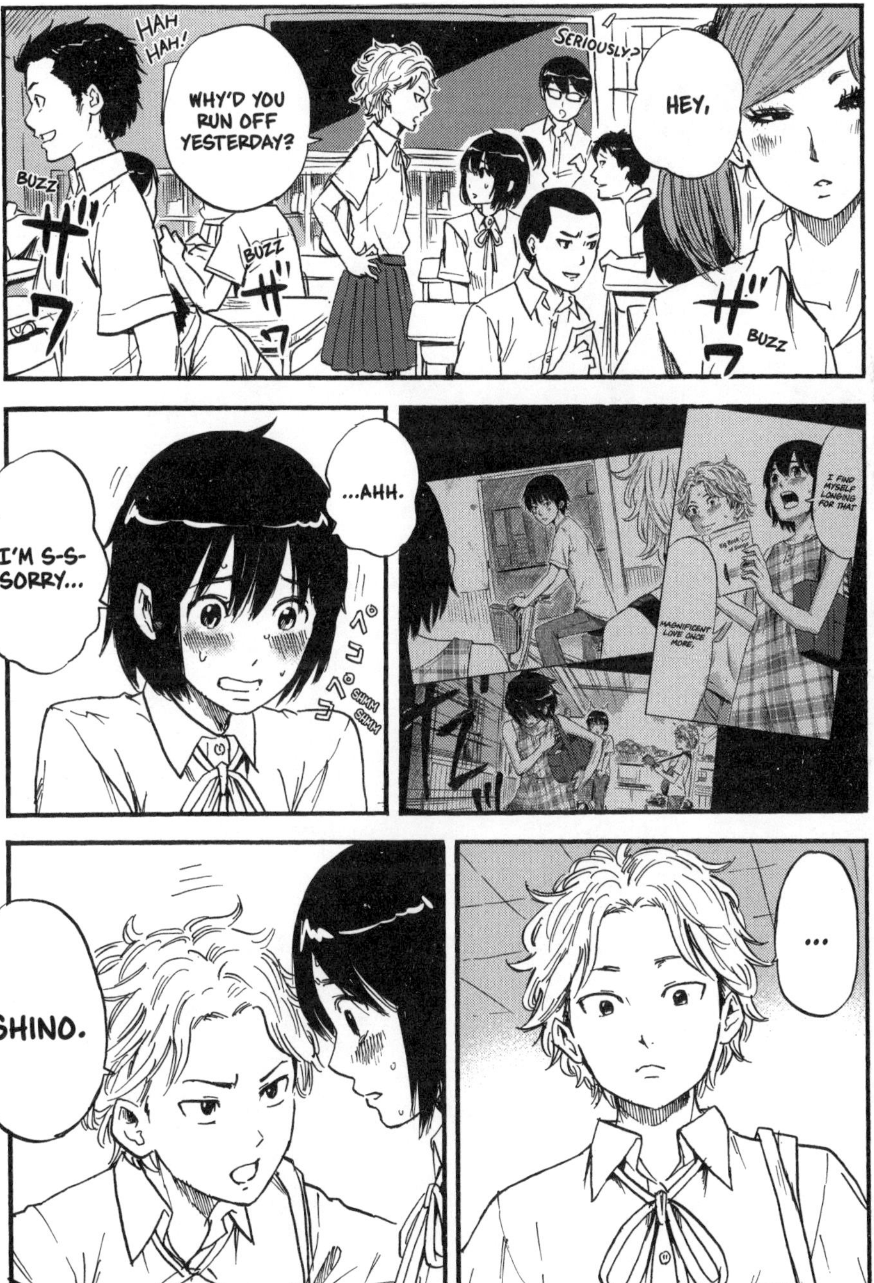
HEY,
SERIOUSLY?
WHY'D YOU RUN OFF YESTERDAY?
HAH HAH!
BUZZ
ザワ
BUZZ
ザワ
BUZZ
ザワ
I FIND MYSELF LONGING FOR THAT
MAGNIFICENT LOVE ONCE MORE.
...AHH.
I'M S-S-SORRY...
ペコペコ
SHMM SHMM
...
SHINO.

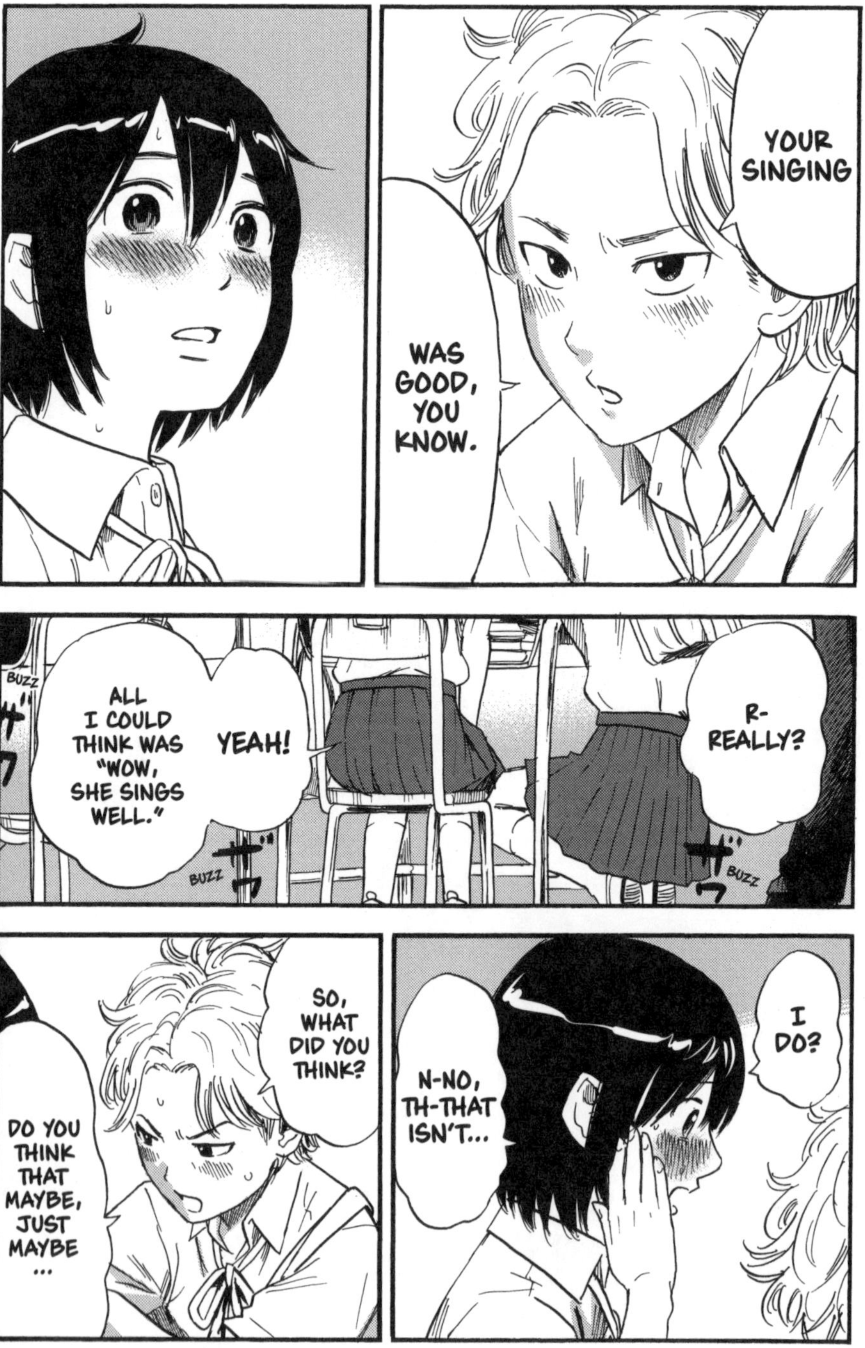
YOUR SINGING
WAS GOOD, YOU KNOW.
R-REALLY?
BUZZ
YEAH!
ALL I COULD THINK WAS "WOW, SHE SINGS WELL."
BUZZ
BUZZ
I DO?
N-NO, TH-THAT ISN'T...
SO, WHAT DID YOU THINK?
DO YOU THINK THAT MAYBE, JUST MAYBE ...

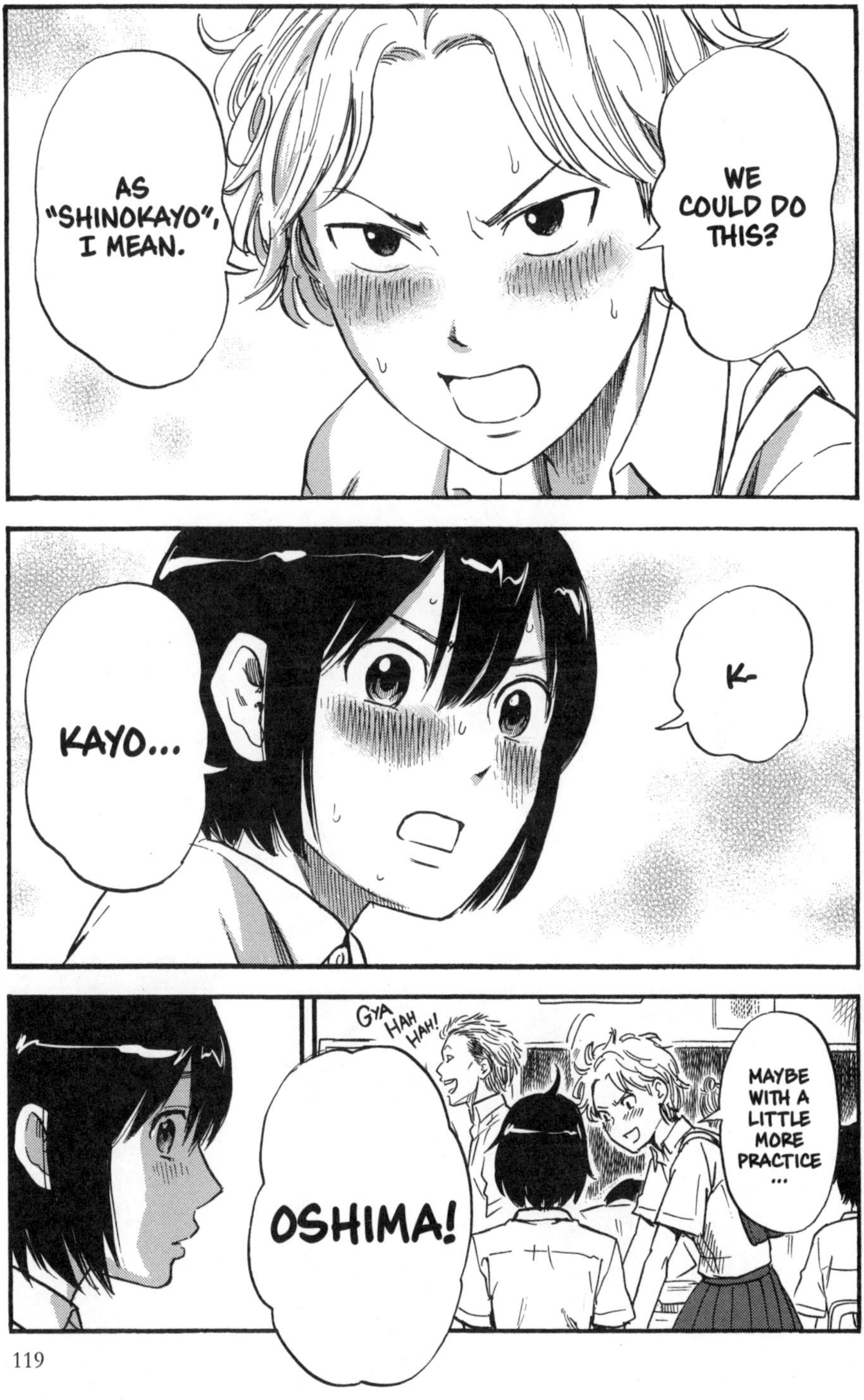
WE COULD DO THIS?
AS "SHINOKAYO", I MEAN.
K-
KAYO...
MAYBE WITH A LITTLE MORE PRACTICE ...
GYA HAH HAH!
OSHIMA!

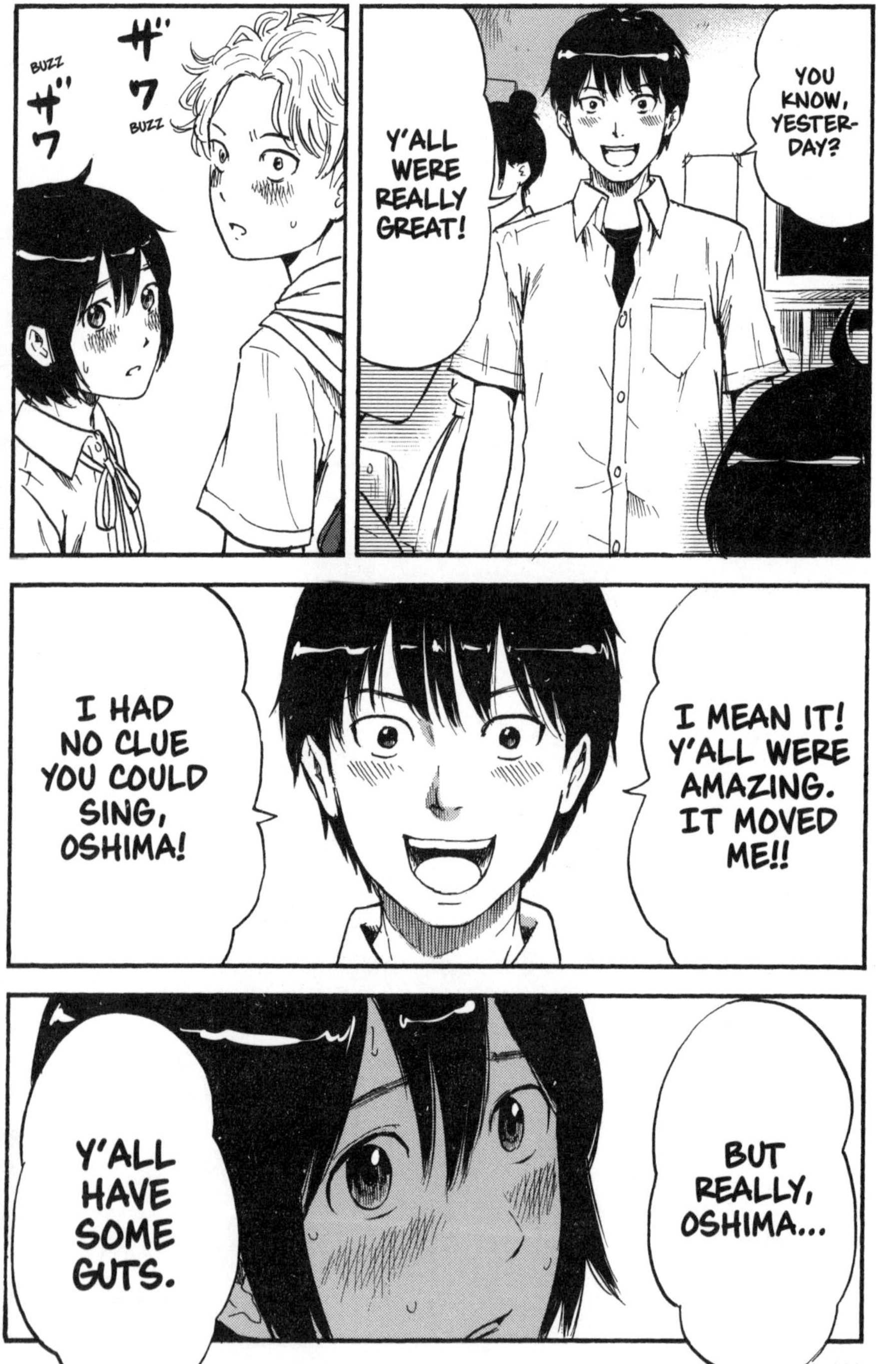
YOU KNOW, YESTER-DAY?
Y'ALL WERE REALLY GREAT!
ザワ
BUZZ
ザワ
BUZZ
I MEAN IT! Y'ALL WERE AMAZING. IT MOVED ME!!
I HAD NO CLUE YOU COULD SING, OSHIMA!
BUT REALLY, OSHIMA...
Y'ALL HAVE SOME GUTS.

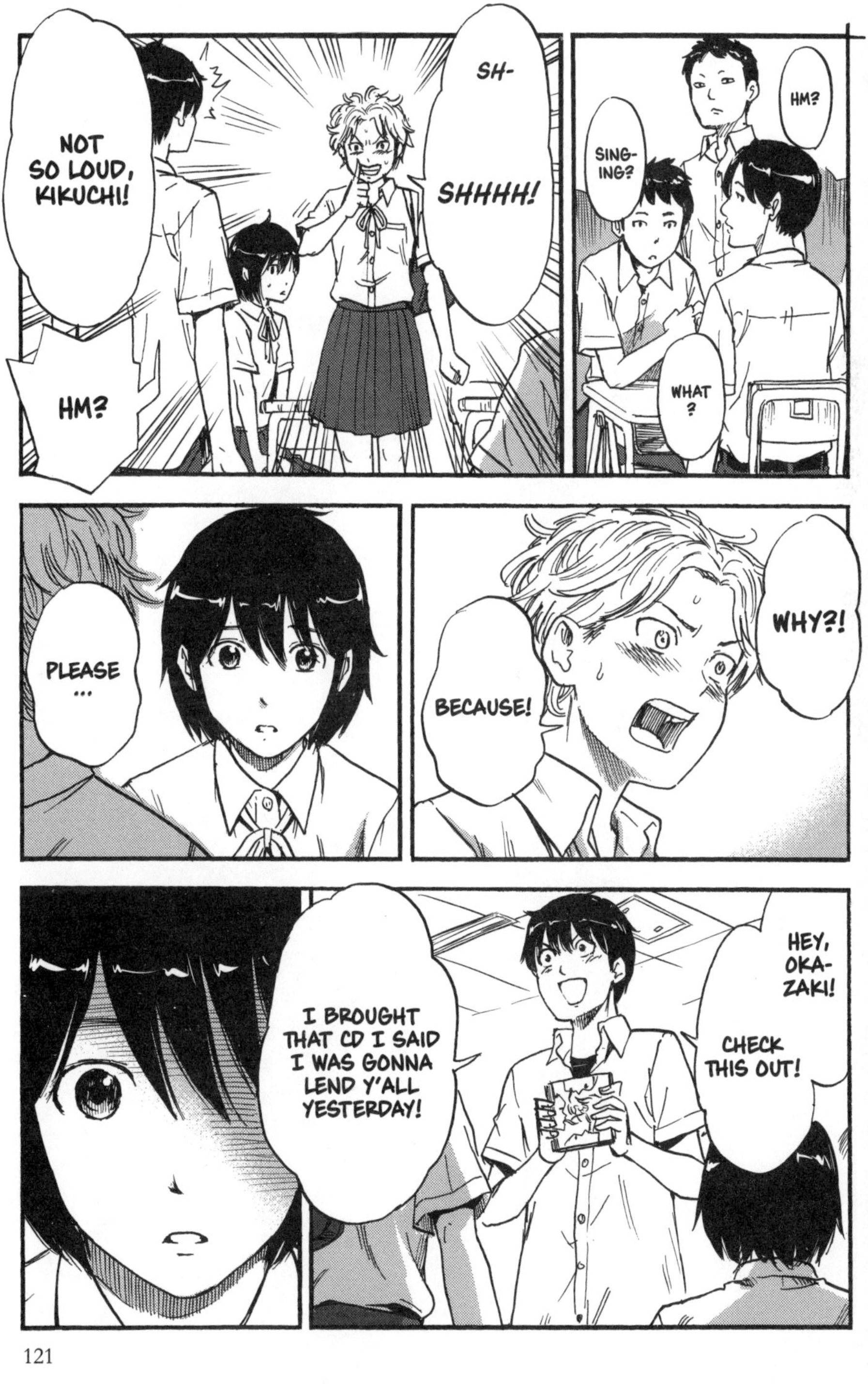
HM?
SING-ING?
WHAT?
SH-
SHHHH!
NOT SO LOUD, KIKUCHI!
HM?
WHY?!
BECAUSE!
PLEASE...
HEY, OKA-ZAKI!
CHECK THIS OUT!
I BROUGHT THAT CD I SAID I WAS GONNA LEND Y'ALL YESTERDAY!

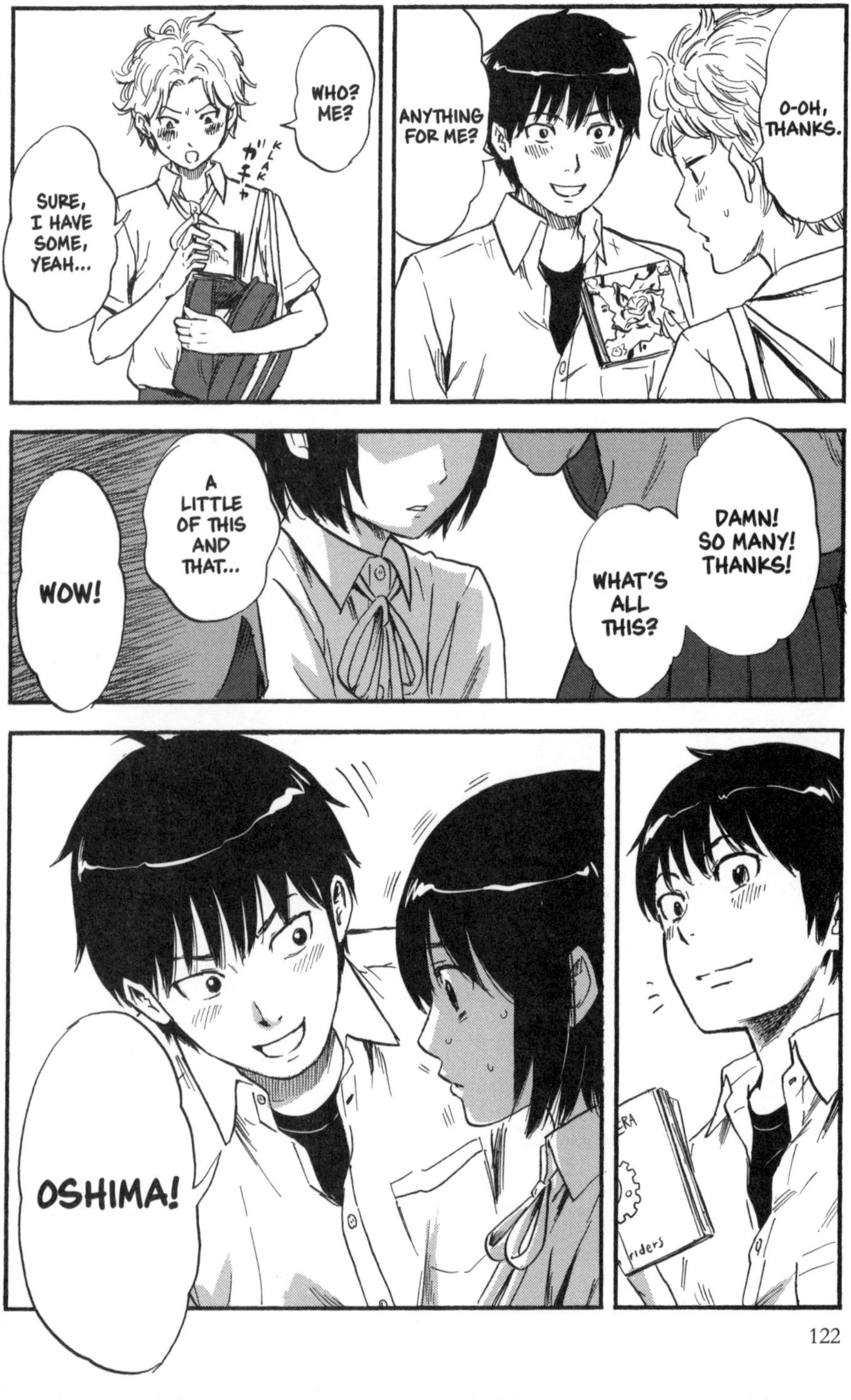
O-OH, THANKS.
ANYTHING FOR ME?
WHO? ME?
ガチャ KLAK
SURE, I HAVE SOME, YEAH...
DAMN! SO MANY! THANKS!
WHAT'S ALL THIS?
A LITTLE OF THIS AND THAT...
WOW!
OSHIMA!

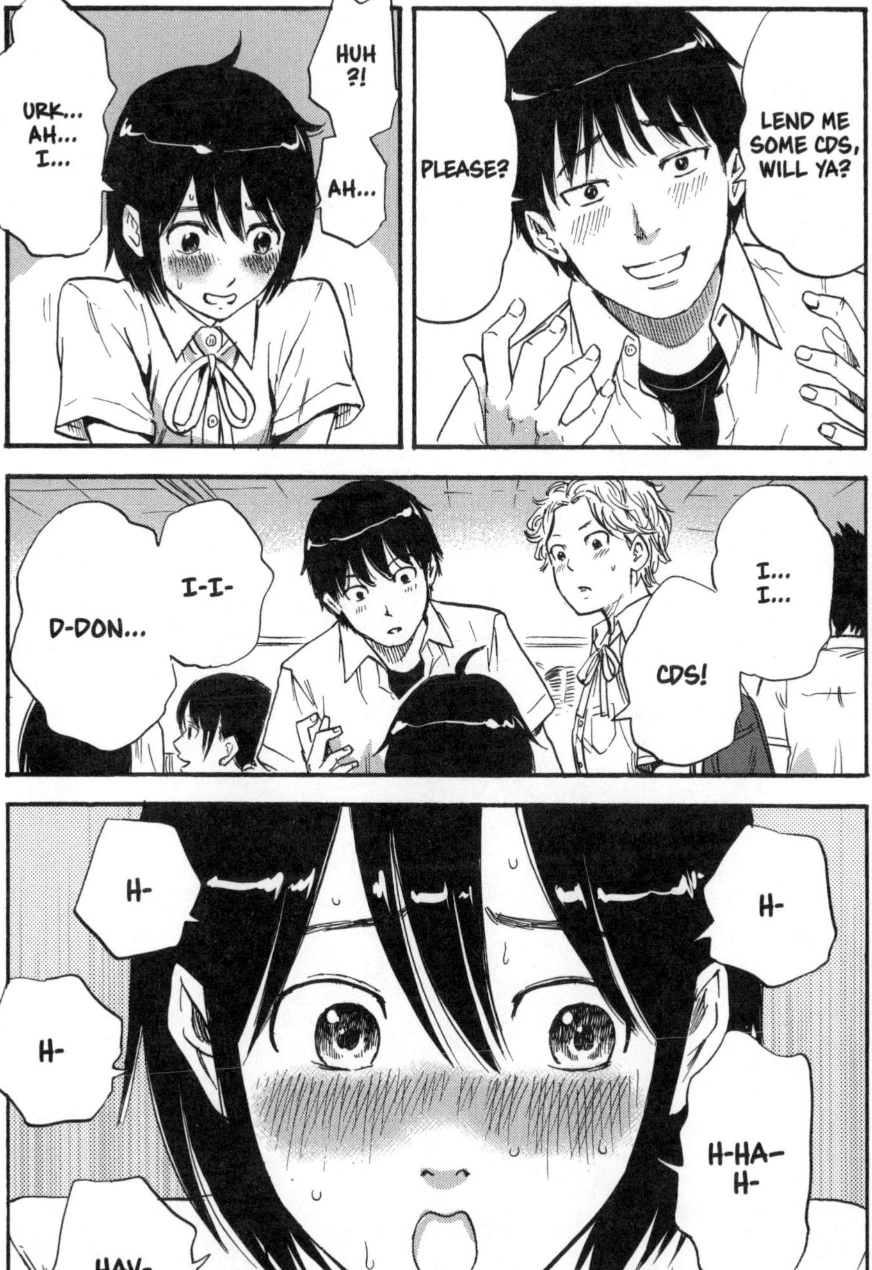
LEND ME SOME CDS, WILL YA?
PLEASE?
HUH ?!
AH...
URK... AH... I...
I... I...
CDS!
I-I-
D-DON...
H-
H-
H-
H-HA-H-
HAV-

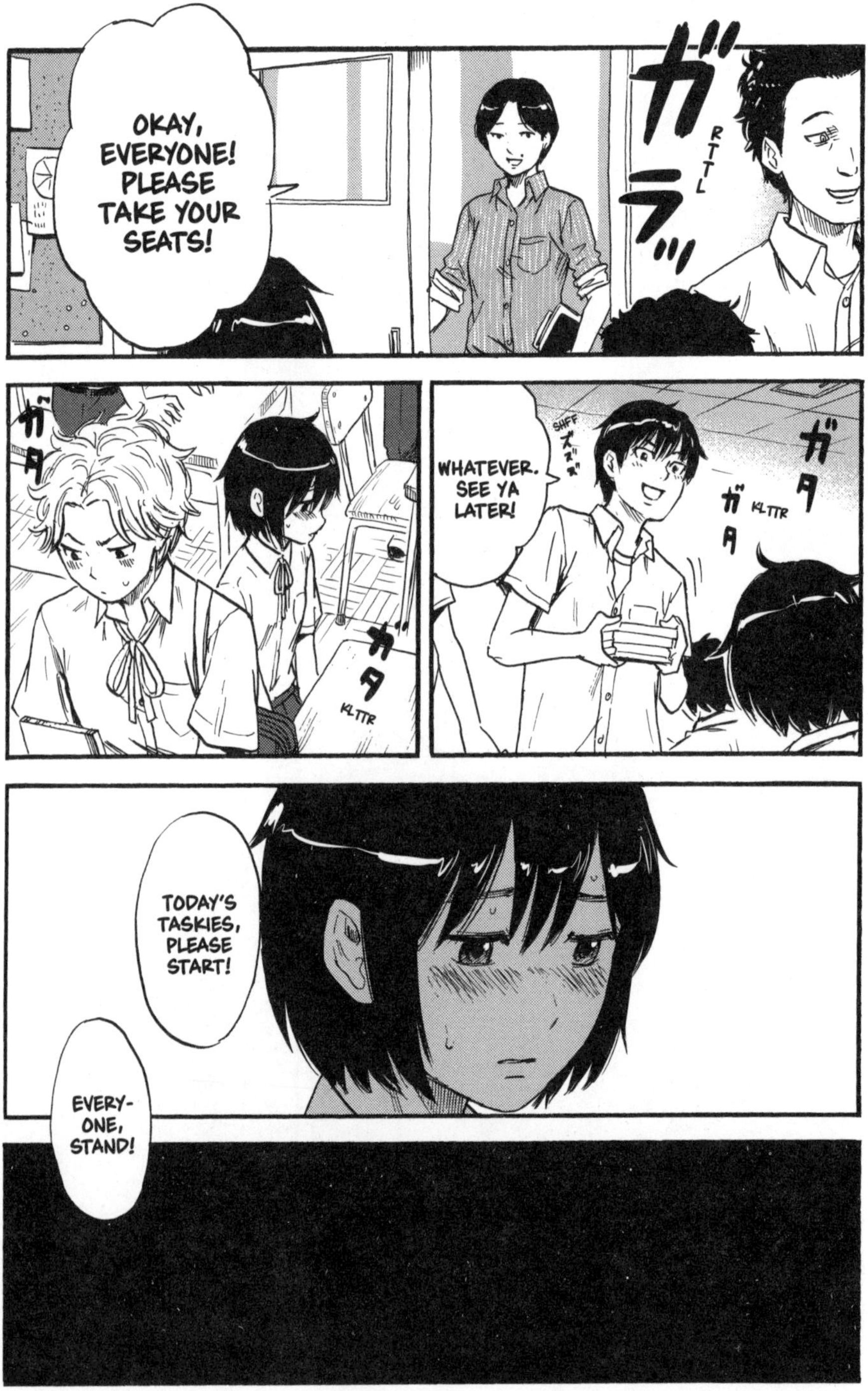
ガラッ
RTTL
OKAY, EVERYONE! PLEASE TAKE YOUR SEATS!
ガタ
ガタ
KLTTR
SHFF
ズズ
WHATEVER. SEE YA LATER!
ガタ
ガタ
KLTTR
TODAY'S TASKIES, PLEASE START!
EVERY-ONE, STAND!

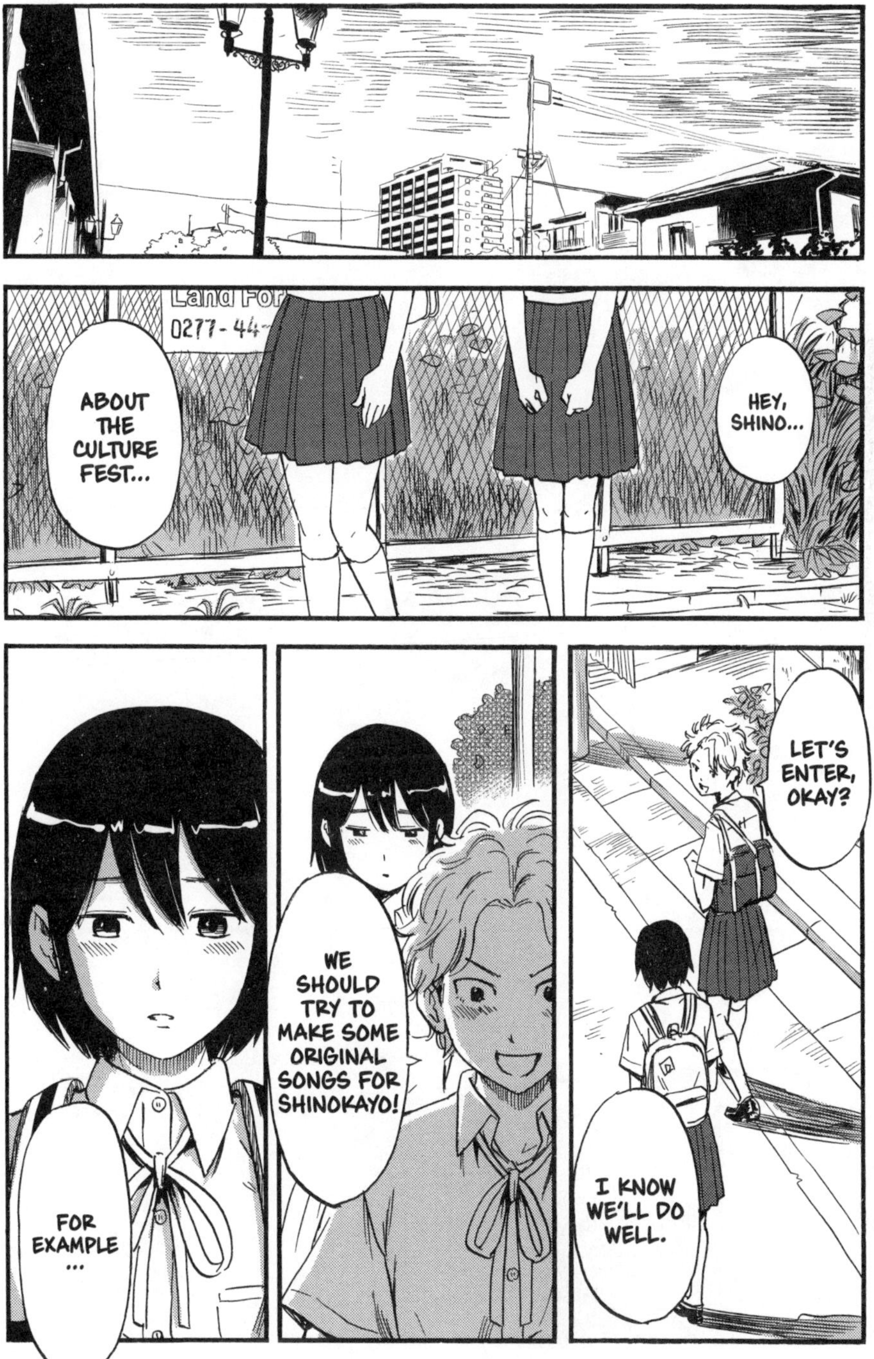
Land For
0277-44-
HEY, SHINO...
ABOUT THE CULTURE FEST...
LET'S ENTER, OKAY?
I KNOW WE'LL DO WELL.
WE SHOULD TRY TO MAKE SOME ORIGINAL SONGS FOR SHINOKAYO!
FOR EXAMPLE ...

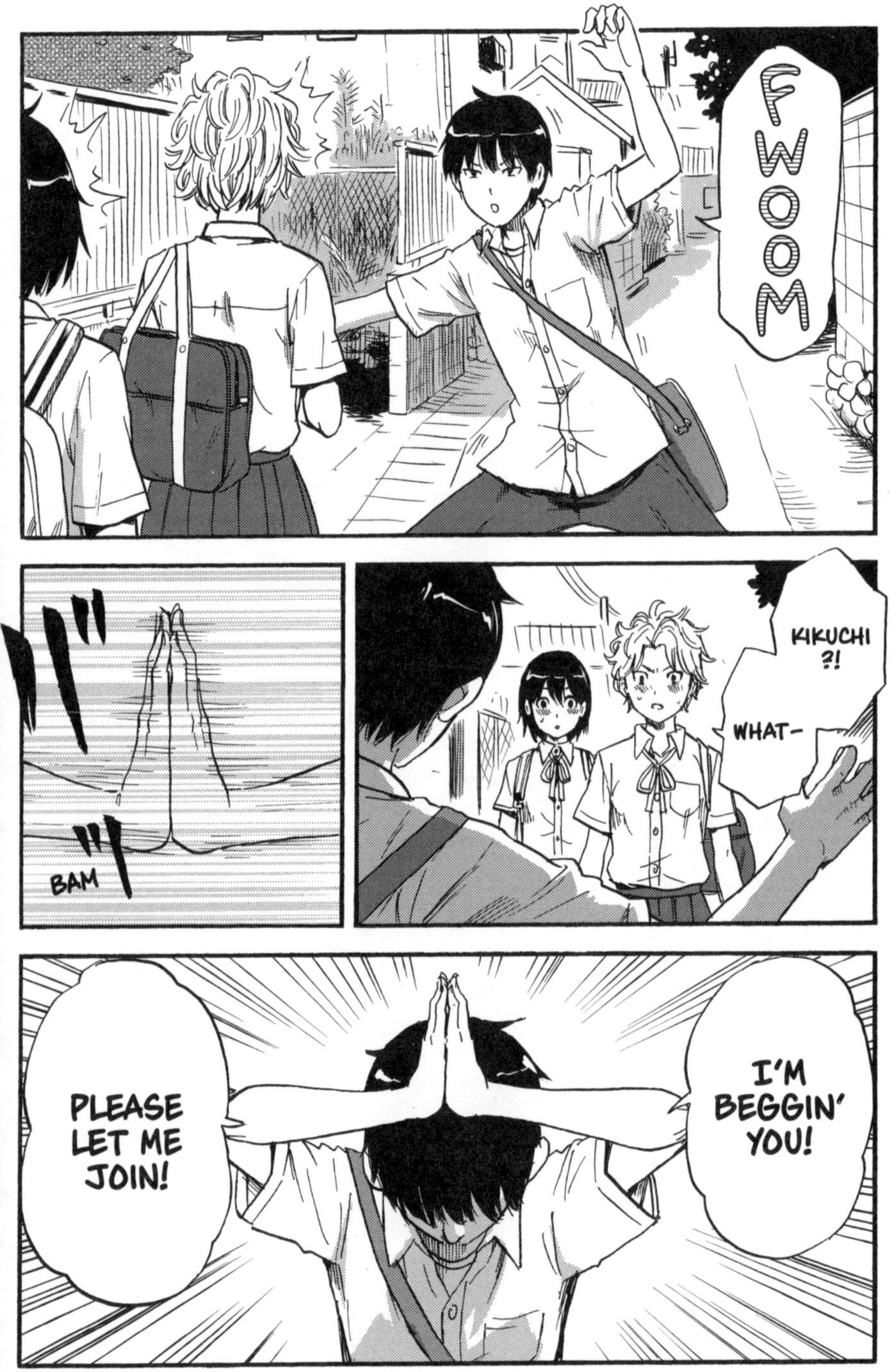
FWOOM
KIKUCHI ?!
WHAT-
BAM
I'M BEGGIN' YOU!
PLEASE LET ME JOIN!

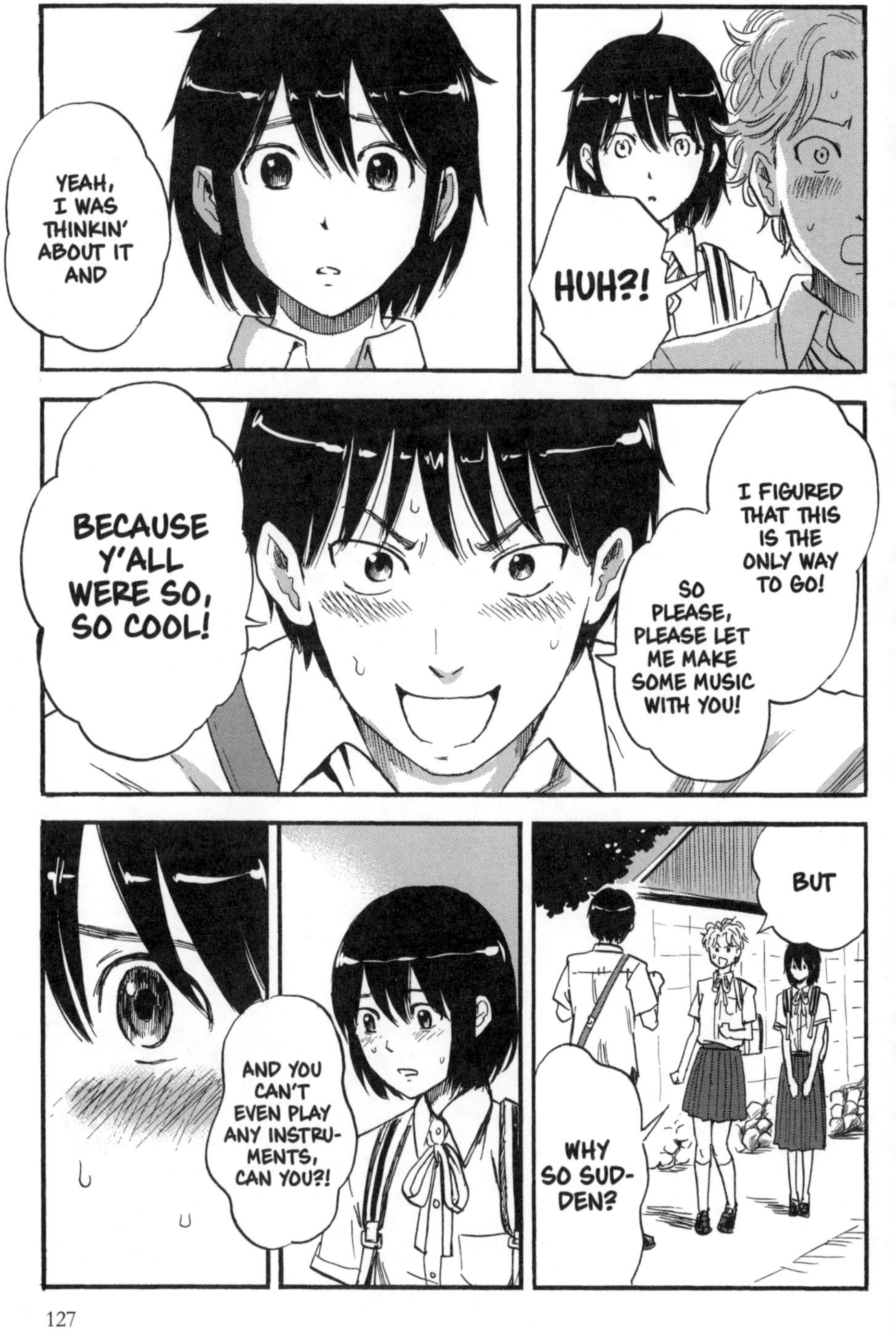
HUH?!
YEAH, I WAS THINKIN' ABOUT IT AND
I FIGURED THAT THIS IS THE ONLY WAY TO GO!
SO PLEASE, PLEASE LET ME MAKE SOME MUSIC WITH YOU!
BECAUSE Y'ALL WERE SO, SO COOL!
BUT
WHY SO SUD-DEN?
AND YOU CAN'T EVEN PLAY ANY INSTRU-MENTS, CAN YOU?!

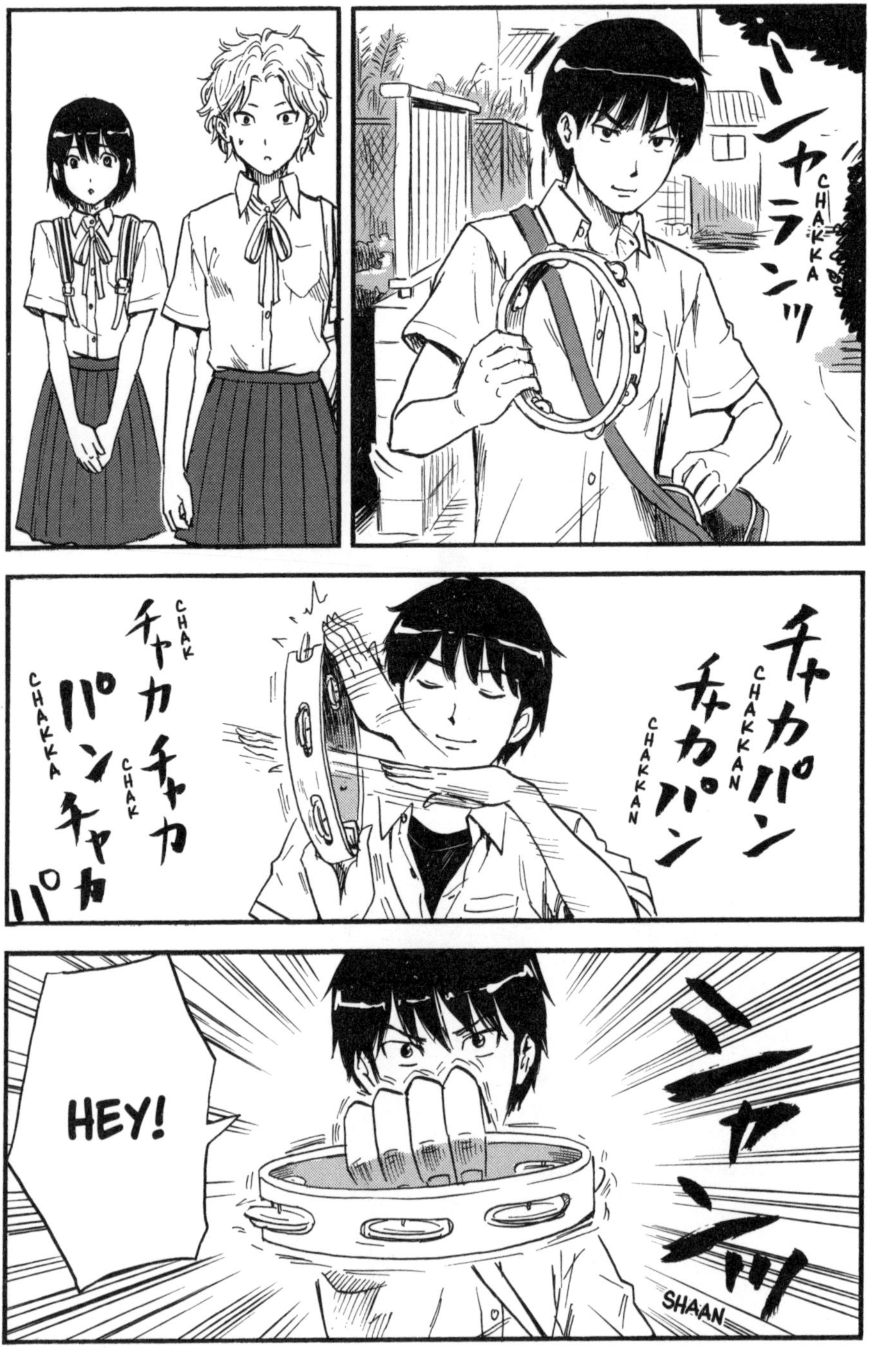
シャランッ
CHAKKA
チャカパン
CHAKKAN
チャカパン
CHAKKAN
チャカ
CHAK
チャカ
CHAK
パン
CHAKKA
チャカ
パ
シャーンッ
SHAAN
HEY!

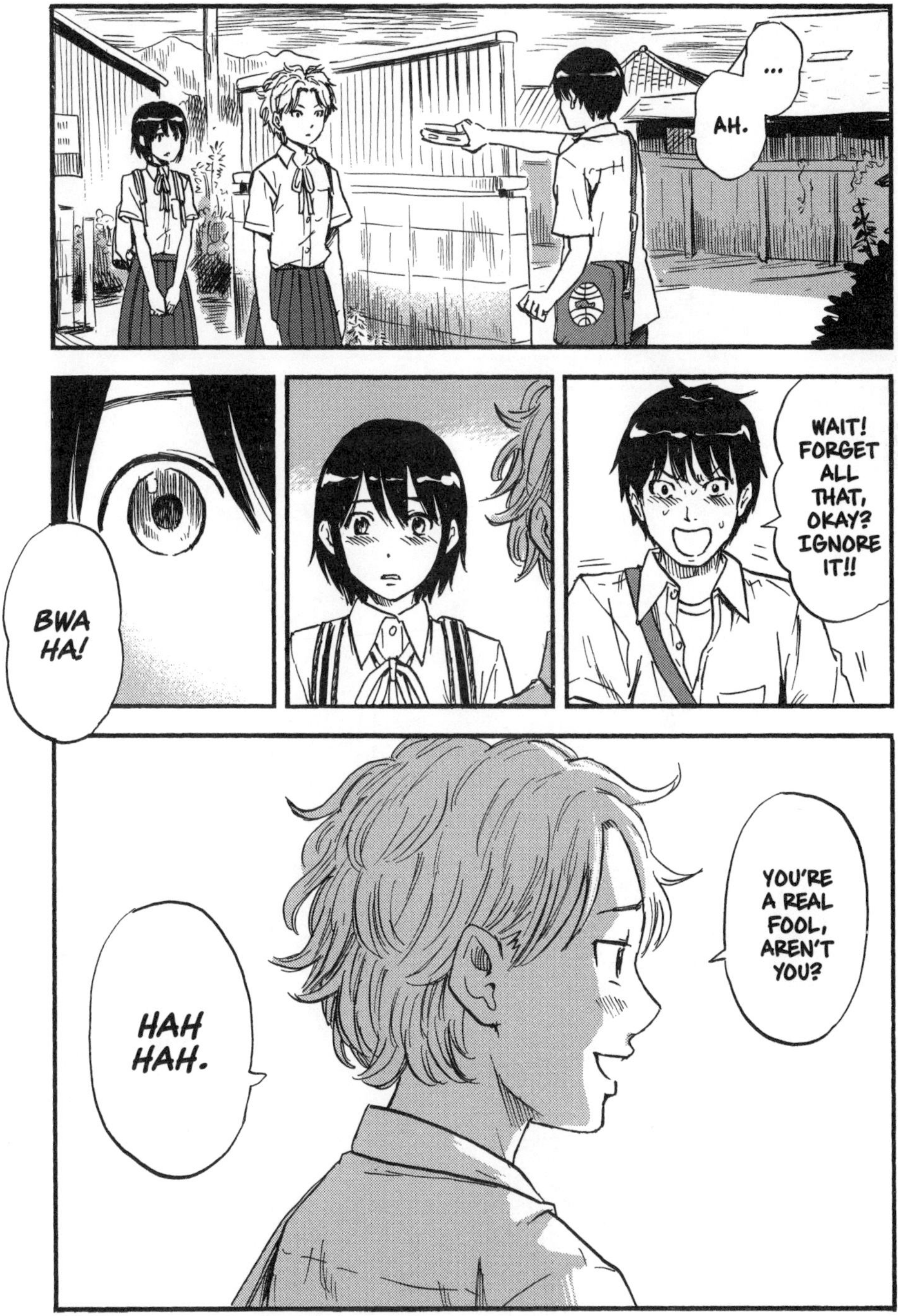
...
AH.
WAIT! FORGET ALL THAT, OKAY? IGNORE IT!!
BWA HA!
YOU'RE A REAL FOOL, AREN'T YOU?
HAH HAH.

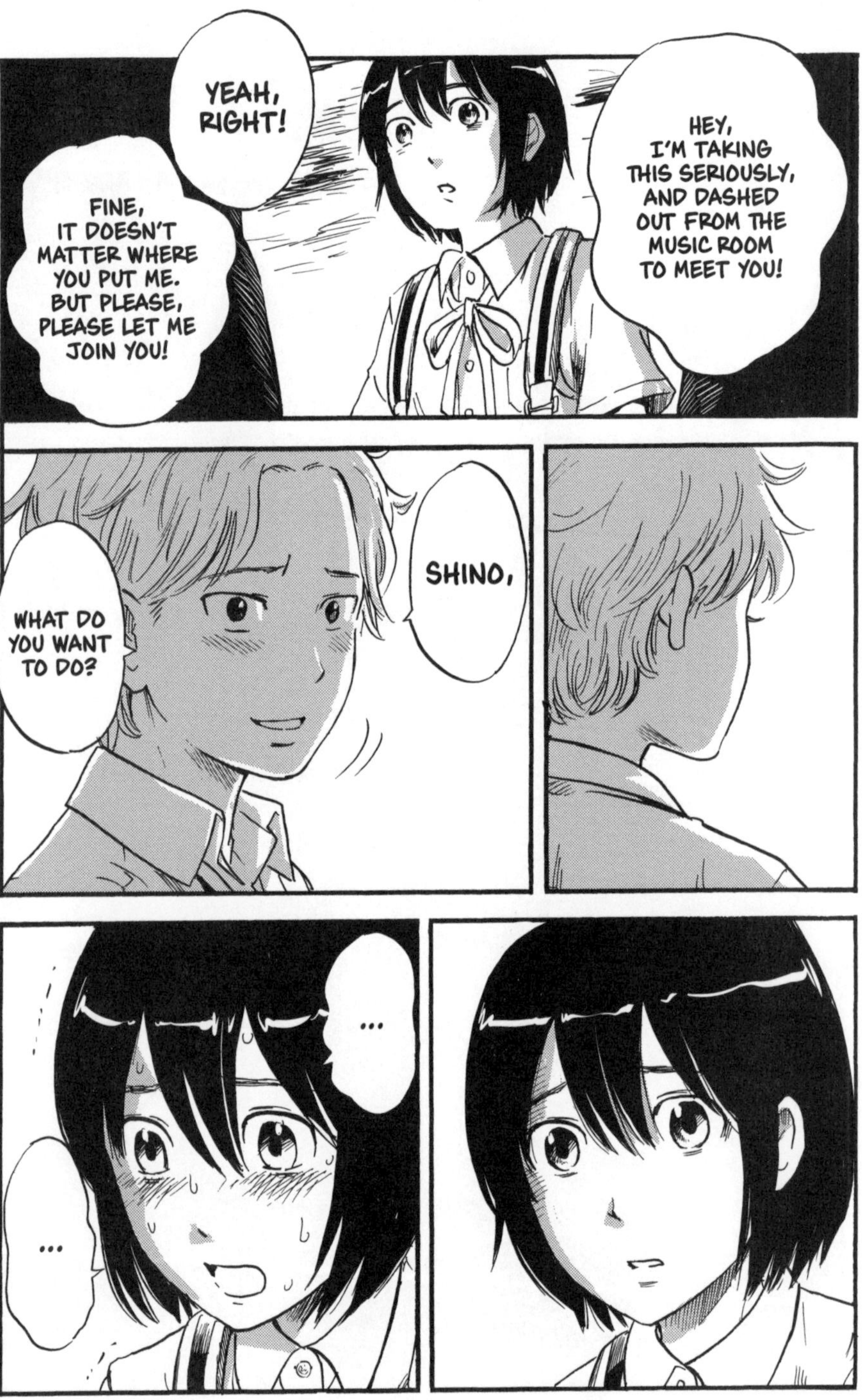
HEY, I'M TAKING THIS SERIOUSLY, AND DASHED OUT FROM THE MUSIC ROOM TO MEET YOU!
YEAH, RIGHT!
FINE, IT DOESN'T MATTER WHERE YOU PUT ME. BUT PLEASE, PLEASE LET ME JOIN YOU!
SHINO,
WHAT DO YOU WANT TO DO?
...
...

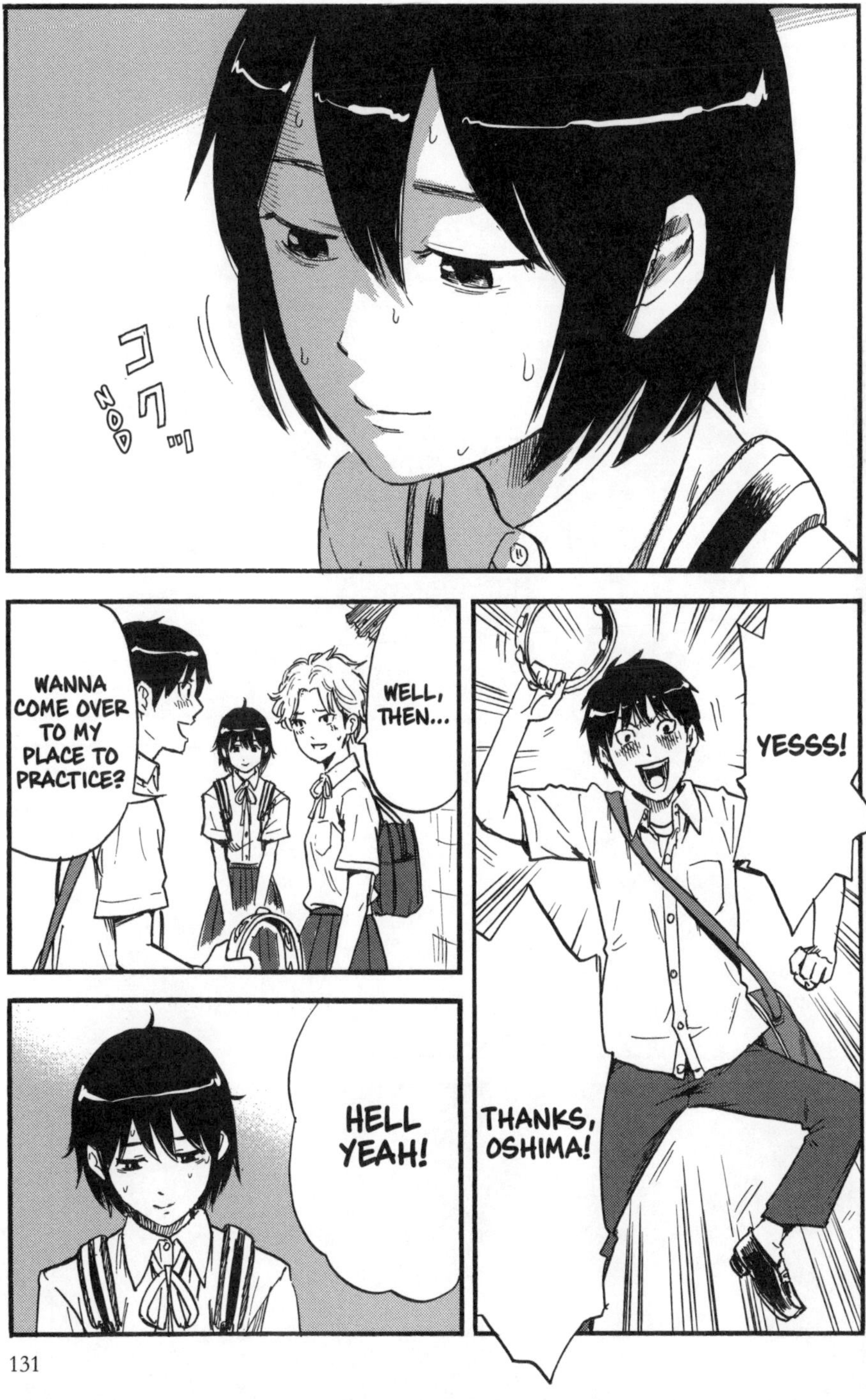
コクッ
NOD
YESSS!
THANKS, OSHIMA!
WELL, THEN...
WANNA COME OVER TO MY PLACE TO PRACTICE?
HELL YEAH!

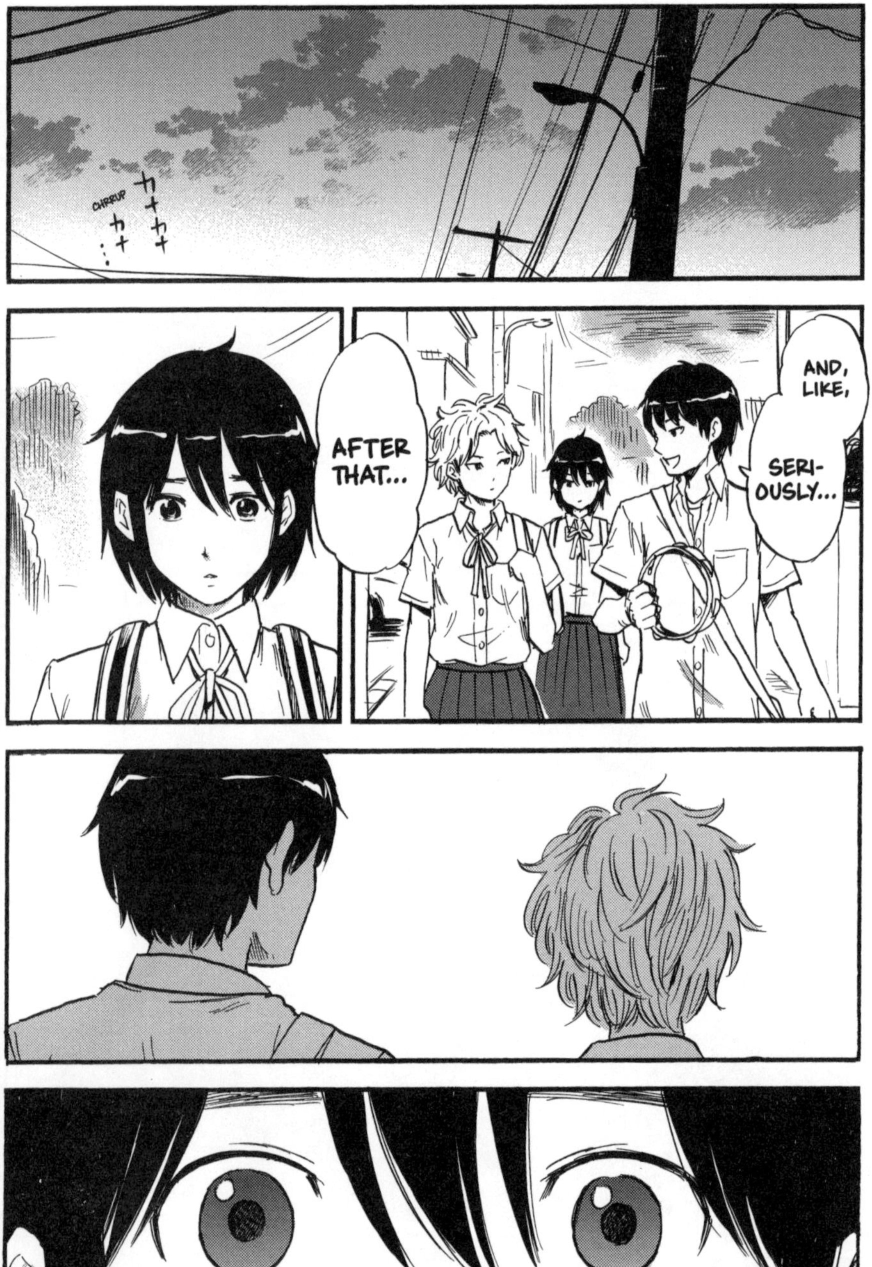
カナカナ
カナ…
CHIRRUP
AND, LIKE, SERIOUSLY...
AFTER THAT...

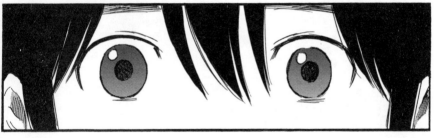

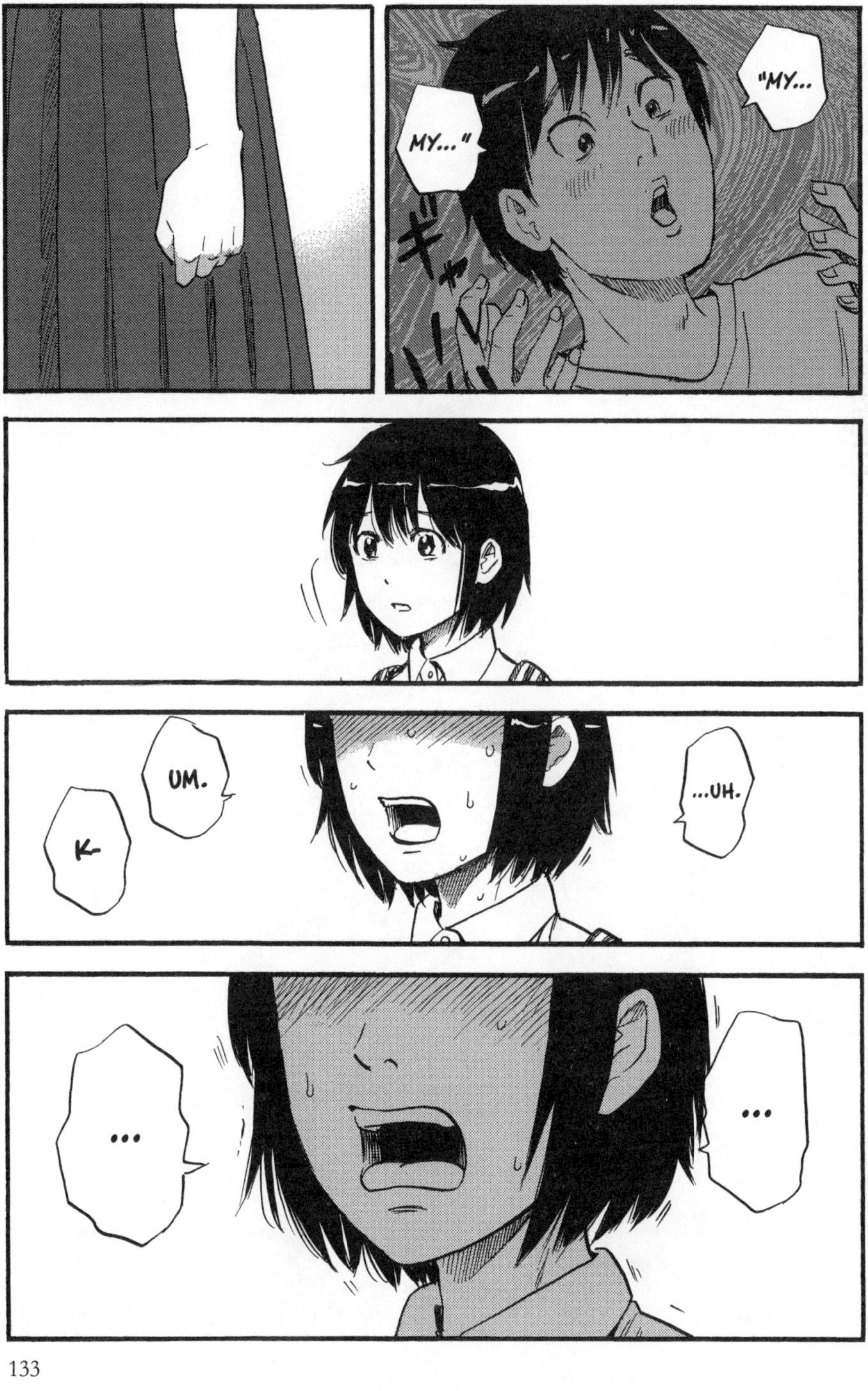
"MY...
MY..."
...UH.
UM.
K-
...
...

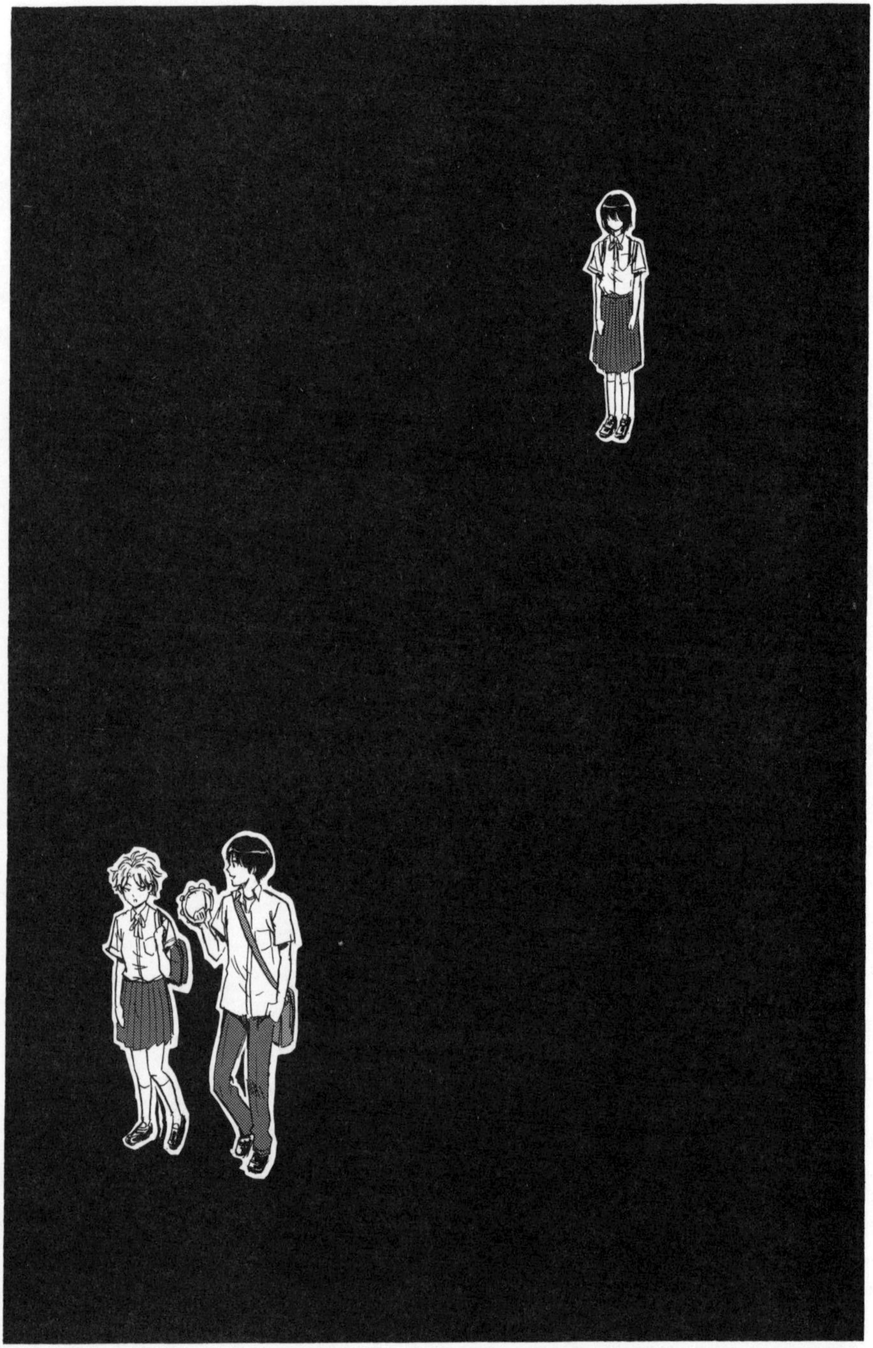

Chapter 8
If You Don't Say Anything,
How Will I Know?

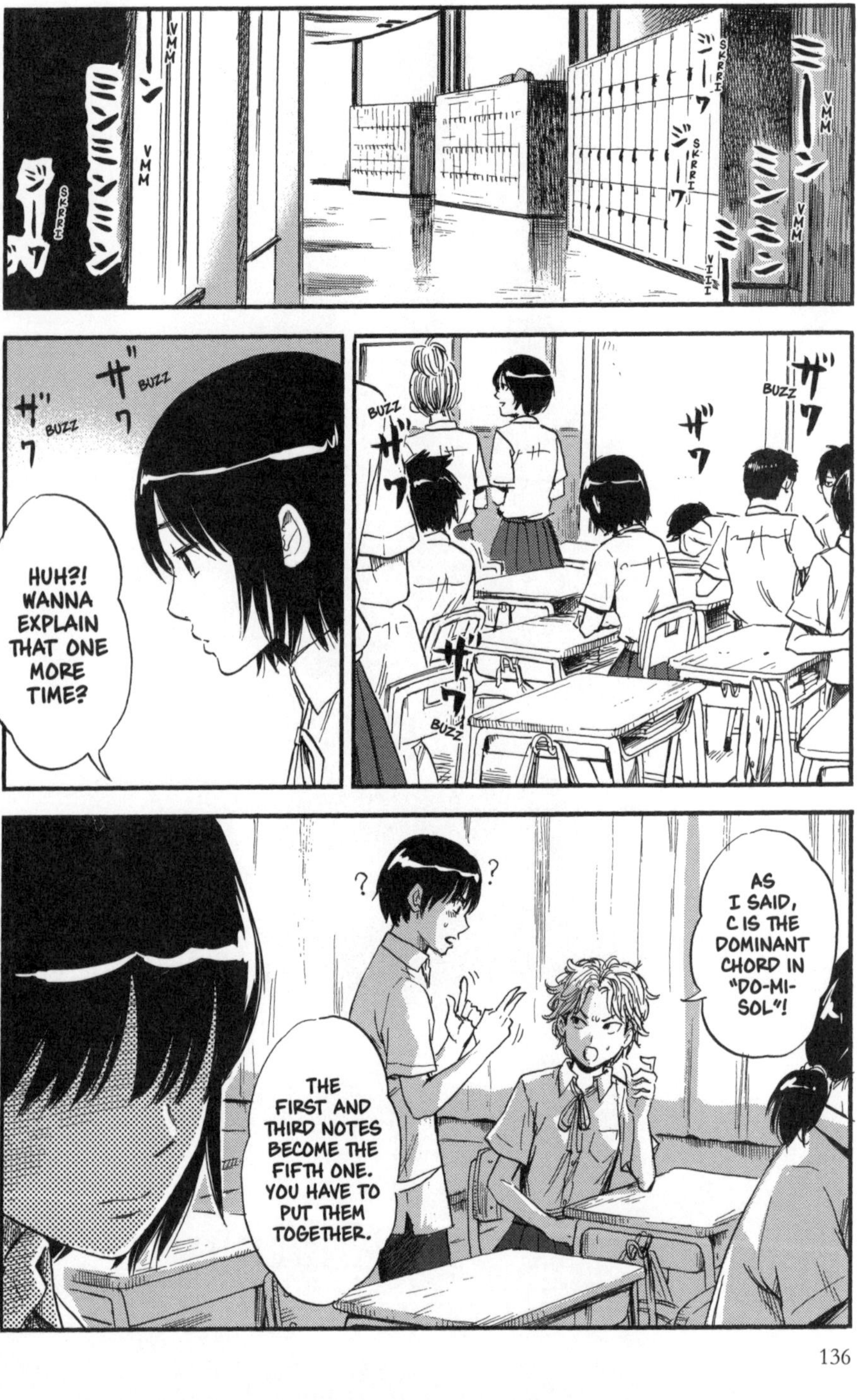
ミーンミンミンミ
VMM
VMM
VIII
ジーワ
SKRRI
ジーワ
SKRRI
ーン
VMM
VMM
ミンミンミン
ジーワ
SKRRI
ザワ
BUZZ
ザワ
ザワ
BUZZ
ザワ
BUZZ
ザワ
BUZZ
ザワ
BUZZ
HUH?! WANNA EXPLAIN THAT ONE MORE TIME?
AS I SAID, C IS THE DOMINANT CHORD IN "DO-MI-SOL"!
THE FIRST AND THIRD NOTES BECOME THE FIFTH ONE. YOU HAVE TO PUT THEM TOGETHER.

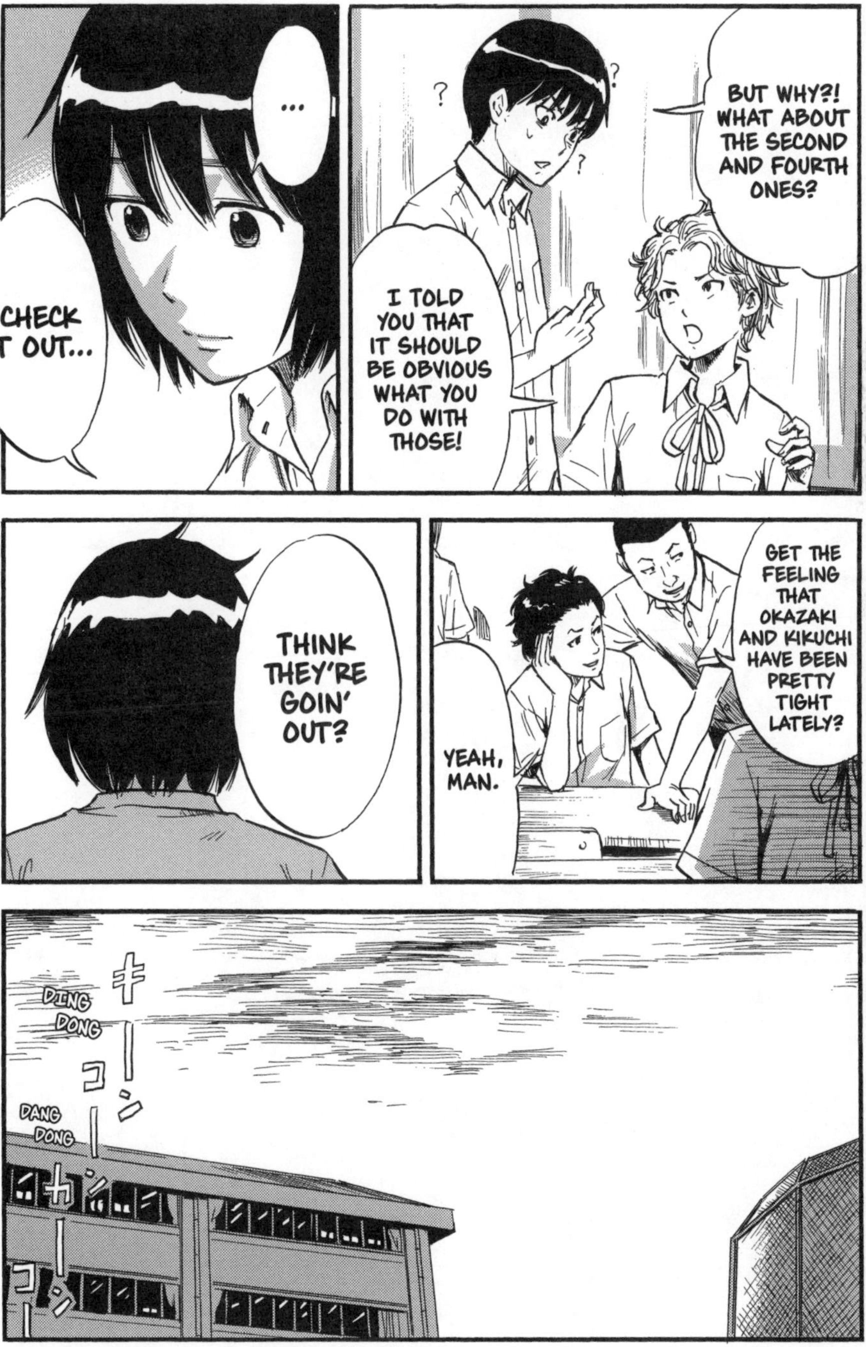

BUT WHY?! WHAT ABOUT THE SECOND AND FOURTH ONES?
I TOLD YOU THAT IT SHOULD BE OBVIOUS WHAT YOU DO WITH THOSE!
...
CHECK IT OUT...
GET THE FEELING THAT OKAZAKI AND KIKUCHI HAVE BEEN PRETTY TIGHT LATELY?
YEAH, MAN.
THINK THEY'RE GOIN' OUT?
キーンコーン
カーンコーン
DING DONG
DANG DONG

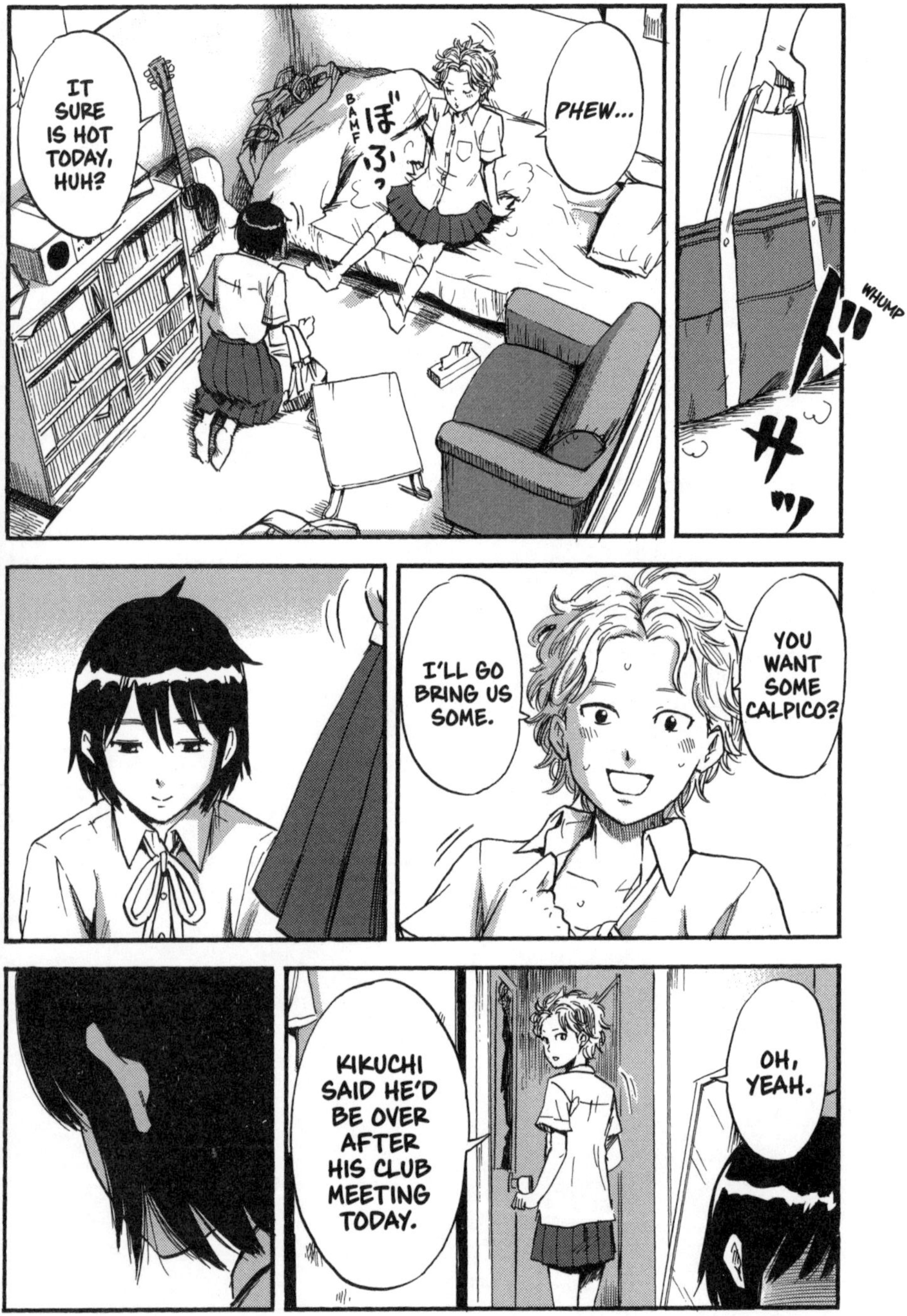
WHUMP
ドッ
ザッ
PHEW...
BAMF
ぼふっ
IT SURE IS HOT TODAY, HUH?
YOU WANT SOME CALPICO?
I'LL GO BRING US SOME.
OH, YEAH.
KIKUCHI SAID HE'D BE OVER AFTER HIS CLUB MEETING TODAY.

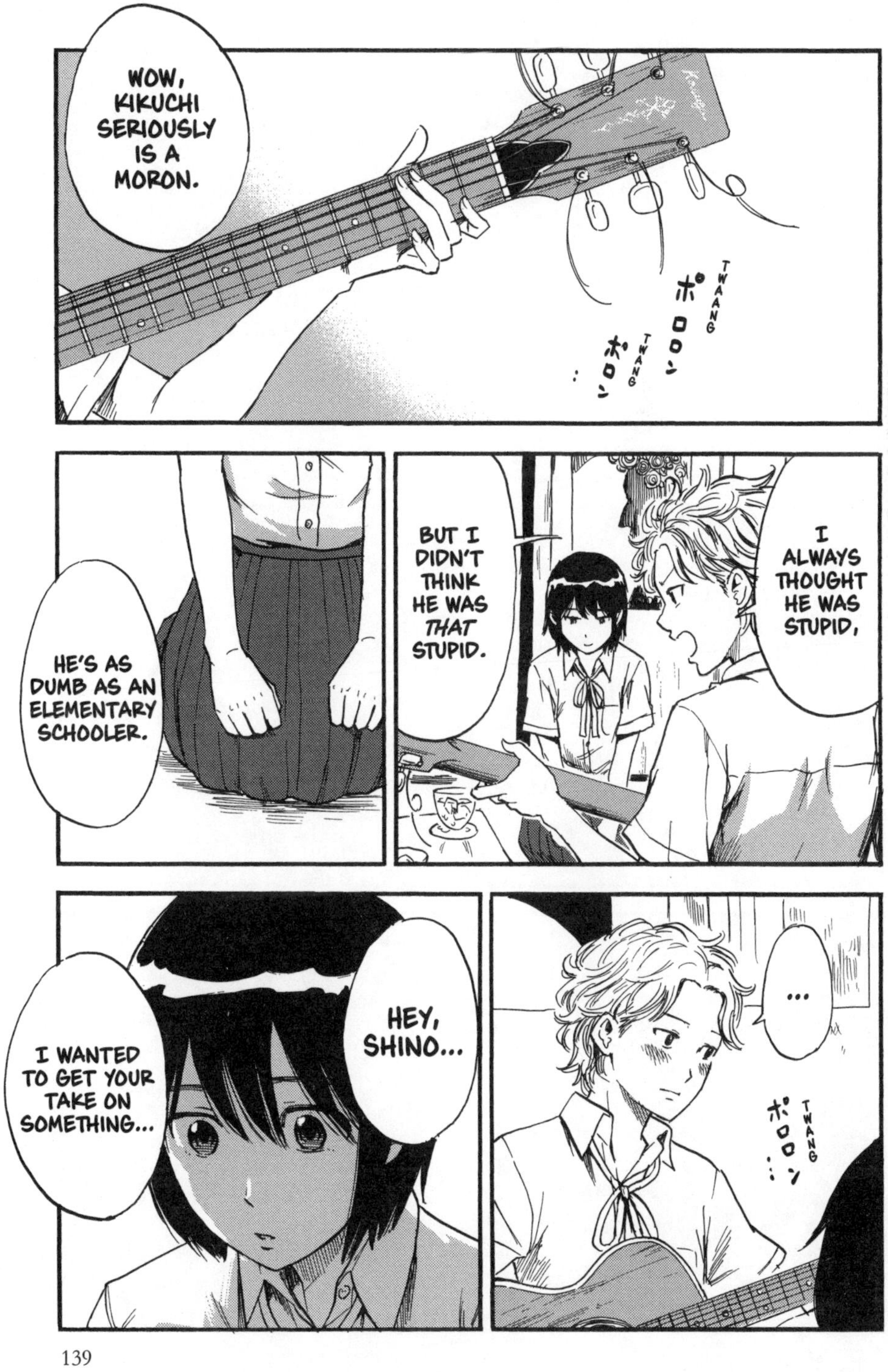
WOW, KIKUCHI SERIOUSLY IS A MORON.
ポロロン
TWAANG
ポロン…
TWANG
I ALWAYS THOUGHT HE WAS STUPID,
BUT I DIDN'T THINK HE WAS *THAT* STUPID.
HE'S AS DUMB AS AN ELEMENTARY SCHOOLER.
…
ポロロン…
TWANG
HEY, SHINO…
I WANTED TO GET YOUR TAKE ON SOMETHING…

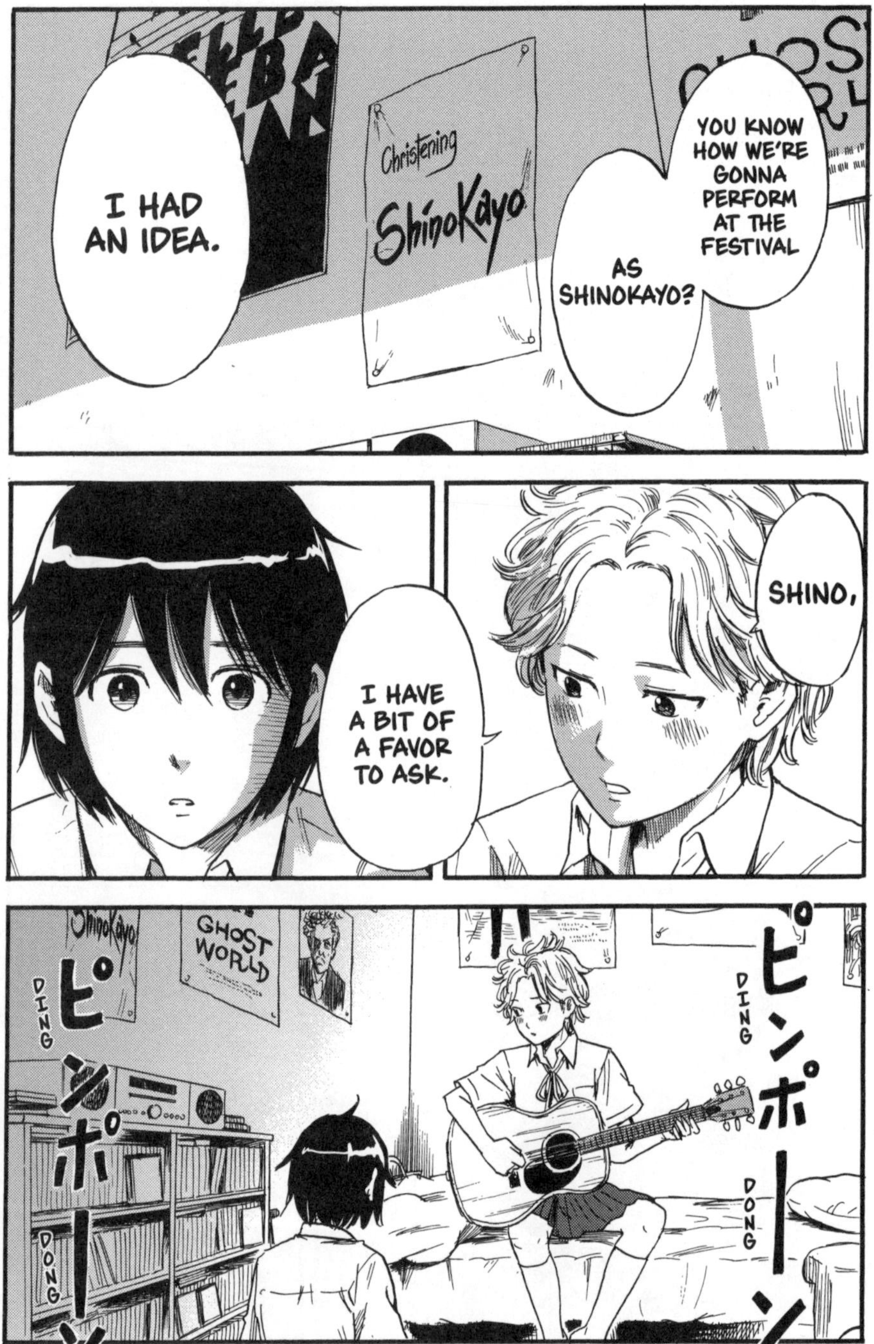
YOU KNOW HOW WE'RE GONNA PERFORM AT THE FESTIVAL
AS SHINOKAYO?
Christening ShinoKayo
I HAD AN IDEA.
SHINO,
I HAVE A BIT OF A FAVOR TO ASK.
ピンポーン
DING DONG
GHOST WORLD
ShinoKayo
ピンポーン
DING DONG

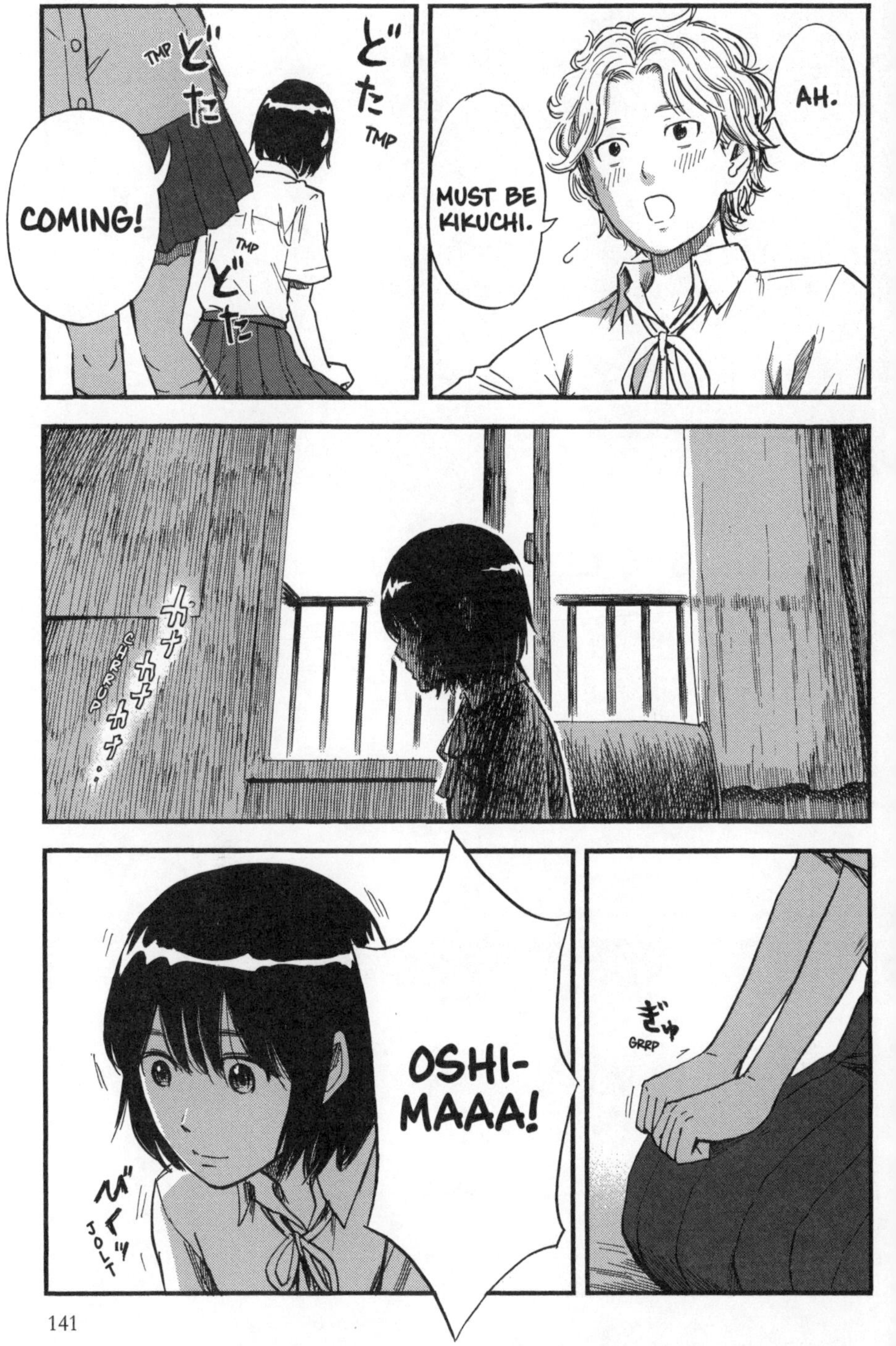
AH.
MUST BE KIKUCHI.
どた
TMP
どた
TMP
COMING!
TMP
どた
カナカナカナ。
CHRRUP
ぎゅ
GRRP
OSHI-MAAA!
JOLT

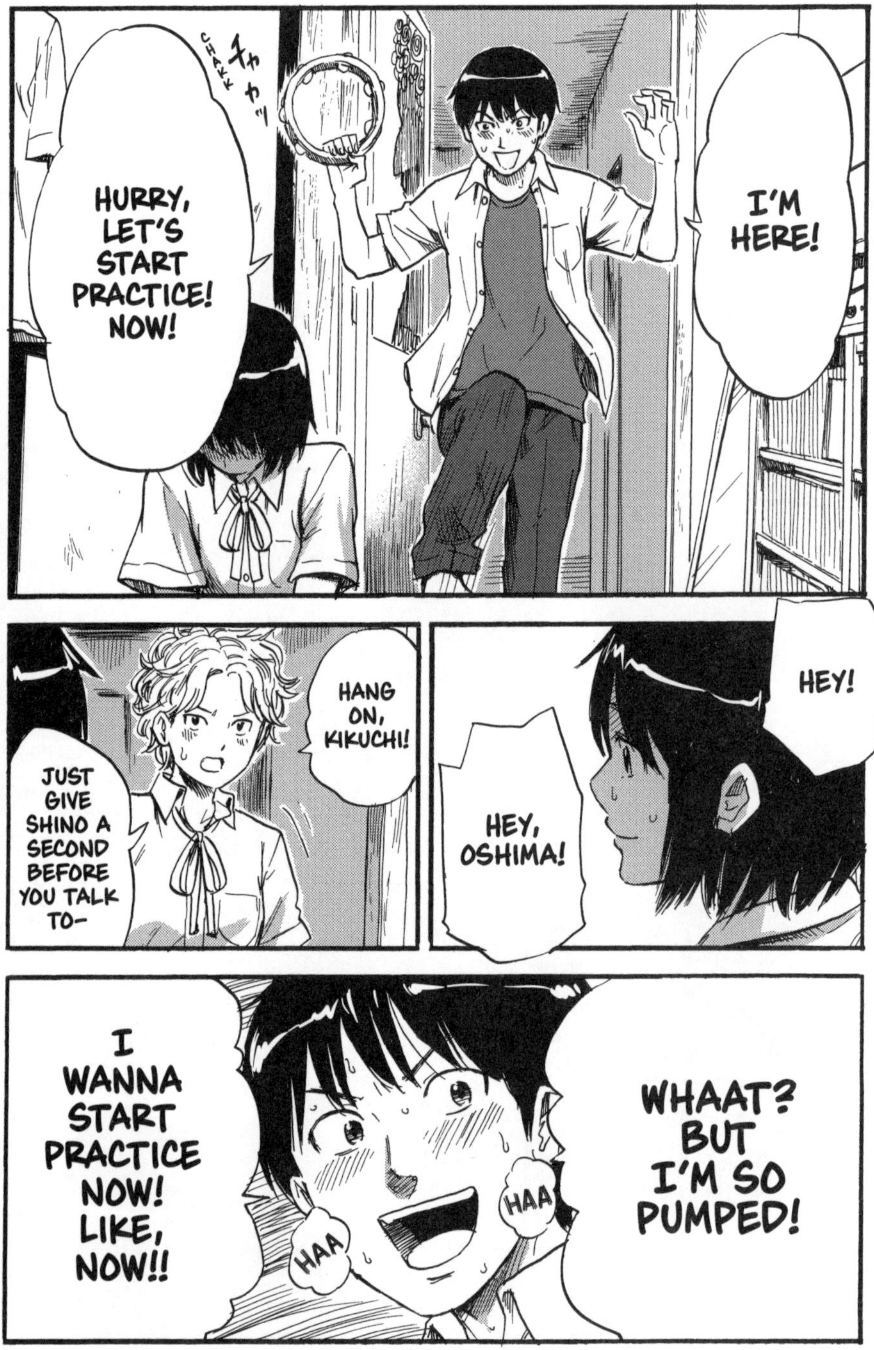
I'M HERE!
チャカッ
CHAKK
HURRY, LET'S START PRACTICE! NOW!
HEY!
HEY, OSHIMA!
HANG ON, KIKUCHI!
JUST GIVE SHINO A SECOND BEFORE YOU TALK TO-
WHAAT? BUT I'M SO PUMPED!
HAA
HAA
I WANNA START PRACTICE NOW! LIKE, NOW!!

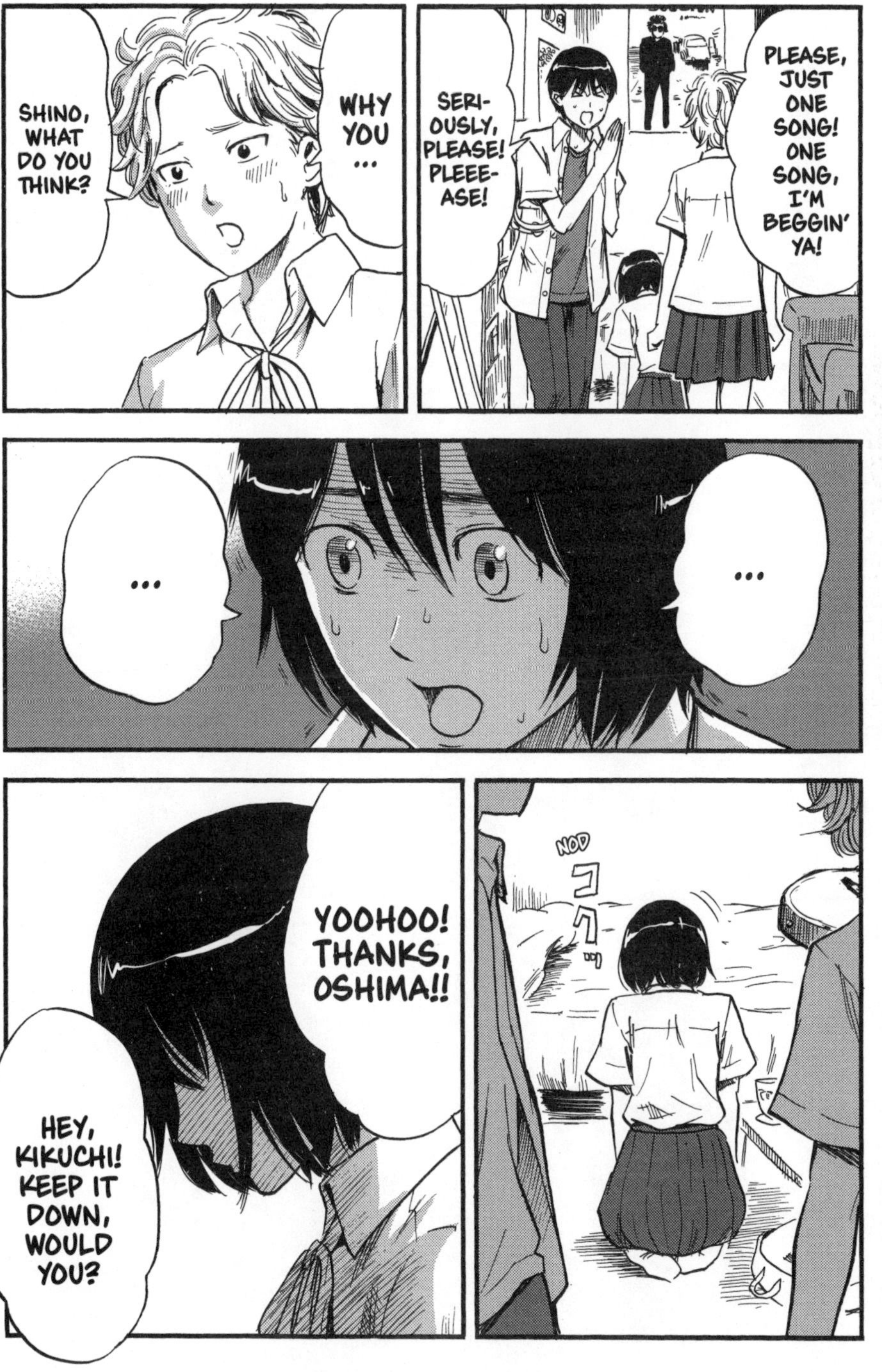
PLEASE, JUST ONE SONG! ONE SONG, I'M BEGGIN' YA!
SERI-OUSLY, PLEASE! PLEEE-ASE!
WHY YOU ...
SHINO, WHAT DO YOU THINK?
...
...
NOD
コクッ
YOOHOO! THANKS, OSHIMA!!
HEY, KIKUCHI! KEEP IT DOWN, WOULD YOU?

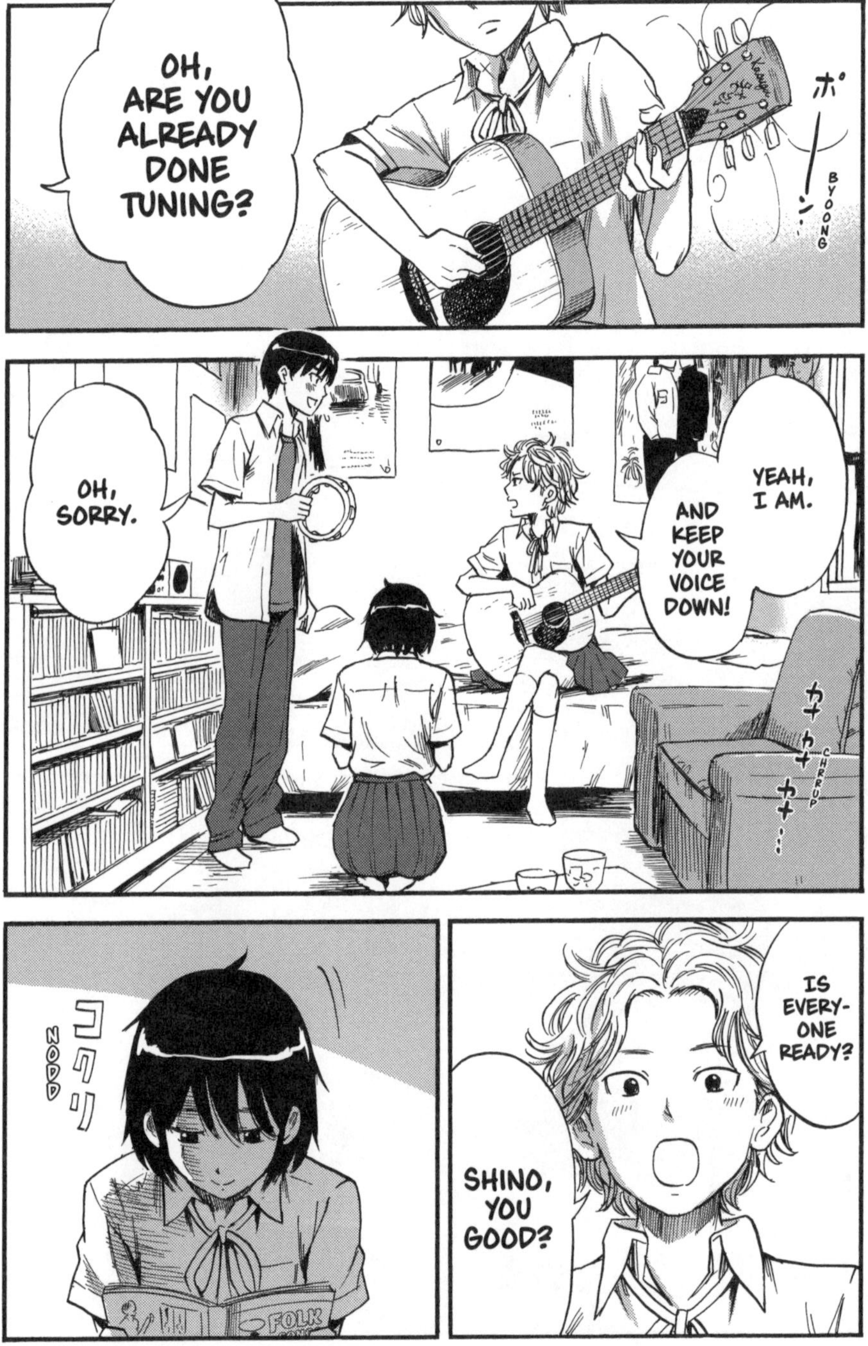
ポーン
BYOONG
OH, ARE YOU ALREADY DONE TUNING?
YEAH, I AM. AND KEEP YOUR VOICE DOWN!
カナカナカナ・・
CHRRUP
OH, SORRY.
IS EVERY-ONE READY?
SHINO, YOU GOOD?
コクリ
NODD
FOLK

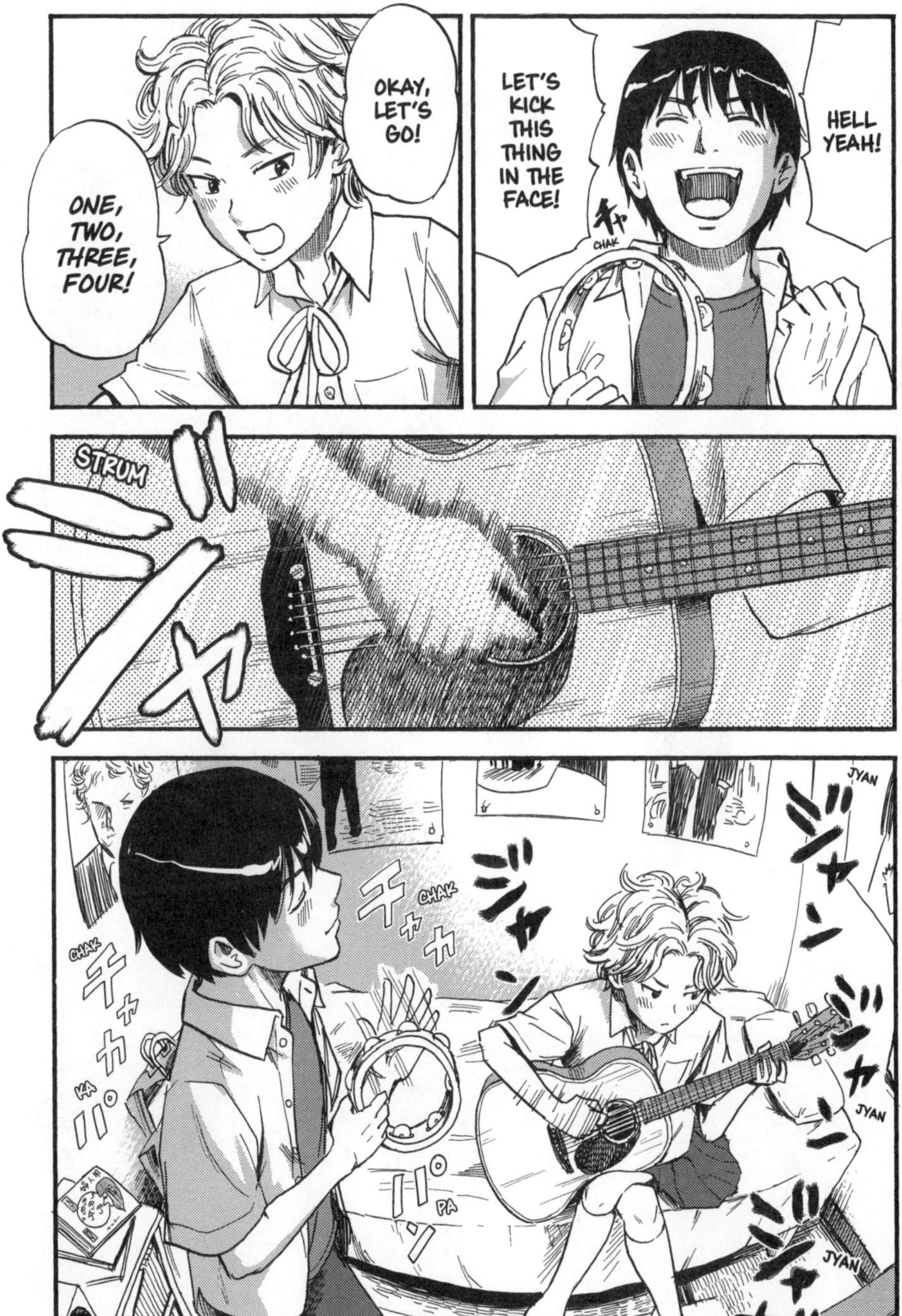
HELL YEAH!
LET'S KICK THIS THING IN THE FACE!
CHAK
OKAY, LET'S GO!
ONE, TWO, THREE, FOUR!
STRUM
JYAN
JYAN
JYAN
CHAK
CHAK
PA
KA

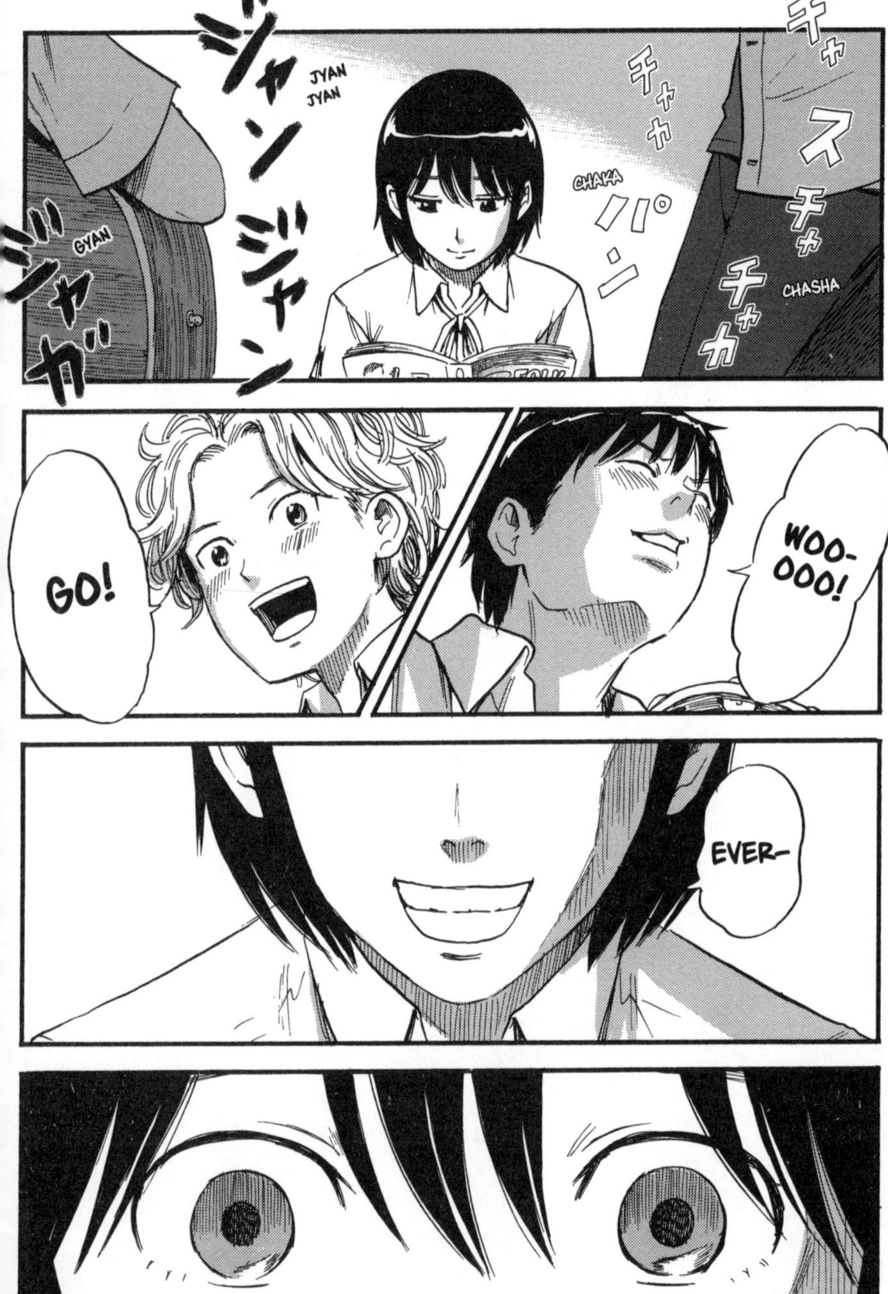

CHASHA
CHAKA
パン
JYAN JYAN
ジャンジャン
GYAN
ジャガ
WOO-OOO!
GO!
EVER-

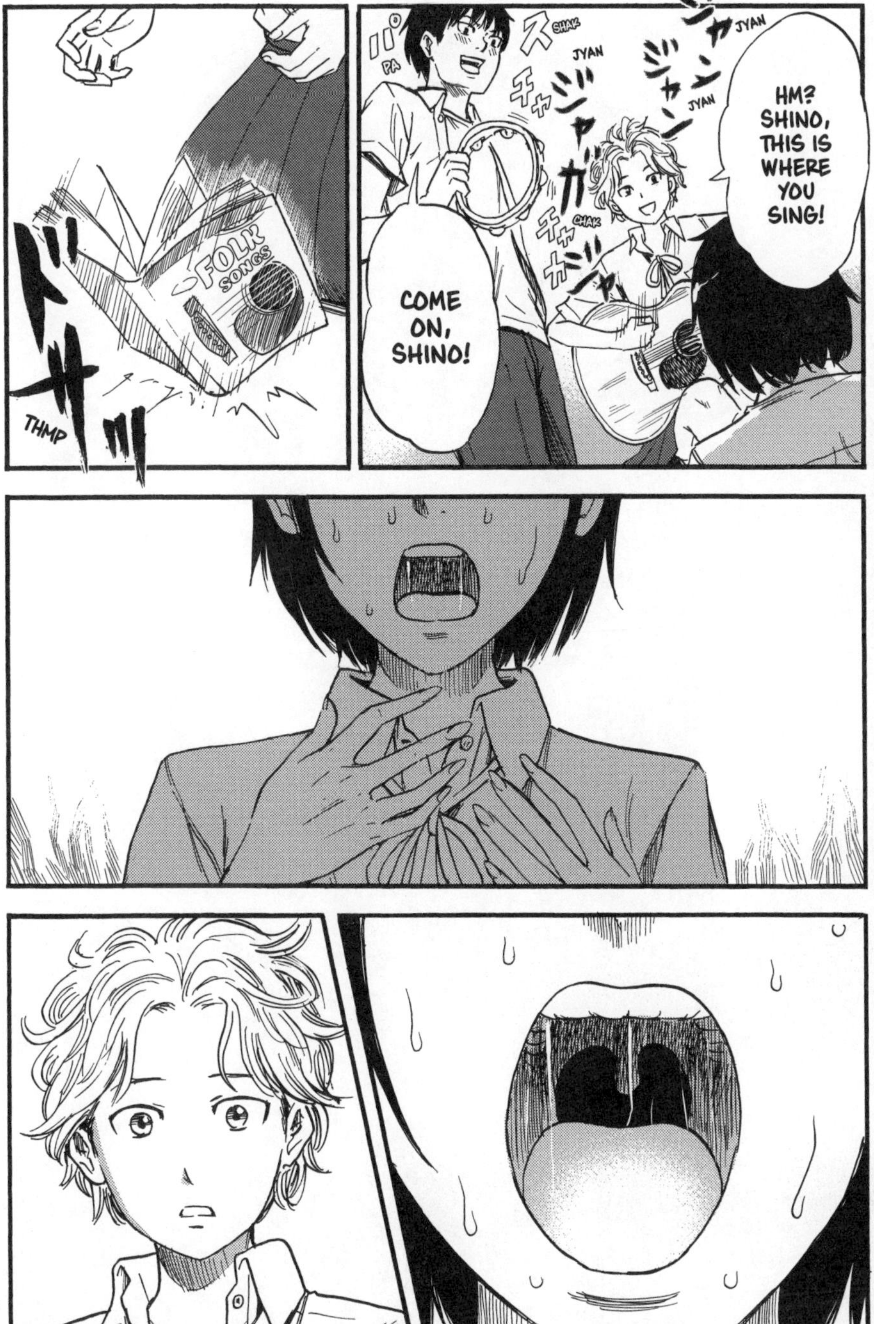
JYAN
HM? SHINO, THIS IS WHERE YOU SING!
JYAN
JYAN
SHAK
PA
CHAK
COME ON, SHINO!
FOLK SONGS
THMP

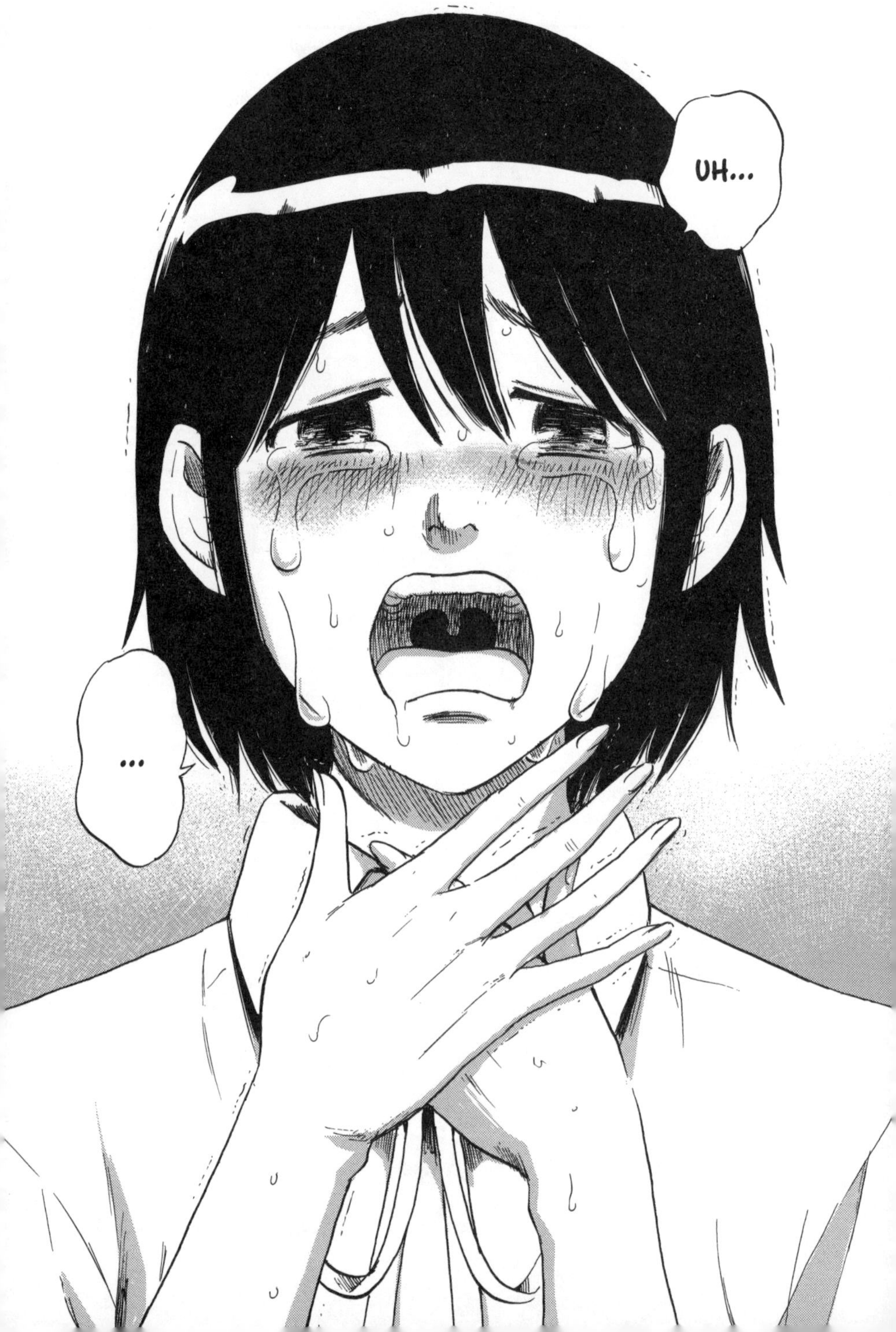
UH...
...

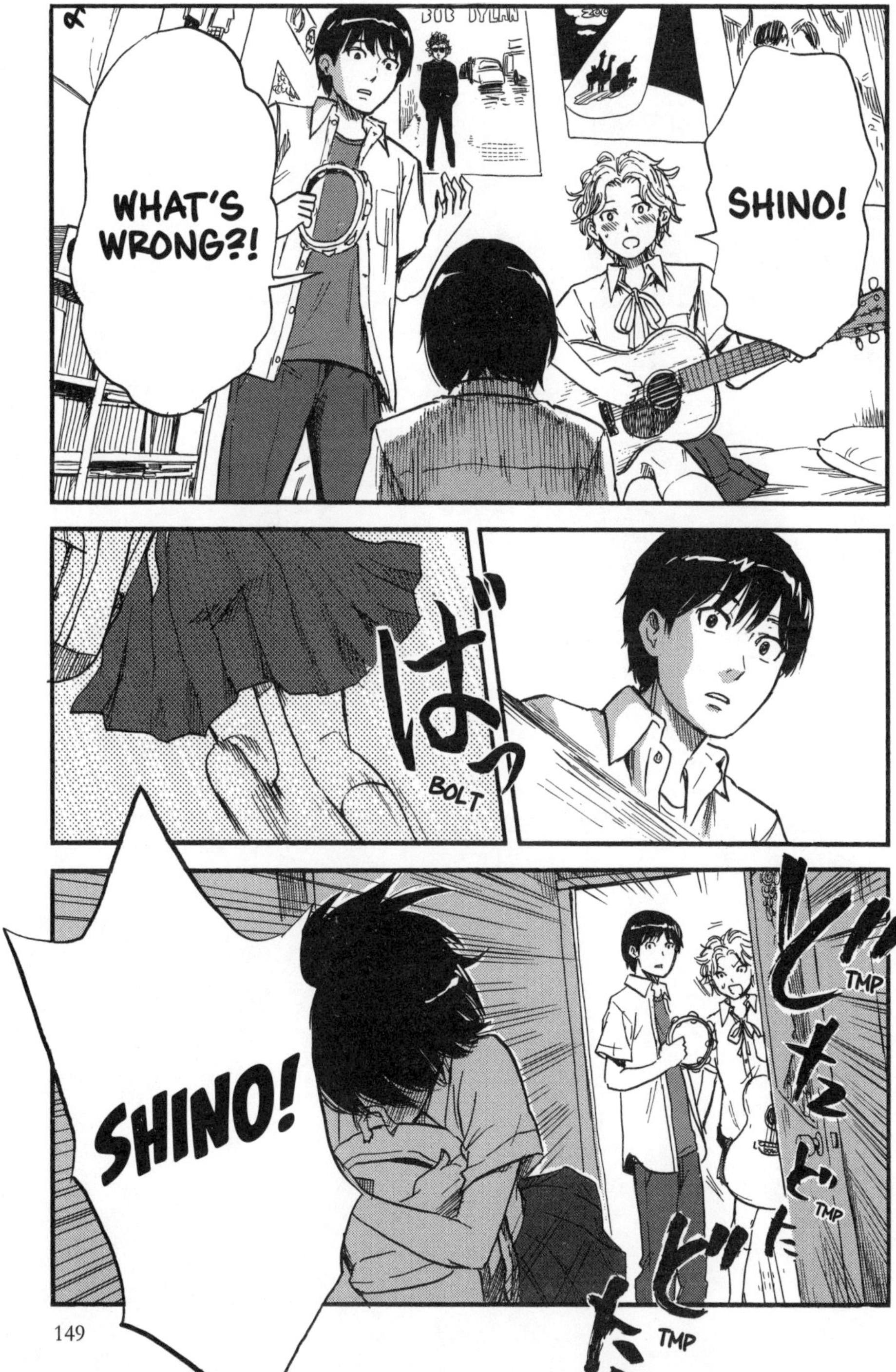
SHINO!
WHAT'S WRONG?!
ばっ
BOLT
どたどたどた
TMP
TMP
TMP
SHINO!

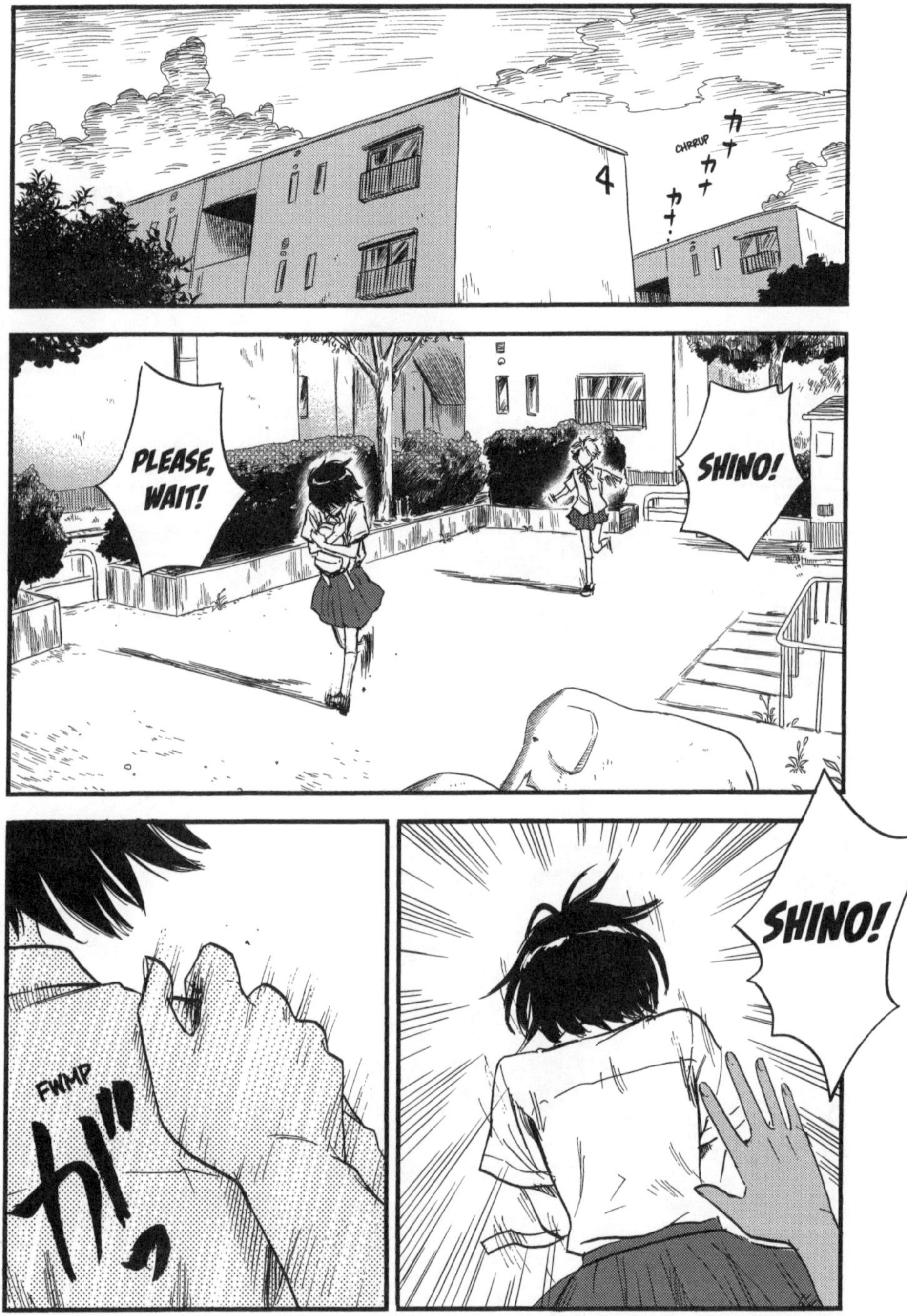
CHRRUP
カナ
カナ
カナ・・
SHINO!
PLEASE, WAIT!
SHINO!
FWMP
ガッ

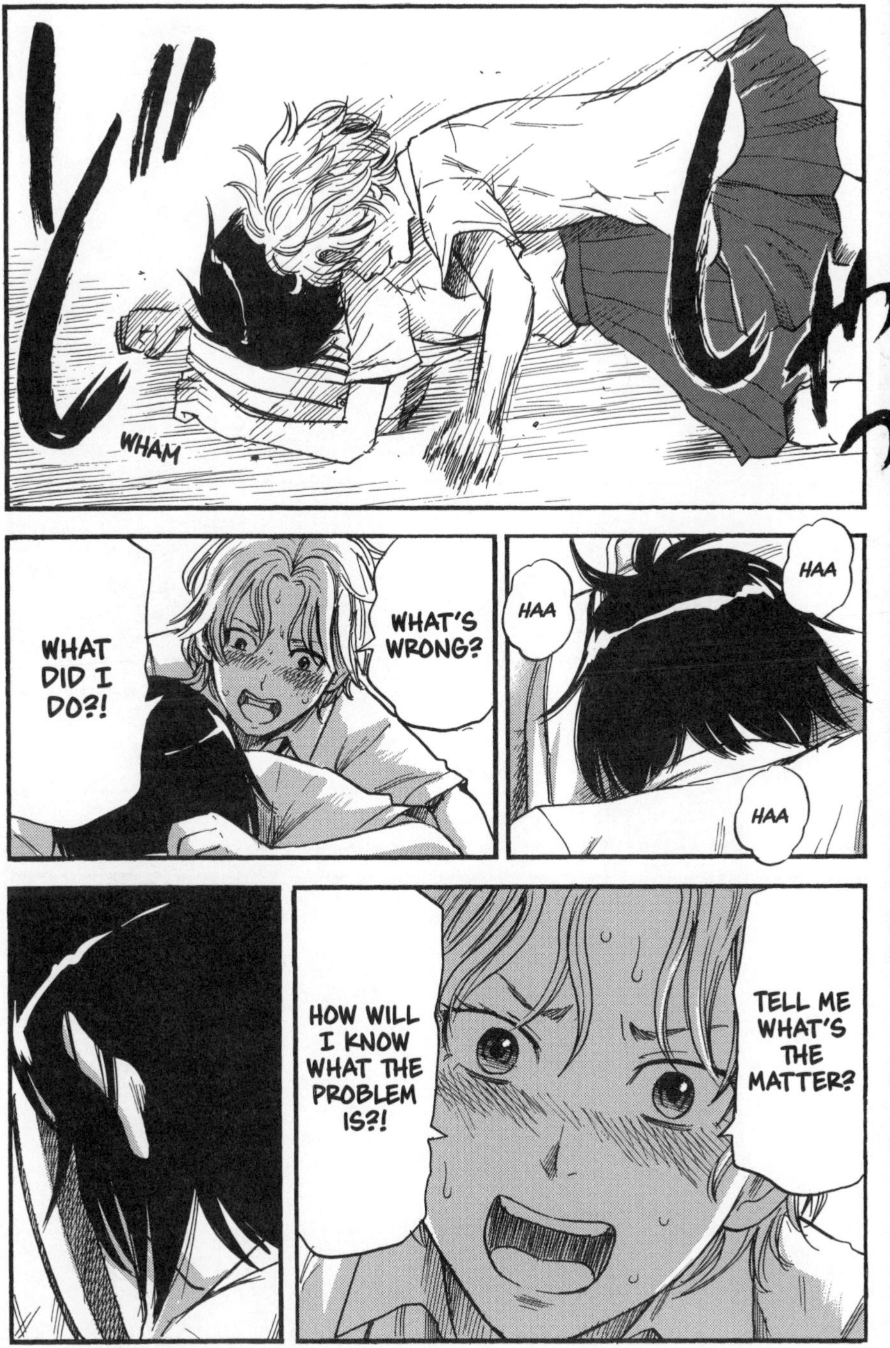
WHAM
HAA
HAA
HAA
WHAT'S WRONG?
WHAT DID I DO?!
TELL ME WHAT'S THE MATTER?
HOW WILL I KNOW WHAT THE PROBLEM IS?!

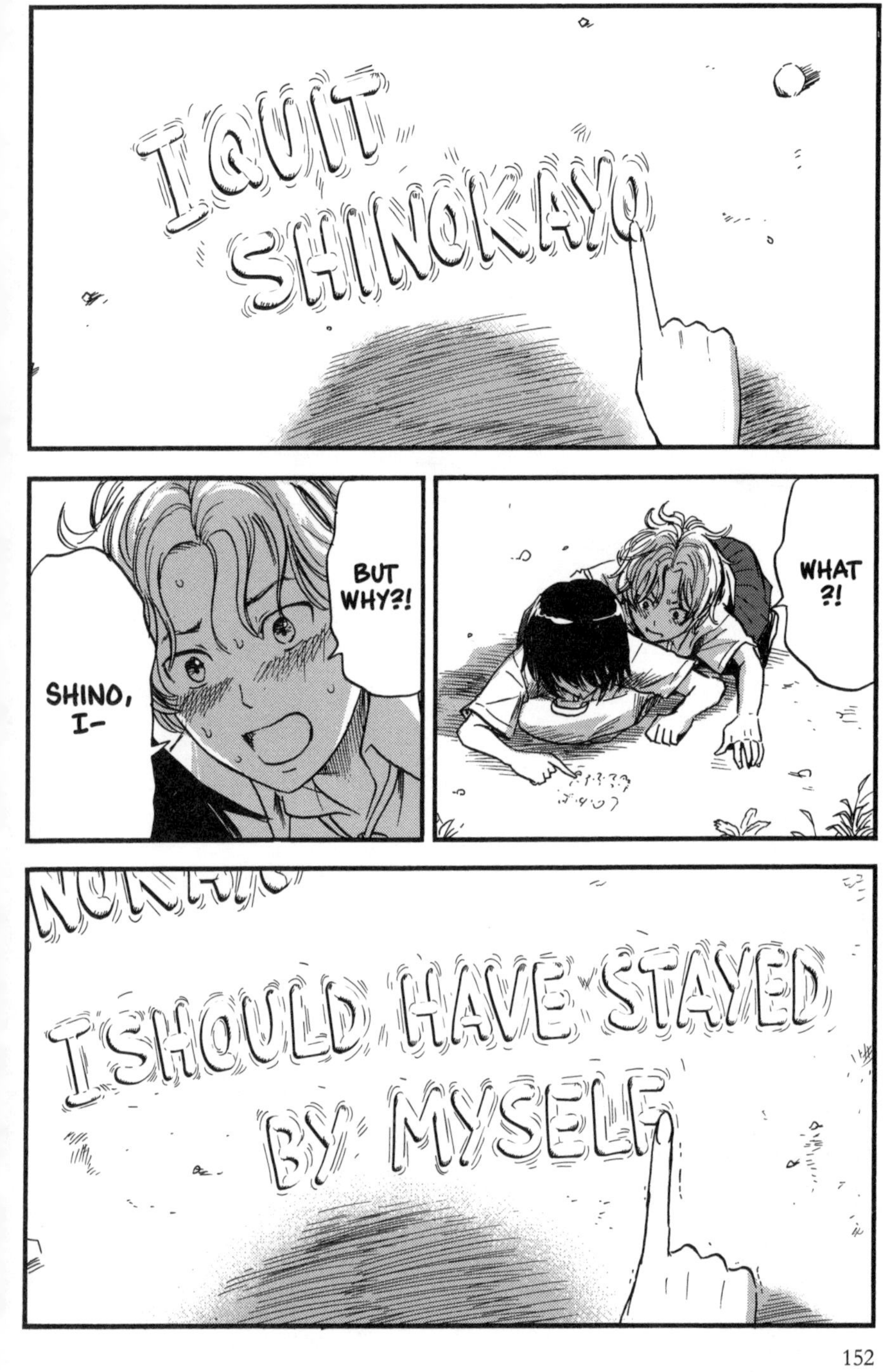
I QUIT SHINOKAYO
WHAT ?!
BUT WHY?!
SHINO, I-
I SHOULD HAVE STAYED BY MYSELF

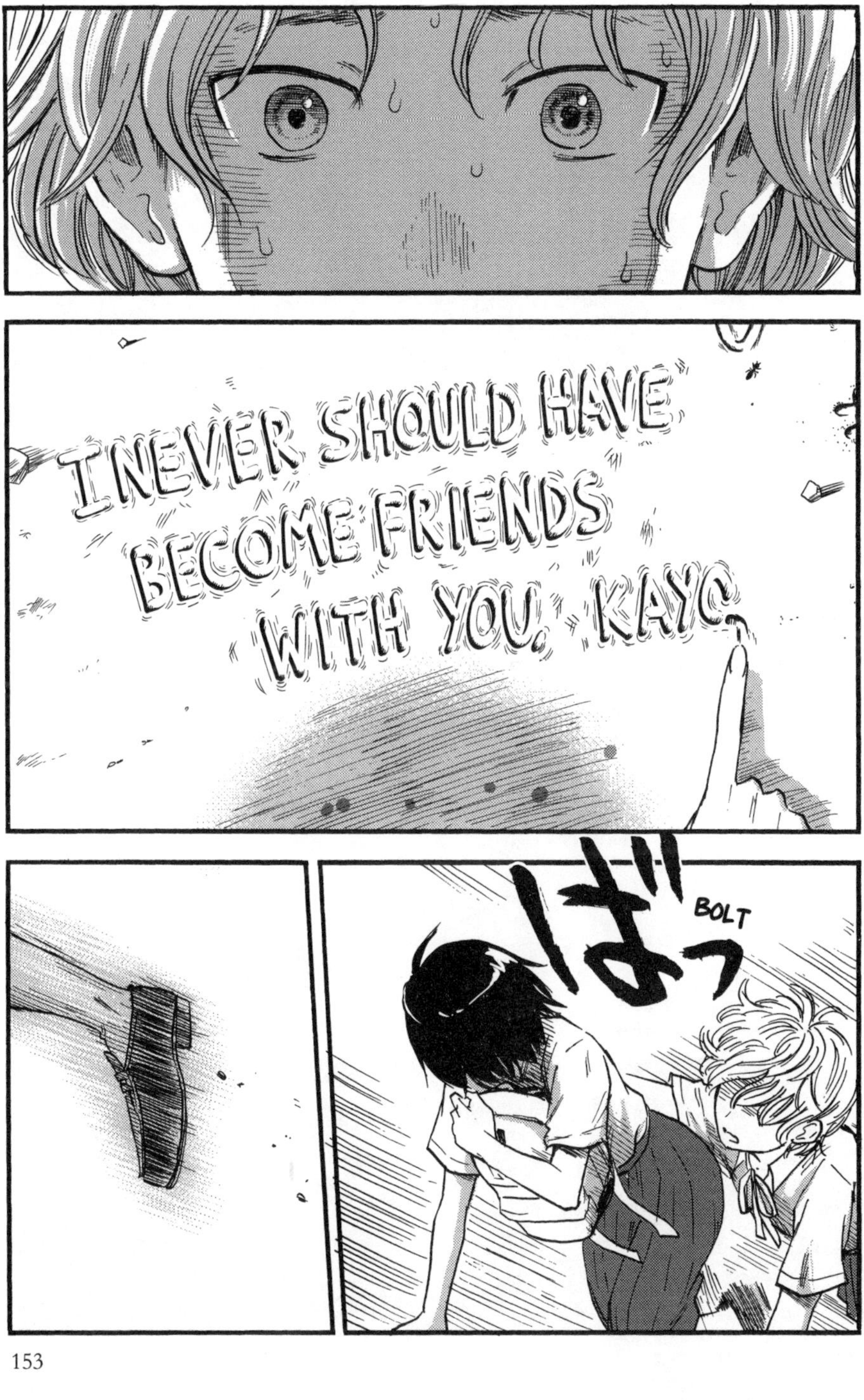
I NEVER SHOULD HAVE BECOME FRIENDS WITH YOU, KAYO
ぼっ
BOLT

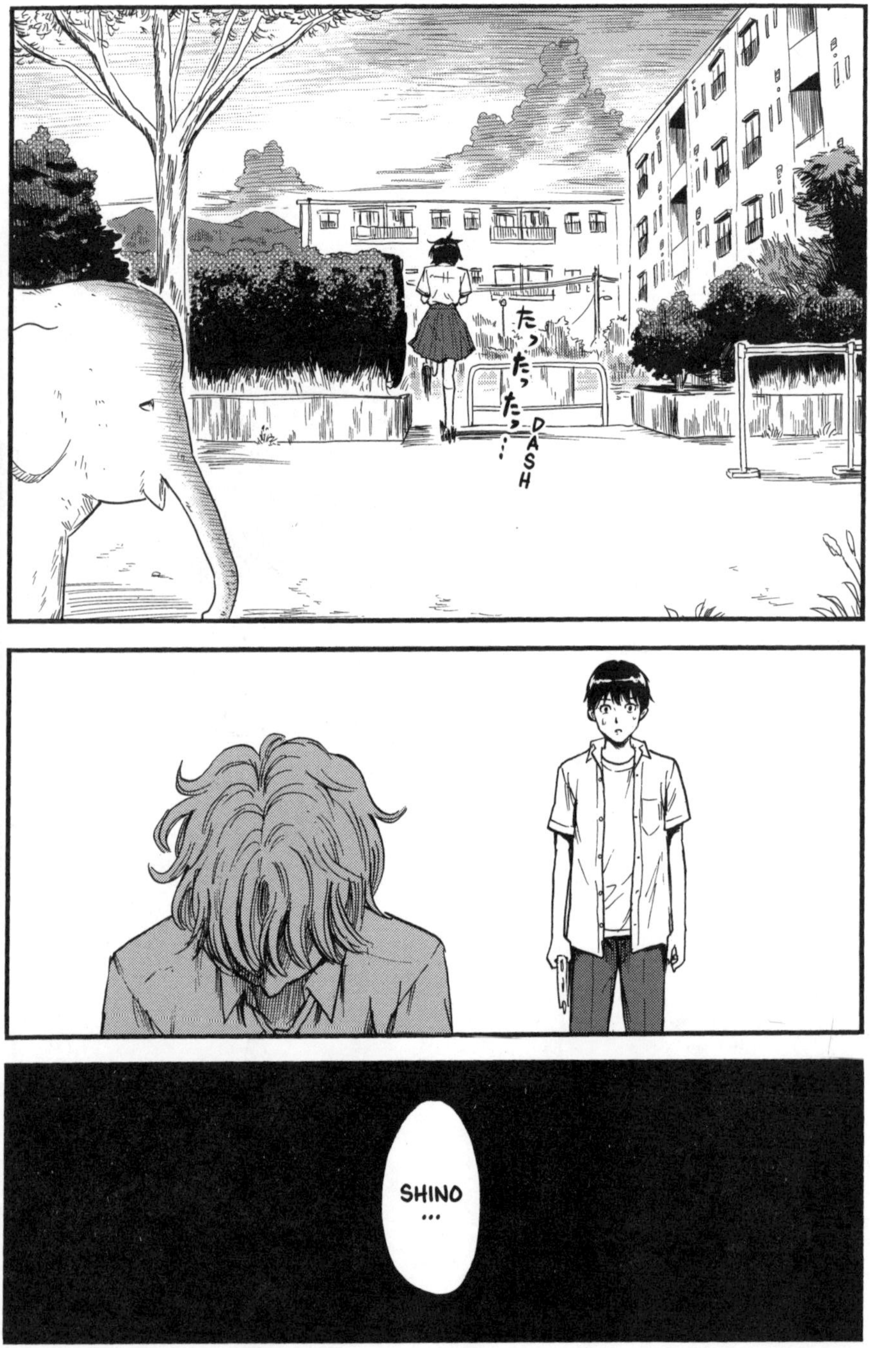
たっ たっ たっ…
DASH
SHINO
...

Chapter 9
It's Been Awhile

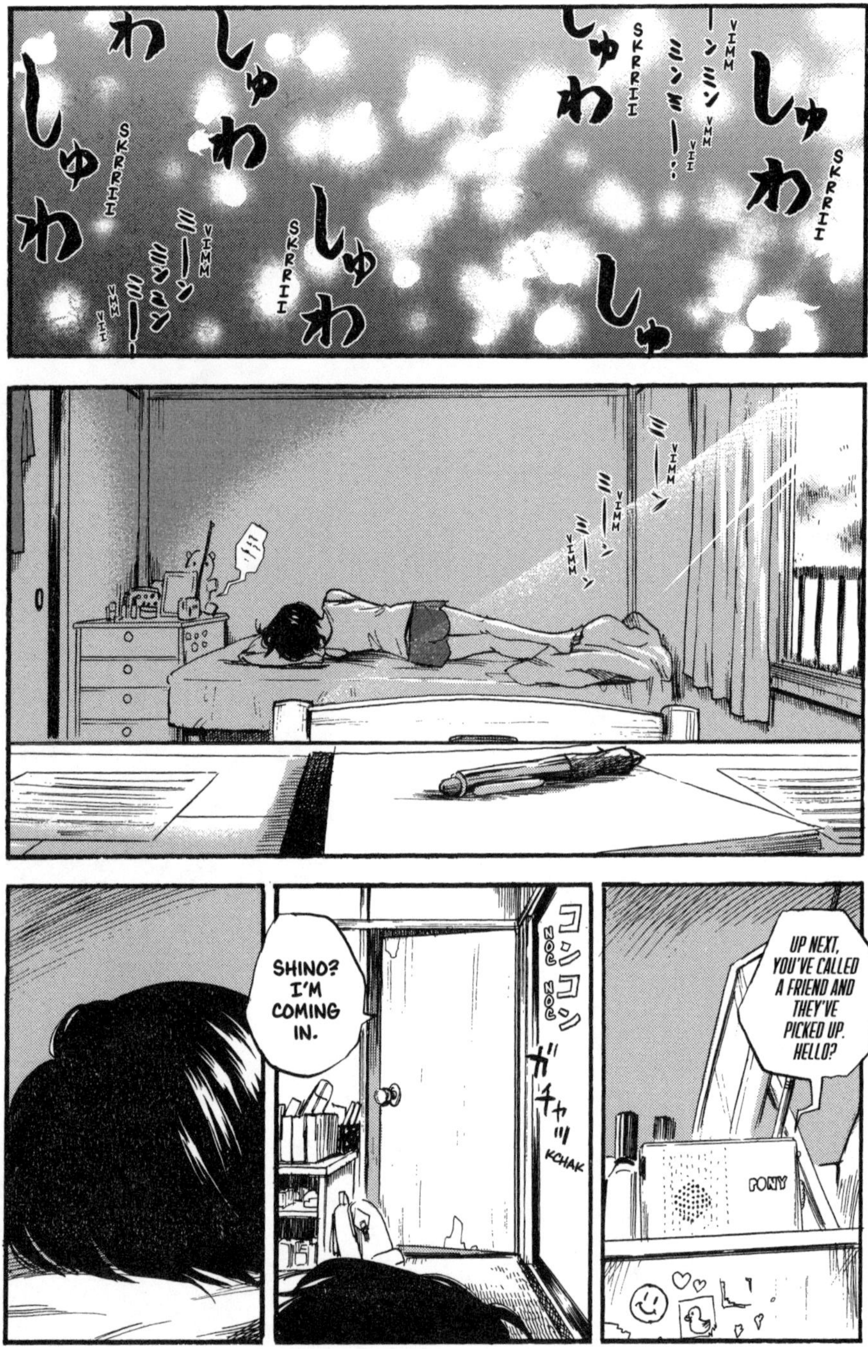
しゅわ
SKRRII
しゅ
ーンミンミンミー…
VIMM VMM VII
しゅわ
SKRRII
しゅわ
SKRRII
ミーンミンミンミー
VIMM VMM VII
わしゅわ
SKRRII
ミーン
VIMM
ミーン
VIMM
ミーン
VIMM
UP NEXT, YOU'VE CALLED A FRIEND AND THEY'VE PICKED UP. HELLO?
PONY
コンコン
NOC NOC
SHINO? I'M COMING IN.
ガチャッ
KCHAK

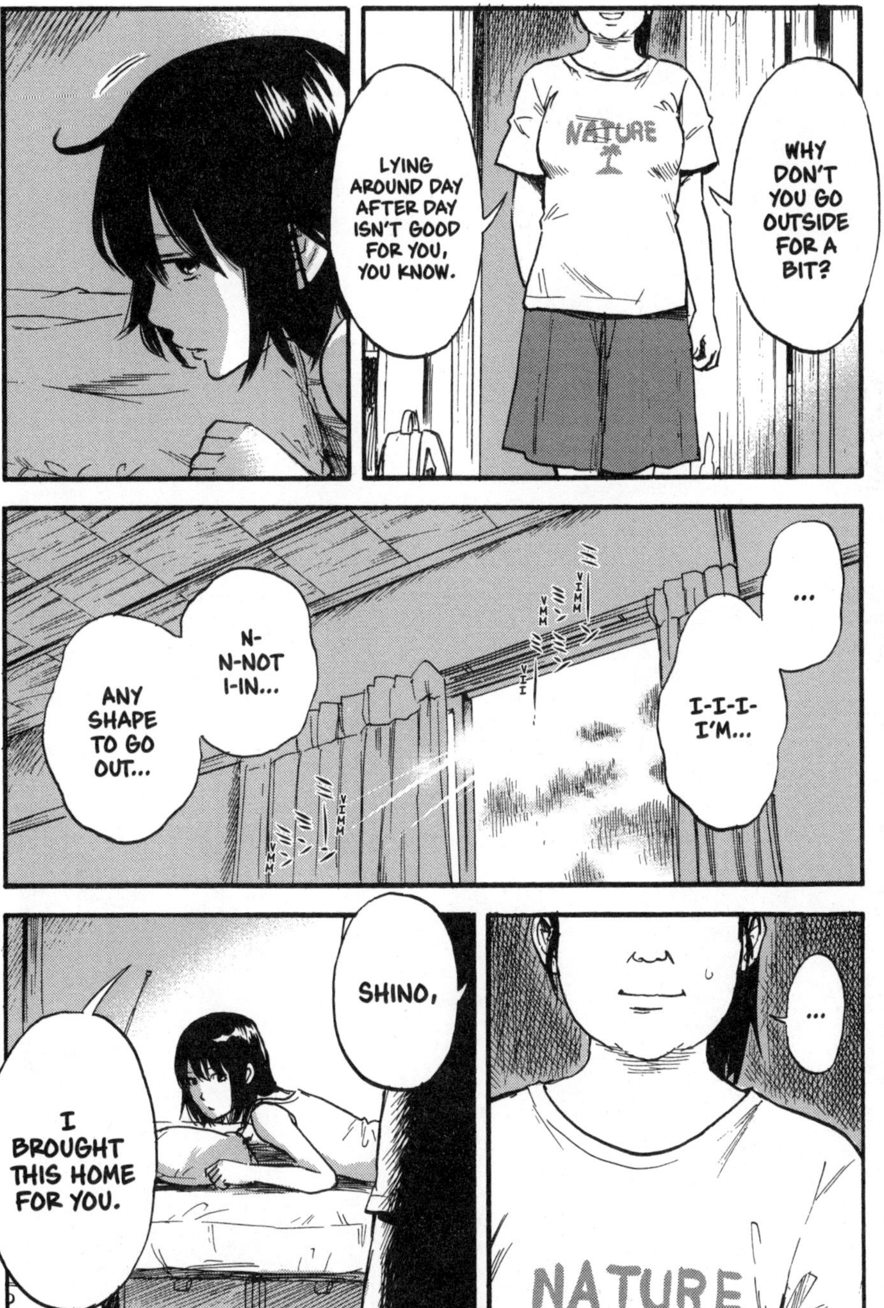
WHY DON'T YOU GO OUTSIDE FOR A BIT?
NATURE
LYING AROUND DAY AFTER DAY ISN'T GOOD FOR YOU, YOU KNOW.
...
I-I-I-I'M...
VIMM
VMM
VII
N-N-NOT I-IN...
ANY SHAPE TO GO OUT...
VIMM
VMM
...
NATURE
SHINO,
I BROUGHT THIS HOME FOR YOU.

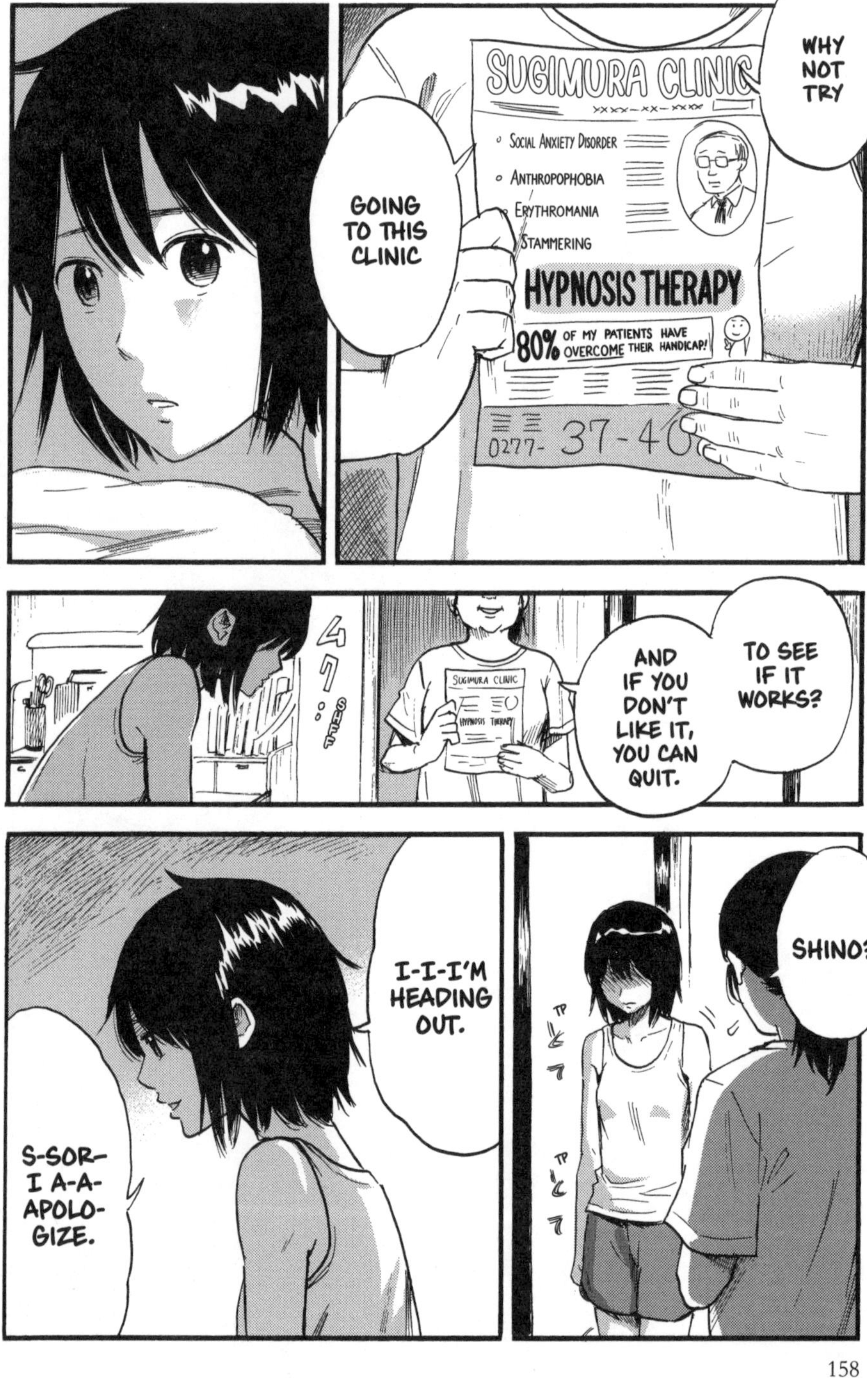
WHY NOT TRY
GOING TO THIS CLINIC
SUGIMURA CLINIC
Social Anxiety Disorder
Anthropophobia
Erythromania
Stammering
HYPNOSIS THERAPY
80% OF MY PATIENTS HAVE OVERCOME THEIR HANDICAP!
0277-37-40
TO SEE IF IT WORKS?
AND IF YOU DON'T LIKE IT, YOU CAN QUIT.
SUGIMURA CLINIC
HYPNOSIS THERAPY
SNIFF
SHINO?
TP
TP
I-I-I'M HEADING OUT.
S-SOR- I A-A-APOLO-GIZE.

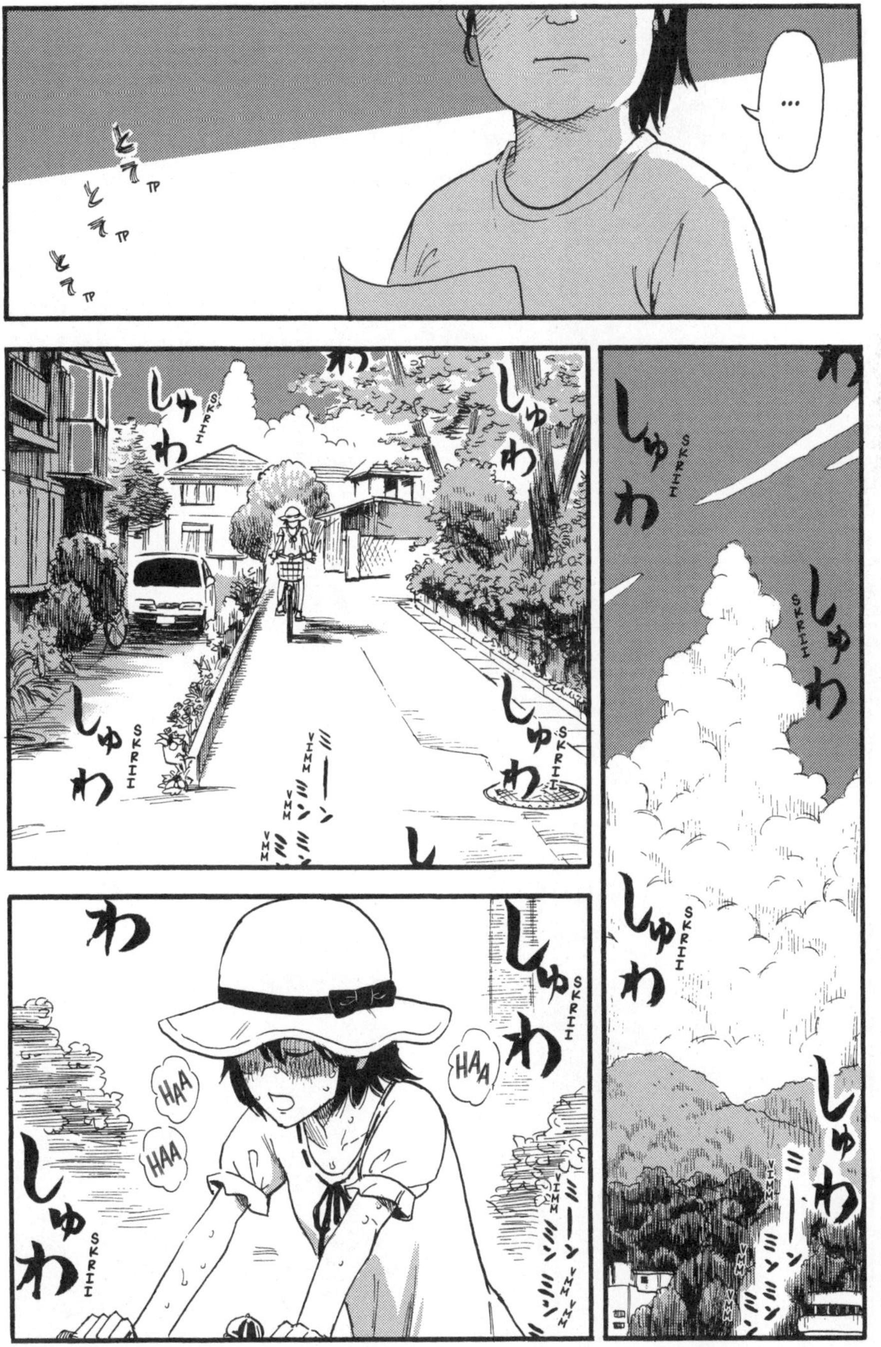
…
とて TP
とて TP
とて TP
わ
しゅわ SKRII
しゅわ SKRII
しゅわ SKRII
しゅわ
ミーン ミン ミン VIMM VMM VMM
わ
しゅわ SKRII
しゅわ SKRII
しゅわ SKRII
ミーン ミン ミ VIMM VMM VMM
わ
しゅわ SKRII
HAA
HAA
HAA
ミーン ミン ミン VIMM VMM VMM
しゅわ SKRII

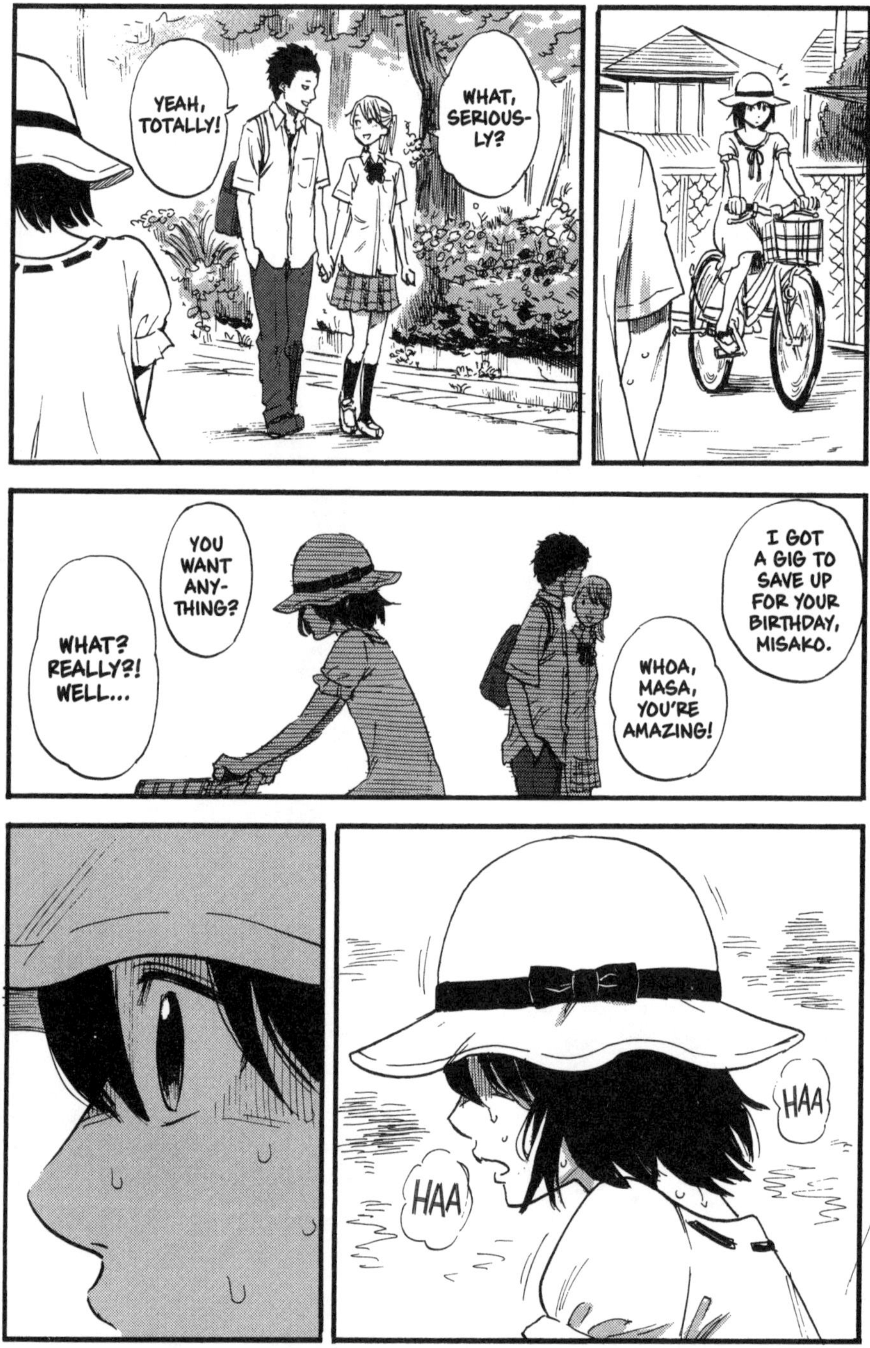
WHAT, SERIOUS-LY?
YEAH, TOTALLY!
I GOT A GIG TO SAVE UP FOR YOUR BIRTHDAY, MISAKO.
WHOA, MASA, YOU'RE AMAZING!
YOU WANT ANY-THING?
WHAT? REALLY?! WELL...
HAA
HAA

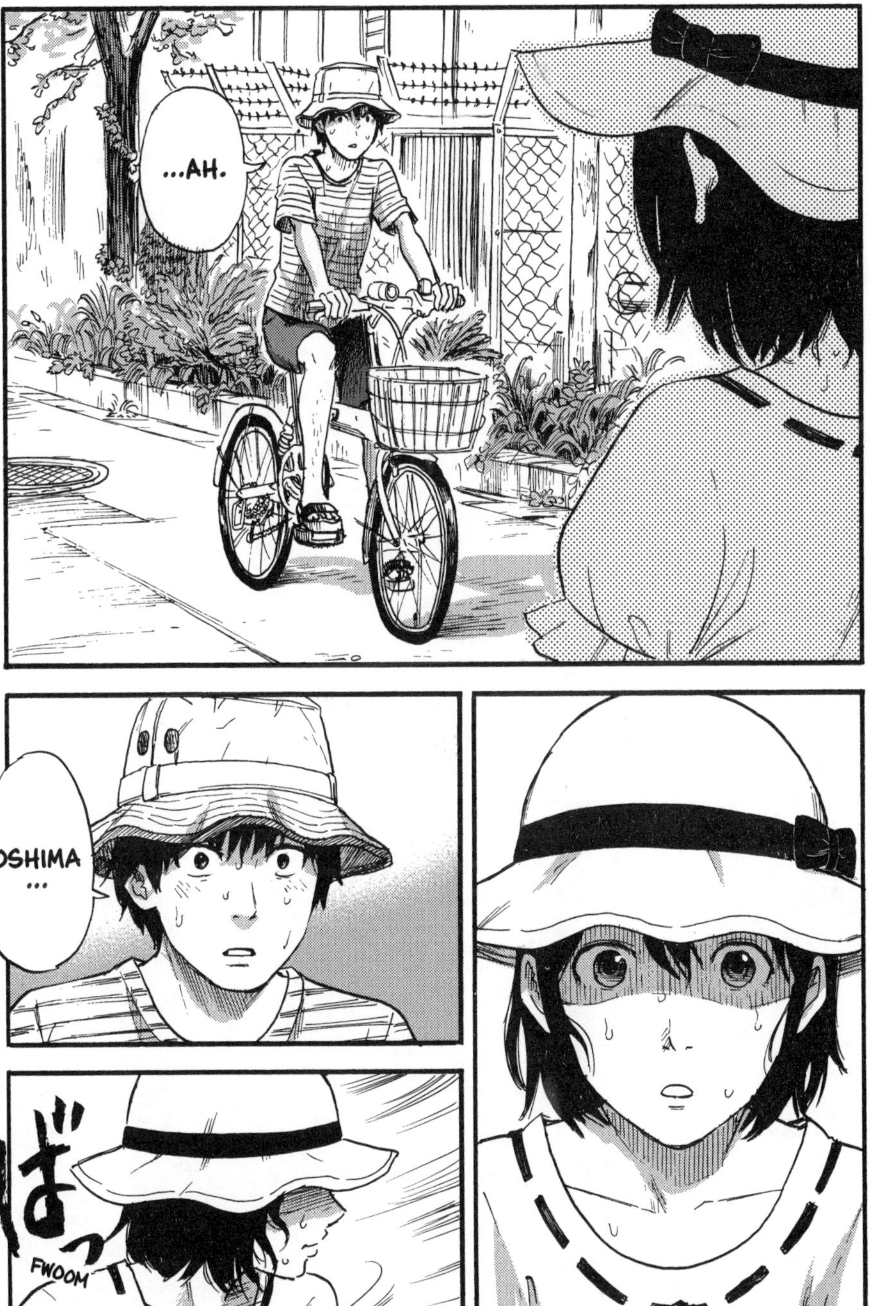
...AH.
OSHIMA ...
ばっ
FWOOM

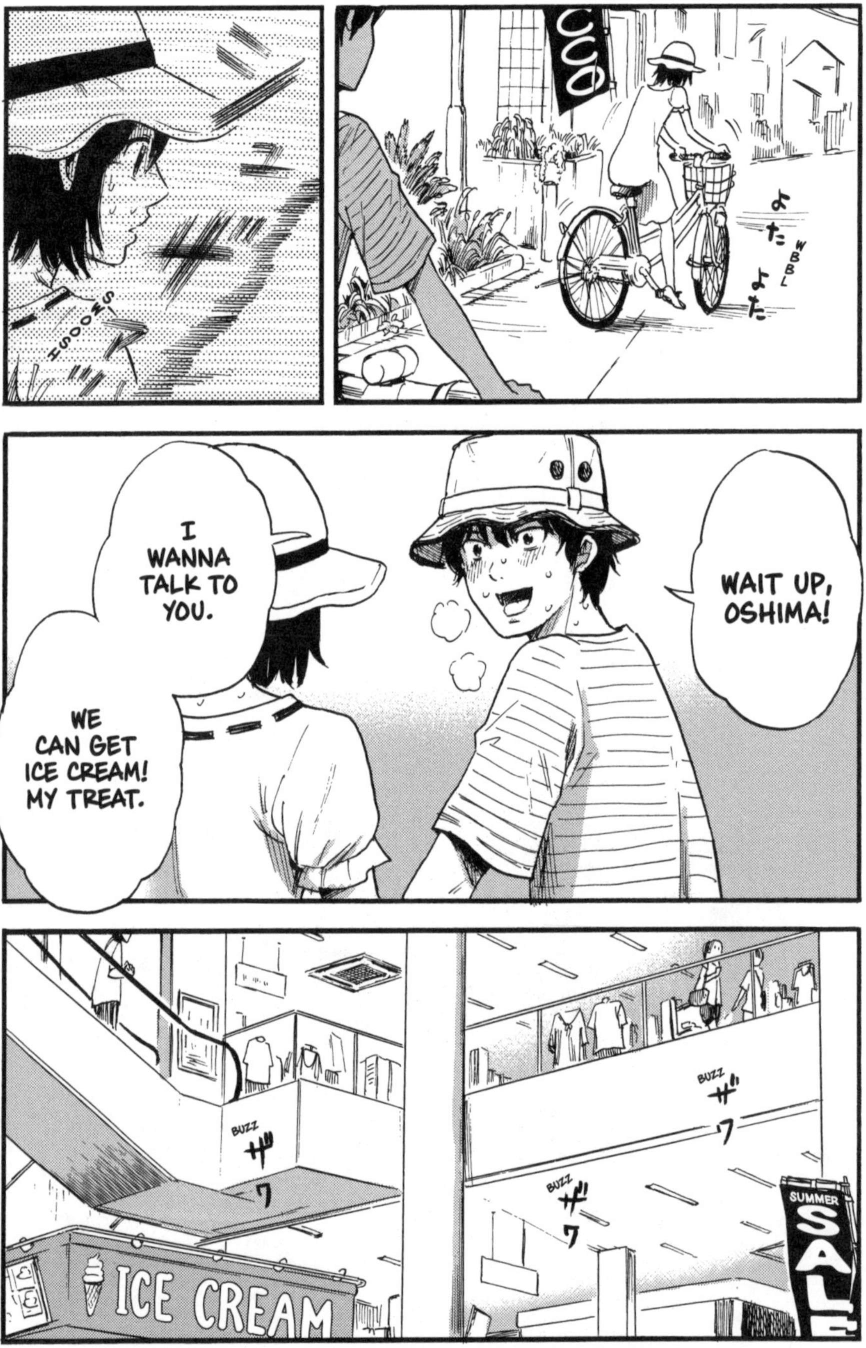
よたよた
WBBL
SWOOSH
WAIT UP, OSHIMA!
I WANNA TALK TO YOU.
WE CAN GET ICE CREAM! MY TREAT.
SUMMER
SAL
BUZZ
ザワ
BUZZ
ザワ
BUZZ
ザワ
ICE CREAM

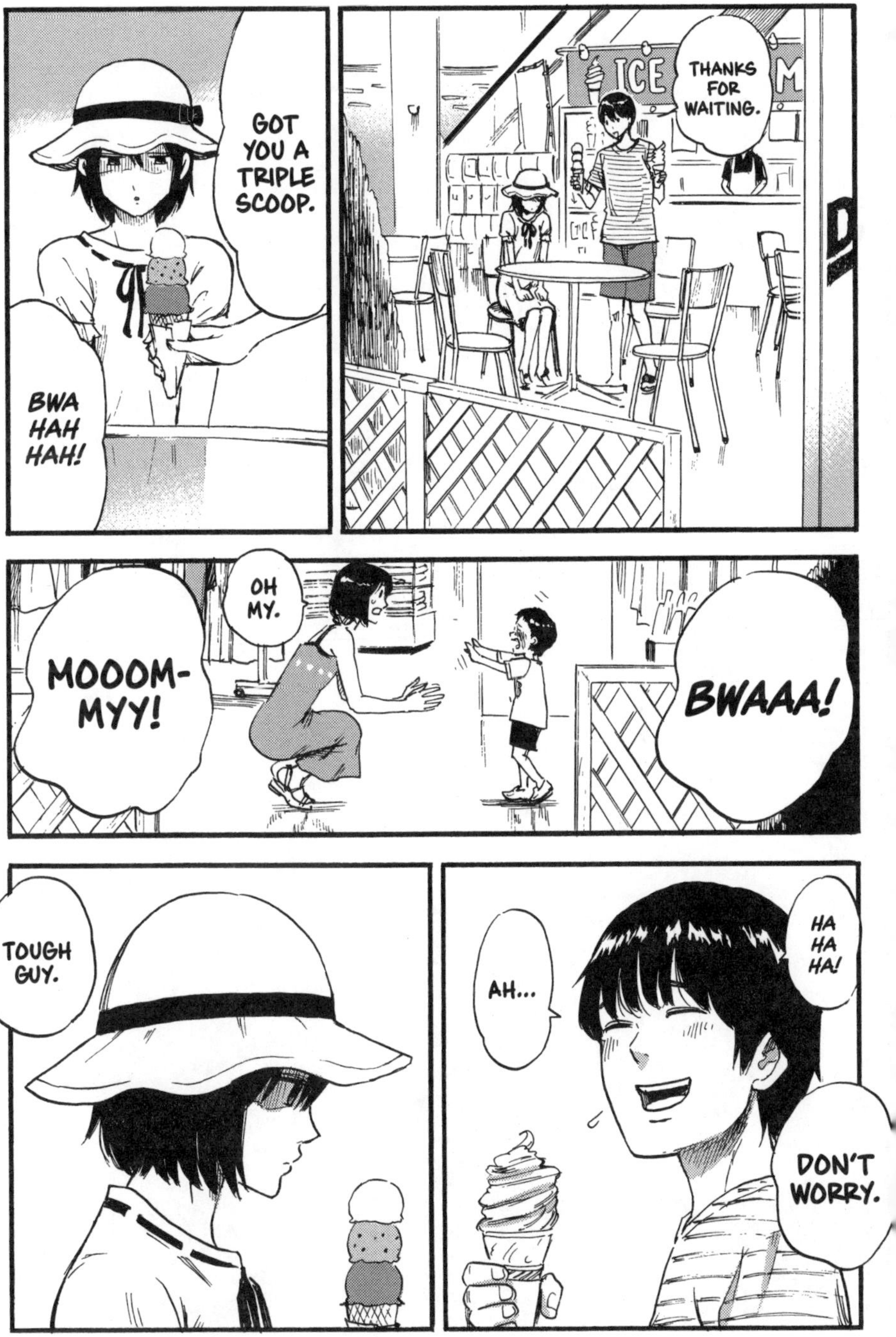
THANKS FOR WAITING.
GOT YOU A TRIPLE SCOOP.
BWA HAH HAH!
BWAAA!
OH MY.
MOOOM-MYY!
HA HA HA!
AH...
DON'T WORRY.
TOUGH GUY.

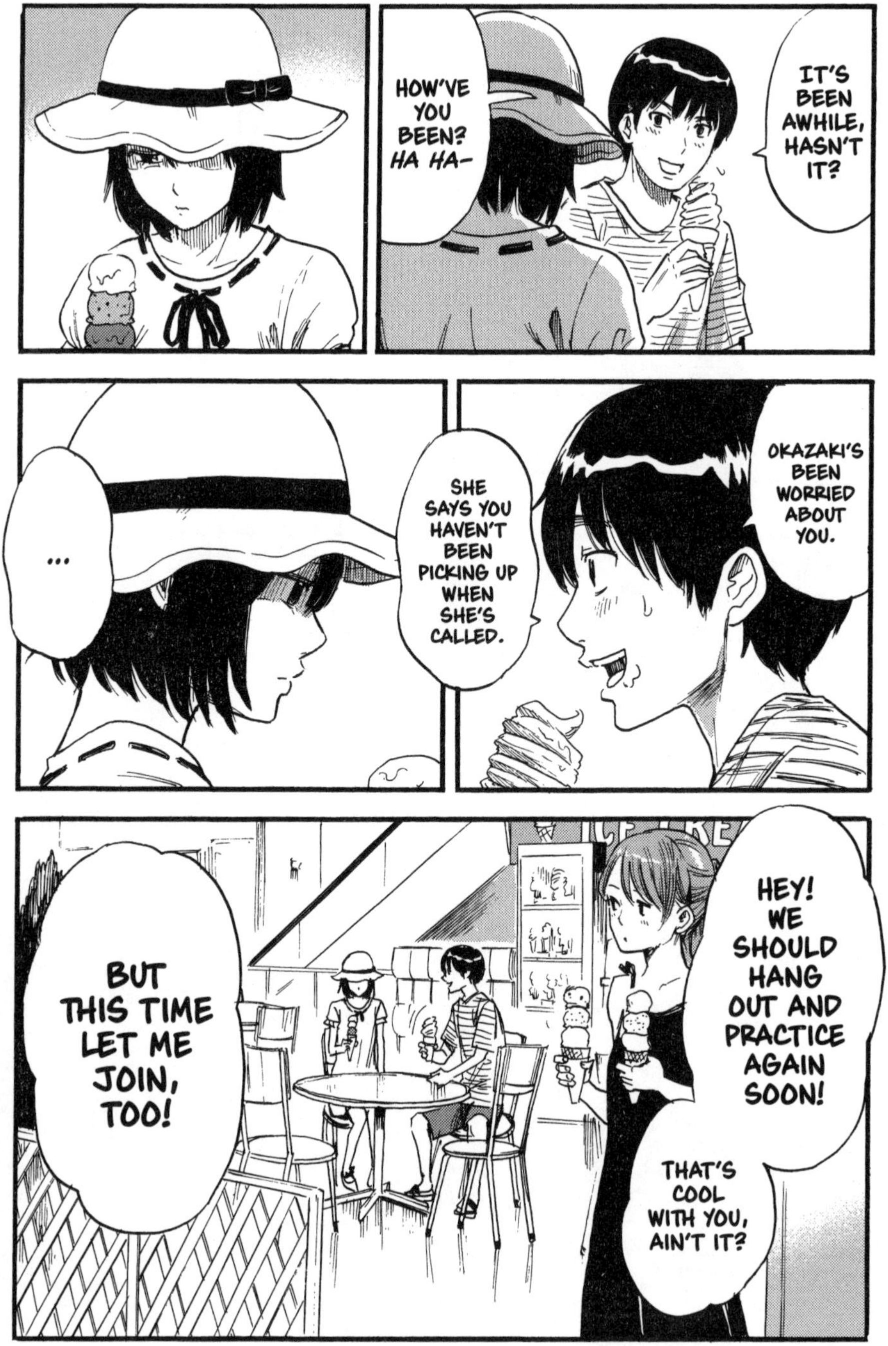
IT'S BEEN AWHILE, HASN'T IT?
HOW'VE YOU BEEN? HA HA-
OKAZAKI'S BEEN WORRIED ABOUT YOU.
SHE SAYS YOU HAVEN'T BEEN PICKING UP WHEN SHE'S CALLED.
...
HEY! WE SHOULD HANG OUT AND PRACTICE AGAIN SOON!
THAT'S COOL WITH YOU, AIN'T IT?
BUT THIS TIME LET ME JOIN, TOO!

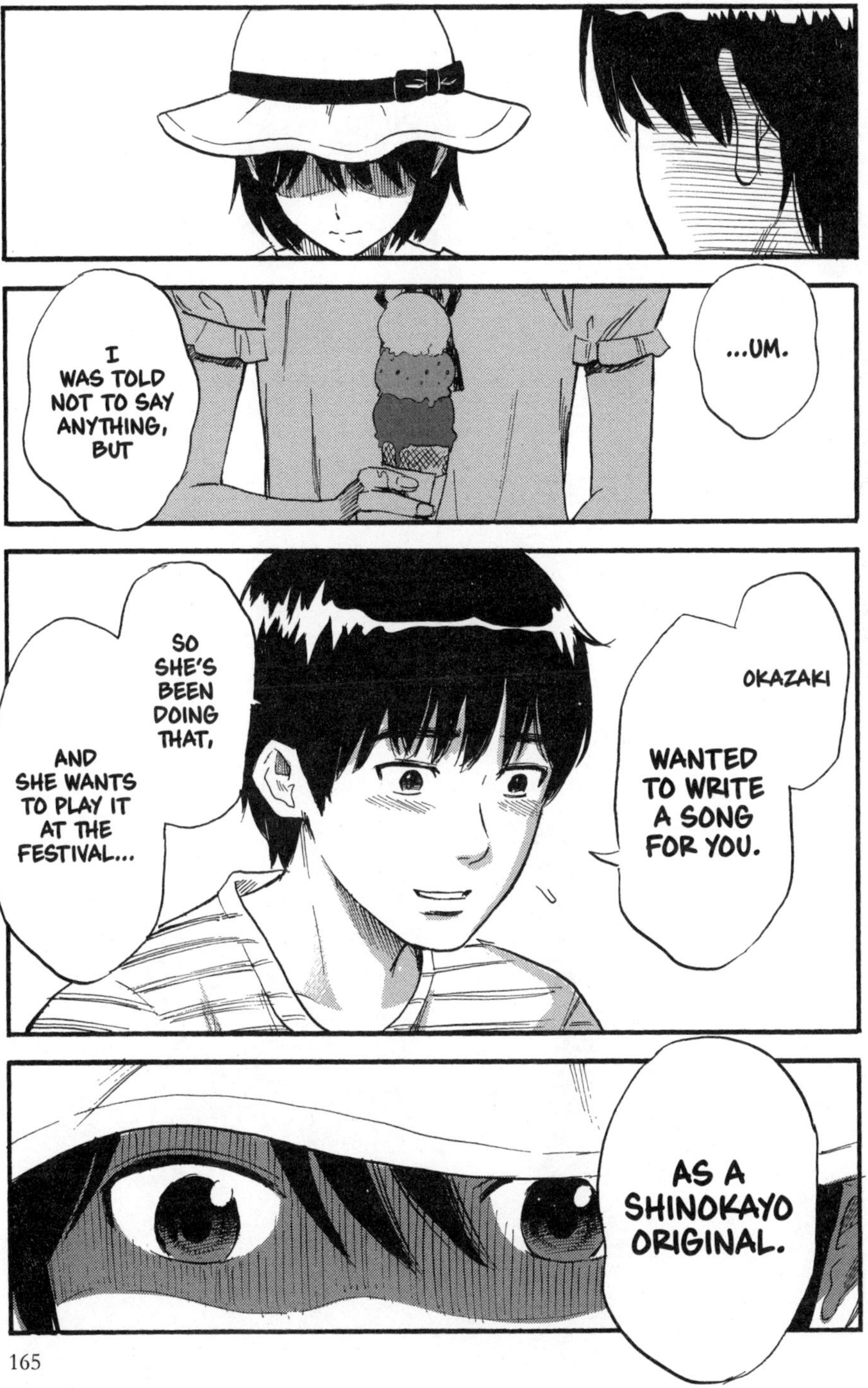
...UM.
I WAS TOLD NOT TO SAY ANYTHING, BUT
OKAZAKI
WANTED TO WRITE A SONG FOR YOU.
SO SHE'S BEEN DOING THAT,
AND SHE WANTS TO PLAY IT AT THE FESTIVAL...
AS A SHINOKAYO ORIGINAL.

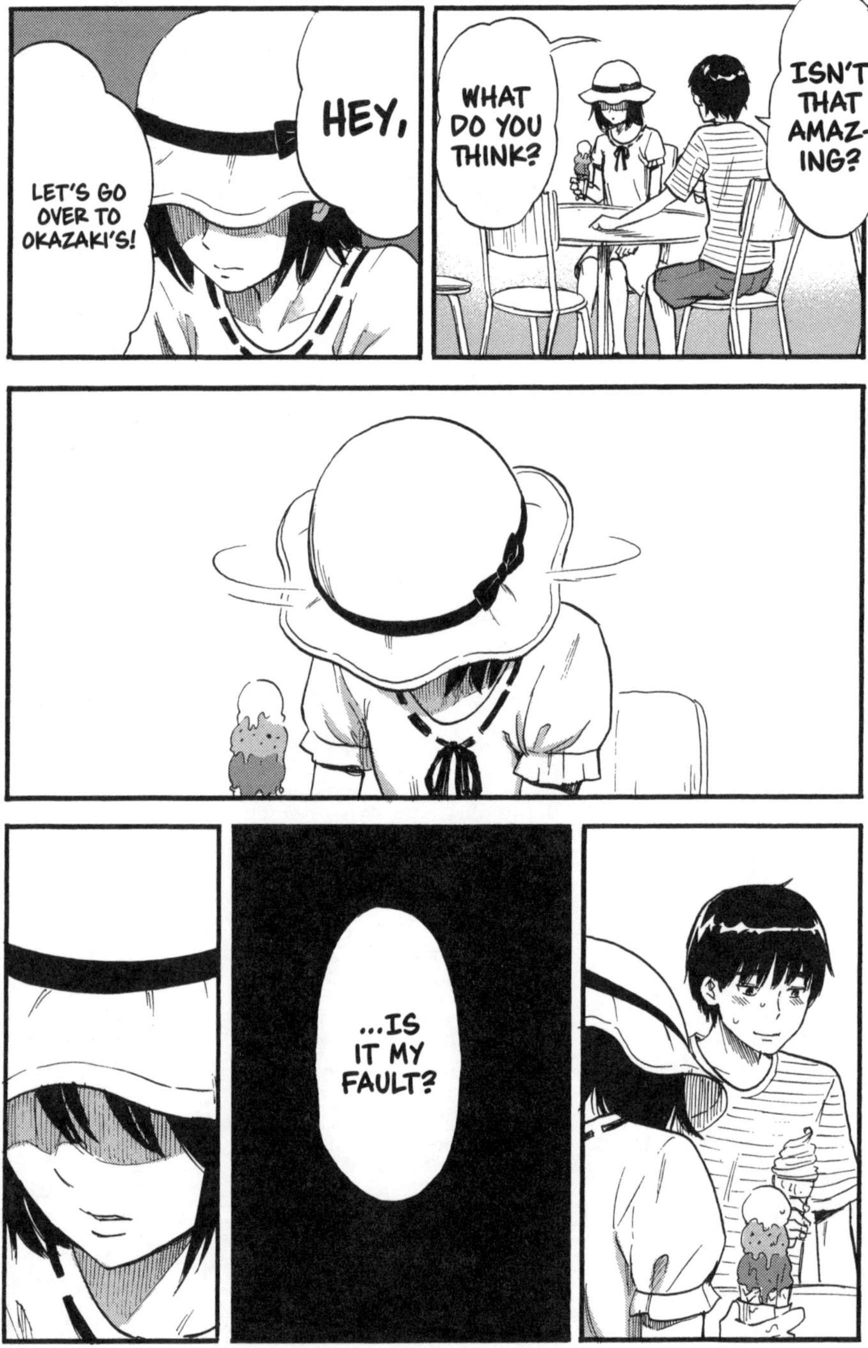
ISN'T THAT AMAZ-ING?
WHAT DO YOU THINK?
HEY,
LET'S GO OVER TO OKAZAKI'S!
...IS IT MY FAULT?

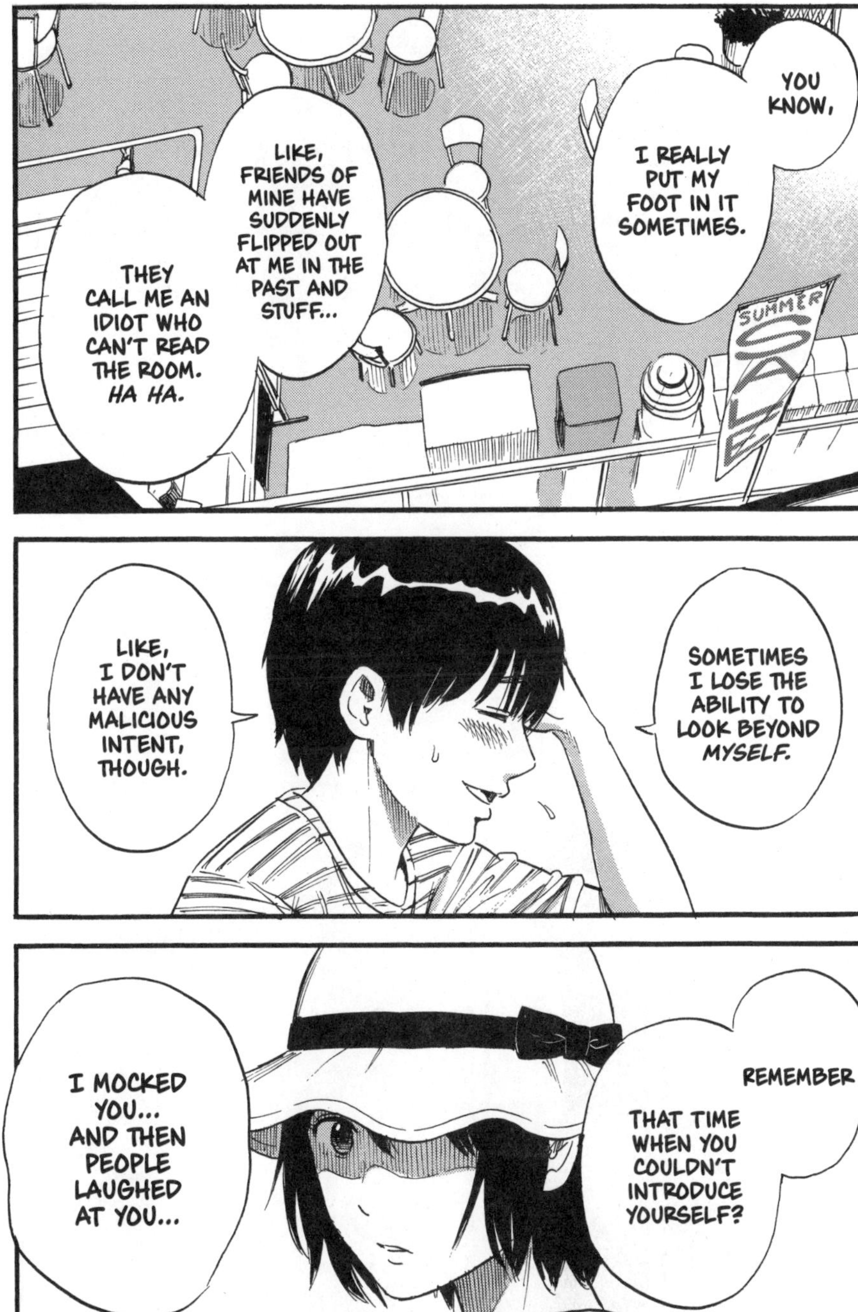
YOU KNOW, I REALLY PUT MY FOOT IN IT SOMETIMES.
SUMMER SALE
LIKE, FRIENDS OF MINE HAVE SUDDENLY FLIPPED OUT AT ME IN THE PAST AND STUFF...
THEY CALL ME AN IDIOT WHO CAN'T READ THE ROOM. *HA HA.*
SOMETIMES I LOSE THE ABILITY TO LOOK BEYOND *MYSELF.*
LIKE, I DON'T HAVE ANY MALICIOUS INTENT, THOUGH.
REMEMBER THAT TIME WHEN YOU COULDN'T INTRODUCE YOURSELF?
I MOCKED YOU... AND THEN PEOPLE LAUGHED AT YOU...

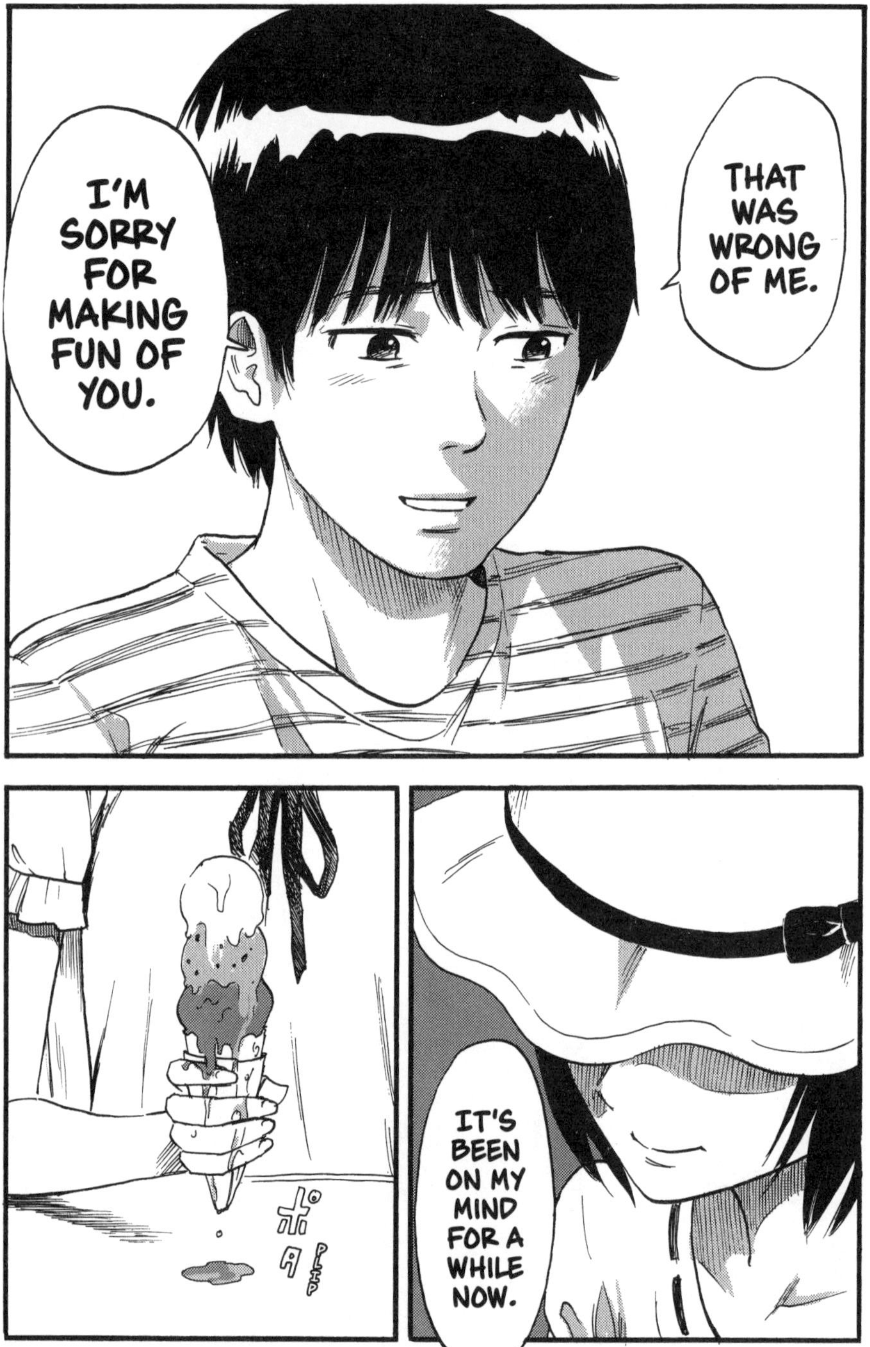
THAT WAS WRONG OF ME.
I'M SORRY FOR MAKING FUN OF YOU.
IT'S BEEN ON MY MIND FOR A WHILE NOW.
ポタ
PLIP

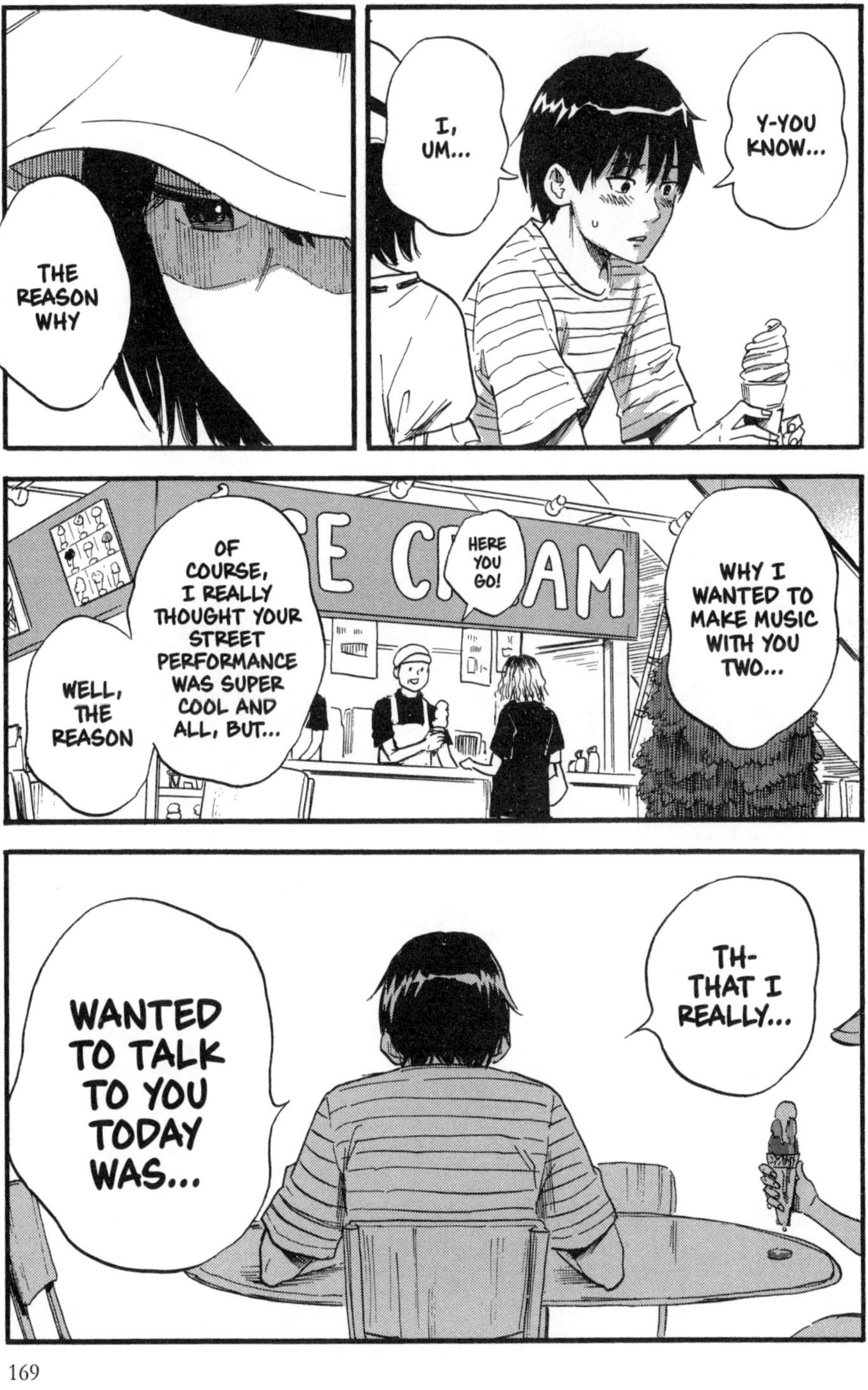
Y-YOU KNOW...
I, UM...
THE REASON WHY
WHY I WANTED TO MAKE MUSIC WITH YOU TWO...
HERE YOU GO!
OF COURSE, I REALLY THOUGHT YOUR STREET PERFORMANCE WAS SUPER COOL AND ALL, BUT...
WELL, THE REASON
TH-THAT I REALLY...
WANTED TO TALK TO YOU TODAY WAS...

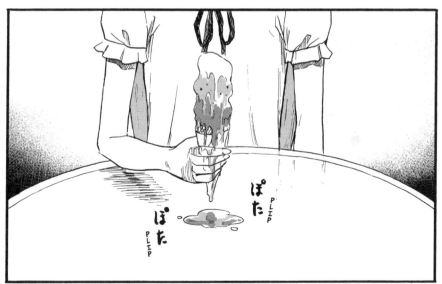

ぽた
PLIP

ぽた
PLIP

ボタッ
PLOP

エ—

UMM... BE-
CAUSE
...

WELL...
OSHIMA

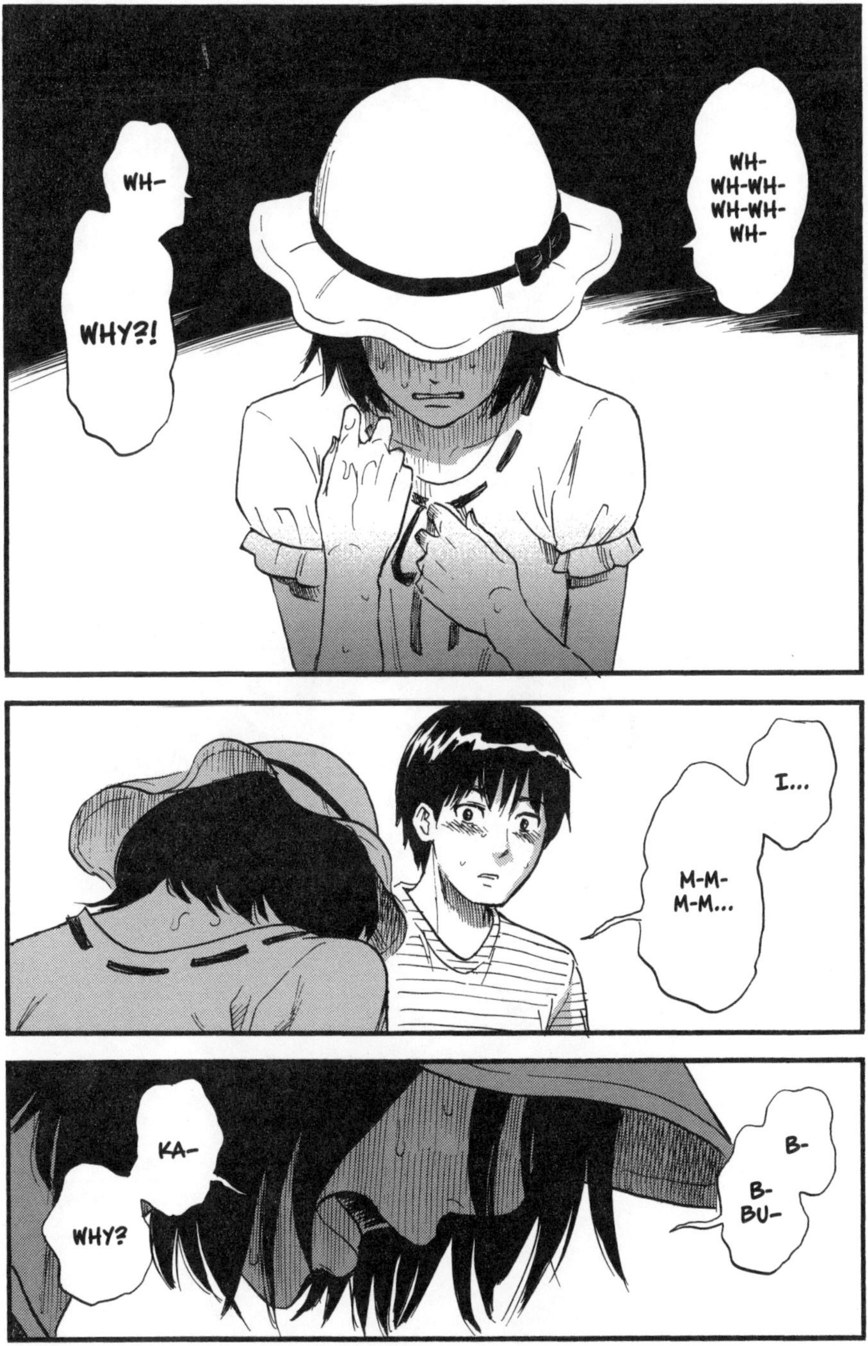
WH- WH-WH- WH-WH- WH-
WH- WHY?!
I... M-M- M-M...
B- B- BU-
KA- WHY?

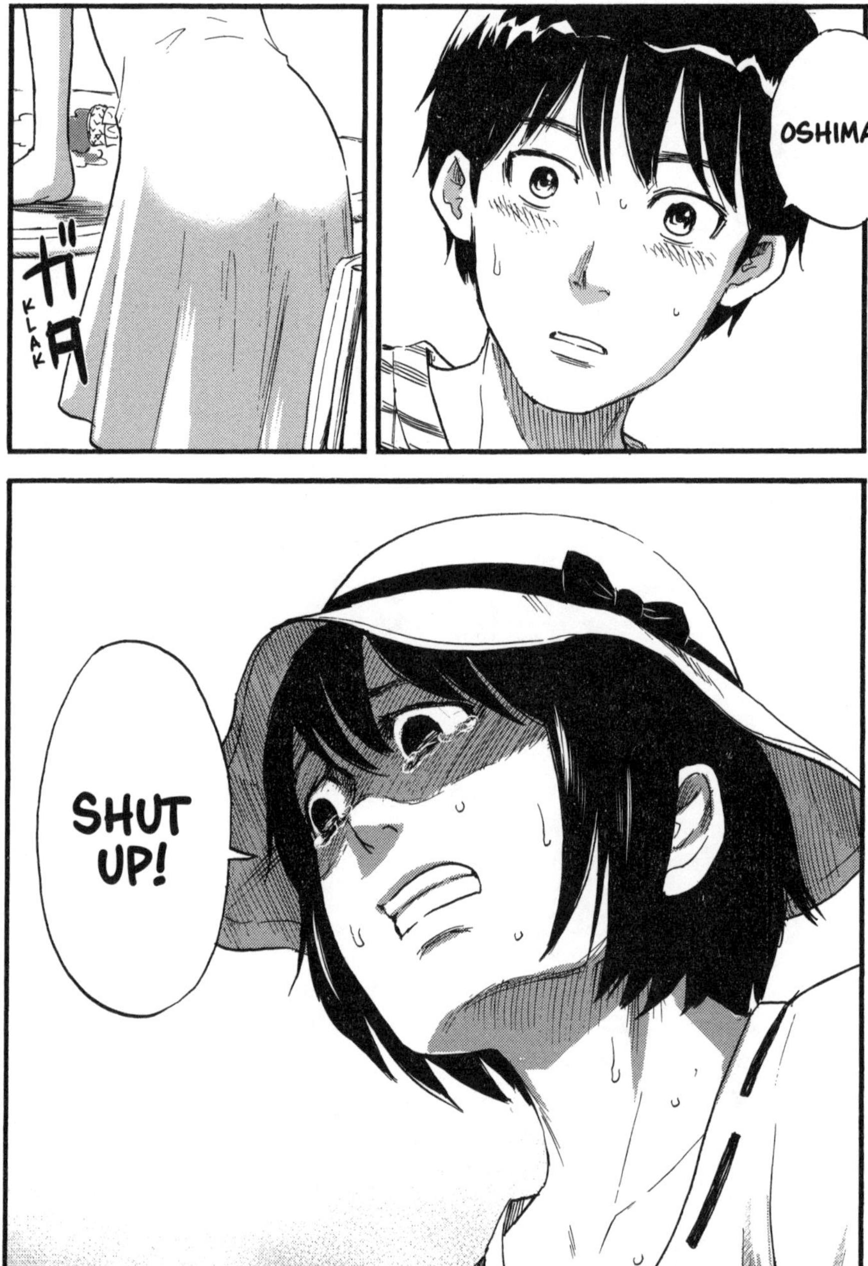
OSHIMA?
ガタ
KLAK
SHUT UP!

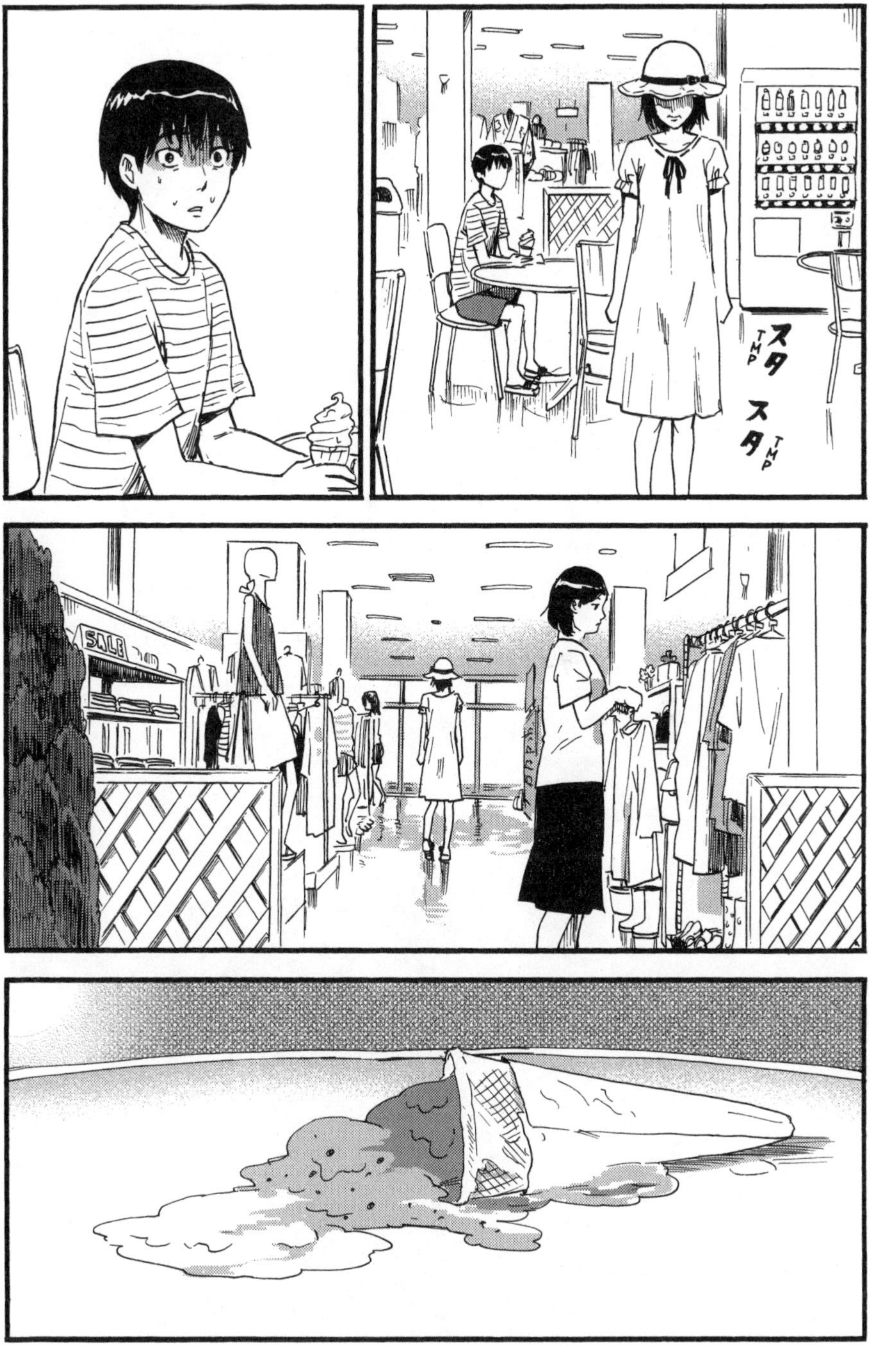
スタ TMP
スタ TMP

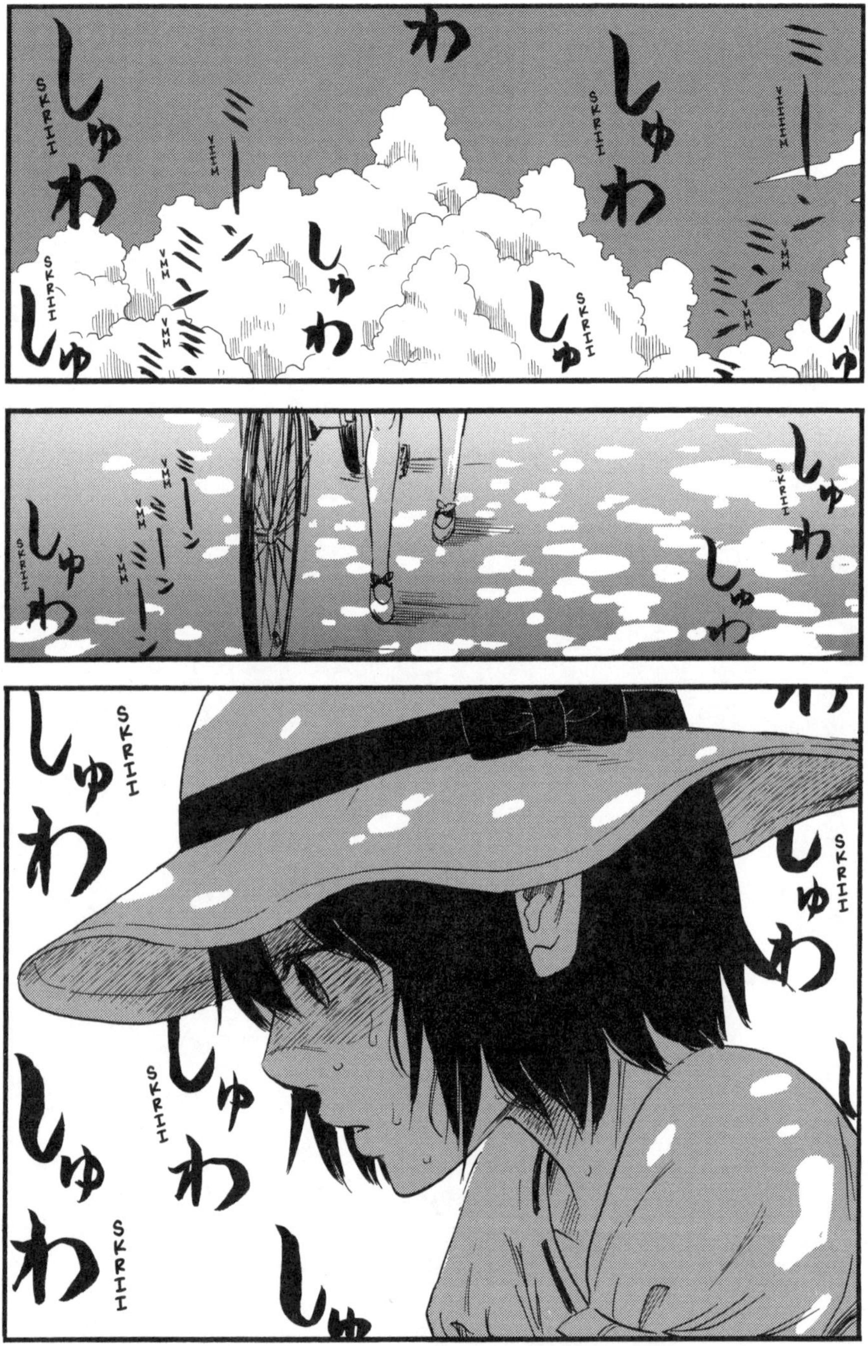
ミーン
VIIIIM
ミン
VMM
ミン
VMM
しゅ
しゅわ
SKRII
わ
しゅ
SKRII
しゅわ
ミーン
VIIM
ミン
VMM
ミン
VMM
しゅわ
SKRII
しゅ
SKRII
しゅわ
SKRII
しゅわ
ミーン
VMM
ミーン
VMM
ミーン
VMM
しゅわ
SKRII
しゅわ
SKRII
しゅ
しゅわ
SKRII
しゅ
しゅわ
SKRII
しゅわ
SKRII

Chapter 10
I Am

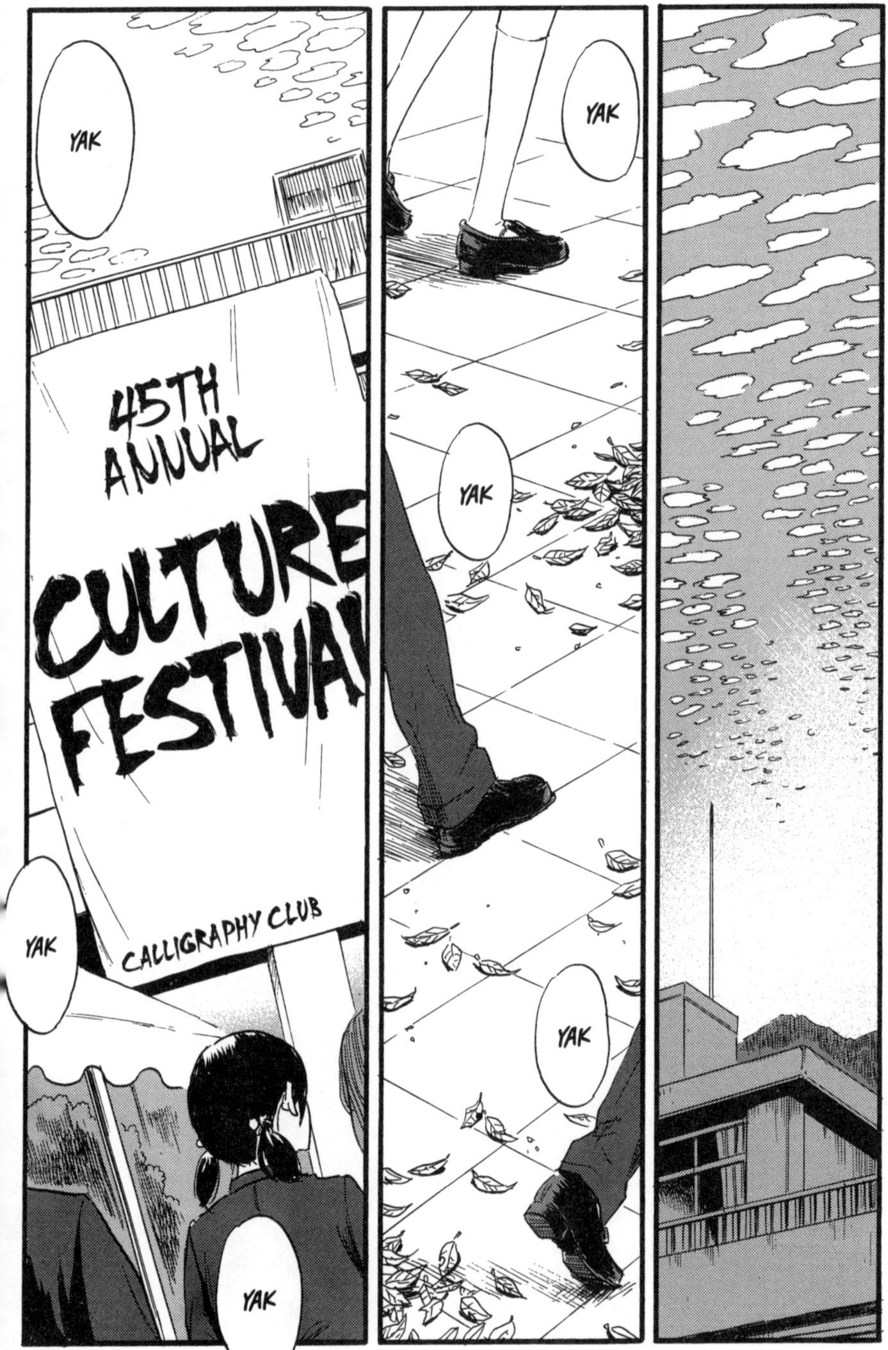
YAK
YAK
YAK
YAK
45TH ANNUAL
CULTURE FESTIVAL
CALLIGRAPHY CLUB
YAK
YAK

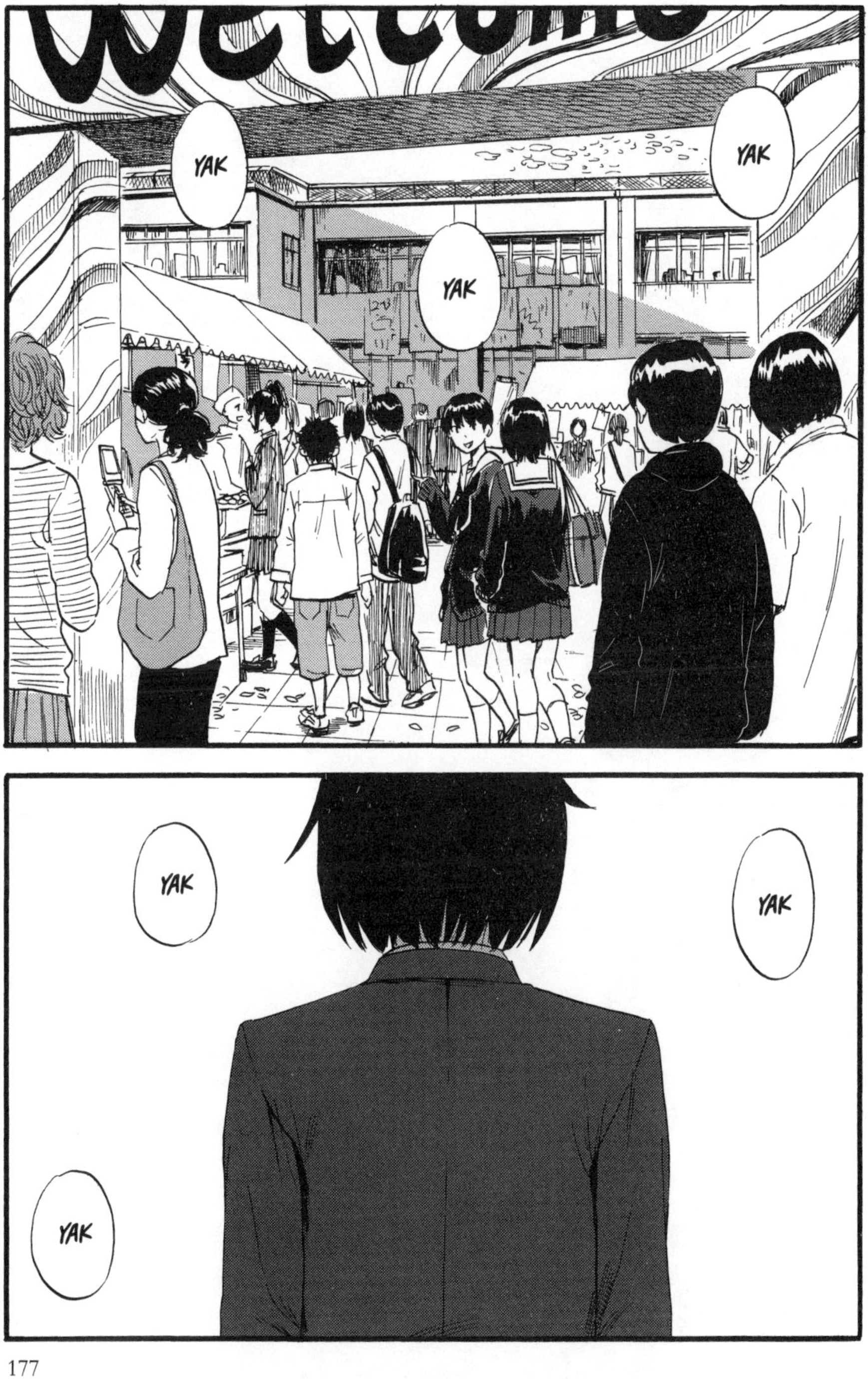
YAK
YAK
YAK
YAK
YAK
YAK

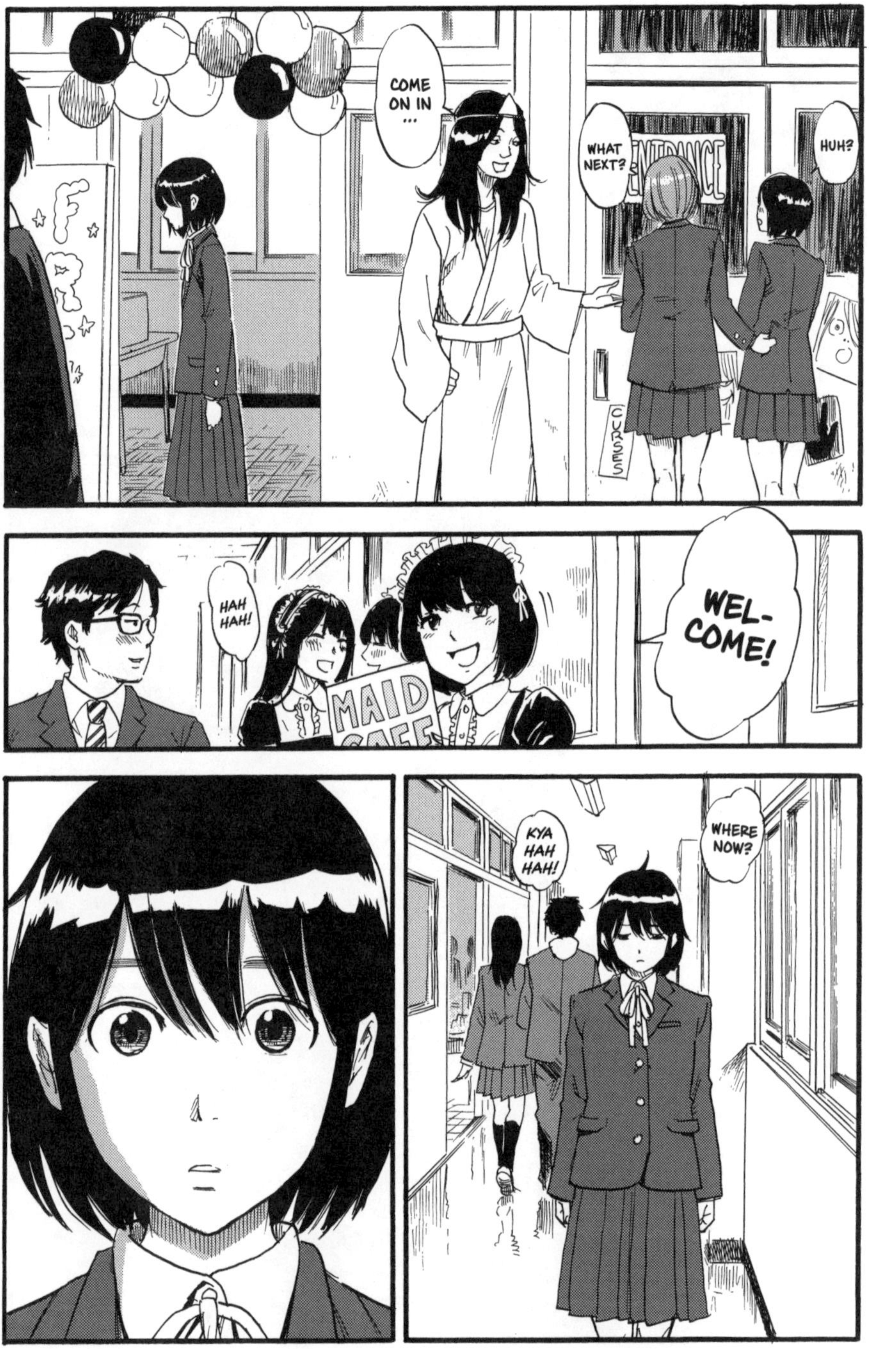
HUH?
WHAT NEXT?
ENTRANCE
CURSES
COME ON IN ...
WEL-COME!
MAID
HAH HAH!
WHERE NOW?
KYA HAH HAH!

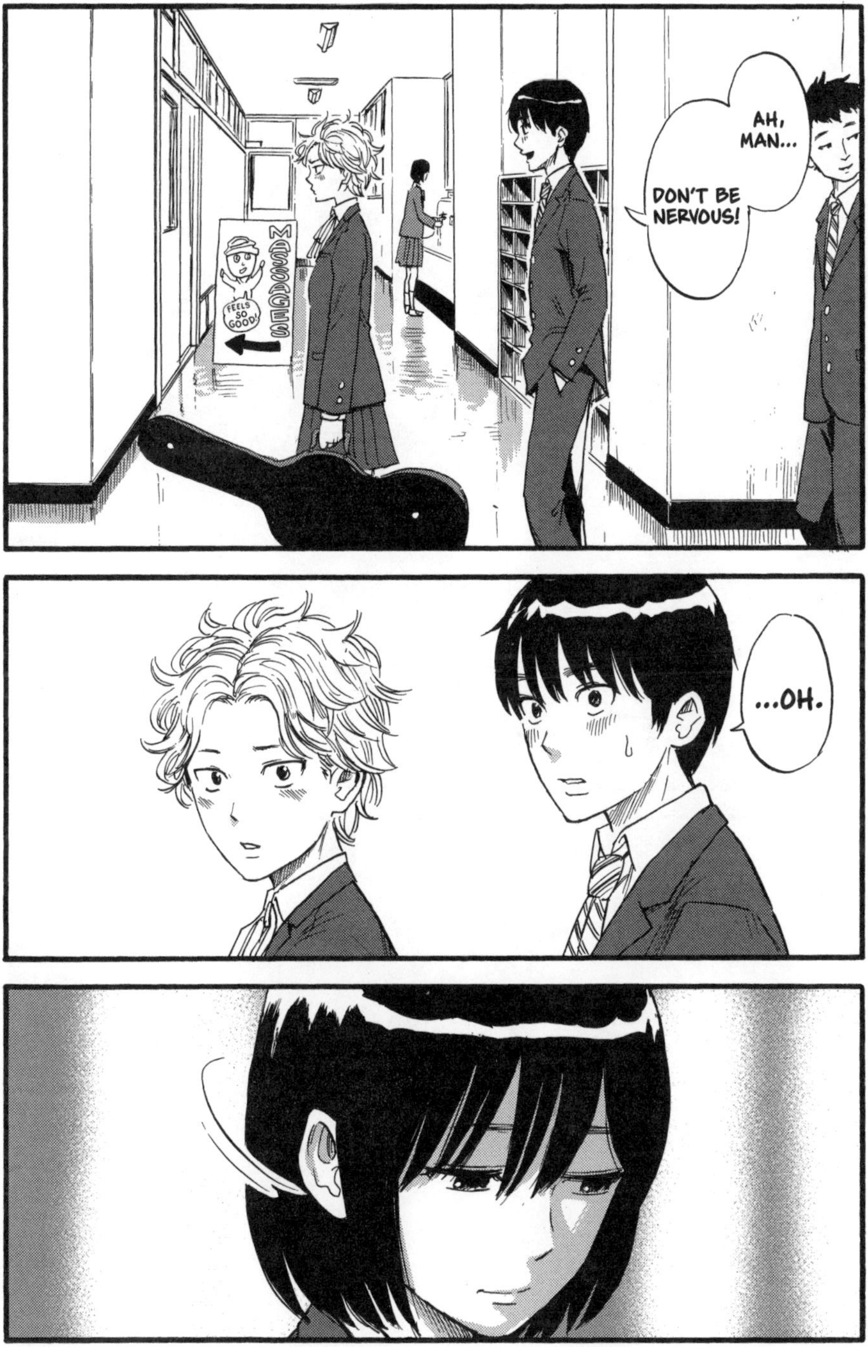
AH, MAN...
DON'T BE NERVOUS!
MASSAGES
FEELS SO GOOD!
...OH.

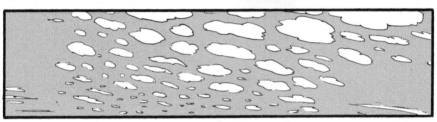

JYAN
JYAAN
ZMM
ZMM
ZMM

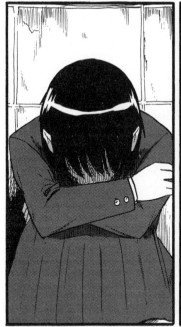

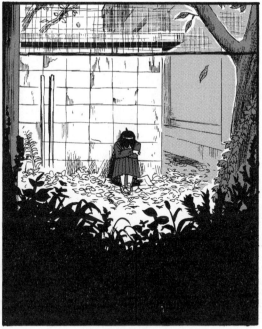

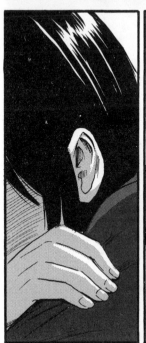

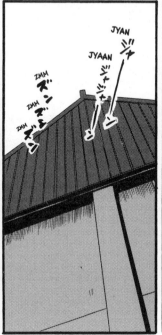

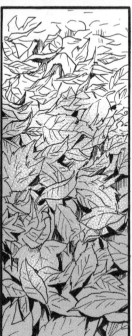

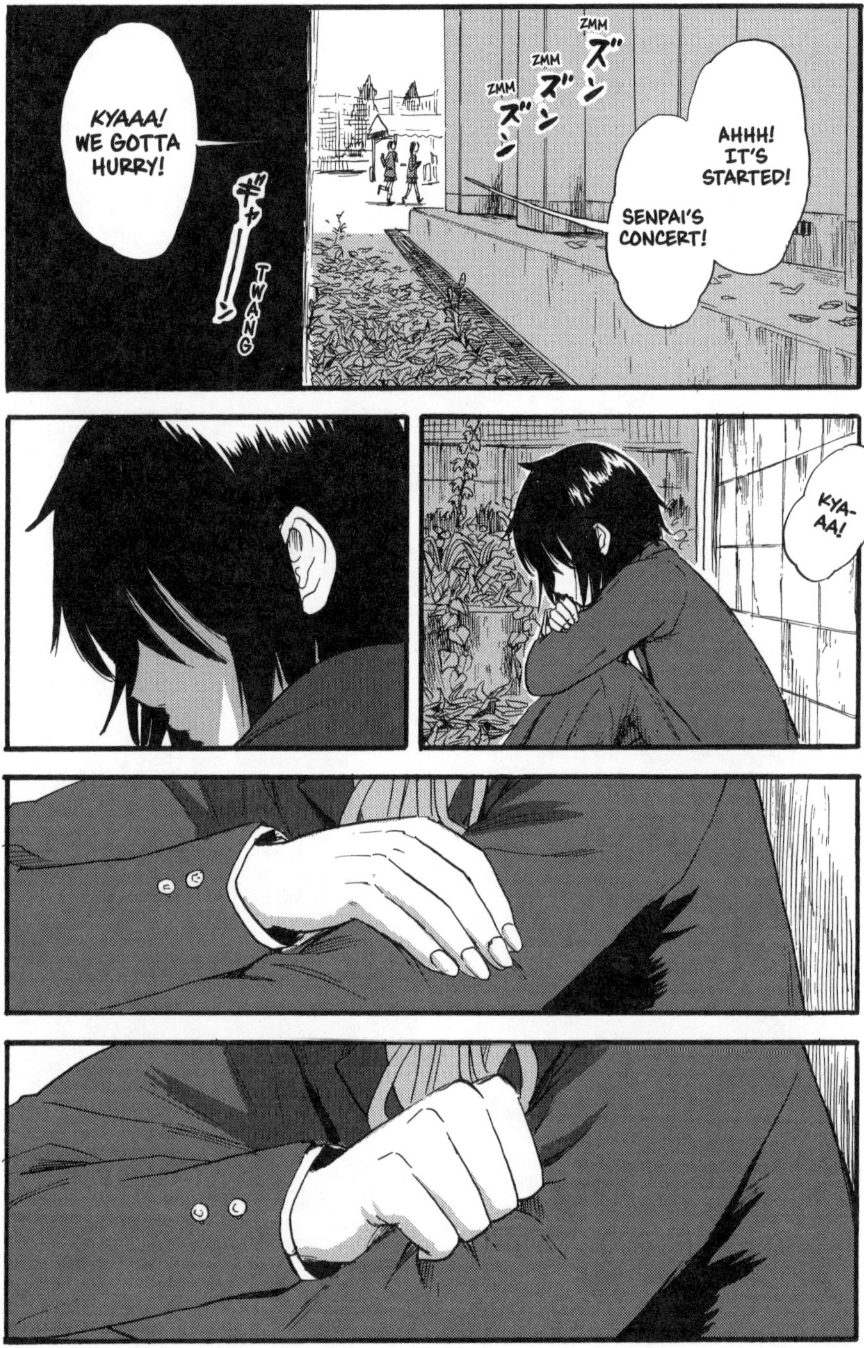
AHHH! IT'S STARTED!
SENPAI'S CONCERT!
ZMM ズン
ZMM ズン
ZMM ズン
KYAAA! WE GOTTA HURRY!
ギャーン
TWANG
KYA-AA!

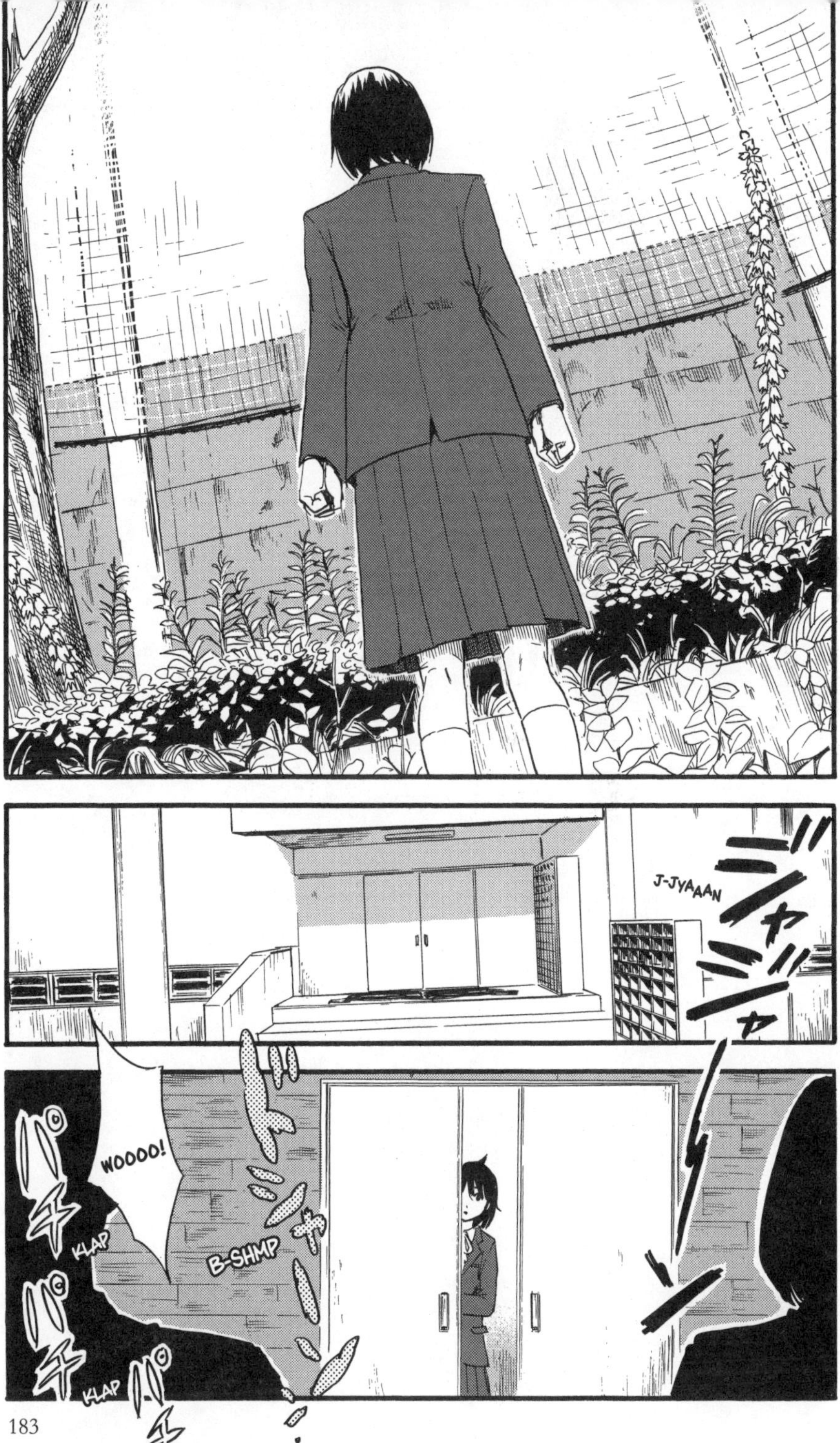
ジャジャーン
J-JYAAAN
B-SHMP
WOOOO!
パチ
KLAP
パチ
KLAP
パチ

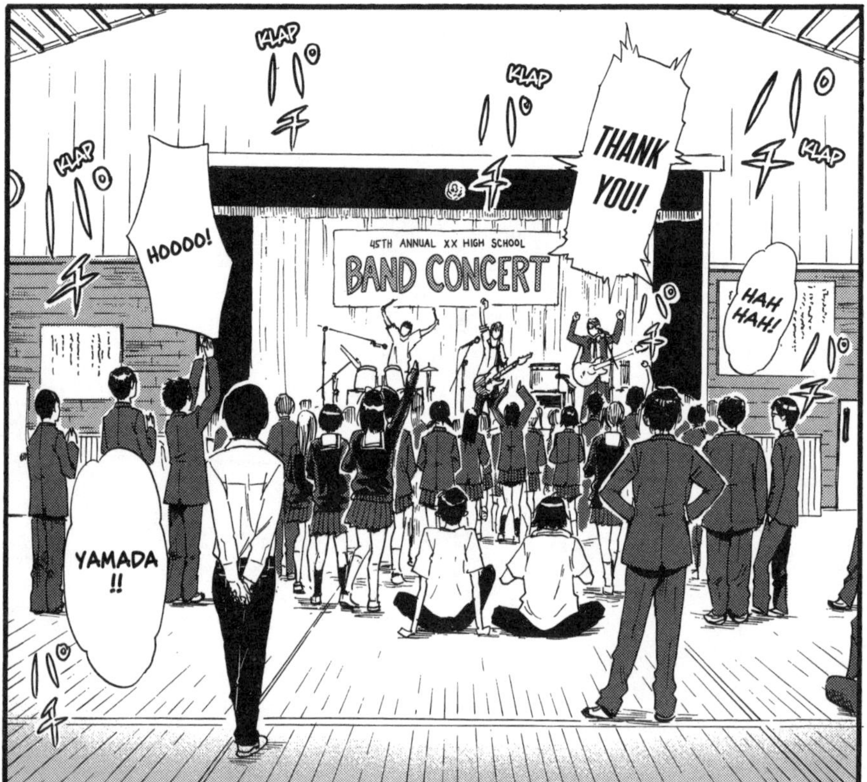
KLAP
KLAP
THANK YOU!
KLAP
KLAP
HAH HAH!
45TH ANNUAL XX HIGH SCHOOL
BAND CONCERT
HOOOO!
YAMADA!!

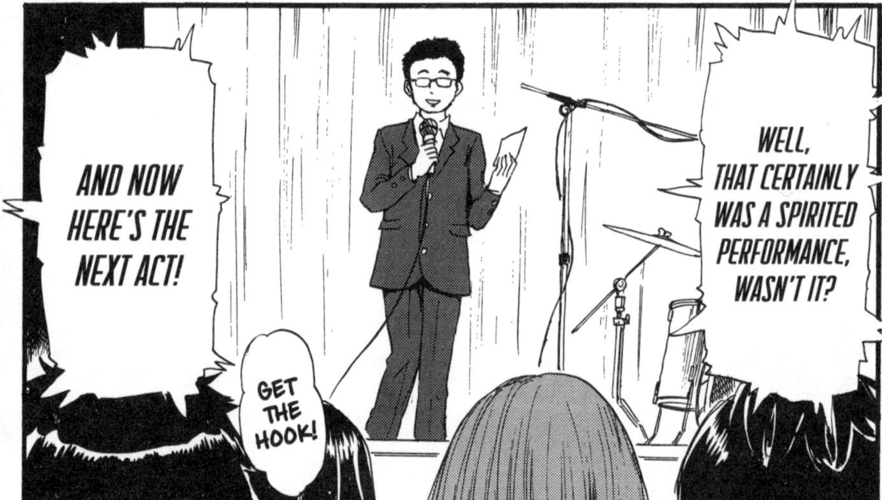
WELL, THAT CERTAINLY WAS A SPIRITED PERFORMANCE, WASN'T IT?
AND NOW HERE'S THE NEXT ACT!
GET THE HOOK!

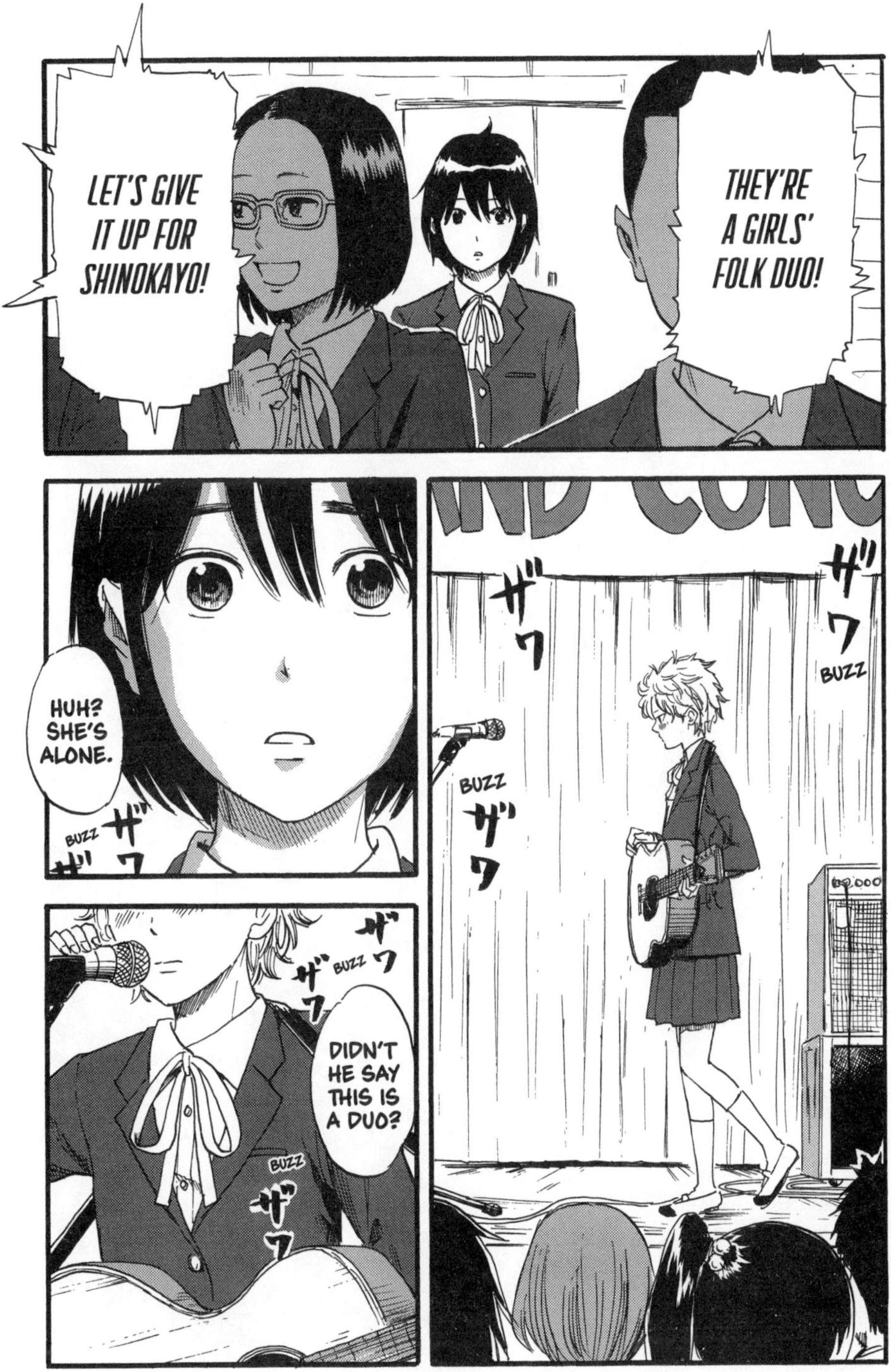
THEY'RE A GIRLS' FOLK DUO!
LET'S GIVE IT UP FOR SHINOKAYO!
ザワ
ザワ
BUZZ
BUZZ
ザワ
HUH? SHE'S ALONE.
BUZZ
ザワ
ザワ
BUZZ
ザワ
DIDN'T HE SAY THIS IS A DUO?
BUZZ
ザワ

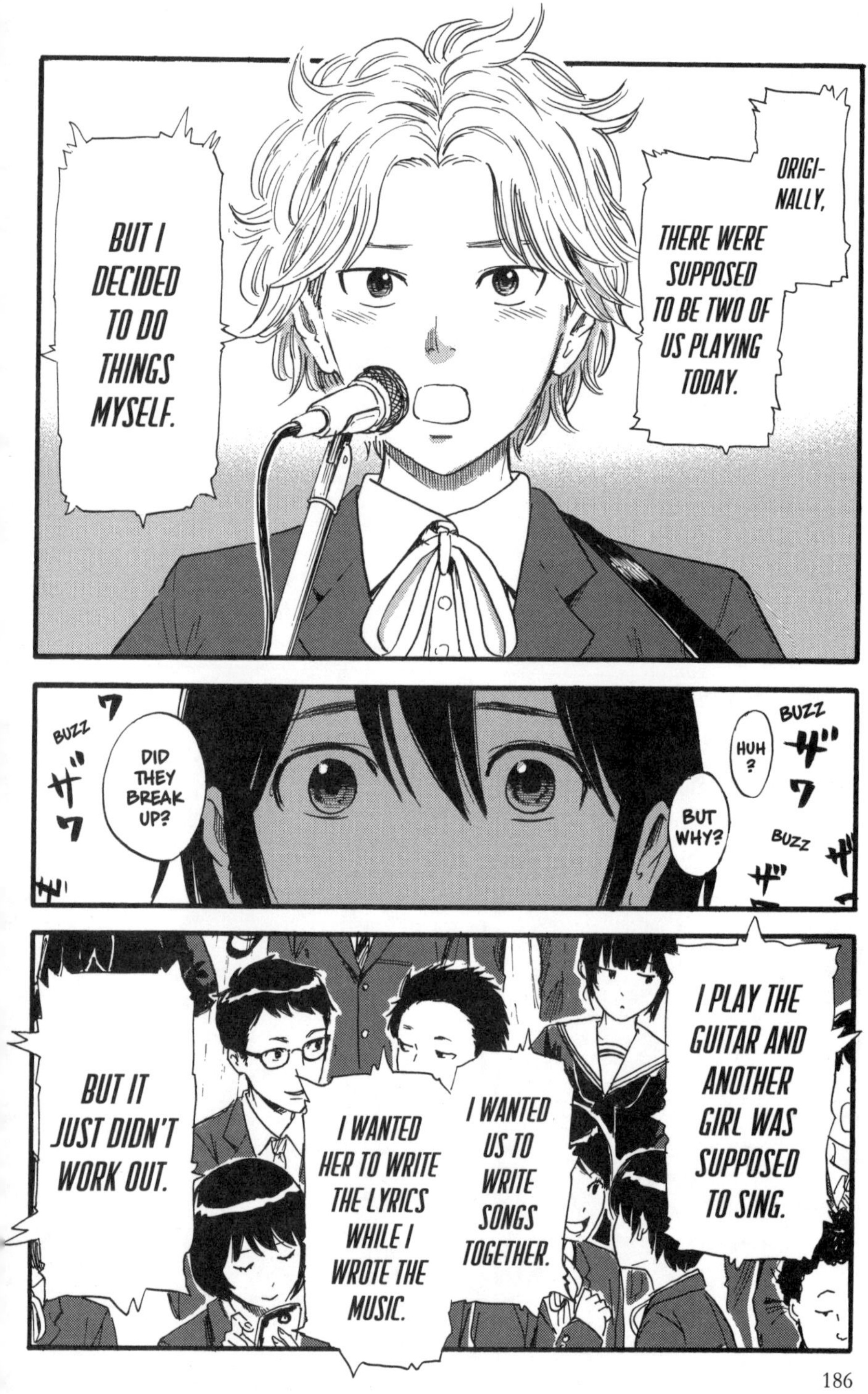
ORIGI-NALLY, THERE WERE SUPPOSED TO BE TWO OF US PLAYING TODAY.
BUT I DECIDED TO DO THINGS MYSELF.
BUZZ
ザワ
HUH?
BUT WHY?
BUZZ
ザワ
DID THEY BREAK UP?
BUZZ
ザワ
I PLAY THE GUITAR AND ANOTHER GIRL WAS SUPPOSED TO SING.
I WANTED US TO WRITE SONGS TOGETHER.
I WANTED HER TO WRITE THE LYRICS WHILE I WROTE THE MUSIC.
BUT IT JUST DIDN'T WORK OUT.

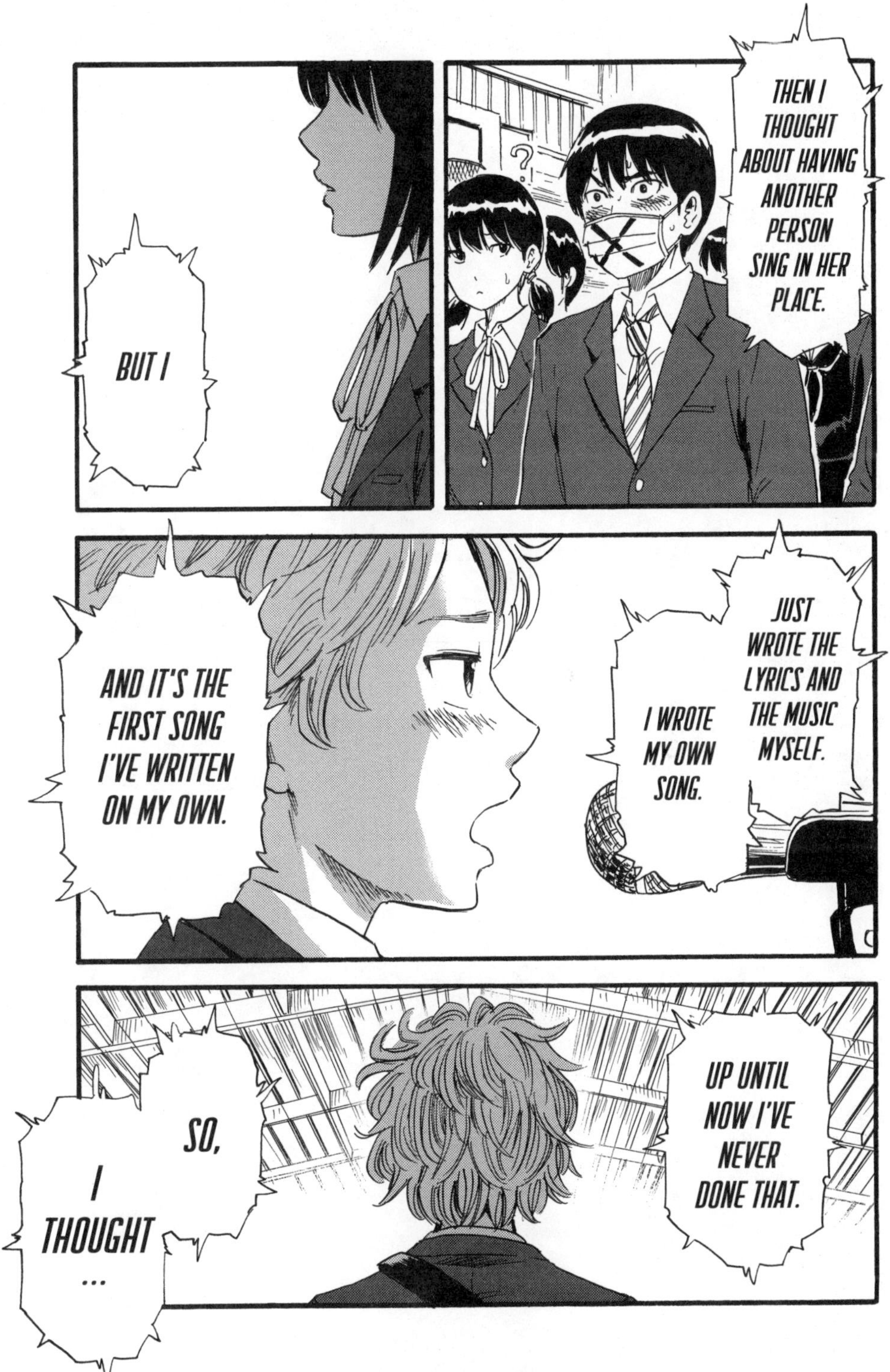
THEN I THOUGHT ABOUT HAVING ANOTHER PERSON SING IN HER PLACE.
BUT I
JUST WROTE THE LYRICS AND THE MUSIC MYSELF.
I WROTE MY OWN SONG.
AND IT'S THE FIRST SONG I'VE WRITTEN ON MY OWN.
UP UNTIL NOW I'VE NEVER DONE THAT.
SO,
I THOUGHT ...

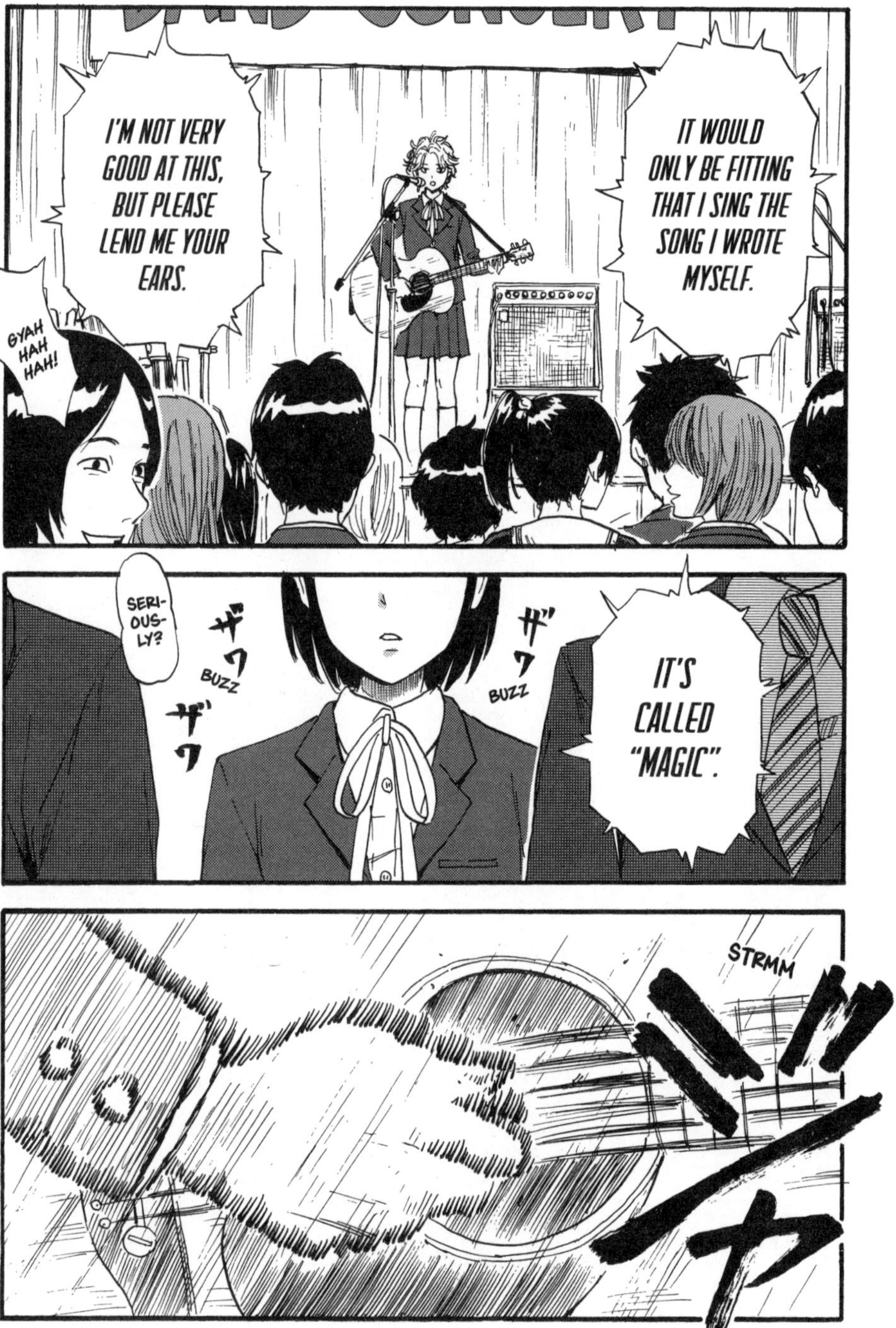
IT WOULD ONLY BE FITTING THAT I SING THE SONG I WROTE MYSELF.
I'M NOT VERY GOOD AT THIS, BUT PLEASE LEND ME YOUR EARS.
GYAH HAH HAH!
IT'S CALLED "MAGIC".
ザワ
BUZZ
ザワ
BUZZ
SERI-OUS-LY?
STRMM

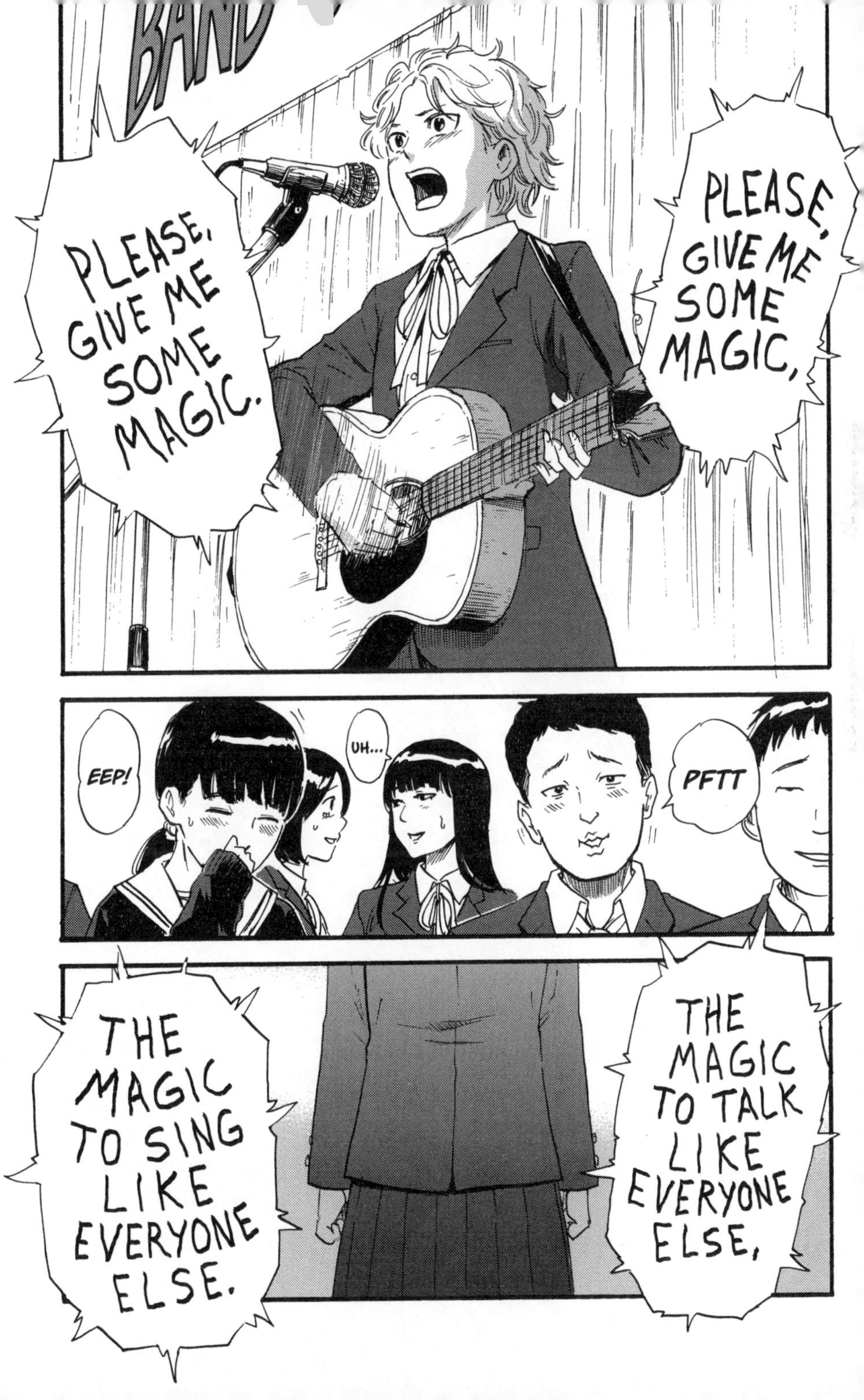
BAND
PLEASE, GIVE ME SOME MAGIC,
PLEASE, GIVE ME SOME MAGIC.
PFTT
UH...
EEP!
THE MAGIC TO TALK LIKE EVERYONE ELSE,
THE MAGIC TO SING LIKE EVERYONE ELSE.

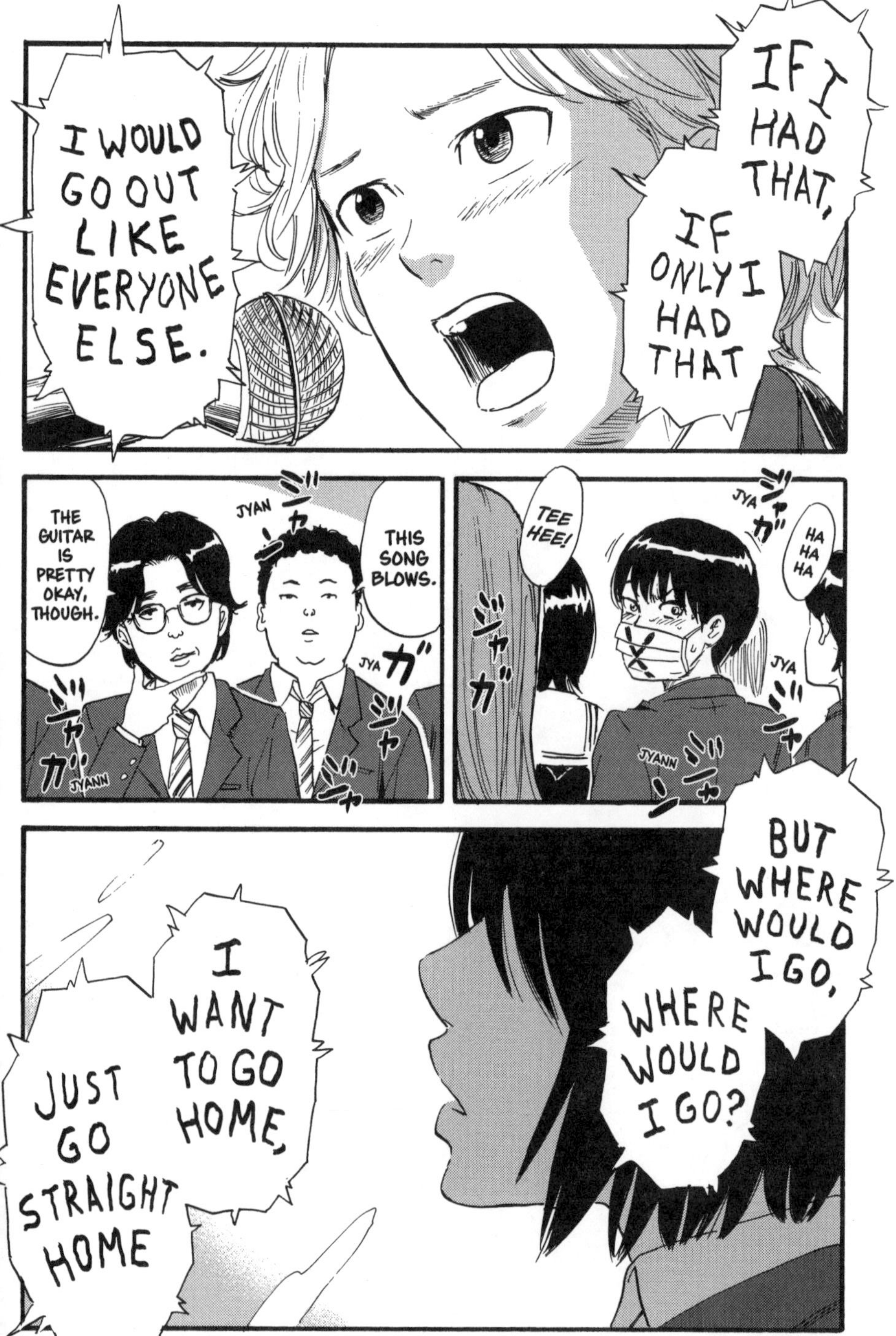

IF I HAD THAT,
IF ONLY I HAD THAT
I WOULD GO OUT LIKE EVERYONE ELSE.
JYA
HA HA HA
TEE HEE!
JYA
JYANN
THIS SONG BLOWS.
JYAN
THE GUITAR IS PRETTY OKAY, THOUGH.
JYA
JYANN
BUT WHERE WOULD I GO,
WHERE WOULD I GO?
I WANT TO GO HOME,
JUST GO STRAIGHT HOME

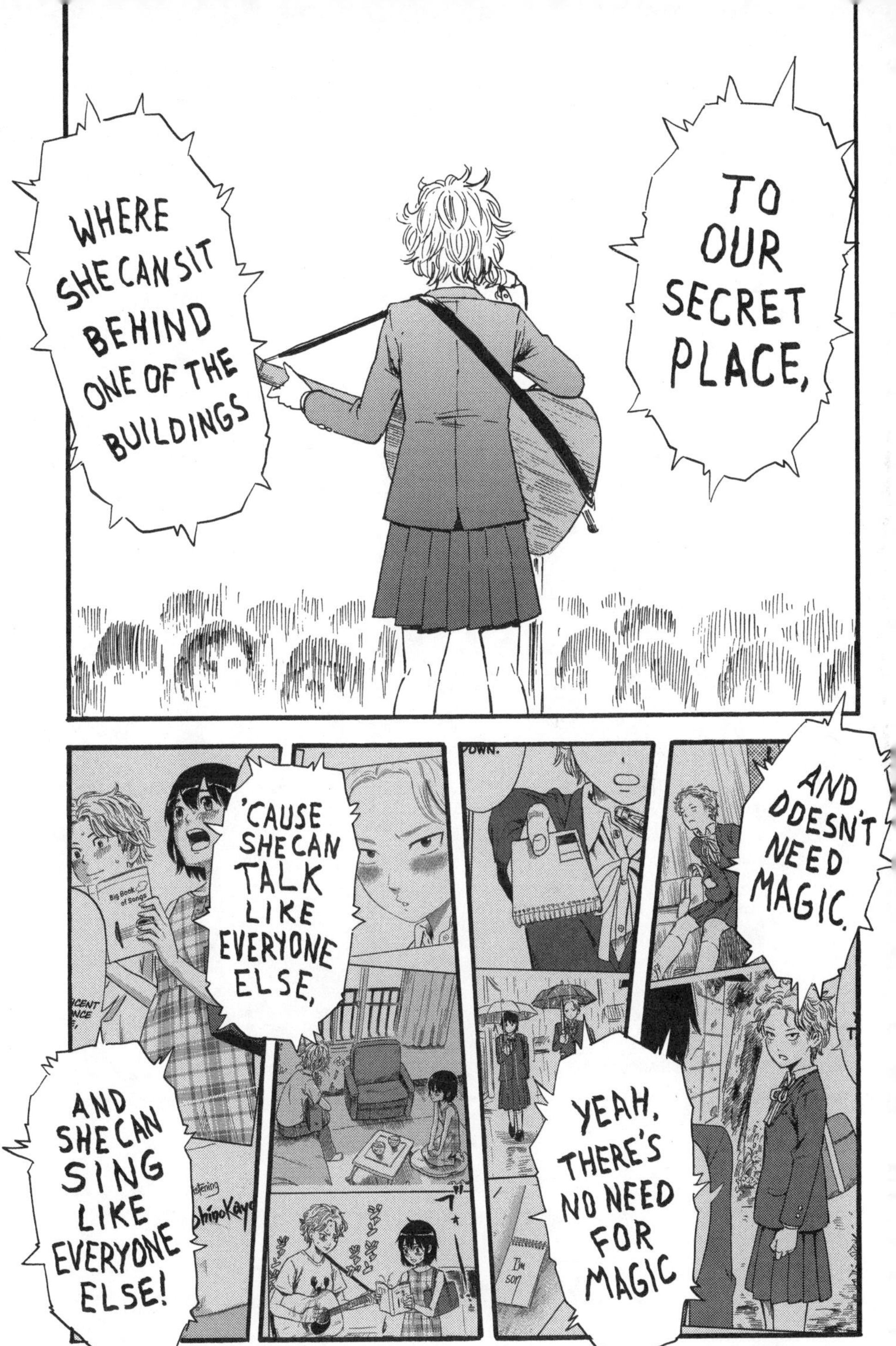
TO OUR SECRET PLACE,
WHERE SHE CAN SIT BEHIND ONE OF THE BUILDINGS
AND DOESN'T NEED MAGIC.
'CAUSE SHE CAN TALK LIKE EVERYONE ELSE,
Big Book of Songs
YEAH, THERE'S NO NEED FOR MAGIC
AND SHE CAN SING LIKE EVERYONE ELSE!

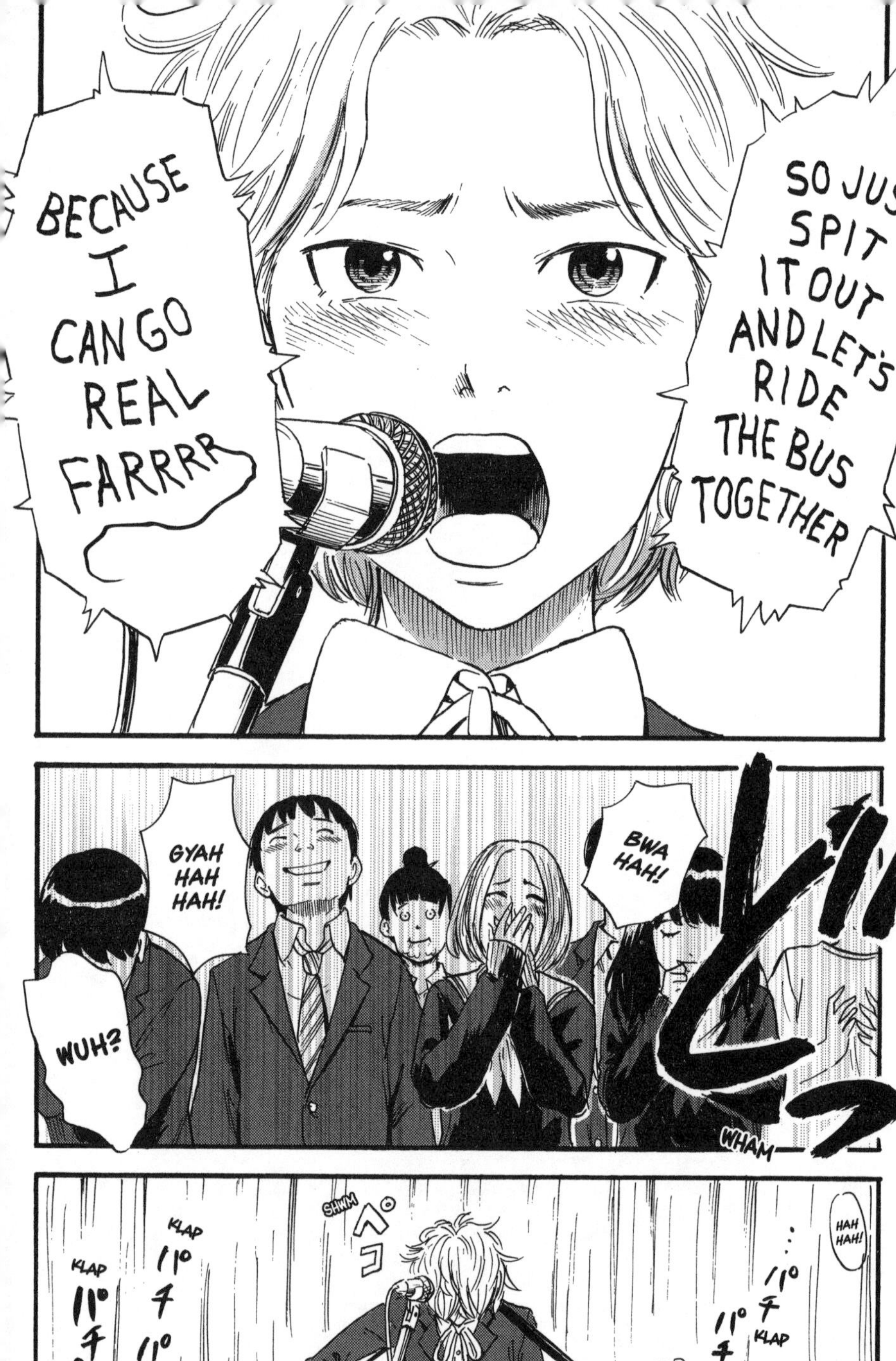
SO JUST SPIT IT OUT AND LET'S RIDE THE BUS TOGETHER
BECAUSE I CAN GO REAL FARRRR
ドッ
WHAM
BWA HAH!
GYAH HAH HAH!
WUH?
HAH HAH!
…
パチパチ
KLAP
ペコ
SHWM
KLAP
パチパチ
KLAP
パチパチパチ

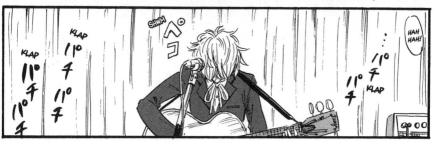

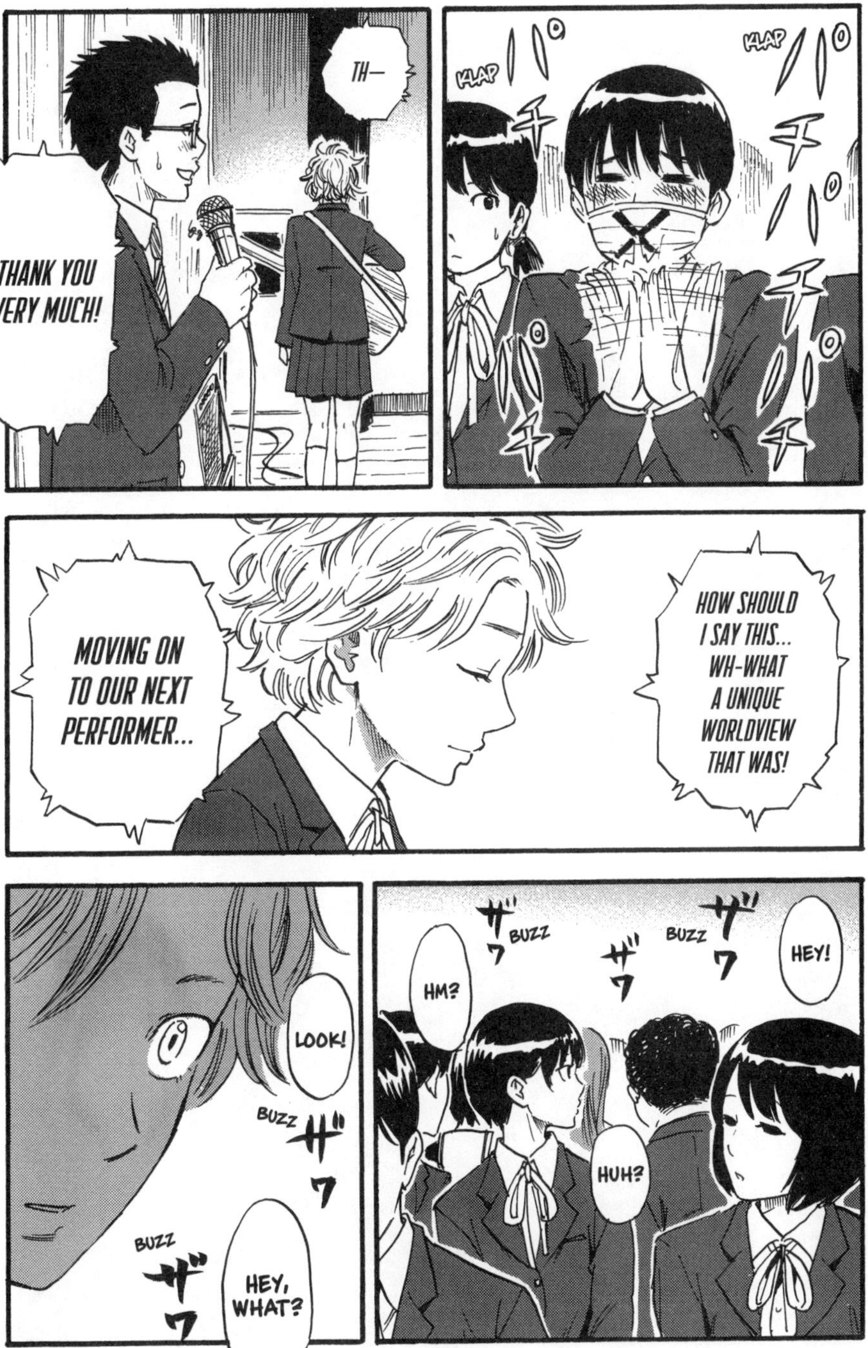
KLAP
KLAP
TH—
THANK YOU VERY MUCH!
HOW SHOULD I SAY THIS... WH-WHAT A UNIQUE WORLDVIEW THAT WAS!
MOVING ON TO OUR NEXT PERFORMER...
HEY!
BUZZ
BUZZ
HM?
HUH?
LOOK!
BUZZ
BUZZ
HEY, WHAT?

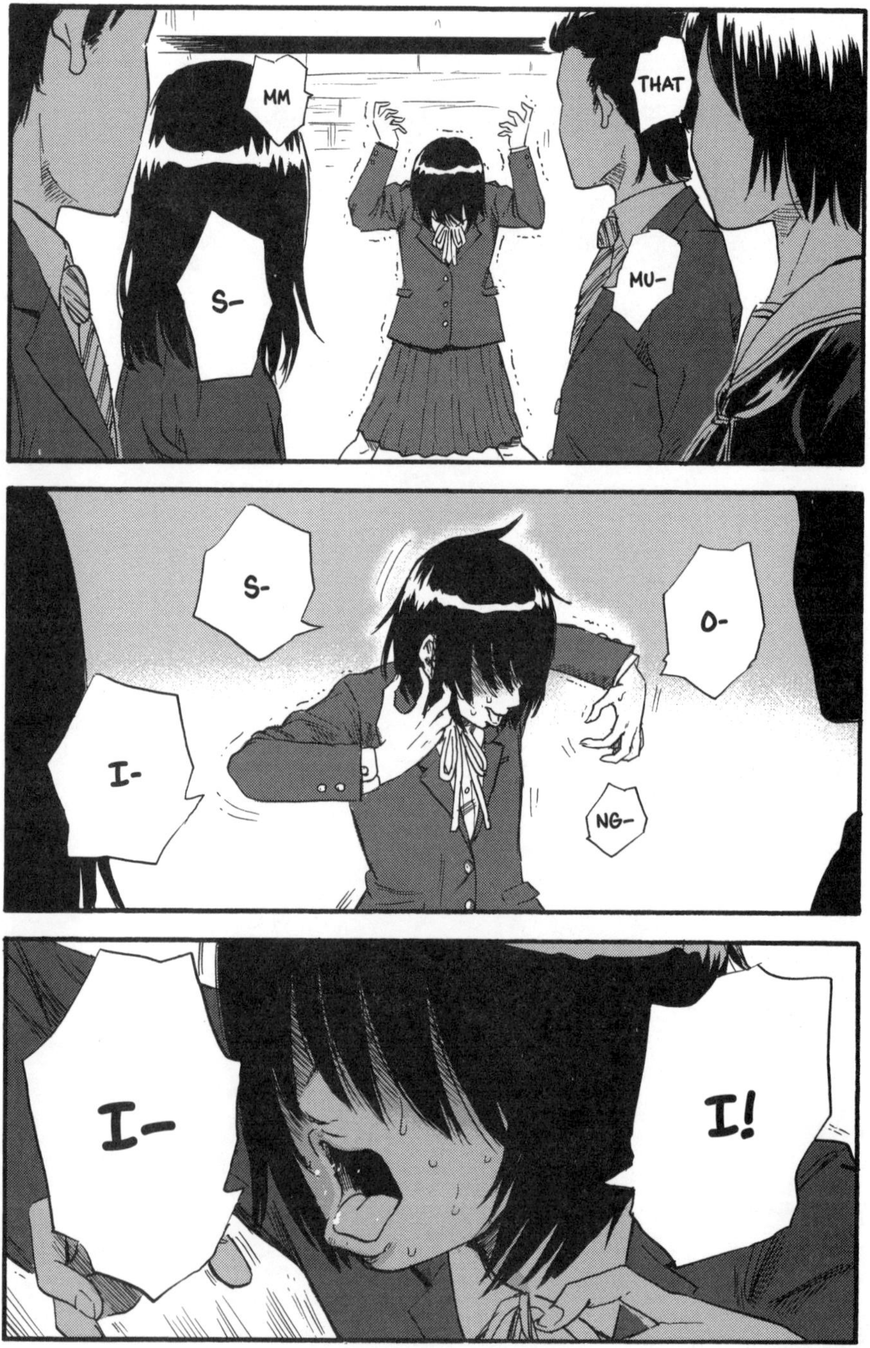
THAT
MU-
MM
S-
O-
NG-
S-
I-
I!
I-

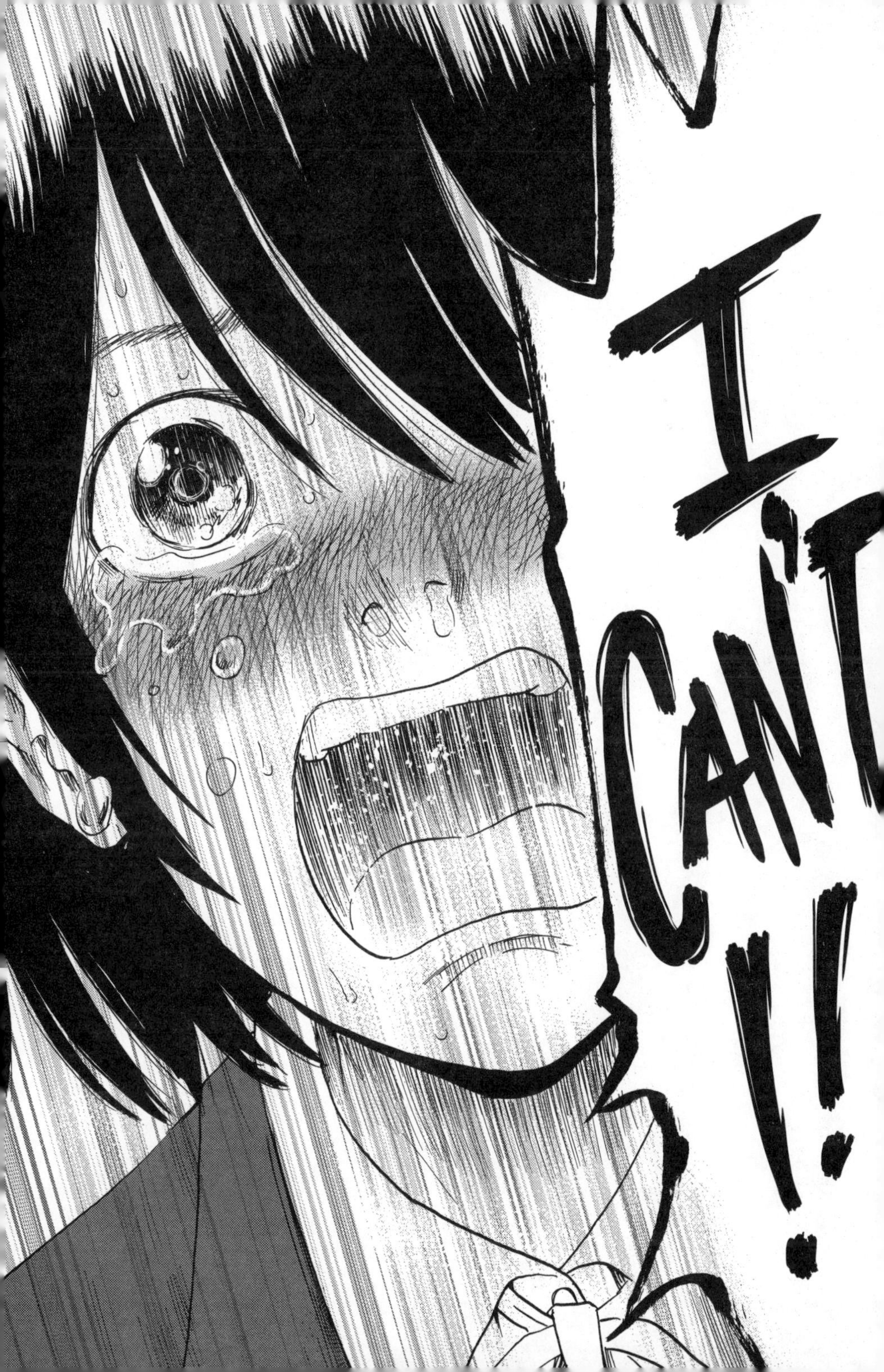
I CAN'T!!

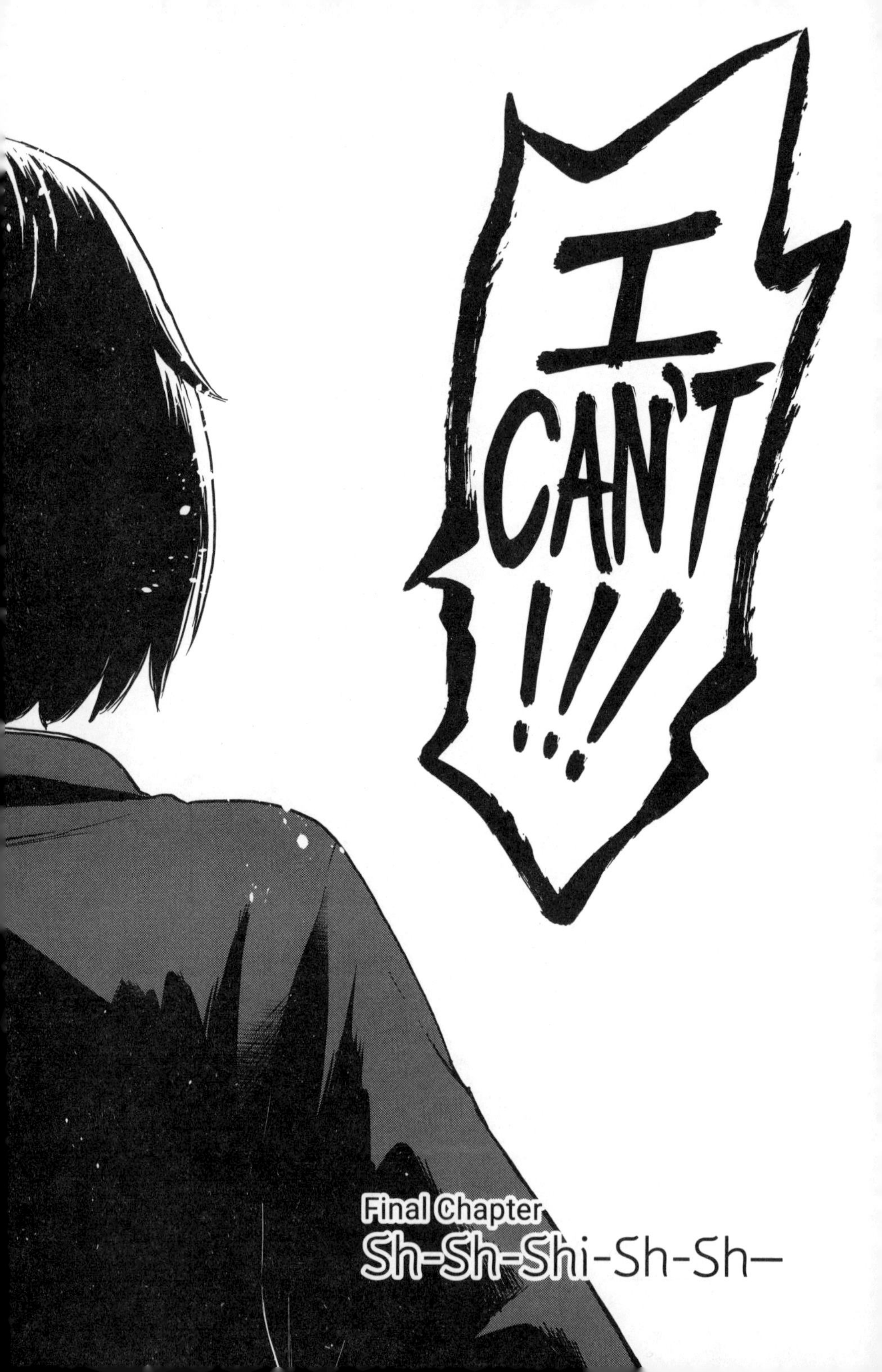
I CAN'T!!!

Final Chapter
Sh-Sh-Shi-Sh-Sh—

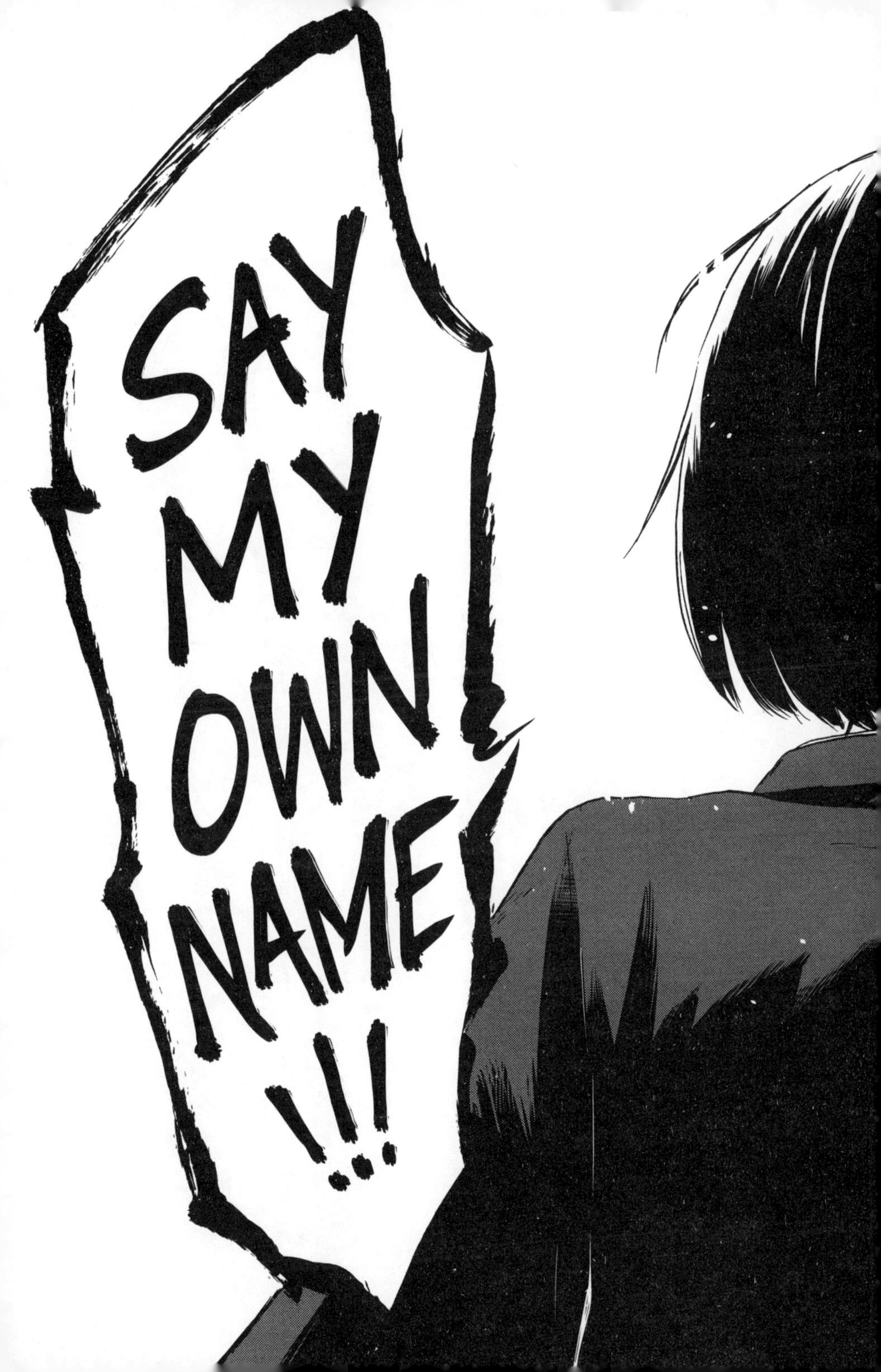
SAY MY OWN NAME!!!

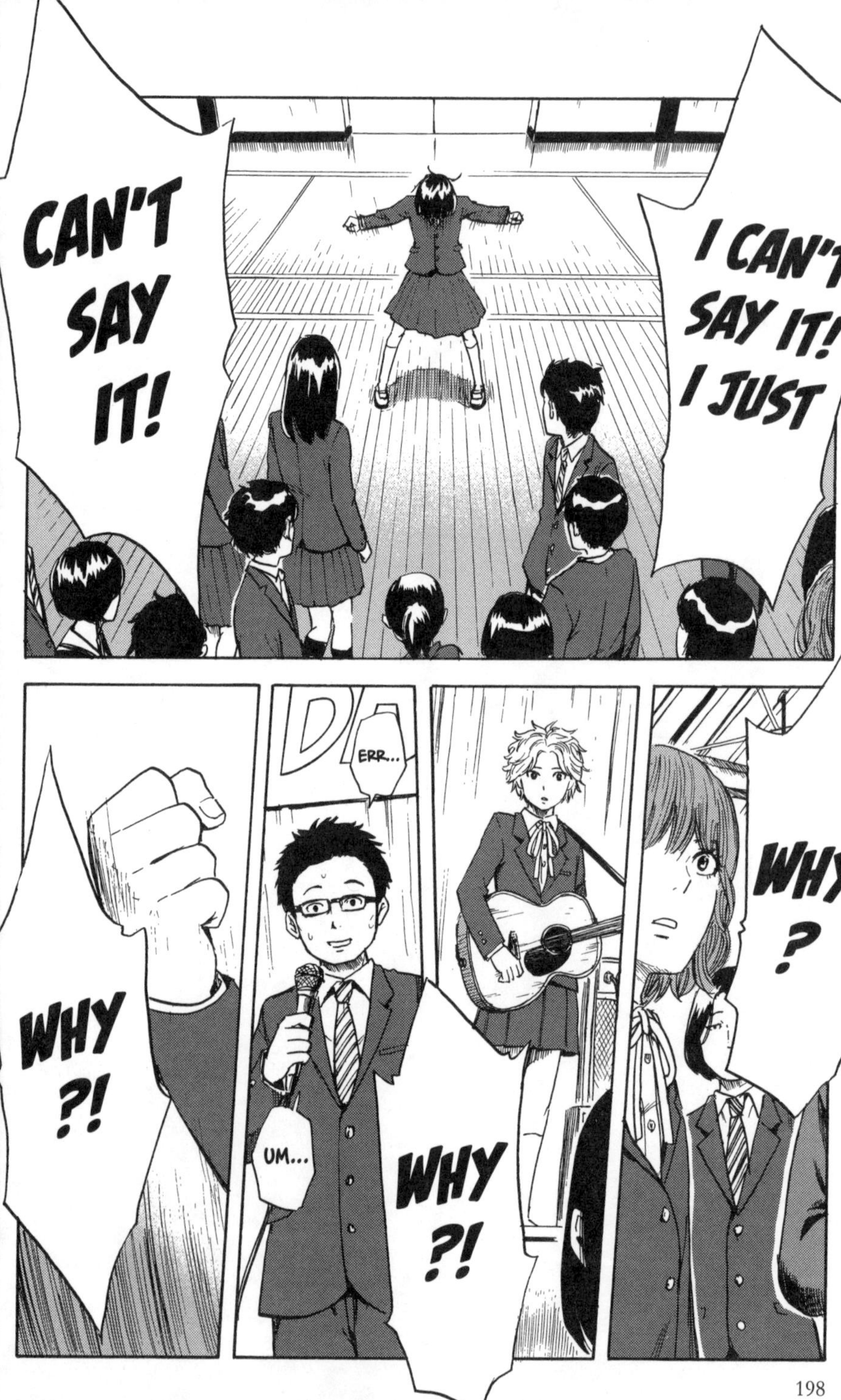
I CAN'T SAY IT! I JUST
CAN'T SAY IT!
WHY?
WHY?!
ERR...
UM...
WHY?!

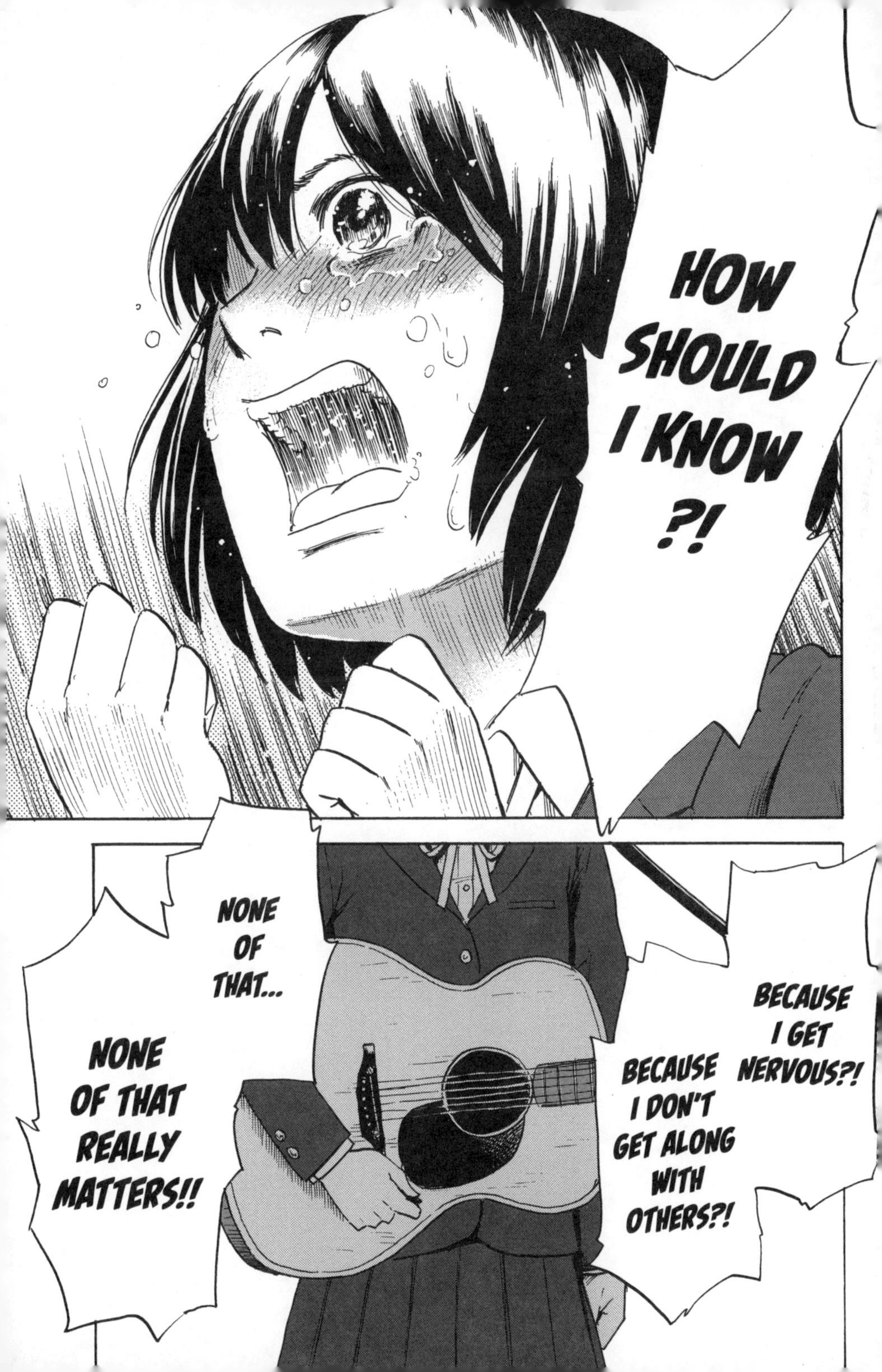
HOW SHOULD I KNOW ?!
BECAUSE I GET NERVOUS?!
BECAUSE I DON'T GET ALONG WITH OTHERS?!
NONE OF THAT...
NONE OF THAT REALLY MATTERS!!

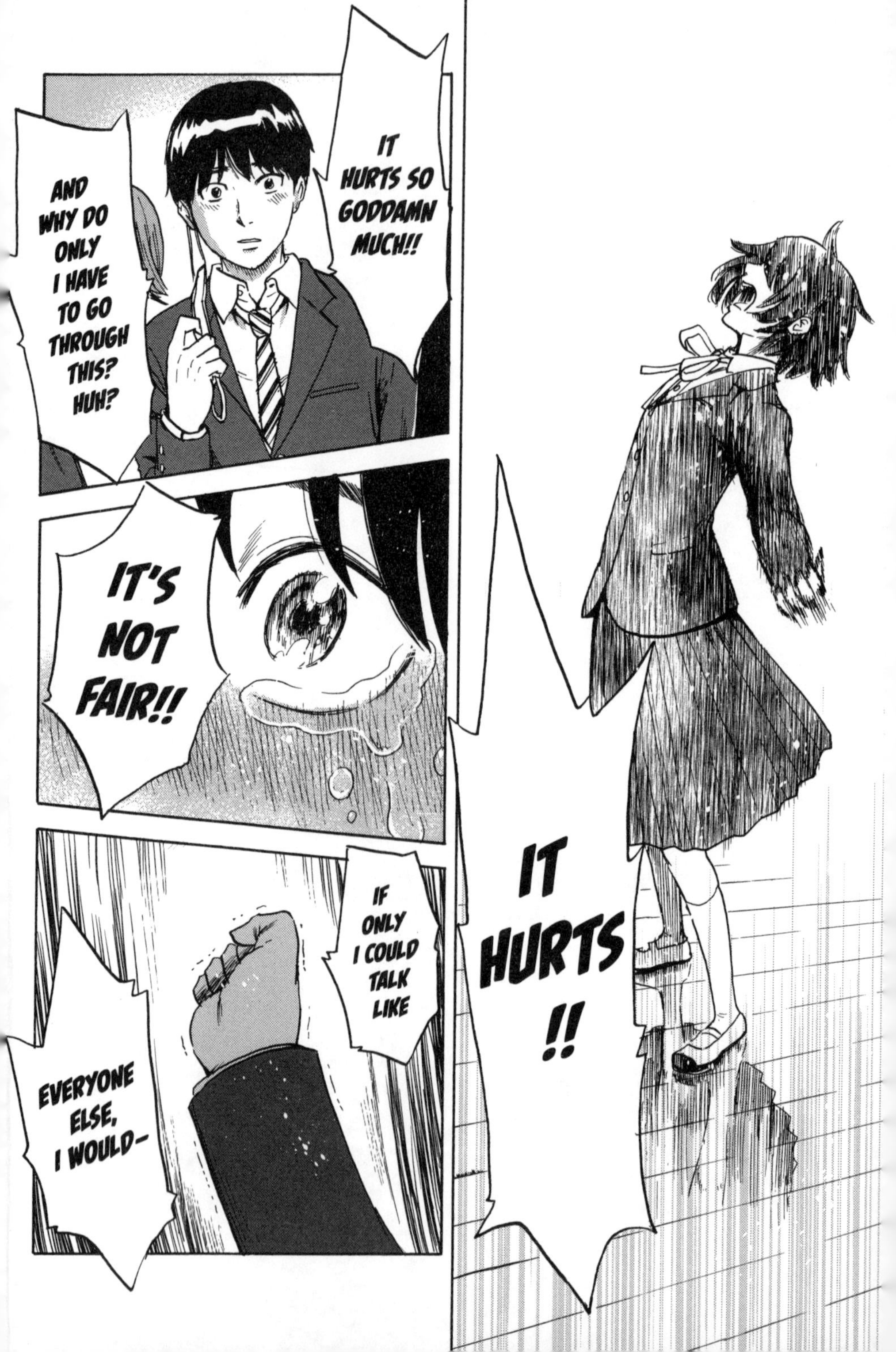
IT HURTS !!
IT HURTS SO GODDAMN MUCH!!
AND WHY DO ONLY I HAVE TO GO THROUGH THIS? HUH?
IT'S NOT FAIR!!
IF ONLY I COULD TALK LIKE
EVERYONE ELSE, I WOULD-

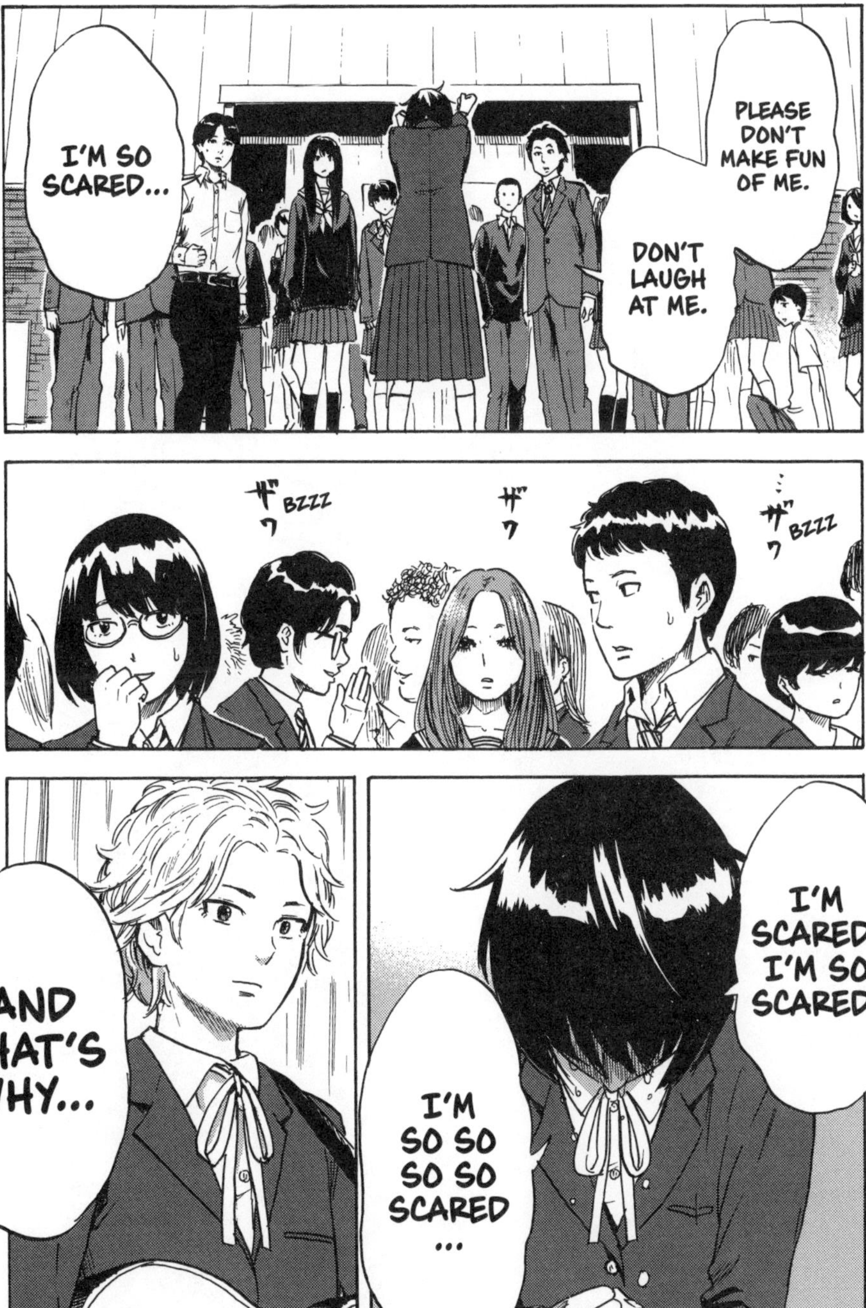
PLEASE DON'T MAKE FUN OF ME.
DON'T LAUGH AT ME.
I'M SO SCARED...
ザワ BZZZ
ザワ
ザワ BZZZ
I'M SCARED! I'M SO SCARED!
I'M SO SO SO SO SCARED ...
AND THAT'S WHY...

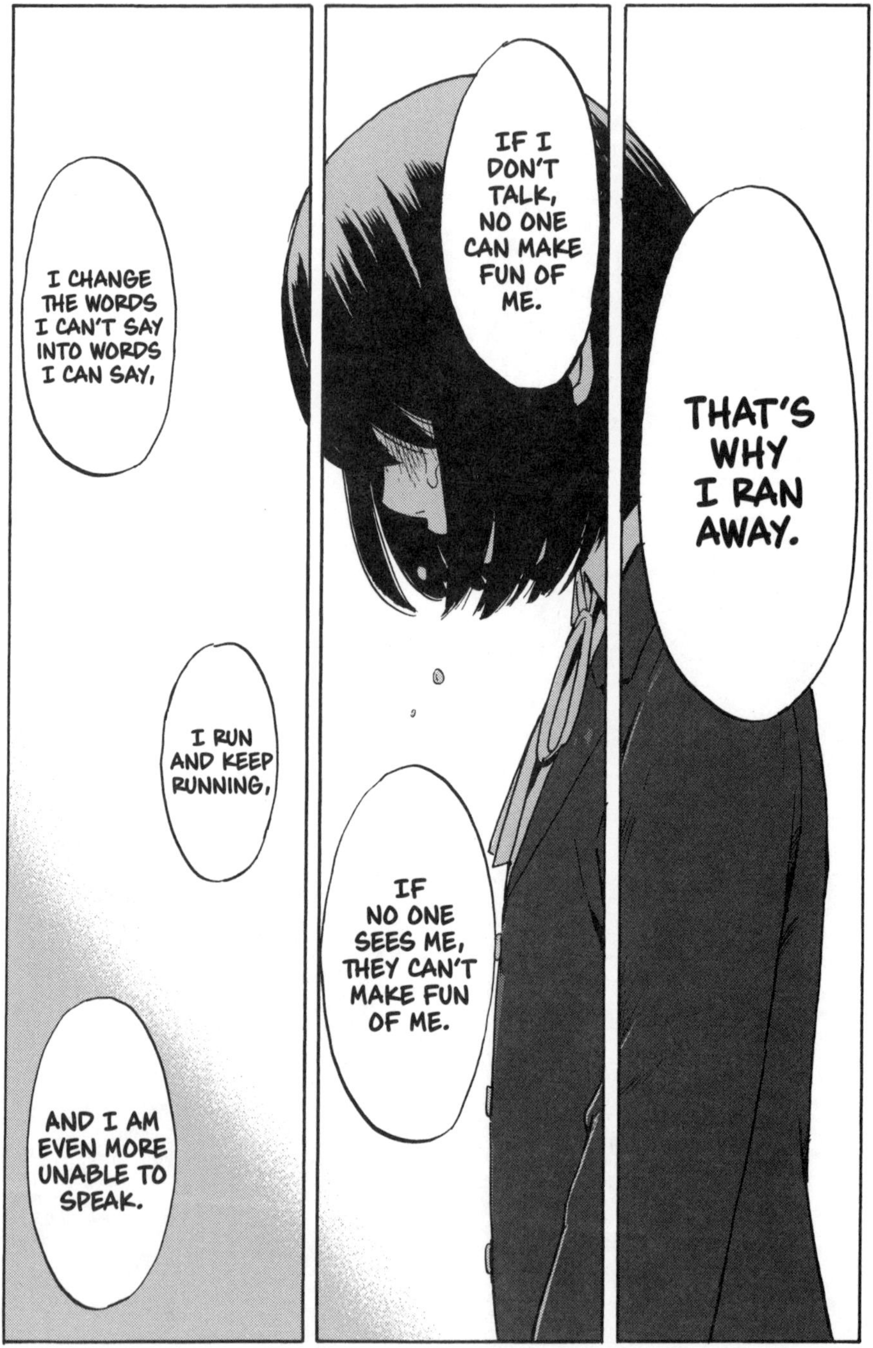
THAT'S WHY I RAN AWAY.
IF I DON'T TALK, NO ONE CAN MAKE FUN OF ME.
IF NO ONE SEES ME, THEY CAN'T MAKE FUN OF ME.
I CHANGE THE WORDS I CAN'T SAY INTO WORDS I CAN SAY,
I RUN AND KEEP RUNNING,
AND I AM EVEN MORE UNABLE TO SPEAK.

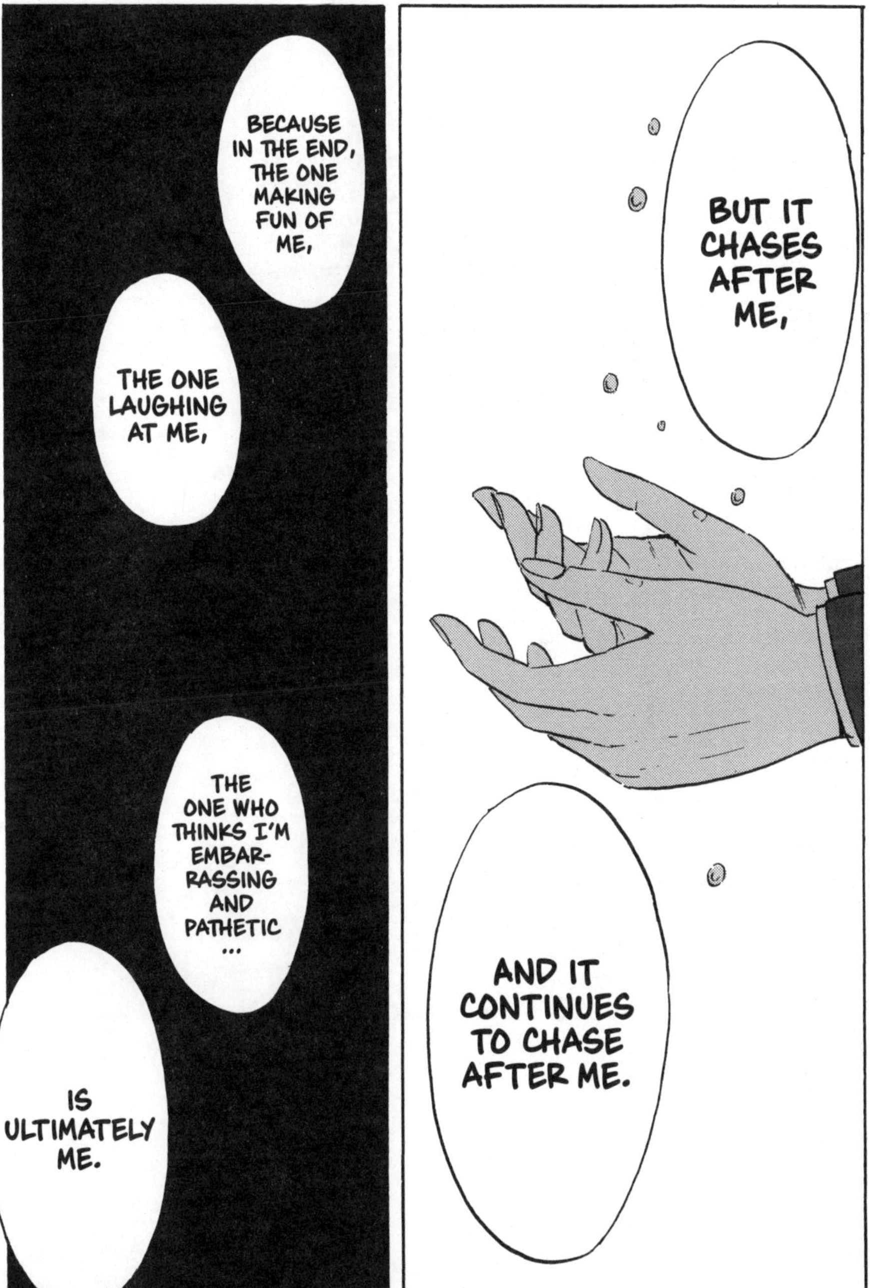
BUT IT CHASES AFTER ME,
AND IT CONTINUES TO CHASE AFTER ME.
BECAUSE IN THE END, THE ONE MAKING FUN OF ME,
THE ONE LAUGHING AT ME,
THE ONE WHO THINKS I'M EMBARRASSING AND PATHETIC...
IS ULTIMATELY ME.

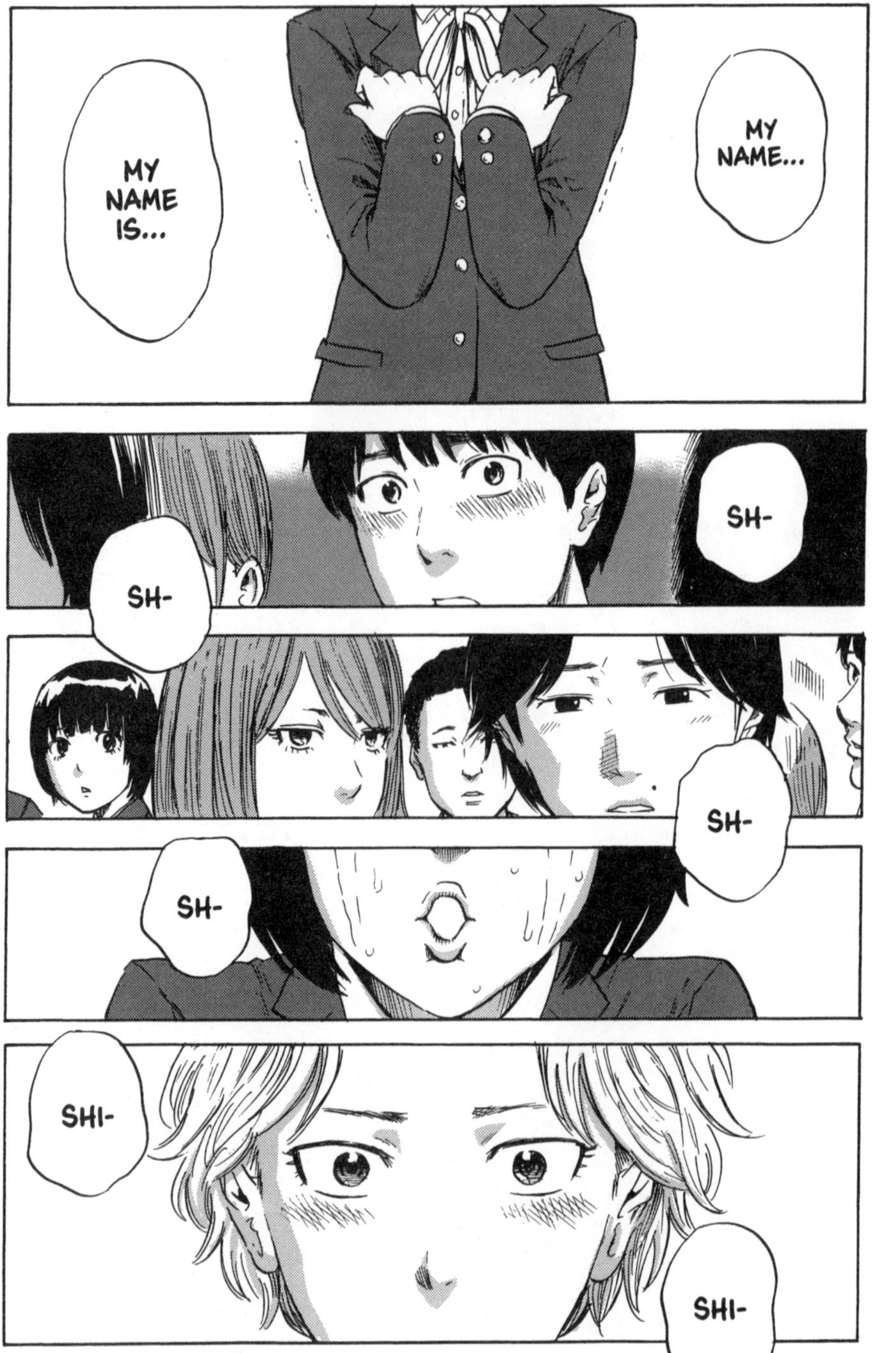
MY NAME...
MY NAME IS...
SH-
SH-
SH-
SH-
SHI-
SHI-

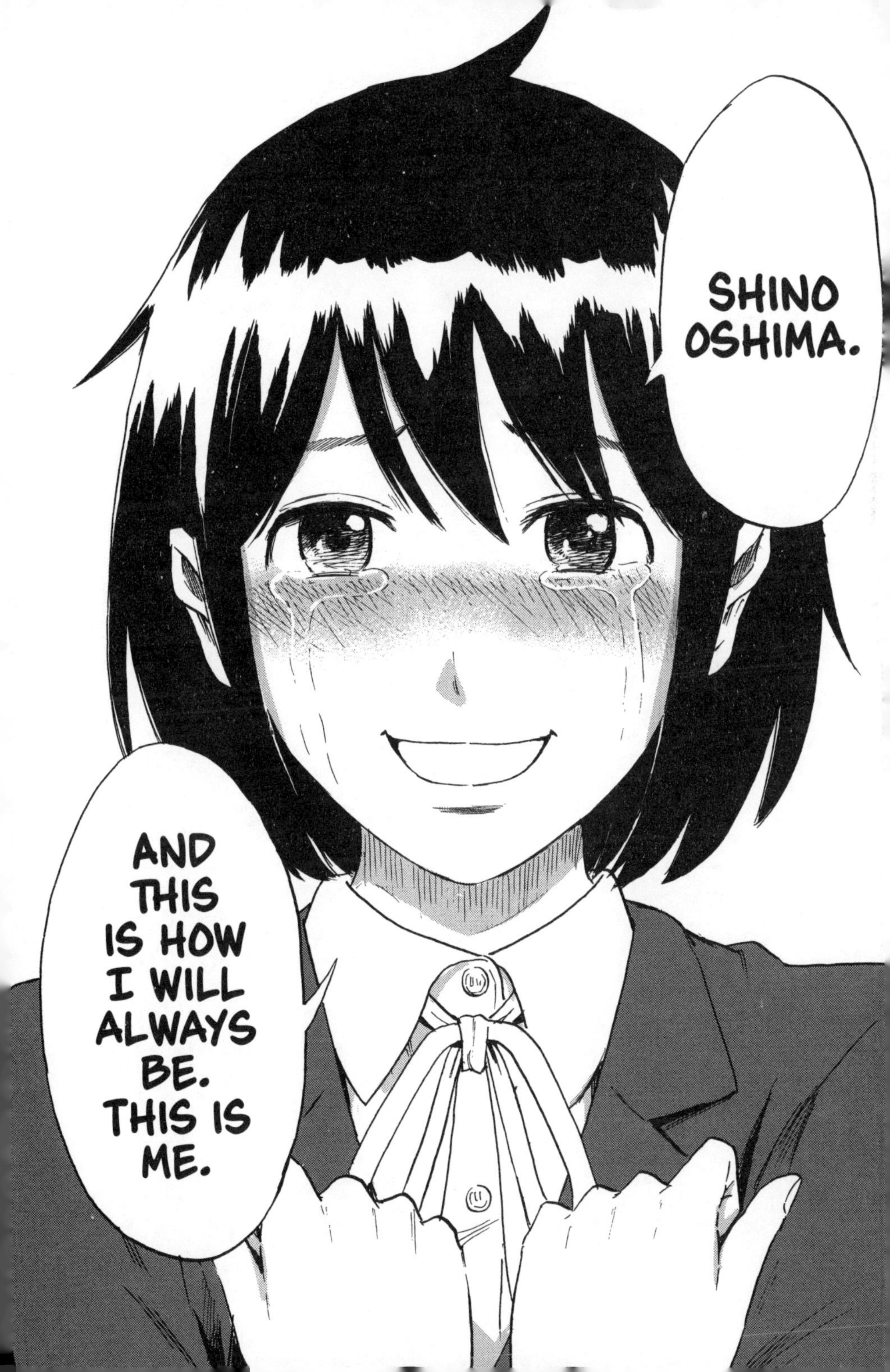
SHINO OSHIMA.
AND THIS IS HOW I WILL ALWAYS BE. THIS IS ME.

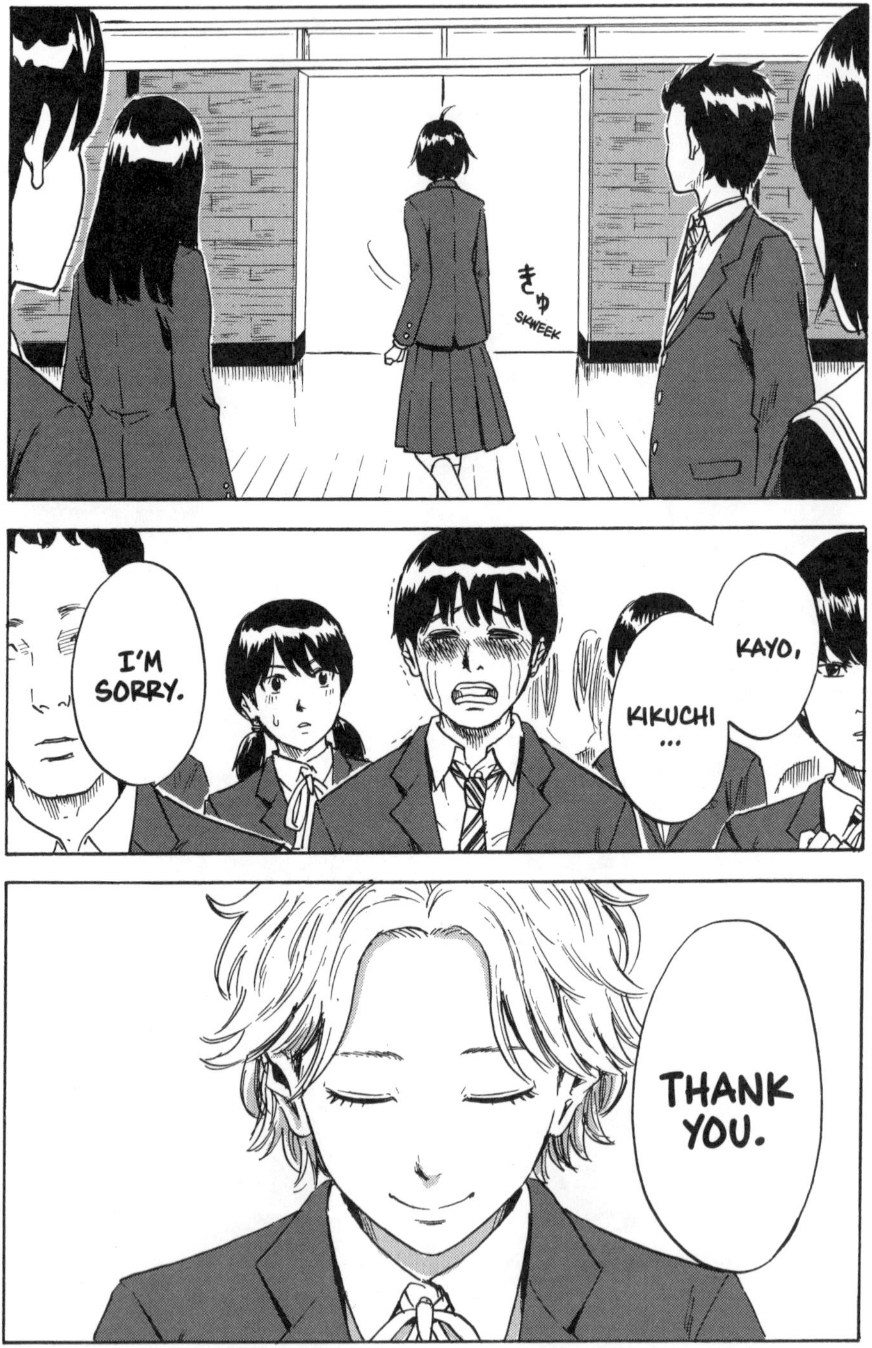
きゅ
SKWEEK
KAYO, KIKUCHI ...
I'M SORRY.
THANK YOU.

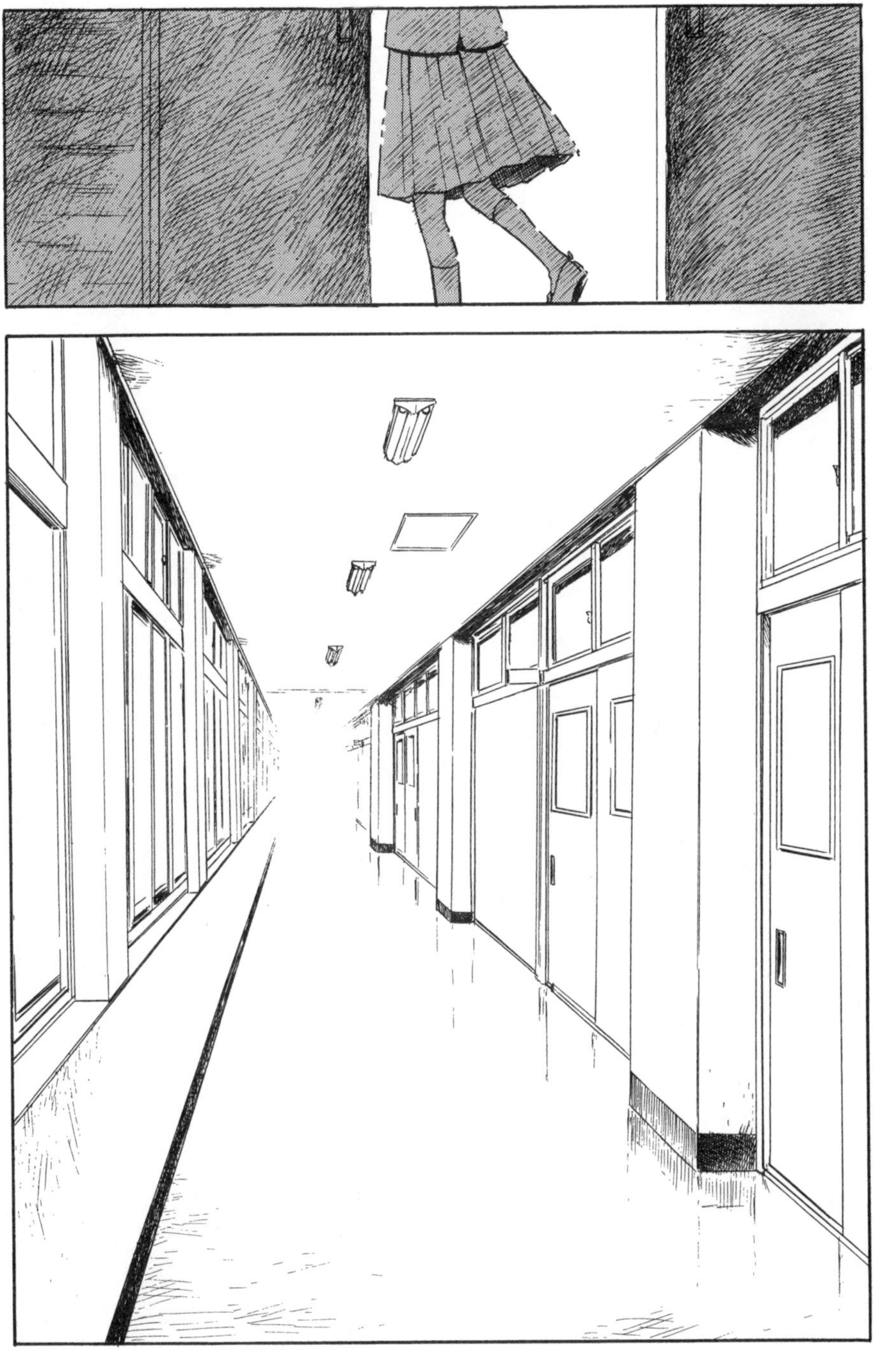

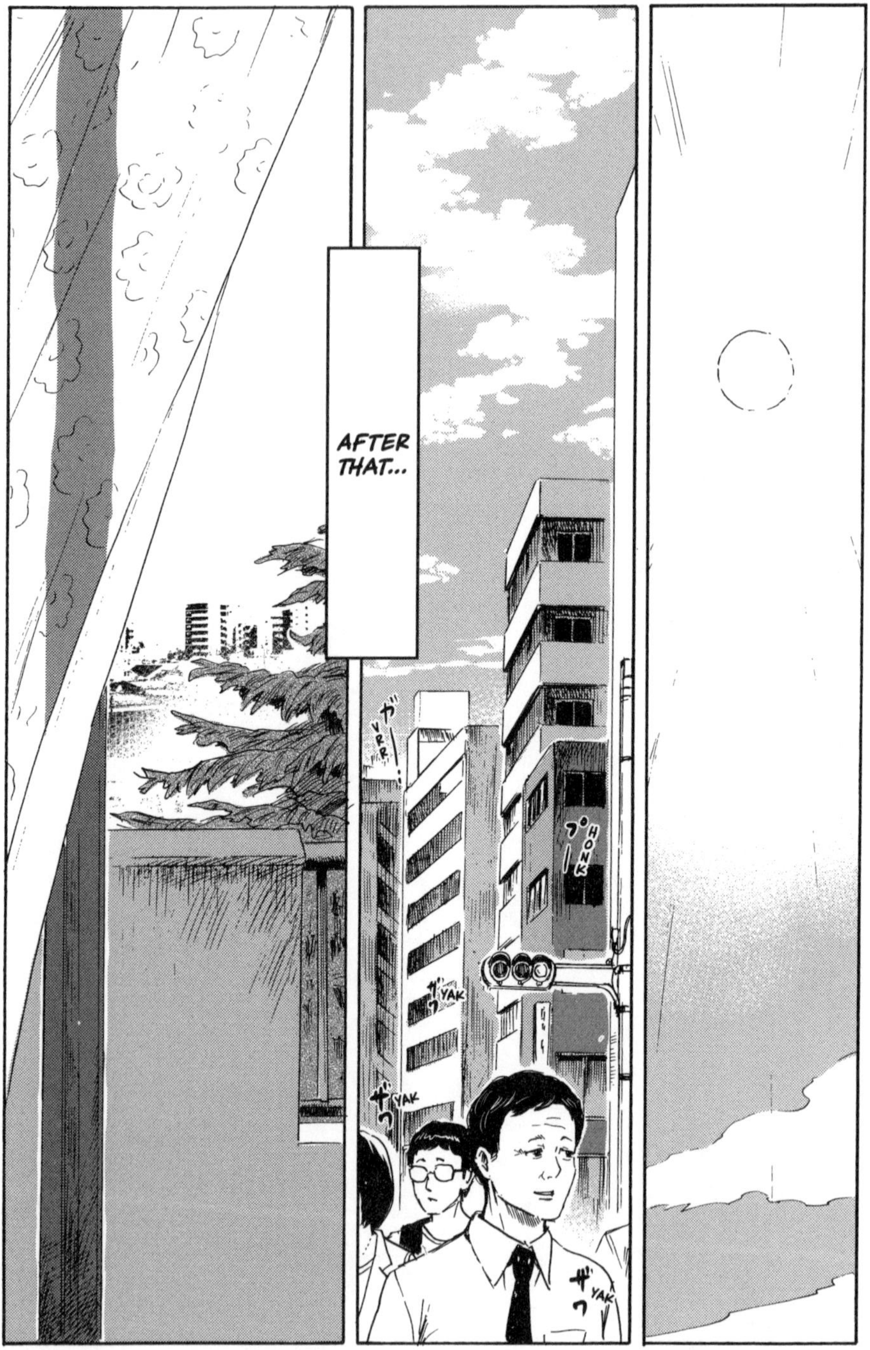
AFTER THAT...
ヴー VRRR
ブー HONK
ザワ YAK
ザワ YAK
ザワ YAK

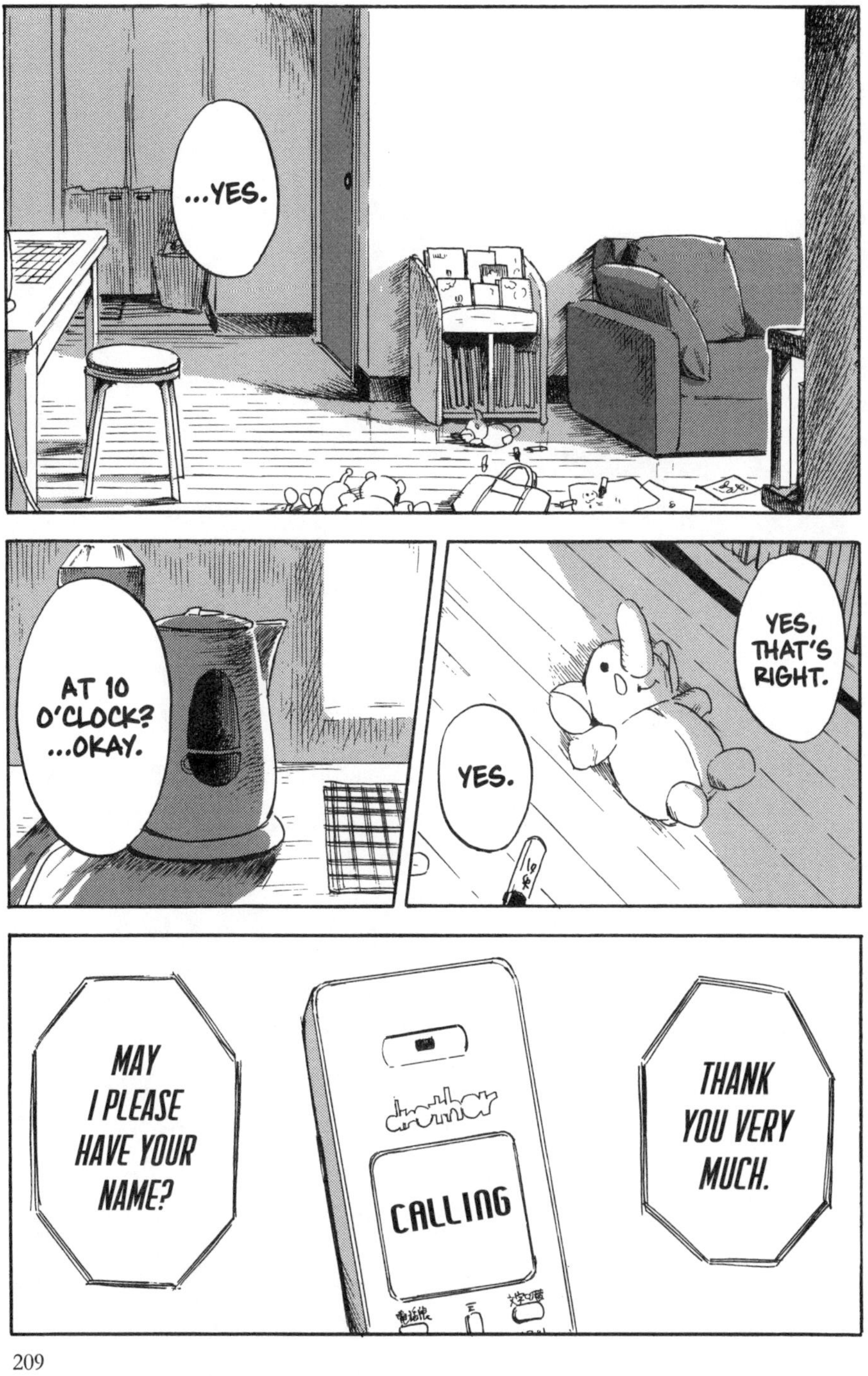
...YES.
YES, THAT'S RIGHT.
YES.
AT 10 O'CLOCK? ...OKAY.
THANK YOU VERY MUCH.
CALLING
MAY I PLEASE HAVE YOUR NAME?

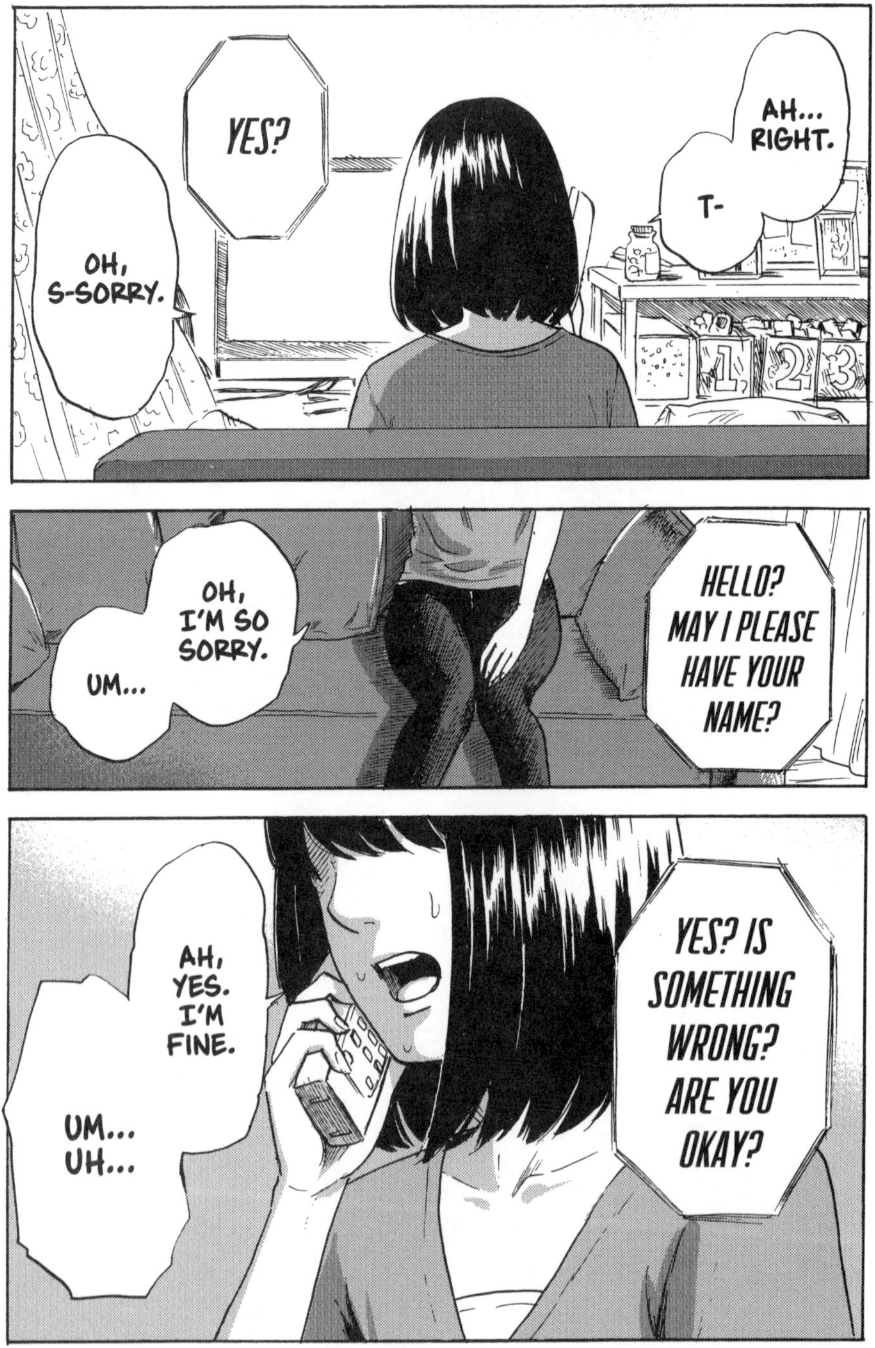
AH... RIGHT.
T-
YES?
OH, S-SORRY.
HELLO? MAY I PLEASE HAVE YOUR NAME?
OH, I'M SO SORRY.
UM...
YES? IS SOMETHING WRONG? ARE YOU OKAY?
AH, YES. I'M FINE.
UM... UH...

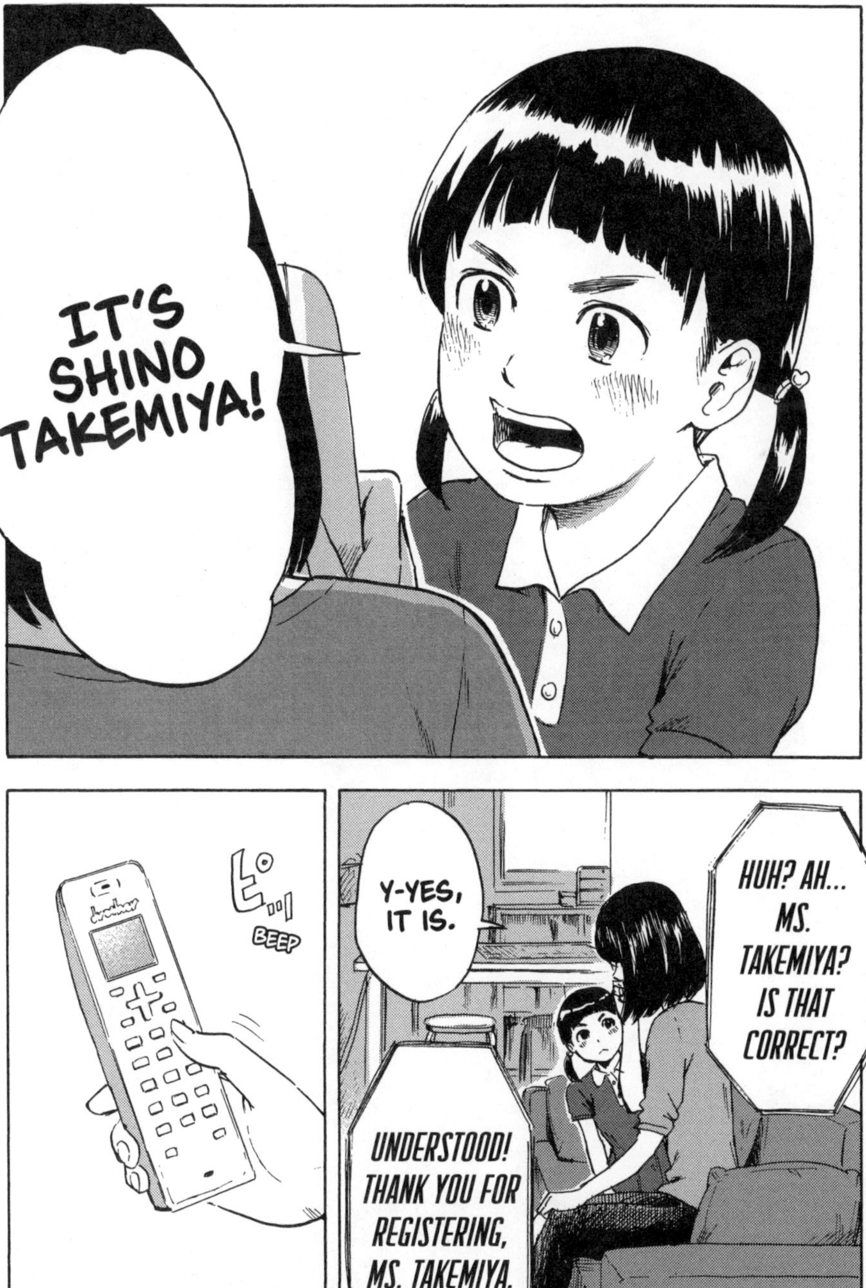
IT'S SHINO TAKEMIYA!
HUH? AH... MS. TAKEMIYA? IS THAT CORRECT?
Y-YES, IT IS.
UNDERSTOOD! THANK YOU FOR REGISTERING, MS. TAKEMIYA.
ピ
BEEP

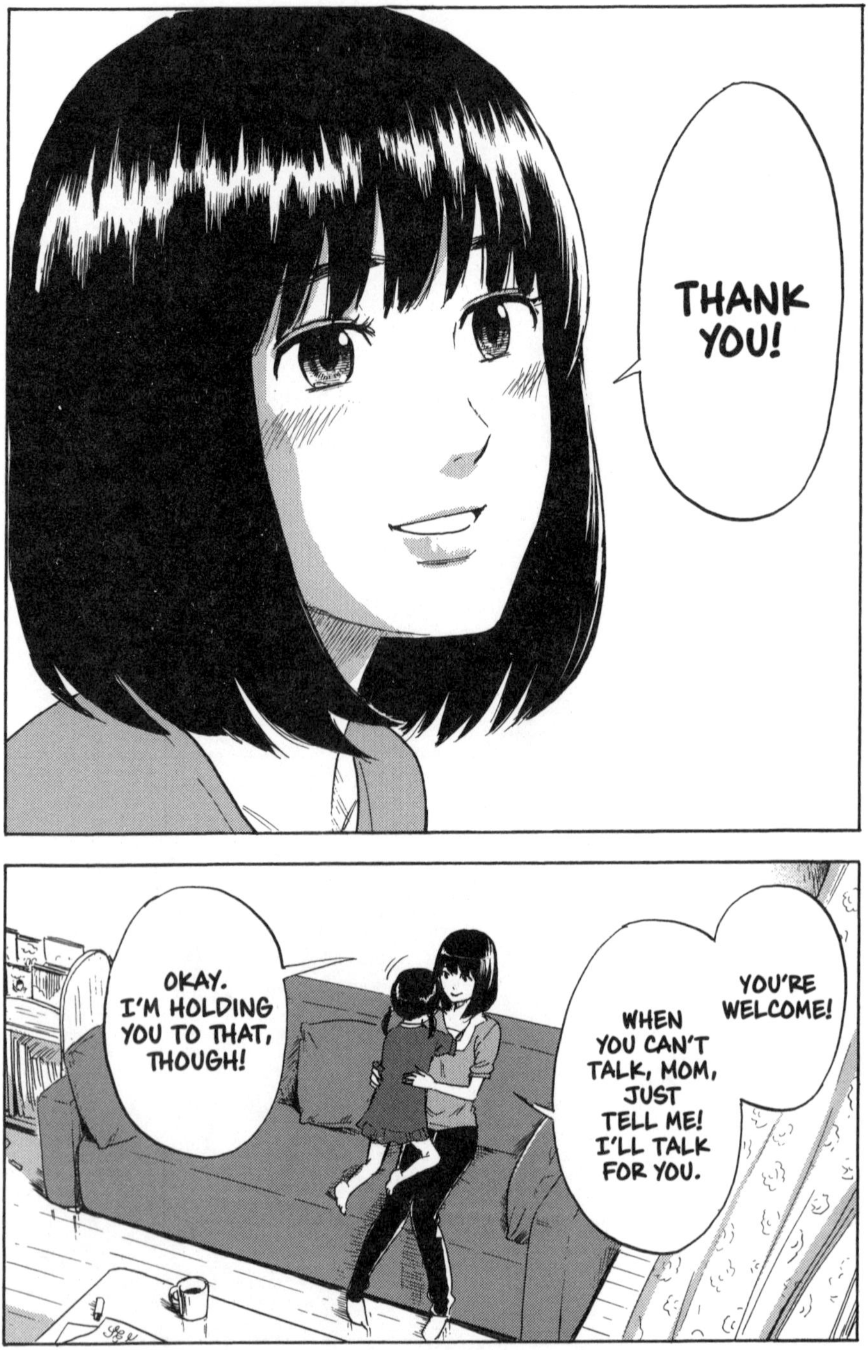
THANK YOU!
YOU'RE WELCOME!
WHEN YOU CAN'T TALK, MOM, JUST TELL ME! I'LL TALK FOR YOU.
OKAY. I'M HOLDING YOU TO THAT, THOUGH!

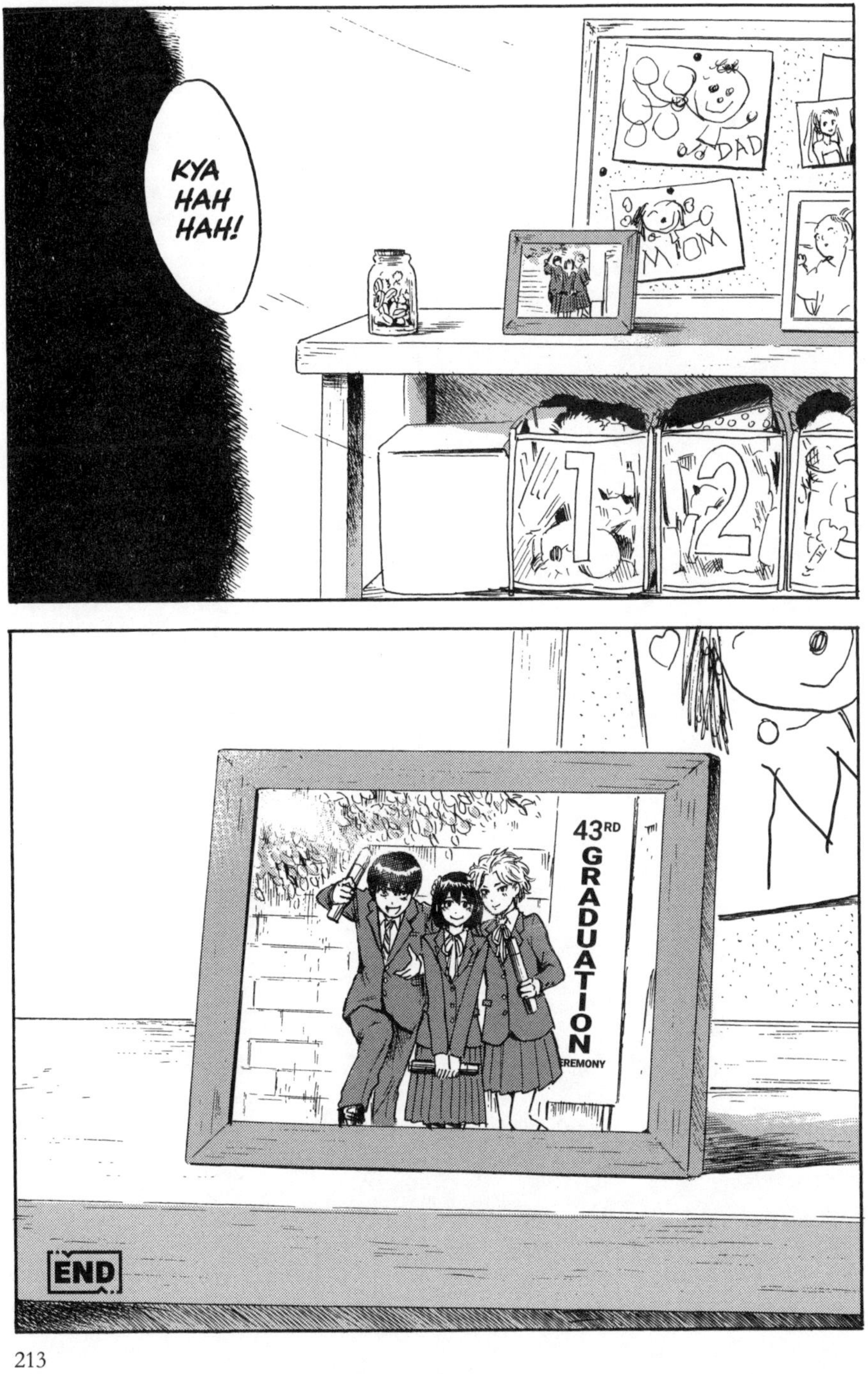
KYA HAH HAH!
DAD
43RD GRADUATION
END

to people, I switched to words that I could say, and left out the ones I couldn't.

I have often heard that "speech holds no catharsis."

Whenever I had to relate an anecdote, in my head I'd choose the perfect interesting or amusing story to talk about, but when it came time to actually speak, I became so terrified of stuttering that I would end up talking until I hit the punchline. And then I would just get bullied harder by those people because of how much they loathed me. But I wouldn't say it was all just bad things that happened to me during this time.

I became incredibly aware about whatever the person on the other end of the conversation would be saying. I was very worried about how they felt towards me, if they thought I was weird and so forth, I developed the ability to extrapolate how that person was feeling through their facial expressions and the gestures they used when they spoke. This came in handy later, as you can imagine, when I drew facial expressions for my manga.

One more thing that happened was that all of the things I wanted to say but couldn't, all of my feelings and thoughts from that time later exploded out of me when I started to draw manga.

That is to say: I now believe that had I not been dysphemic, I might not have been able to become a mangaka.

I'm not saying that due to dysphemia alone that I would have become a mangaka, to be clear. But I do think that when I take into account the dysphemia as a characteristic as well as my own personality, the two have become inseparable.

But to me, it became manga every once in a while. Not everyone is the same that way,

I suppose. After all, as long as you have one thing that can change your world, regardless of how big or small it is, as long as you have that one thing even for a moment, you can live. It may be dramatic and not necessarily big, but it can keep you going.

I did not use the words "stuttering" or "speech impediment" once within this manga. Why? Because I didn't want to make this story solely about either of those things.

As I drew it, I thought, "as long as it can hit home with anyone, yet it still remains a story about one person, that's good enough for me."

I am deeply grateful to my editor Murakami, my designers Kumochi and Dobashi, my little brother who assisted me, and to my wife, who decided that the word Shino would first write for Kayo would be "dick." Thank you so much.

—Shuzo Oshimi